LISA SCOTTOLINE:
THE FIRST TWO NOVELS

LISA SCOTTOLINE: THE FIRST TWO NOVELS

Everywhere That Mary Went

and

Final Appeal

LISA SCOTTOLINE

HarperCollins*Publishers*

LISA SCOTTOLINE: THE FIRST TWO NOVELS. Copyright © 2004 by Lisa Scottoline. All rights reserved. Printed in the United States of America. No part of this book may be used or reproduced in any manner whatsoever without written permission except in the case of brief quotations embodied in critical articles and reviews. For information, address HarperCollins Publishers Inc., 10 East 53rd Street, New York, NY 10022.

Everywhere That Mary Went and *Final Appeal* were originally published in 1993 and 1994 respectively, by HarperCollins Publishers Inc.

Designed by Elliott Beard

ISBN 0-06-075345-5

CONTENTS

EVERYWHERE THAT MARY WENT

For Franca, and for Kiki

ONE

"All rise! All persons having business before this Honorable Judge of the United States District Court are admonished to draw near and be heard!" trumpets the courtroom deputy.

Instantly, sports pages vanish into briefcases and legal briefs are tossed atop the stock quotes. Three rows of pricey lawyers leap to their wingtips and come to attention before a vacant mahogany dais. Never before has a piece of furniture commanded such respect.

"The District Court for the Eastern District of Pennsylvania is now in session! God save the United States and this honorable court!" The deputy casts an eye in the direction of the dais and pauses significantly. "The Honorable William A. Bitterman, presiding."

Judge Bitterman sweeps onto the dais on cue and stands behind his desk like a stout regent surveying his serfdom. His eyes, mere slits sunk deep into too-solid flesh, scan the courtroom from on high. I can read his mind: Everything is in order. The counsel tables gleam. The marble floor sparkles. The air-conditioning freezes the blood of lesser life forms. And speaking of same, the lawyers wait and wait.

"You won't mind the delay, counsel," the judge says indifferently, sinking into a soft leather throne. "After all, waiting is billable too."

An uncertain chuckle circulates among the crowd in the back of the courtroom. None of us defense lawyers likes to admit it, but we will bill the time—we have to bill it to someone and it might as well be you. The plaintiffs' bar doesn't sweat it. A contingency fee has more cushion than an air bag.

"Well, well, well," the judge mutters, without explanation, as he skims the motion papers on his desk. Judge Bitterman might have been handsome in a former life, but his enormous weight has pushed his features to the upper third of his face, leaving beneath a chin as bulbous as a bullfrog's. Rumor has it he gained the weight when his wife left him years ago, but there's no excuse for his temperament, which is congenitally lousy. Because of it my best friend, Judy Carrier, calls him Bitter Man.

"Good morning, Your Honor," I say, taking my seat at counsel table. I try to sound perky and bright, and not at all how I feel, which is nervous and fearful. I'm wearing my navy-blue Man Suit; it's perfect for that special occasion when a girl wants to look like a man, like in court or at the auto mechanic's. The reason I'm nervous is that this oral argument is only my second—the partners in my law firm hog the arguments for themselves. They expect associates to learn how to argue by watching them do it. Which is like saying you can learn to ride a bike by watching other people ride them.

"Good morning, Your Honor," says opposing counsel, Bernie Starankovic. Starankovic blinks a lot and wears a bad suit. I feel a twinge of guilt for what I'm about to say about him in open court—that he's too incompetent to represent our client's employees in a class action for age discrimination. If I win this motion, the class action will evaporate, our client's liability will plunge from megabucks to chump change, and its aged ex-employees will end up living on Social Security and 9-Lives. Defense lawyers consider this a victory.

"Good morning, class," replies Judge Bitterman. I force a fraudulent chuckle. The boys in the back do likewise.

"Ha-ha-ha!" Starankovic laughs loudly. "Ha-ha-ha!" The bogus sound caroms harshly off the walls of the cavernous courtroom, ricocheting like a subatomic particle long after everyone has fallen silent.

"Duly noted, Mr. Starankovic," says Bitter Man dryly, and Starankovic wilts into his chair. The judge's eyes shift in my direction. "Miz DiNunzio!"

"Yes, Your Honor!" I pop up and grin, like an overeducated jack-in-the-box. Popping up and grinning isn't something they taught me in law school, but they should have, since it's a damn sight more useful than Property. I learned it on the job, and it's become a conditioned response to more stimuli than you can count. I'm up for partnership in two months.

"You've done your homework for this morning, haven't you, Miz DiNunzio? I expect no less from a former student of mine."

Bitter Man's chubby lips part in a smile, but it's not a friendly one. I recognize the smile from when I did time as his research assistant, during my second year at Penn. I spent three afternoons a week finding cases for his soporific article on federal court jurisdiction. No matter how good the cases, they were never good enough for him. He always smiled that smile right before he tore into me, in the true Socratic tradition, asking me question after question until he had proven, as a matter of logic, that I was taking up too much space in the universe.

"Miz DiNunzio? Are you with us?" the judge asks.

I nod, in a caffeinated way. My nervousness intensifies. Red, angry blotches burst into bloom, one by one, beneath my starchy blouse. In two minutes, my chest will look like a thatch of crimson roses on a snow-covered field. Very attractive.

Bitter Man turns to Starankovic. "Mr. Starankovic, we've never met, but I trust you've done your homework too. After all, you're fighting for your life today, aren't you? Or at least the next best thing—a very large contingency fee."

Starankovic springs to his feet, blinking rhythmically. "The fee is of no moment to me, Your Honor, I can assure you. My only concern is for my clients, a veritable generation of golden-agers who have been ruthlessly victimized by defendant cor-poration, at a time in their lives when they should be able to relax, relying on the fact that their hard-earned pensions—"

"Very good, Mr. Starankovic. You get an A for enthusiasm," Bitter Man snaps, which shuts Starankovic down in mid-homily. Then the judge studies the motion papers before him, ignoring us both.

I'm not sure whether to remain standing, so I steal a glance at Starankovic. He's swaying stiffly, like a sunflower before a thunderstorm. I take a chance and sit down.

"Miz DiNunzio!" says Bitter Man.

"Yes, Your Honor!" I pop up and grin.

"Approach the podium!"

I hear Starankovic snicker, which proves he doesn't deserve my sympathy. I walk to the lectern with apparent confidence and adjust the microphone to girl height. "May it please the Court, my name is Mary DiNunzio—"

"Miz DiNunzio," Bitter Man says. "I have your name, re-member?"

"Yes, Your Honor. Sorry, Your Honor." I clear my throat to the sound of muffled laughter. "As you may know, Your Honor, I'm presenting this Motion to Strike Class Action Allegations on behalf of Harbison's The Hardware People. Harbison's is a national chain of hardware stores. It employs over—"

"I don't need the prospectus, Miz DiNunzio. I've heard of the company."

"Yes, Your Honor."

"I'd have to be deaf, dumb, and blind not to have heard of the company, after that inane jingle of theirs. You know their jingle."

"Their jingle?"

"Yes, their jingle. Their anthem. Their team song. I hear it everywhere—on my television, on my car radio—every fifteen minutes. You said you represent them, Miz DiNunzio, so I'm sure you know it. Do you?"

I nod uncertainly.

"Then sing it."

"*Sing it*, Your Honor?"

"You heard me," he says evenly.

A hush settles over the back of the courtroom. Each one of them is thanking God he's not in my pumps. I look down at the podium. My heart is pounding, my ears tingling. I curse Bitter Man, for humiliating me, and Richard Nixon, for appointing him to the federal bench.

"Pretty please? With a cherry on top?" The judge's voice is thick with sarcasm.

Not a soul in the gallery laughs. The courtroom deputy avoids my eye, busily examining the buttons of the tape recorder. Christ. It'll be on tape. "Your Honor—"

"Miz DiNunzio!" Bitter Man is suddenly furious; he looks like a volcano about to blow. "Sing!"

The courtroom is as quiet and stone-cold as death.

I close my eyes. I want to be somewhere else, anywhere else but here. I'm back in my girlhood, back in midnight mass on Christmas Eve, lost in the airy heights of "Ave Maria." I open my mouth and the notes fly out, unexpectedly clear and strong. They soar high over the congregation like the hymn, lovely and resonant in the wintry air. "Harbison's The Hardware People. We take the haaaaaard out of hardware!"

When I open my eyes, Bitter Man's anger has evaporated. "That was quite . . . beautiful," he says.

I can't tell if he's being sarcastic, and I don't care. "May I begin my argument, Your Honor?"

"You may."

So I do, and the argument sounds punchy and right, fueled

by my fury at the judge. I rattle off the local court rules that Starankovic has broken, then segue into my cases, transforming each into the parable of the Careless Lawyer Who Undermined Our System of Justice. Bitterman begins to bare his canines in an encouraging way, which means he's either happy or hungry. I finish my argument and return to counsel table.

"Your Honor, if I may respond," Starankovic says. He pushes down the shiny pants that are static-clinging to his socks and walks to the podium like a Christian into the Roman Colosseum. "May it please the Court, I'm Bernard—"

"Save it, Mr. Starankovic. We both know that defense counsel is right on the law. Your conduct as class counsel has been a disgrace—even my law clerks could do better. How could you miss the deadline on your motion for class certification? It's the one thing you have to do and you couldn't even do that right."

"But Your Honor . . ."

Bitter Man holds up a hand that looks like a mound of Play-Doh. "Stifle, Mr. Starankovic, as Archie Bunker used to say." He glances around the room to see if anyone appreciates his joke. The gallery is too terrified to laugh, but the courtroom deputy smiles broadly. Your tax dollars at work.

"Yes, Your Honor." Starankovic bows slightly.

"Now, Mr. Starankovic, even though Miz DiNunzio thinks she has you, you and I know that I have total discretion in deciding whether to grant her motion. I may grant it or I may deny it purely as a matter of my own inherent powers. Am I right?"

Starankovic nods.

"Of course I am. So your work is cut out for you. Your job is to give me your best argument. Give me one good reason why I shouldn't grant Miz DiNunzio's motion."

Starankovic blinks rapidly. "Your Honor, if I may, the class is composed—"

Bitter Man holds up a finger. "I said, one good reason."

"I was about to, Your Honor. The class is composed of some five hundred employees, and counting—"

"No. No. You're not listening, Mr. Starankovic. Repeat after me. 'The one good reason . . .'"

Starankovic licks his dry lips. "The one good reason . . ."

" 'You shouldn't grant the motion . . .'"

"You shouldn't grant the motion . . ."

" 'Is . . .'" Bitter Man finishes with a flourish, waving his hand in the air like a conductor.

"Is . . ."

"No, you idiot! I'm not going to finish the sentence for you. *You* finish the sentence."

"I knew that, Your Honor. I'm sorry." The man is sweating bullets. "It's hard to explain. I—"

"*One good reason!*" the judge bellows.

Starankovic jumps.

The courtroom deputy looks down. The gallery holds its breath. I wonder why judges like Bitter Man get appointments for life. The answer is: because of presidents like Nixon. Someday the electorate will make this connection, I know it.

"I made some mistakes, Your Honor, I admit it," Starankovic blurts out. "I was having a rough time, my mother had just passed, and I missed a lot of deadlines. Not just on this case—on others too. But it won't happen again, Your Honor, you have my word on that."

Bitter Man's face is a mask of exaggerated disbelief. He grabs the sides of the dais and leans way over. "*This* is your best argument? *This* is the one good reason?"

Starankovic swallows hard.

I feel awful. I almost wish I'd never brought the motion in the first place.

"*This* is the best you can come up with? The one good reason I shouldn't grant the motion is that you were making a lot of mistakes at the time—*and this was just one of them*?"

"Your Honor, it's not like—"

"Mr. Starankovic, you said your only concern was for your clients. Isn't that right?"

"Yes, Your Honor."

"Do you care enough to give them the best lawyer possible?"

"Yes, Your Honor."

"Would the best lawyer possible fail to file his motion for class certification on time?"

"No . . . Your Honor."

"But you failed to do so, didn't you?"

Starankovic blinks madly.

"Didn't you?"

Starankovic opens his mouth, but nothing comes out.

"Didn't you fail to do so, Mr. Starankovic? Yes or no will do."

"Yes," he says quietly.

"Then you are not the best lawyer possible, are you?"

There is silence as Starankovic looks down. He can't bring himself to say it. He shakes his head once, then again.

Socrates would have stopped there, but Bitter Man is just warming up. He drags Starankovic through every deadline he blew and every phone call he failed to return. I can barely witness the spectacle; the back rows are shocked into silence. Poor Starankovic torques this way and that, eyelids aflutter, but Bitterman's canines are sunk deep in his neck, pinning him to the floor. There's nowhere to run, nowhere to hide. There's only pain and suffering.

When it's over, Bitter Man issues his decision from the bench. With a puffy smile, he says, "Motion granted."

"Thank you, Your Honor," I say, dry-mouthed.

"Thank you, Your Honor," says Starankovic, hemorrhaging freely. He shoots me a look that could kill.

"Next!" says Bitter Man.

I stuff my papers in my briefcase and turn to go, as another corporate shill takes my place at counsel table. The pews are jam-packed with us, padded shoulder to padded shoulder, because the argument schedule is so late. I hurry by the freshly shaved suits in rep ties and collar pins. I feel like I'm fleeing the scene of a murder. I avoid the eyes of the men in the gallery, some amused, others curious. I don't want to think about who sat among them at this time last year.

I promised myself.

I'm almost past the back row when someone grabs my elbow. It's the only other woman in this horde of pinstriped testosterone, and her red-lacquered nails dig into my arm.

"This has gone far enough!" the woman says.

"What do you mean?" My chest still feels tight, blotchy. I have a promise to keep and I'm failing fast. I try to avoid looking at the pew where she sits, but I can't help it. It's where my husband sat with his first-grade class and watched me argue my first motion. The rich mahogany of the pew has been burnished to a high luster, like a casket.

"He hates us! He hates women lawyers!" she says. She punches the bridge of her glasses with a finger. "I think it's high time we did something about it."

I only half hear her. All I can think about is Mike. He sat right in this row and had to quiet the class as they fidgeted, whispered, and giggled through the entire argument. He sat at the end of the pew, his arm rested right here. I touch the knobby arm rest with my fingertips. It feels just like his shoulder used to feel: strong, solid. As if it would never give way. I don't want to move my hand.

"We have to file a complaint of judicial misconduct. It's the only thing that will stop him. I know the procedure. You file the complaint with the Clerk of the Third Circuit, then it goes to the Chief Judge and . . ."

Her words grow faint. My fingertips on the shoulder of wood put me in touch with Mike, and in touch with that day. It was a morning like this one. My first argument in court. I remember my own nervous excitement, presenting the motion almost automatically, in a blur. Bitter Man ruled for me in the end, which caused the first-graders to burst into giddy applause. Mike's face was lit up by a proud smile that didn't fade even when Bitter Man went ballistic, pounding his gavel. . . .

Crack! Crack! Crack!

Reality.

I pull my hand from the cold, glossy wood of the pew. Mike isn't here, Mike is gone. I feel my chest flush violently. "I have to go."

"Wait? How will I find you? I need you to sign the complaint," the woman says, grasping at my arm. "I have at least two other incidents. If we don't do something about this, no one else will!"

"Let me go, I have to go." I yank my arm from her grasp and bang through the courtroom doors.

My promise is broken; my head is flooded with a memory. Mike and I celebrated the night I won the motion. We made love, so sweetly, and then ate pizza, a reverse of our usual order. Afterward he told me he felt sorry for the employees whose discrimination case I had gotten dismissed.

"You're a softie," I said.

"But you love me for it," he said.

Which was true. Two months later, Mike was dead.

And I began to notice a softer-hearted voice than usual creeping into my own consciousness. I don't know for sure whose voice it is, but I think the voice is Mike, talking to me still. It says the things he would say, it's picked up where he left off. Lately it's been whispering to me that my on-the-job sins are piling up. That each hash mark for the corporate defense is a black mark for my soul.

Judgment day will come, it says. *It's just a matter of time.*

TWO

It's exactly 11:47 when I get back to my office at Stalling &
Webb, one of Philadelphia's holy trinity of corporate mega-
firms. I can't help but know the time exactly, given the view
from my office. It's a regulation associate cubicle except for the
fact that the window behind my desk is entirely consumed by
the immense yellow clock face on top of Philadelphia's City
Hall, which is directly across the street. If you have to have a
clock looming over your shoulder as you work, it's one of the
nicest: an old-timey clock, round as the moon and almost as
large. Ornate hands, curlicued with Victorian ironwork, move
precisely on time, silently pointing to Roman numerals of
somber black. Nobody senior to me wanted this office because
of the clock, but I didn't mind it. I always know what time it
is, which is good for a lawyer. As Socrates said, time is money.

I swivel around in my chair and look at the clock. 11:48.
11:49. I don't like it so much anymore, though I'm not sure
why. 11:50. *It's only a matter of time.*

"Snap out of it, Mare," says a distinctive voice from the
doorway. My secretary, Brent Polk, comes in with a stack of
yellow message slips and coffee on a tray. Brent's a slim, good-
looking man with hazel eyes and a thatch of jet-black hair. He's

also gay, but only Judy and I are privy to that bit of job-threat-ening information. Judy nicknamed him Bent in honor of his sexual preference; he loves it, but we can't call him that around the other secretaries. They think he has a girlfriend in Massa-chusetts and can't decide whether to get married. The perfect camouflage—a man who won't commit. He blends right in.

"Coffee, what a great idea. Brent, you're a man among men."

"Don't I wish." He sets the coffee and the messages down on my desk. "Look, I even have the tray today. Aren't you proud of me?" Brent's ticked off because one of Stalling's command-ments is THOU SHALT NOT CARRY COFFEE WITHOUT A TRAY because it will stain the carpets, and he got reprimanded last week for not using one.

I pick up the YOU WANT IT WHEN? mug gratefully. All the coffee mugs talk back at Stalling, because the employees can't.

"Now listen, Mare, you got another call from Mystery Man. This is ridiculous. We should change your phone numbers. It's been going on for a year."

"Don't exaggerate. It hasn't been a year."

"Yes it has, off and on. It seems like it's more often now, too—this guy must have nothing better to do. Are you getting more calls at home?"

"When did he call?" Lately I've noticed the calls have fallen into a pattern, occurring when I get back to the office or home from work. I get the feeling that someone knows when I'm coming and going, which is not a good feeling to have. If Brent knew the whole story, he'd call out the National Guard. But I'm not sure the whole thing isn't coincidental.

"What difference does it make when he called? He called."

"Let's hold off. I've had the same phone number since I started here. All the clients know it. I hate to change for no good reason. People hate that."

"Arrrrgh," he growls in frustration, and reaches for my throat.

"Back, back. I'm telling you: You don't screw up your clients without good cause. Then they go away, and you're broke."

"But, Mary, it's sceevy. Did you ever think about what this guy's doing when you answer the phone?" He wrinkles his nose in disgust. "I had an Uncle Morty who—"

"Brent, please."

"Well it's the truth."

"All right. Let it sit for a while. If it keeps on happening, we'll change the numbers, okay?"

"Yes, bwana," he says with a sigh.

"Good."

His dark eyes light up wickedly. "Wait'll the big kahuna hears you won that motion. He and Delia are gonna celebrate tonight at the Four Seasons." Brent's connected like nobody's business at Stalling. The latest dirt is that the senior partner on the *Harbison's* case, Sam Berkowitz, is having an affair with his secretary. "I figure she'll leave at five and he'll leave ten minutes later. This time I'm gonna win. I can feel it."

"What do you mean, you're going to win?"

"You want in? It's only a buck." Brent pulls a wrinkled piece of steno paper out of his pants pocket and reads from it. "I bet he could wait ten minutes, but Janet says only five. Maggie bet he'll tough it out for half an hour. Lucinda says they'll leave together, but she's crazy. He's got his position to think of. Not *that* position, *this* position." He laughs.

"You mean you have a pool going?"

"Yeah." He slips the paper back into his pocket.

"You're shameless. You don't know they're having an affair."

"What, are you kidding? Everybody knows it."

"But he's married."

Brent rolls his eyes. "So was I."

"You were young. It's different."

"Please. I can't believe you've lived this long, you're so naive. Take a look at Delia next time you're up there. She's edible."

"She's okay-looking, but—"

"Okay-looking? She's a knockout. I'm gay, dear, not blind, and neither is Berkowitz. He's got the hots. Everybody's talking about it. Where there's smoke, there's fire."

I make a finger crucifix and ward him off with it. "Blasphemer! The man is chairman of the department!"

"Oh, excuse me, I forgot. Your idol, Berkowitz, King of Kings. You know what I heard about him?"

"What?"

"You have to promise not to freak when I tell you, or I'm not going to tell you anything else. Ever again." He wags a finger at me through a too-long shirtsleeve. Black, of course, the only color he wears. "Especially about this partnership crap."

"What did you hear?"

"Promise, Mary."

"Tell me! We're talking my job here."

He leans over my desk. I can smell the Obsession on his neck. "I heard that no matter what they say, Berkowitz is authorizing only two partners from litigation. Two, not three. Two, and that's it."

"Not three? They said three!"

"Yeah? Well that was then and this is now. They don't want to divide up that pie any more than they have to."

"So they're just going to fire one of us? I can't believe it."

"Here we go. I knew I shouldn't have told you."

"How are they going to choose between the three of us? We all have the same evaluations, and we all bill over two thousand hours a year. We've indentured ourselves to this fucking firm, now they're gonna lop one of us off?" I rub my forehead on the front, where it's beginning to pound. I'm convinced that this is the partnership lobe. It's right next to the bar exam lobe and the SAT lobe.

"It won't be you, Mare. You just won a big motion."

"What about Judy?"

"Judy's got it made. They need her to crank out those briefs."

"And Ned Waters, what about him? I don't want to see any of us fired, for Christ's sake. It'll be impossible to get another job. It's not like the eighties, when you could pick and choose."

"Listen to me, you're working my last nerve. Are you having lunch with Judy today?"

"Of course."

"Good. Go early. Talk it over with her. She'll straighten you out."

And she tries to, as we sit at a wobbly table by the wall in the Bellyfiller, a dingy restaurant in the basement of our office building. Judy drags me here all the time because the sandwiches are huge and the pickles are free. She doesn't mind that the atmosphere is dark and cruddy, the big-screen TV attracts all the wrong people, and the sawdust on the floor sometimes crawls.

"You're letting this make you nuts, Mary!" She throws up her long arms, with their Boeing-sized wingspan. Judy Carrier is six feet tall, and from northern California, where the women grow like sequoias.

"I can't help it."

"Why? You just won a motion, you dufus. You're undefeated. We should be celebrating."

"How can you be so relaxed about this?"

"How can you be so worried about it?"

I laugh. "Don't you ever worry, Judy?"

She thinks a minute. "Sure. When my father is belaying. Then I worry. His attention wanders, and he—"

"What's belaying?"

"You know, when you climb, you designate one person to—"

"I'm not talking about rock climbing. I mean about work, about partnership. Don't you ever worry about whether we'll make it?"

"Making partner is nothing compared with rock climbing,"

she says earnestly. "You make a mistake rock climbing and you're fucked."

"I'm sure."

"You should come sometime. I'll take you." She turns around and looks for our waitress for the third time in five minutes.

"Right. When pigs fly."

She turns back. "What did you say?"

"Nothing. So you really don't worry about making partner?"

"Nope."

"Why?"

"Because we're both good lawyers. You do the discrimination defense and I'm the entire appellate brief department. We'll make it." Judy grins easily, showing the many gaps between her teeth, which are somehow not unattractive on her. In fact, men look her over all the time, but she disregards them cheerfully. She loves Kurt, the sculptor she lives with, who has most recently hacked Judy's buttercup-yellow hair into a chunky Dutch-boy cut. She calls it a work in progress.

"You think it's that easy?"

"I know it is. Do the work, the rest will come. You'll see—"

"Here it is, ladies," interrupts our waitress, who hates us. Not that we're special; the waitresses here hate all the customers. She slides the plates off her arm and they clatter onto the center of the table. Then she stalks off, leaving Judy and me to sort the orders. We move the heavy plates around like bumper cars.

"Girl food coming at you," Judy says, pushing the garden salad and diet Coke to me. "Yuck."

"Gimme a break. If I were ten feet tall I could eat like a lumberjack too." I slide her the hoagie with double meat, a side order of potato salad, and a vanilla milkshake.

"But you're not. You're a little Italian shortie. Where I come from, we use you people for doorstops." Judy bites eagerly into her hoagie. She starts at the end, like the sword-swallower in the circus. "Actually, there *is* one thing I'm worried about," she says, chomping away.

"What?"

"You. I'm worried about you."

"Me?" I can't tell if she's kidding.

"Yes."

"The phony phone calls?" I take a gulp of soda. It tastes like aspartame.

"No, they'll go away. I'm talking real danger," she says, wiggling her eyebrows comically. "Ned Waters is after you."

"Oh, jeez. Don't start, Jude."

"He wants it, Mare. Better buy some new undies." Judy likes sex and talks about it frankly and naturally. Since I was raised a Catholic, I know her attitude is perverted and evil. Faxed from Satan himself.

"Judith, keep it clean."

She leans over confidentially. "Be prepared to deal with the man, because it's true. I heard it from Delia the Stone Fox."

"Delia? Berkowitz's secretary? How does she know?"

"She heard it from Annie Zirilli From South Philly."

I laugh. Judy loves to make up nicknames. Half the time, I don't know who she's talking about. "You mean Barton's secretary?"

"Right. Annie saw him mooning around his office yesterday and started up a conversation with him. He told her he's interested in someone but won't say who. He said the girl—that's what he said, too, the *girl*— doesn't even know herself, because he's too scared to tell her. Too *scared*, can you believe this guy? What a horse's ass!" She stabs at her milkshake with a straw.

"He's shy."

"In a kid, it's shyness. In a man, it's dysfunction. And I bet money you're the lucky victim, because he always tries to sit next to you at department meetings. Plus I've seen the way he looks at you." She makes googly eyes.

"Bull. If he were interested, he would have followed up in law school. After our big date."

"But you met Mike."

"Ned didn't know that. He didn't even call back."

Judy shakes her head. "Sounds just like Waters. A torrid love affair of the mind. This guy has intimacy issues out the wazoo, I'm telling you. He's too cool. Cool Waters, that's him. Run for cover." She plows into her potato salad with a soup-spoon, like a bulldozer clearing heavy snow.

I watch her eat, thinking about Ned Waters. I still say he's shy, but it doesn't square with how handsome he is. Strong, masculine features, a smattering of large freckles, and unusual eyes of light green. "He has nice eyes."

"If you like Rosemary's baby."

"Come on. He was a hunk in law school."

"It's tough to be a hunk in law school, Mare. If your pupils respond to light, you can screw half the class."

I smile, remembering back to school when I had dinner with Ned. I was surprised when he asked me out, but not when he didn't call back, because he was so quiet on the date. He barely said a word; I yammered away to fill the silences. Of course, I didn't sleep with him or anything; that would have required 12,736 more dates, and even then I wouldn't have enjoyed it. Enjoying it didn't happen until Mike.

After lunch, Judy and I take a walk around the block, since it's a warm day in spring and Philadelphia's infamous humidity has yet to set in. We window-shop, checking out the displays at Laura Ashley, Banana Republic, and Borders, a chic bookstore on Walnut Street. I like Borders, because it's made reading fashionable, and I like to read. Judy likes Borders because it has an espresso bar with big cookies. Big as flapjacks, she likes to say. I treat her to a big cookie, and we walk back to the office, with me feeling like the stumpy mommy to a child on growth hormones.

THREE

A black-mirrored elevator whisks us to the top of a black-mirrored monolith that is home to a major oil company, an investment banking house, and Stalling & Webb. Stalling has the building's top seven floors, which always remind me of the seven deadly sins I learned in parochial school. Sloth is the bottom floor, where Judy gets off, and the next stops are Anger, Gluttony, Envy, Lust, and Avarice. Pride is the penthouse. I get off on Envy, which is where Martin H. Chatham IV, the junior partner on *Harbison's*, has his office. I'll tell him about the big victory after I freshen up.

Stalling's ladies' rooms are like heaven. They're clean, palatial, all done in cumulus white. The Corian countertop boasts eight generous basins, each lined with fake gold. At the end of the countertop is a white cabinet stocked with all-you-can-eat toiletries—free Tampax, Band-Aids, mouthwash, and dental floss. There's even Neutrogena, which I use liberally.

I wash my face as the secretaries joke around with me. They started to be nicer to me after Mike died, killed by a hit-and-run driver as he rode his bike along the Schuylkill River. I became a Young Widow, a character many of them recognized from their romance paperbacks. The lawyers, who have no time to read anything, barely remarked Mike's passing, which was fine with me. It's private.

I blot my face with a pebbled paper towel and take off.

Martin's on the telephone but waves me in. I sit down in one of the Shaker chairs facing his Shaker desk. Everything in Martin's office is tasteful, in a Thomas Moser kind of way, except for the owls. Needlepointed owls stare from the pillows, ceramic owls glare from the bookshelves. I used to think the owls were a high-prep fetish, like whales, but there's a better explanation. Martin is boredom personified and must know it, so he's seized on an interest to make himself interesting. The owls fill the vacuum where his personality should be. Now everyone knows him as Martin, the Guy Who Likes Owls. See what I mean?

"I'm listening, Stuart," Martin says into the telephone.

Listening is Martin's forte. He listened when I told him my idea for this motion, even as he winced with distaste. Martin's of the gentleman's school of litigation, which considers it bad form to put your client's interests ahead of your squash partner's. It was Berkowitz who green-lighted the motion, because Berkowitz is a real lawyer and doesn't know from squash.

"Good enough, Stuart. Take care, big guy." Martin hangs up the telephone and immediately puts a finger to his lips, a tacit *whoooo!* He makes a note in his red day journal to bill his time and another in his blue telephone log to bill the call. Later, Martin will bill for the time it takes him to write a file memo about the call, and he'll bill for the cost of duplicating the memo. Martin makes $265 every hour and 15 cents every page. In the name of the Father, of the Son, and of the Holy Ghost.

"So, Mary, how did it go?" he asks blandly.

"Very well."

"Good news?" His washed-out blue eyes flicker with interest.

"We won, Martin."

"We won? We *won?*"

"He ruled from the bench. The class action is no more."

"Good God, Mary!" Martin pumps me for every detail of the argument. I edit out the "Ave Maria" and give him the colorized version, in which I star as Partnership Material, No Question. When I'm finished, Martin calls to see if Berkowitz is in. Then he grabs his suit jacket, because THOU SHALT NOT WALK AROUND THE HALLS WITHOUT A JACKET, and dashes out.

I walk back to my office. I've done my job, which is to make Martin look good. That's why he goes alone to Berkowitz's office, to take credit for the win. Likewise, since Martin's raison d'être is to make Berkowitz look good, he'll let Berkowitz take the credit when he telephones Harbison's General Counsel. Because Berkowitz has made the GC look good to his CEO, the GC will send him more cases. ASAP. And partners who bring in the most business make the most money. You get the picture: The knee bone's connected to the thigh bone, the thigh bone's connected to the hip bone, and so on.

I should feel happy, but I don't. The victory lights up my Partnership Tote Board big-time, but it comes at a price. If Brent's information is right, my partnership could cost the firing of either of two fine lawyers, one of whom is my best friend.

And don't forget about the Harbison employees, says the little Mike-voice, come back again. *They were fired just when their pensions were about to vest, and the only mistake they made was choosing a lousy lawyer. Now they don't even have him anymore. Is that what you went to law school for?*

I try to shake off the voice when I hit my office. 2:25. I run out the day's string, listlessly dealing with the mail. I ask Brent to divide it into Good and Evil, with Good on the right and Evil on the left. The Good mail is advance sheets, which are paperback books summarizing recent court decisions. I'm supposed to read the Good mail, but if I did, cobwebs as heavy as suspension cables would grow from my butt to the chair. Instead, I put them in my out box so the messengers will shovel them onto someone else's desk. That's why they're Good.

The Evil Mail is everything else. It's Evil because your opponent's trying to fuck you. There's only one lawyerly response: Fuck back. For example, last week, in a case for Noone Pharmaceuticals, opposing counsel tried to fuck us into a settlement by threatening to publish company memoranda in the newspaper. So I'm writing a motion asking the Court to restrict the use of company documents to the lawsuit and to award Noone my fees in preparing the motion. This is primo fucking back, and you have to fuck back. If you don't fuck back, you'll get fucked.

Believe it or not, I usually enjoy this aspect of my profession, the head-banging and the back-fucking, but not today. Anxiety gnaws at the edges of my brain and I can't focus on the Evil mail. I turn to the unfinished brief for Noone. I read it over and over but the argument sounds like a verbal Mobius strip: Judge, you should restrict the documents to the lawsuit because documents should be restricted to lawsuits. I can't tell if it's a failure of concentration or of writing. I pack the draft in my briefcase and leave the office at dusk.

The remainder of the day's sunlight is blocked prematurely by Philadelphia's new and improved skyline. Developers went crazy after City Council permitted buildings to be taller than William Penn's hat, with the result that the city streets get dark too soon and there's a lot of empty office buildings sprouting like mushrooms in the gloom.

The air cools down rapidly as I reach Rittenhouse Square. I'm shivering like all the other superannuated yuppies, except that I refuse to wear Reeboks. If my shoes were too uncomfortable to walk in, I wouldn't buy them.

The square looks just like it does every evening this time of year. The old people huddle together on the benches, clucking worriedly about the young people, with their orange-striped hair and nose rings, as well as the homeless, with their shopping carts and superb tans. Runners circle the square for the umpteenth time. Walkers stride by in fast-forward, plugged into Walkmans. A pale young man on a bench looks me up and down, and then I remember.

Is someone watching me?

I look backward over my shoulder at the pale man on the bench, but he's joined by a girlfriend in a black beret. I look at the other people as I pass through the square, but they all look normal enough. Is one of them the someone? Does one of them call me and do God-knows-what when I answer? My step quickens involuntarily.

I hurry inside when I reach my building. It's quiet in the entrance hall, the kind of absolute silence that settles in when a big old house is empty. I'm the only tenant here. My landlords are an elderly couple who live on the first two floors of the house. They're nice people, hand-holders after fifty years of marriage, off on another Love Boat cruise. I pick up my bills and catalogs from the floor and make sure the front door's locked.

I climb the stairs, wondering if the telephone will ring after I get in. I unlock the door and switch on the living room light. I glance at the telephone, but it's sitting there like a properly inanimate object. I breathe a sigh of relief and drop my briefcase with a thud.

"Honey, I'm home."

The tabby cat doesn't even look up from the windowsill. She's not deaf, she's indifferent. She wouldn't care if Godzilla drove a Corvette through the door, she's waiting for Mike to come home. In winter, the windowpane is dotted with her nose prints. In summer, her gray hairs cling to the screen.

"He's not coming back," I tell her. It's a reminder to both of us since the episode this morning in court.

I kick off my shoes and join her at the window, looking out at the apartments across the street. Most have plants on their windowsills, starved for light in the northern exposure. One has a turquoise Bianchi bike hanging in the window, like an advertisement to break in, and another has an antique rake. Most of my neighbors are home, cooking dinner or listening to music. The window directly across from mine has the shade drawn; it looks dark inside. I wonder if the person who lives there is the one who's been calling me. It's hard to imagine, since Mike knew all our neighbors. He was the friendly one.

"Come on, Alice. Let's close up." I nudge the cat and she jumps to the living room rug, her hindquarters twitching.

I yank on the string of the knife-edged blinds, which tumble to the windowsill with a *zzziiip*. I pad over to the other window, flat-footed without my heels, and am about to pull down the blinds when I hear the ignition of a car outside the window.

Strange. I didn't see a driver walk to the car, and it's not a car I recognize.

I let down the blinds but peek between them at the car. It's too dark out for me to see the driver.

The car's headlights blaze to life as it pulls out of its parking space and glides down the street. I don't know the make of the car; I'm not good at that. It's big, though, like the boats my father used to drive. An Oldsmobile, maybe. Before they tried to convince us that they're not the boats our fathers used to drive.

I watch the car disappear, as the telephone rings loudly.

I flinch at the sound. Is it the someone?

I pick up the receiver cautiously. "Hello?"

But the only response is static—a static I hear on many of the calls. It's him. My heart begins to pound as I put two and two together for the first time.

"Is this a car phone, you bastard? Are you watching my house, you sick—"

The tirade is severed by the dial tone.

"Fuck you!" I shout into the dead receiver.

Alice blinks up at me, in disapproval.

FOUR

"Taste, *cara*," says my mother, holding out a wooden spoon with tomato sauce.

"Mmmm. *Perfetto*." I'm at my parents' row house in South Philly the next day, playing hooky because my twin sister's on parole from the convent. She only gets out once a year under the rules of her cloistered order, and isn't permitted phone calls or mail. I hate the convent for taking my twin from me. I can't believe that God, even if he does exist, would want to divide us.

"You all right, Maria?" My mother frowns behind her thick glasses, which make her brown eyes look supernaturally large. She's half blind from sewing lampshades in the basement of this very house, her childhood home. The kitchen is the only thing that's changed since then; the furniture and fixtures remain the same, stop-time. We still use the tinny black switchplate like a bulletin board, leaving notes among the dog-eared mass cards, a photo of JFK, and a frond of dried-out palm.

"I'm fine, Ma. I'm fine." I wouldn't dream of telling her I think I'm being watched. She's like a supersensitive instrument, the kind that calibrates air pressure—or lies. She has a jumpy needle, and the news would send it into the red zone.

"Maria? They're not treating you good at that office?" She

scrutinizes me, the wooden spoon resting against her stretch pants like Excalibur in its scabbard.

"I've just been busy. It's almost time for them to decide who makes partner."

"*Dio mio!* They're lucky to have you! Lucky! The nuns said you were a genius! A genius!" A scowl contorts her delicate features. Even at seventy-three, she makes up in the morning and gets her hair done every Saturday at the corner, where they tease it to hide her bald spot.

"Catholic school standards, Ma."

"I should go up there to that fancy office! I should tell them how lucky they are to have my daughter be their lawyer!" She unsheaths the spoon and waves it recklessly in the air.

"No, Ma. Please." I touch her forearm to calm her. Her skin feels papery.

"They should burn in hell!" She trembles with agitation. I wrap my arms around her, surprised at her frailty.

"It's all right. Don't worry."

"Whaddaya two doing, the fox-trot?" jokes my father, puffing his cigar as he walks into the kitchen. He looks roly-poly in a thin short-sleeved shirt. It's almost transparent, made from some obscure synthetic fiber, and he's got the dago T-shirt on underneath. My father has dressed this way for as long as I can remember. When he's dressed up, that is.

"Out! Out of the kitchen with that cigar!" my mother shouts—of necessity, because my father never wears his hearing aid.

"Don't shoot!" He puts up both hands, then returns to the baseball game blaring in the living room.

My mother's magnified eyes are an inch from my nose. "When is he going to stop with those cigars? When?"

"He's been smoking cigars for sixty years, Ma. You think he'll quit soon?"

Suddenly, there's a commotion at the front door and I hear Angie shouting a greeting to my father. My mother and I hurry into the living room, where Angie is taking off her sweater.

"Hello, beautiful," she says, with a laugh. She always calls me that. It's her joke, since we're identical twins.

"Angie!" I lock her in a bear hug.

"Hey, that's too tight, let me go."

"No."

"Mare . . ."

"Not until you tell me you miss me."

"Ma, get her off of me, please."

"Let your sister alone. You're too old for that. Too old." My mother swats me in the arm with the spoon.

"Too old to hug my own twin? Since when?"

She hits me again.

"Ouch! What is this, *Mommy Dearest?*" I let Angie go.

"Yeah, grow up," she says, with a short laugh. Her eyes look large and luminous under a short haircut—our childhood pixie resurrected. She's dressed in jeans and a Penn sweatshirt just like mine, having left her Halloween costume back at the convent. We're twins again, but for the hair and the fact that Angie looks rested and serene, with a solid spiritual core.

"Look at her, Ma, she looks so good!" I say. "Angie, you look great!"

"Stop, you." Angie can't take a compliment, never could.

"Turn around. Let me see."

She does a obligatory swish-turn in her jeans.

"You wearing underwear?"

She laughs gaily. For a split second, it's a snapshot of the twin I grew up with. I catch glimpses of the old Angie only now and then. The rest of the time, she's a twin I hardly know.

"*Basta*, Maria! *Basta!*" chides my mother happily.

"So you're out of uniform. I can't believe it."

"I changed at a Hojo's after I left." She sets her purse on the floor.

"Why?"

"No special reason. Tired of you making all those habit jokes, I guess."

"Me?"

"You."

"Well I love the sweatshirt. You look like yourself again."

"Like I didn't know you'd say that," Angie says.

"Look at this hair!" My mother runs an arthritic hand through Angie's hair. "So soft. Just like a baby's."

Angie smiles, and I wonder why she's so accepting of my mother's touch and not my own.

"Look at this hair, Matty!" my mother shouts delightedly. "Just like a baby's!"

My father smiles. "You got your baby back, Mama."

Angie positively glows in my mother's arms. "I can't get over how good you look, Ange. I think I'm in love," I say.

"Will you stop already?" She wiggles away from my mother, still smiling.

"Plus I'm not used to you looking so much better than me. You look like the *after* picture and I look like the *before*."

"That's because you work too hard."

"Tell me about it."

"Did you make a partner yet?"

"No, they decide in two months. I'm going crazy. I hate life." I wish I could tell her about the partnership rumors and the strange car, but we won't have any time alone unless I waylay her.

"And it's a hit! Out to right field! Might be deep enough . . . It is!" screams the Phillies announcer, Richie Ashburn, but my father's too excited at seeing Angie again to look at the television. My parents miss Angie, even though they're proud of her decision. They're proud of both their twins, the one who serves God, and the other who serves Mammon.

We troop into the kitchen to talk and drink percolated coffee from chipped cups. That's all we'll do today, as Richie Ashburn calls a high-decibel double-header to an empty living room. I start the ball rolling over the first cup, whining about my case-load, but my father quickly takes over the conversation. He can't hear when others talk, so his only choice is to filibuster. None of us minds this much, least of all my mother, who foot-notes his narrative of their courtship.

My father takes a breather after lunch and my mother holds forth about the new butcher, who doesn't trim off enough fat. She tells a few stories of her own, mostly about our childhood, and I realize how badly she needs to talk to someone who can hear her. Angie must know this too, for she doesn't look bored, and, truth to tell, I'm not either. But we both draw the line after dinner, when she launches into the story of a maiden aunt's gallbladder operation. Angie seizes the opportunity to head for the bathroom and I follow her upstairs, hoping to get her alone. I reach the bathroom door just as she's about to close it.

"Ange, wait. It's me." I stick my foot in the door.

"What are you doing?" Angie looks at me through the crack.

"I want to talk to you."

"Move your foot. I'll be right out."

"What am I, the Boston Strangler? Let me in."

"I have to go to the bathroom."

"Number one or number two?"

"Mary, we're not kids anymore."

"Right. Number one or number two?"

She shakes her head. "Number one."

"Okay. So number one, you can let me in."

"It can't wait two minutes?"

"I don't want Mom to hear. Will you open the goddamn door?"

So she does, and I take a precarious seat on the curved edge of the tub, an old claw-and-ballfoot. Angie stands above me with her hands on her hips. "What is it?" she says.

"You can pee if you have to."

"I can wait. Why don't you tell me what you have to say."

A little ember of anger starts to glow inside my chest. "What's the big deal, Angie? We took baths together until we were ten years old. Now you won't let me in the bathroom?"

She closes the lid on the toilet seat and sits down on it with a quiet sigh. The old Angie would have snapped back, would have given as good as she got, but that Angie went into the convent and never came out. "Is something the matter?" she asks patiently.

By now my teeth are on edge. "No."

"Look, Mary, let's not fight. What's the matter?"

I look down at the tiny white octagons that make up the tile floor. The grout between them is pure as sugar. My father, a tile setter until he popped a disc in his back, regrouts the bathroom every year. The porcelain gleams like something you'd find at Trump Tower. My father does beautiful work.

"It's beautiful, isn't it?" Angie says.

I smile. We used to be able to read each other's minds; I guess Angie can still read mine. "What was it Pop always said?"

" 'It's not a job, it's a *craft*.' "

"Right." I look up, and her face has softened. I take a deep breath. "I don't know where to start, Ange. So much is going on. At work. At home. I feel tense all the time."

"What's happening?"

"It's the last couple of weeks until they decide who's partner. I heard they're only picking two of us. Everything I do is under the microscope. Plus I've been getting these phony phone calls. And last night I could swear a car was watching me from across the street."

She frowns. "Are you sure?"

"Yeah."

"But why would anybody be watching you? You're not involved in any trouble, are you? I mean, in the work you do?"

"I don't do any criminal cases, if that's what you mean. Stalling would never touch anything like that."

From downstairs, my mother calls, "Angela! Maria! Dessert!"

Angie gets up. "Maybe it's your imagination. You always had a vivid imagination, you know."

"I did not."

"Oh, really? What about the time you hung garlic in our room, after that vampire movie we saw? It was on our bulletin board for a whole year. A foot-long ring of garlic."

"So?"

"So my sweaters smelled like pesto."

"But we never got any vampires."

She laughs. "You look stressed, Mary. You need to relax. So what if they don't make you partner? You're a great lawyer. You can get another job."

"Oh, yeah? Being passed over isn't much of a recommendation, and the market in Philly is tight. Even the big firms are laying people off."

"You need to stay calm. I'm sure everything will turn out all right. I would tell you that it's in God's hands, but I know what you'd say."

"Girls, your coffee's getting cold!" calls my mother.

"She's waiting for us," Angie says. "And I still have to go to the bathroom."

I get up, reluctantly. "I wish we could get time to talk, Ange. We never talk. I don't even know how you're doing. Are you okay?"

"I'm fine," she says, with a pat smile, the same smile you'd give to a bank teller.

"Really?"

"Really. Now go. I have to pee." She ushers me out the door. "I'll pray for you," she calls from inside.

"Terrific," I mumble, walking down the stairs to a darkened living room. The double-header is over, and my father is standing in front of the television watching the Phillies leave the field. Red, blue, and green lights flicker across his face in the dark. Despite the carnival on his features, I can see he's dejected. "They lose again, Pop?"

He doesn't hear me.

"They lose, Pop?" I shout.

He nods and turns off the ancient television with a sigh. It makes a small electrical crackle; then the room falls oddly silent. I hadn't realized how loud the volume was. He yanks the chattery pull chain on the floor lamp and the room lights up instantly, very bright. They must have a zillion-watt bulb in the lamp; the parchment shade is brown around the middle. I'm about to say something when I remember it might be because of my mother's eyesight.

"You want some cannoli, honey?" my father asks tenderly. He throws an arm around my shoulder.

"You got the chocolate chip, don't you? 'Cause if you don't, I'm leaving. I've had it with the service at this place."

"What kinda father would I be that I don't have the chocolate chip? Huh?" He gives me a squeeze and we walk into the kitchen together.

My mother clucks about the cold coffee as we sit down, and Angie joins us at the table. My father's soft shoulders slump over his coffee. We carry on the conversation around him, and my mother chatters anxiously through dessert. Something's wrong, but I can't figure out what it is. Angie senses it too, because after my father declines a cannoli for the second time, she gives me a discreet nudge.

"Pop," I say, "Have a cannoli. I'm eating alone here."

He doesn't even look up. I don't know if he doesn't hear me or what. Angie and I exchange glances.

"Pop!" Angie shouts. "You okay?"

My mother touches my hand. "Let him be. He's just tired."

My father looks up, and his milky brown eyes are wet. He squeezes them with two calloused fingers.

My mother deftly passes him a napkin. "Isn't that right, Matty? You're tired?"

"Ah, yeah. I'm tired." He nods.

"You're leading the witness, Ma," I say.

She waves me off like an annoying fly. "Your father and I were talking about Frank Rizzo last night. Remember, it was this time of year, Rizzo had the heart attack. It's a sin. He coulda been mayor again."

My father seems lost in thought. He says, half to himself, "So sudden. So young. We couldn't prepare."

"It's a sin," repeats my mother, rubbing his back. With her lipstick all gone, her lips look bloodless.

"Pop, Rizzo was almost eighty," I say, but Angie's look silences me. Her eyes tell me who they're grieving for. The one who loved percolated coffee, the Phillies, and even an occasional cigar—Mike. I feel a stab of pain inside; I wonder when this will stop happening. I rise stiffly. "I better get going. It's a school night."

My parents huddle together at the table, looking frozen and small.

Angie clears her throat. "Me too. I have to change back."

I walk to the screen door with its silly scroll-work D, looking out into the cool, foggy night. I remember nights like this from when I was little. The neighbors would sit out in beach chairs, the women gossiping in Italian and the men playing *mora*. Angie and I would sit on the marble stoop in our matching pajamas like twin mascots. It was a long time ago.

I wish I could feel that air again.

I open the screen door and walk down the front steps onto the sidewalk. The air is chilled from the fog, which hangs as low as the thick silver stanchions put in to thwart parking on the sidewalk. A dumb idea—all it does is force people to double-park on the main streets. Like my father says, in South Philly the cars are bigger than the houses.

Suddenly a powerful car barrels by, driving much too fast

for this narrow street. It comes so near the curb in front of me that I feel a cold chill in its wake.

"Hey, buddy!" I shout after him, then do a double-take. It looks just like the car from last night.

I run into the middle of the street, squinting in the darkness. I catch sight of the car's flame-red taillights as it turns right at the top of the street and disappears into the dark. My father comes out of the house, followed by my mother.

"Pop! Did you see that car? What kind of car was that? Was that an Oldsmobile?"

"What?" He cups a hand behind his ear, making a lumpy silhouette in front of the screen door.

"Ma! Did you see that car?"

"What car?" she hollers, from behind her bulletproof glasses.

Behind them both, at a distance, is Angie.

FIVE

"I would say this is Evil mail, wouldn't you?" Brent asks grimly. He holds up a piece of white paper that reads:

CONGRATULATIONS ON YOUR
PARTNERSHIP, MARY

The letters are typed in capitals. It looks computer-generated, like the laser printers we use at Stalling. State-of-the-art. The paper is smooth. The note is unsigned.

I read it again. "Weird."

"Very."

"It's not a nice note, is it?"

"No." Brent's face looks tight.

"Who do you think it's from?"

"I have no idea. There's no return address, either."

"Let me see." I take the envelope, a plain white business envelope, and flip it over. On the front is my name and Stalling's address in capital letters. Also laser-printed. The stamp is a tiny American flag. "I don't understand."

"I do."

"What?"

"I think somebody's jealous of you, that's what I think. The news about your motion is all over the department. Everybody knows you won before Bitterman. It was a big deal for an associate. I even heard it in the secretaries' lunchroom, so you know the lawyers are talking about it."

"Really?"

"Sure. You're a star, kid. Your enemies will be comin' out of the woodwork now. It just proves my theory."

"What theory?"

"I never told you my theory?"

"You told me your cancellation theory, about how assholes marry each other. You never told me your theory about hate mail."

"Well. My theory is that you find out who your true friends are when something good happens to you. Everybody loves you when something bad happens to you. Then you're easy to love."

"That's sick, Brent."

"But true. And this is a good example. There must be somebody who you think is your friend, but who isn't really. Not a true friend. They're jealous as shit of you, secretly competing with you. Whoever it is, they smile in your face."

His words make me uneasy. "Who?"

"Think about it. Who's competing with you right now to make partner? Judy and Ned. We know it can't be Judy, so that leaves Ned. I never liked that guy." He looks bitter.

My thoughts race ahead. Is the note connected to the car? To the phone calls? Is it one person or more than one? Holy Christ. I hand Brent the envelope. I don't even want it in my hand.

It's getting worse, says the Mike-voice. *First the calls. Then the car. Now a note.*

"Mary? You okay?"

I plop down into my chair. "I think this has something to do with the phone calls."

"Mystery Man?"

"Brent, something's the matter."

"What?"

"Close the door, okay?"

"Mare, what's going on?" He shuts the door and sinks into one of the chairs opposite my desk.

"I think somebody might be watching me. Following me."

"What?" His eyes widen.

I tell Brent about the car on my street and then at my parents' house. He barely lets me finish before he has a conniption. "You have to call the cops! Right this instant!" He points to the telephone on my desk. "What are you waiting for?"

"I can't do that. I'm not even sure about the car. Maybe I'm imagining—"

"Mary, you're not imagining *this!*" He waves the note in the air like a warning flag.

"I can't just call the cops. Can you imagine? Cops asking everyone in the department—even partners—about me? That would be terrific right now, right before the election."

"Mare, what's the matter with you? Someone is stalking you and you're worried about making partner?"

"They're not *stalking* me, you don't have to make it sound like that."

At that moment, my telephone rings and we exchange uneasy looks. Brent takes charge. "Let Lucinda get it. And they *are* stalking you. What do you think it's called when someone follows you around?"

The phone rings again, and Brent looks at it angrily. "Fuck! Can't she get off her ass for once? I pick up for *her!*"

The phone rings a third time.

I reach for it, but Brent heads me off. "No, let me. If it's that asshole, I'm gonna scream my fucking head off." He snatches up the receiver. "Ms. DiNunzio's office," he says, in a crisp telephone tenor. Then his face blanches. "Okay. Right now." He nods, hanging up.

"What?"

"Berkowitz wants to see you."

"Why? Is something the matter? Was that him?"

"It was Delia. She said he wants to see you right away."

"Great. This is all I need." I dig in my purse for my compact and check my reflection in its round mirror. A circle of dirty-blond hair, shoulder length. A circle of dark brown eye, an extended-wear contact lens afloat on its cornea. A circle of whitish teeth, straightened into Chiclets by orthodonture paid for in installments. Mike used to say I was pretty, but I don't feel pretty today.

"What are you doing? Get going! You're worse than Jack with that mirror," Brent says. Jack is his lover of five years, a bartender at Mr. Bill's, a gay bar on Locust Street. Judy calls him Jack Off, but Brent claims he thought of it first. "Go, girl, you'll be late!"

Berkowitz's corner office is on Pride, and Delia's desk blocks its entrance like a walnut barricade. She types as she listens to the teaching of Chairman Berkowitz through dictating earphones. Even the ugly headset doesn't mar her good looks. Lustrous red hair, a perfect nose, the sexiest pout in legal history. Brent is right. Delia *is* a stone fox.

"Hi, Delia."

"I'm busy." She doesn't look up but continues to hit the keys of her word processor with spiky acrylic nails. *Click-click-click-click*. It sounds like a hail on a rooftop. Too bad it will look like *jciywegwebcniquywgxnmai*. I know, I've seen her work.

"Oh. Sorry."

"He's in there." *Click-click-click. Oreuhbalkejeopn?*

"I'll just go in, then."

"Suit yourself."

This is even more attitude than I'm used to from Delia; I wonder what's bothering her. I walk to the open doorway of Berkowitz's office, but his brawny back is to the door. A tailored English suit strains at its shoulder seams as Berkowitz hunches over. The only time Burberrys has dressed a major appliance.

"Go in already!" snaps Delia.

The command startles me into the sanctum sanctorum. Berkowitz is on the telephone and doesn't turn around. I walk the three city blocks to his desk and sit down in a massive leather wing chair. The decor here screams Street Kid Who Made God—I mean, Good. The desk is a baroque French antique with a surface that was polished by a Zamboni. The high-backed desk chair could have belonged to the Sun King. Photographs of Berkowitz's first, second, and third sets of children adorn curly-legged mahogany end tables. I feel like a scullery maid at Versailles.

"I don't care, Lloyd! I don't give *one flying fuck!*" Berkowitz bellows into the telephone, as he swivels around in his chair. "You tell that little bastard if he thinks he's going to fuck me, he has another thing coming! We can take his fucking little *pisher* of a firm, and we will!" Berkowitz is so engrossed in making what constitutes Terroristic Threats under the Pennsylvania Crimes Code that he's oblivious to me altogether. This is why Judy calls him Jerkowitz, but I think she's being unfair. Berkowitz grew up in tough West Philly and made it to the peaky-peak on sheer brainpower and force of will. If your Fortune 500 Company is in deep shit, he's one of the few lawyers in the country who can save your sorry ass. Guaranteed. But not in writing.

"Where the fuck does he get off? I told him what the agenda was, and he tries to make a fool out of me! He'll be offa this committee so goddamn fast it'll make his head spin!" Berkowitz is yelling at one of his apostles on the Rules Committee, which he chairs. It's a twelve-man panel of federal judges and prominent litigators that meets at our offices to propose changes in federal court rules. If something didn't go

well at a recent meeting, heads will roll, and balls too. Everything rolling, off down the hall.

"Don't tell me to calm down! I *am* calm! . . . No! No! No!
You deal with him then!"

Berkowitz slams down the telephone receiver. The glaze in
his eyes tells me he's back on Girard Avenue, decades ago,
fighting off the punks who want a peek at his foreskin. Or lack
thereof.

Berkowitz shakes his head, his face still florid. "Can you believe this fucking guy? Can you fucking believe this guy?"

I gather the question is rhetorical and say nothing.

He rubs his eyes irritably and leans back in his chair. His
look says, Heavy is the head that wears the crown. "You want
my job, Mary, Mary, Quite Contrary?"

"What?"

"I'm asking you. You want it?" He isn't smiling.

"I don't understand."

"Do you want to be here someday? Run the department,
head the committees? When I was your age, I wanted to be me
so bad I was on fire." He gazes out of a massive window at the
best view in the city. From his vantage point, you can see all
the way to the Delaware River and the snaky black border it
makes between Pennsylvania and New Jersey. An occasional
tourist ferry travels in slow motion under the Ben Franklin
Bridge. We ain't the port of call we used to be.

"I would have killed to be me," Berkowitz says absently. Suddenly he snatches a pack of Marlboros from his desk and lights
one up, belching out a puff of smoke so thick it looks like the In-
dustrial Revolution took place in his office. I pretend the smoke
doesn't bother me, which it does, mightily. I try not to breathe.

"But you're not interested in this shit and neither am I.
You're wondering why I called you up here." He takes a slow
drag on the cigarette and squints at me through the smoke.

I nod, yes.

"Two reasons. One: That was a helluva result you got on the motion before Bitterman. I saw him at the Rules Committee meeting"—at this he winces—"and he told me you had great potential."

"Uh . . . thank you."

"He's an ugly bastard, isn't he?"

I laugh.

"Two: Harbison's GC is sending me a new case. You know how they like to spread their business around, get all the firms competing with each other. They sent the case to Masterson originally, but the GC thinks we can do a better job. We can, right?"

"Right." So we stole a case from Masterson, Moss & Dunbar, the firm at the apex of the holy trinity. We must have snaked them with our win before Bitter Man and some pillow talk by Berkowitz. He doesn't say these things, but I don't need a crib sheet to translate Latin One.

"It's another age discrimination case. They demoted a CFO, so it's very high-profile. And they won't settle. They want to crush the bastard." Berkowitz blows an enormous cloud of smoke upward, which is something he does at meetings when he thinks he's being considerate. "I'm assigning the case to you, Mary Mary. You make all the calls, just be sure you blind-copy me on the correspondence. I don't want to look like a smacked ass if the GC calls. There's a pretrial conference scheduled for today at three-thirty. It's your baby. Any questions?" He sucks on the cigarette throttled between his thick knuckles. Its red tip flashes on like a stoplight.

"And . . . Martin?"

"Forget Martin!" he says, breathing smoke. "You don't need Martin, do you?"

"No, I just . . . I thought he handled your matters."

"Well, he doesn't. I told him the other day. He's fine with it. You want this case or don't you?"

"I do. I do."

"Good. Then we're married." He erupts into laughter.

I laugh too, with relief and wonder.

"Now get out of my office. Can't you see I'm a busy man?"

I laugh again, but the meeting is over. I get up to leave.

"By the way, Ned Waters was in here bitching today. He heard that only two of you will be making partner in June. You hear anything like that, Mary, Queen of Scots?"

"No," I lie.

"Fine," he replies, knowing I'm lying. "It's not true."

"Good," I reply, knowing he's lying.

As I leave his office, I see that Delia's headset is off, resting at the base of her neck like a cheap choker. As I walk by, she's sipping tea in a genteel way from a white china cup. An affectation she's picked up from Berkowitz, who likes to stub out his Marlboro in the saucer.

"See you later, Delia."

"Ready to play with the big boys, Mary?" She looks daggers at me over the delicate cup.

Her expression bewilders me. "Guess so."

"You'd better be." Her lovely eyes glitter with hostility as she sets the cup down. It makes an unhappy sound when it crashes into the saucer.

"Are you mad at me for something, Delia?"

"You, Mary? Never. You're little Miss Perfect. Hail Mary, full of grace. He forgot that one, didn't he? But that's not one he'd know."

Before I can react, Berkowitz's hulking frame appears in the doorway. His cigarette is burnt all the way down to the V between his index and middle fingers, but he seems heedless of it. "Delia, I need you in here," he says gruffly.

"But I'm having a nice conversation with Mary, Mr. Berkowitz." Her full lips curve upward in a sly smile.

"Now!" It sounds like a gunshot.

I jump, but Delia doesn't. Still smiling, she stands up and unfolds slowly, from her perky breasts on down. She and Berkowitz lock eyes, with him looking the stern principal to her naughty schoolgirl. As I turn to go, I hear the door of Berkowitz's office close behind them.

SIX

"Oh-ho!" Brent whoops behind the closed door of my office. "She's jealous of you, Mare. Sammie's giving you your big chance, and it's killing her. This ain't a law firm, it's a mini-series!"

"You think she's jealous?"

"That girl needs a spanking, and I bet I know who's gonna—"

"Jealous enough to send me that note?"

His face falls. "My God, Mary. I didn't think of that."

"Is she capable of it?"

"I only know what I hear about her. Sure, she's the type to send a hate note—she'd do it in a minute. But follow you around in a car? That's a bit much. I'd sooner believe that of Waters. And he has more of a reason. It's his partnership you'd take." Brent bites at a thumbnail.

"I don't think it's Ned."

"Why?"

"Something tells me it's not him. I don't know; if anything, he seems kind of vulnerable. And why not Delia? Look, I don't know if she's having an affair with Berkowitz, and it doesn't matter. What if she has a crush on him and he's favoring me? Maybe that's enough to piss her off."

"They're having an affair, Mare. He left five minutes after her Monday night. Janet won four bucks."

I flash on the way Berkowitz looked at Delia before they closed the door. "Okay. So maybe they're having an affair. That would make her even more jealous, wouldn't it?"

He shakes his head, examining the ragged nail. "It's not her," he says with certainty.

"How do you know?"

"No typos."

So he's seen her work, too.

A while later, Judy drags me to the Bellyfiller for lunch, which is fine, because I'm not hungry. The place is packed with middle managers. They sit behind combination meat sandwiches, pretending not to be interested in the soap opera on the big-screen TV. I tell Judy about the car that drove by my parents' house and about the note in the morning mail. It sounds more farfetched than the soap and takes almost as long to tell. Judy's finished dessert by the time I've finished the story.

"Brent's right," she says with finality. "I think Ned wrote the note. It makes the most sense. He wants to make partner so bad he can taste it."

"More than we do?"

"Sure. He has a famous daddy to live up to, remember? And the firm is his whole life. It's all he has."

Judy's words echo inside my head. It's all *I* have, too. That must be why I obsess over it and she doesn't. I take a gulp of water from a smudgy glass.

"We don't know enough to say whether the car's connected to the note, but it seems more likely than not. And for some reason, call it sexism, I find it hard to believe that a woman would be stalking you in a car. So Delia's out."

"Yeah, I guess." I feel tense and confused. On the big-screen TV, a gigantic nurse looks tense and confused. My life, parodied before my eyes. I try to block out the TV, but it's as hard to ignore as the huge clock in my office window. Big, scary things seem to be everywhere I go lately, like a nightmare of Claes Oldenburg's.

"Do you ever see the car in the daytime?"

"No."

"That's consistent with someone who works during the day."

"Everybody at Stalling, in other words."

Judy thinks a minute. "Have you thought about calling the cops?"

"Brent wants me to, but I hate to do that. The last thing I need right now is an investigation in the department. I might as well kiss my career good-bye."

"Hmmm. I see your point. Let's not do the freak yet, let's see if it blows over. I'll be your bodyguard in the meantime. How does that sound?"

I consider this. "I can't afford to feed you."

"Very funny."

On the TV, two monster nurses are discussing whether somebody will live through the week. Their glossy mouths are the size of swimming pools. A commercial for a mile-high can of Crisco comes on.

"Mary?"

"Yeah?"

"You look spaced. Listen, it's okay to be upset about this. I don't blame you. It's spooky."

"It's not just the car, Jude. It's everything."

"What do you mean?" She sets down her milkshake.

"I don't know what I mean. What I mean doesn't make sense."

"So tell me what you're thinking. It doesn't matter if it makes sense."

I look at Judy's blue eyes, so wide-set and uncluttered. I'm reminded of how different we are. There's a whole country between us. She's so free and openhearted, like the West Coast, and I'm so—well, East. Burdened with my own history, dark and falling apart. "I don't know. Forget it, Jude. It's stupid."

"Come on, Mary. Let's talk about it."

"I don't know."

"Try it."

"All right." I take another gulp of water. "It's just that lately, like after my argument for Harbison's, I hear this . . . voice. Not that I'm hearing voices, like Son of Sam or something, not like that."

"No German shepherds," she says with a smile.

"No. Sometimes the voice sounds like Mike, you know? Not the tone of it, I mean, but what it says. It sounds just like something he would say. Something right. Am I explaining this okay?"

"You're doing fine."

I take a deep breath. "You know the expression, what goes around comes around?"

She nods patiently. Her long silver earrings swing back and forth.

"Sometimes I think that the car, and now the note, are happening for a reason. And I think it's going to get worse unless I change something. Do something different, do something better. I think Mike, or the voice—whoever, is trying to tell me that."

She frowns deeply. "You think you did something to cause the note? And the guy in the car?"

It strikes a chord. That's exactly how I feel. I nod yes, and am surprised to feel my chest blotching up.

"That's crazy. You didn't do anything, Mary. Somebody's jealous of you. It's not your fault."

I feel flushed and hot. There's no water left in my glass.

"What is this, some Italian thing? Some Mediterranean version of karma?"

"I don't know."

Judy looks sympathetic. "It's nothing you did, Mary. You did not cause this. You are not responsible for it. If it doesn't go away, which I sincerely hope it does, we'll deal with it. We'll figure it out together."

Judy gives me a bone-crushing squeeze and we leave the restaurant. We decide not to walk around after lunch, and she buys us both some shoestring licorice from a candy store on the basement level. She says it'll cheer me up, but she ends up being wrong about that.

I'm back at my desk at 1:58, wrestling with my fears and the Noone brief. After it's finished, I send it along to the partner in charge, Timothy Jameson. I do a good job because every partner gets a vote in the partnership election, and I can't afford to screw anything up at this point. I tally the votes for the third time today—I'm like an anorexic, counting the same few calories over and over. If Berkowitz votes for me, I might have the requisite votes right there, but there's a faction that hates Berkowitz, and Jameson's in it. The election will be close. My head begins to thunder.

In the afternoon, I'm in the chambers of the Honorable Morton A. Weinstein, resident genius of the district court. Judy calls him Einstein, naturally. Einstein is stoop-shouldered, with a frizzy pate of silvery hair. Steely half-moon reading glasses make him look even smarter. He's flanked by a geeky law clerk who mousses with margarine. Even the geeks want to look like Pat Riley.

We're sitting at a chestnut-veneer conference table to discuss my new case, *Hart v. Harbison's*, which, to my dismay, is a stone-cold loser. I'd spent the cab ride to the courthouse skimming the thin case file as I looked out the window for the dark car. I don't know which worried me more. I've seen bad discrimination cases in my time—evidence of the shitting upon of every minority in the rainbow—but *Hart* is the worst. I'd settle the case instantly if it were up to me, but I have a mission. Search, destroy, and petition for costs.

To make matters worse, there's a cherub posing as plaintiff's counsel. He can't be more than a year out of law school, and his face is as tender and soft as a newborn's. His hair, a wispy strawberry blond, brings out the rosy hue of his cheeks. His briefcase is spanking new; his bow tie looks clipped on. My job is to ignore all this cutehood and yank out his nuts with the roots intact.

"Young man," interrupts Einstein, "I'm sorry. I didn't catch your name."

"Oh, jeez. I'm sorry, Your Honor." He blushes charmingly. "I'm new at this, I probably forgot to say it. My name is Henry Hart. Henry Hart, Junior."

"Is the plaintiff your father, Henry?" asks Einstein.

"Yes. They call me Hank. I just got my mother to stop calling me Little Hank, if you can believe that. I have to remind her that I'm twenty-four now." He smiles, utterly without guile.

I can't believe what I'm hearing. Harbison's did this to the child's *father*? And I have to justify it?

"Twenty-four, my, my." Einstein turns to his law clerk and chuckles. "Was I ever twenty-four, Neil?"

Neil doesn't miss a beat. "Come on, Judge. You're not that old."

"No? I remember the big one. World War II. I was a navigator in the Eastern Theater. Flying B-24's out of Italy."

"The flying boxcars!" says Hank.

Einstein looks delighted. "How do you know about the flying boxcars?"

"My father flew a B-29 out of England."

"Well, I'm impressed. I look forward to meeting him, even under these circumstances." Einstein's gaze lingers warmly on Hank's face. "Now, is this your first pretrial conference, Hank?"

"Yes, sir."

Einstein touches Hank's sleeve lightly. "Well, son, it's nothing to be afraid of. All I want to do is to hear both of you out. Maybe see if we can settle this matter."

"Right, sir."

"Go ahead and outline the facts for me. You needn't rush."

"Okay, Your Honor. Thanks." Hank glances down at his notes. "The facts in this case are simple. My father worked at Harbison's for thirty-two years, as long as I can remember. He's an accountant. He started out in Harbison's bookkeeping department." Hank rechecks his notes. "He got promotion after promotion and a salary increase each time. He entered management in 1982. He was promoted to chief financial officer in 1988, reporting directly to the chief executive officer, Franklin Stapleton. But as soon as he turned sixty-five, Your Honor, Mr. Stapleton told him he had to retire. In clear violation of the Age Discrimination in Employment Act." Hank glares at me accusingly.

I scribble on my legal pad to avoid his stare. I write: *I hate my job. I'm moving to New Jersey to grow tomatoes in the sun.*

"Go on, Hank," says Einstein.

"Of course, my father refused. He was at the peak of his skill and experience, and he needed the income besides. So, in retaliation, Harbison's demoted him. They stripped him of his title, his office, and his pride, Your Honor. They busted him down to office manager of their store in the King of Prussia mall. So, after serving Harbison's for thirty years, after reporting directly to the chief executive officer, they had him peddling eye bolts, Your Honor. In the mall." His boyish chest heaves up and down with outrage.

The chambers are silent. I write: *The beach would be nice. I could look for dimes in the sand with a metal detector.*

"Well, Henry, I was about to give you a lecture on the relative wisdom of representing relatives," Einstein says with a smile, "but your dad has found a very fine lawyer in you."

"Thank you, sir." Hank blushes again.

The judge frowns at me over the rimless edge of his half-glasses. "Ms. DiNunzio, you represent Harbison's in this matter?"

I nod yes. I feel like the devil in disguise.

"That's quite a story I just heard. I'm sure the jury will be as impressed with it as I am."

I clear my throat as if I know what I'm going to say, but I have no idea. "Your Honor, I just got this case today. We're new counsel."

Einstein frowns again. This frown says, You are making excuses, and that is reprehensible.

What's a girl to do? I parrot back what I read in the file on the way over. "As you know, Your Honor, there are two sides to every story. Harbison's denies that it made such statements to plaintiff and that it demoted plaintiff on account of his age. Harbison's position is that it demoted plaintiff because his management style was abrasive and, in particular, he was verbally abusive to company employees."

"That's a lie and you know it!" Hank shouts, and leaps to his feet.

An appalled Einstein clamps a firm hand on Hank's arm. "Sit down."

Hank eases back into his chair. "I'm sorry, Your Honor."

Einstein snatches off his reading glasses and tosses them onto the file in front of him. The judge plays by the rules, which don't provide for name-calling in chambers. He can barely look up, he's so offended. "It's not *me* you owe the apology to, young man," he says finally.

"That's all right, Your Honor," I break in. "I'd be upset too, if it were my father." I mean this sincerely, but it sounds condescending. Unwittingly, I've exploited the only weakness in Hank's case—that he is his father's son.

The point, however inadvertent, is not lost on Einstein. The tables turn that fast. The judge replaces his glasses and, without looking at Hank, asks coldly, "Henry, is your father interested in settling this matter?"

"Yes, Your Honor."

"Ms. DiNunzio, is Harbison's interested in settling this matter?"

"No, Your Honor."

Einstein snaps open his black Month-at-a-Glance and thumbs rapidly through the pages. "The deadline for discovery is two months from today. You go to trial July thirteenth. I'll send you both my Scheduling Order. Exchange exhibits and expert reports in a timely manner. I do not expect to hear from either of you regarding extensions of time. That's it, counsel."

We leave Einstein's chambers. Hank flees ahead of me to the elevator bank. As he forces his way into an elevator, I see that he's in tears.

"Hank, wait!" I call out, running to the elevator. But the stainless steel doors close as I reach it, and I'm left staring at the ribbon of black crepe between them. I press the DOWN button.

I hear the voice. It sounds harsher now, less like Mike. *What goes around comes around. You made an angel weep, now you're getting it back. A phone call greets you at the door. An anonymous note shows up in your mail. And a dark car is tracking your every move.*

Pong! The elevator bell rings out, silencing the voice.

The doors rattle open. The only person in the elevator is a steroid freak in a muscle shirt and mirrored sunglasses. Acne dots his shoulders and his hips jut forward suggestively as he leans against the side of the elevator. "Come on in, honey," he drawls. "The water's fine."

"Uh, no. I'm going up."

"Maybe next time, sugar."

As soon as the doors close, I punch the DOWN button again. I slip thankfully into the next elevator, packed with honest citizens wearing yellow JUROR buttons. I grab a cab back to the office and spend most of the ride as I did before, looking out the windows, peering anxiously at every dark sedan on Market Street. When I get back to the office, Brent's desk is empty. He has his opera lesson tonight; he says there's more to life than shorthand.

I go into my office to empty my briefcase.

There, sitting at my desk, bent over my papers, is Ned Waters.

SEVEN

Ned's green eyes flash with alarm as he looks up. The big clock glows faintly behind him. "Mary. I was just leaving you a note."

"A note?" My throat catches. Did Ned send the note I got this morning? Does he drive a dark car?

"I thought you left for the day. Your secretary was gone, so I couldn't leave a message."

"He studies opera singing."

"Opera, huh?" Ned rises awkwardly. He replaces one of my ballpoints in their mug and snatches a piece of paper from my desk.

"Is that the note?" I set my briefcase on the file cabinet.

"Yeah." He crumples it up and stuffs it into his jacket pocket. "But you won't need it now. I can tell you what it says. I thought you might like to grab some dinner."

"Dinner?" I don't know what else to say, so I stare at him open-mouthed, like a trout.

"I heard you won an important motion. We could celebrate."

"You want to celebrate my winning a motion?"

"Sure. Why wouldn't I?"

"Maybe because we're competing with each other. You know, for partnership."

He looks stung. "I didn't even think of that, Mary."

I sigh, suddenly exhausted by the intrigue, the guessing, the strangeness of my life of late. "I don't get it, Ned. The last time we had dinner was in law school."

He looks down for a minute, studying his wingtips. When he meets my eye, his gaze is almost feline in its directness. "I wanted to call you back, but by the time I got my courage up, you were practically engaged."

It sounds genuine. I feel flattered and wary at the same time. I don't know what to say, so I don't say anything. I try not to look like a trout, however.

"Isn't that right?"

"Not exactly. I met Mike after you and I went out. And I didn't get engaged all that fast."

"No? You looked to me like you fell pretty hard. I remember seeing you doing research in the library, you looked like you were on cloud nine. Unless it was the sheer joy of working for Bitterman."

"Not likely."

"How could you stand that guy? I know he's supposed to be a legal genius, but what a jerk. I heard from Malone he was a tyrant in the courtroom."

"And out of it. He threw a fit when I wouldn't do the research for his second article. Reamed me out in his chambers."

"Why?"

"The law should be my first love, he said."

"But it wasn't."

I think of Mike.

Ned clears his throat. "Anyway, you looked like a woman in love, even to somebody as dense as me. I figured I didn't have a prayer, so I settled for being friends. What a guy, huh?"

"What a guy."

His hands shift inside the pockets of his bumpy seersucker

jacket. "So. Please don't make this any harder than it is. Let me take you to dinner."

"I don't really go out, Ned. I mean, I don't know if you're talking about going out, but I—"

"Why do we have to label it anything? Let's just have dinner together. We're old friends, classmates, and we went out once. I've been remiss in not getting hold of you sooner, but—well, there was a lot going on." He shrugs uncomfortably. "Let's go eat, huh?"

I can't decide. The silence is excruciating.

"Come on. It won't kill you."

"Tell me one thing. What kind of car do you drive?"

"Talk about a non sequitur!" he says, with a deep laugh. It's a merry sound, happy and relieved, and shows his teeth to advantage. They're white and even, I bet they grew in that way. "Okay, I confess. I drive a Miata."

"What color?"

"White."

"Do you have a car phone?"

"You want to see my W-2? I can afford dinner, you know."

"That's not why I'm asking, and we'll split dinner."

"So why are you asking? And no, we won't."

"Just tell me, okay? Please."

"Of course I don't have a car phone. The Miata is as pretentious as I get."

So I agree, reluctantly.

Dinner turns out to be no fun at all in the beginning, when I'm busy worrying about whether Ned rents the car he follows me around in. Then he orders me a Tanqueray-and-tonic, and it eases my anxiety on impact. I begin to enjoy the restaurant, an elegant one overlooking Rittenhouse Square, and Ned's conversation, which comes more easily than it used to. In fact, he's changed a lot, as far as I can tell. He seems freer, more lively. We trade firm gossip, and he confides that he's always been intrigued by Judy. An enigma, he calls her. I find this funny, since she's no fan of his either. By the refill of my drink, I confess that Judy calls him Cool.

"Why does she call me that? I'm not cool at all."

"You *are* cool, Cool."

"Am not."

"Are too."

He laughs. "This is mature."

"Admit it! Look at you, you're a preppie hunk. You're like a J. Crew catalog, only alive." I realize I'm flirting, even as I speak. It not only scares the shit out of me, it makes me feel profoundly guilty. I celebrated my first motion with Mike, and here I am, celebrating my second with Ned. And I'm still Mike's wife, inside. I clam up.

Ned doesn't notice my silence and launches into his life story. He tells me about his wealthy Main Line family and his father, who's the managing partner of the Masterson firm. When he's finished his Dover sole, he changes the subject, as if he suddenly became aware that he'd been soliloquizing. "Only two months to go until P-day. June 1st, the partnership election."

I move a radish around on my plate.

"I didn't think June would be a good month for you. Isn't that when your husband—"

"Yes." The anniversary of Mike's death is June 28, but I didn't think Ned knew that. "How did you—"

"I remember. I went to the funeral."

"You did?" I'm not sure I want to talk about this.

"I didn't think you'd mind. I wanted to go. Mike seemed like a very nice guy. I'm sorry."

"I didn't think you ever met him."

"Sure I did. You introduced us when he came by school to meet you for lunch. He rode his bike over. He rode a bike, right?"

I nod yes. I line up my forks, squaring the tines off at the top.

"I'm sorry. I guess I shouldn't have mentioned—"

"No, it's fine."

"Well. Let's see, at least one good thing will happen in June."

"What's that?"

"You're making partner."

"Please. You make it sound like a done deal."

"It is. You're a shoo-in. You don't have a thing to worry about."

Then I remember what Berkowitz said about Ned's coming in to see him. "I heard they were only making two partners in litigation, not three. Did you hear that?"

"I try not to believe every rumor I hear, there are so many flying around. First I heard they were making three, then I heard it was down to two. This morning I heard that the Washington office was going to push through one of the lateral hires. It's ridiculous." He shakes his head.

"A lateral? In Washington? Shit."

"I'm sure they'll make three from Philly, Mary. The department's had a great year."

"Yeah. I guess." I note that he doesn't mention his meeting with Berkowitz on this very subject. I regard this as a material omission, and it makes me doubt him all the way through the dessert, shaved chocolate somethings.

Later, Ned insists on walking me home, since it's only a few blocks from his house. We walk in silence on this muggy night, so humid that the air forms halos around the mercury vapor lights. Rittenhouse Square is almost deserted. The runners have run home, the walkers have walked. Only the homeless remain, sleeping on the park benches as we go by. I look around for the dark car, but it's nowhere in sight.

Suddenly, before we've reached my doorstep, Ned kisses me. I'm totally unprepared for it, and his hesitant peck lands on my right eyebrow. I feel mortified. I worry about whether my neighbors saw. I worry about whether Alice saw. I even worry about whether Mike saw. I hurry inside, muttering a hasty good-bye to Ned, who looks concerned and sorry as I close the door.

I gather my mail from the floor and am about to stick it under my arm when I remember that, as of this morning, the United States mail is no longer my friend. I set down my brief-case and look through the letters, holding my breath. Bills: Philadelphia Electric, Greater Media Cable, Allstate, *Vanity Fair*. Two more catalogs, sent to DiNunziatoi and O'Nunzion respectively, and then a small white envelope, with no return address. My name is on the front, spelled correctly in block let-ters, and so is my home address. The stamp is an unfurled American flag.

Just like the note at work. I swallow hard.

I run my finger across the front. Laser-printed, not typed.

I tear open the envelope. Inside is a small white piece of paper:

I'M THE PERFECT ANSWER TO ALL YOUR REAL ESTATE NEEDS!
And here's the perfect recipe:
Artichoke Dip
1 8oz. can artichoke hearts
1 cup mayo
1 cup parmesan cheese
garlic powder optional
Mash artichokes, mix everything together. Bake at 350 for 30 minutes. Serve with pita bread!
Call SHERRY SIMMONS at JEFMAR REALTY!

Christ. Artichoke dip.

I crush the paper and trudge up the carpeted stairs. I'm get-ting so paranoid I'm losing it. What's the matter with me?

Mike hasn't been gone for a year and I'm kissing another man. What's the matter with Ned? Is he trying to start up a romance, when one of us is about to be fired and the other canonized? I unlock my door with a sigh and flick on the light switch. I toss my briefcase onto the couch and plop down next to it, opening up the first bill.

Philadelphia Electric. You need a Ph.D. to break the code on your rate charges. I'm trying to decipher the tiny numbers when the phone on the end table rings. I pick it up without thinking. "Hello?"

There's no response. No static.

I'm not paranoid. It's real. "Leave me alone, you fucking asshole!"

But the only reply is a click.

"Goddamn it!"

I slam down the phone, my chest tight, and then grab it from the hook just as quickly. I hear the high whine of the dial tone. It runs interference for me, like a swift and burly lineman. See if you can get through that, you prick. Alice, who's been dozing like the Sphinx on the quilted couch, blinks slowly and goes back to sleep.

Get a grip, girl. I keep hold of the phone. The dial tone gives way to a woman's voice, speaking patiently and sweetly, like a young mother to a toddler. "If you want to make a call," she says, "please hang up and try again. If you need assistance, please hang up and dial your operator."

I lean back and breathe easier, listening to the young mother's voice. She sings her lullaby again. I let it enter and pacify me.

But she's squelched by a jarring BRRRRRRRRRRR.

I sit bolt upright.

"Goddamn you!" Furious, I get up and shove the receiver between the cushions of the couch. Alice's eyes open wide, ears flat against her sleek head. Then she leaps out of harm's way.

"Goddamn you to hell!"

I smother the receiver with another cushion, and another, so that the couch looks like it's been trashed. But still I can hear the sound.

It won't leave my head.

EIGHT

I can't sleep. I adjust the light level, the covers, the air-conditioning. I take off my T-shirt and put it back on again. I gather my hair in a ponytail on top of my head, then yank it out. I try everything. Nothing works.

My head is full of visions, faces that swim up at me out of the dark. Starankovic's wounded mask. A baby-faced Hank, tears coursing down his cheeks. Ned, with his cat's eyes, lying with me like an incubus. Finally, Mike's robust face appears, with its coarse, working-class nose stuck in the middle. Framed by untamable brown curls, animated by eyes full of love. *But you love me for it*, he'd said. I bury my head under the pillow, which helps no more than the cushions over the telephone.

I feel wretched as I watch the night bleed into the dawn. Angry. Tired. Guilty. I feel the need to do penance, to make up for my date with Ned, so I get up to clean the bathroom. Penance, if you don't know, is the notion that the soul can be Martinized While-U-Wait, like a camel skirt. Probably the most bizarre concept I've ever heard, after original sin. The idea that a child's soul turns black the instant of its birth is something even Angie couldn't make me understand. But I scrub behind the toilet seat just the same. Despite my best efforts, I'm still Catholic after all these years.

I scuff into the living room in my pink slippers, dust mops for the feet, and exhume the telephone receiver. I hang it up and rearrange the cushions on the couch. Alice watches me, looking faintly suspicious.

"Who asked you?" I say.

I scuff into the kitchen and crack a pressurized can of Maxwell House. The can opens with a fragrant hiss, then the telephone rings.

"Fuck!" I send the can opener spinning across the kitchen counter. Is it the caller? At this hour? I pound into the living room, my adrenaline pumping, and tear the receiver from the cradle. "Who is this?"

"Mary? It's Ned!"

"Oh, jeez."

"I know it's early, but that's quite a greeting."

"Someone keeps calling me and hanging up. It's not you, is it?" I'm only half joking.

"Did you push star sixty-nine?"

"What's that?"

"If you push star sixty-nine after someone calls you, the phone calls them back."

"How do you know that?"

"I'm cool, remember?"

"Oh. Yeah." I cringe.

"Okay. Well. Let me say why I'm calling before I lose my nerve altogether. I wanted to tell you that I'm sorry about what happened after dinner. About pushing things like that. I couldn't sleep, I felt like such a bozo. I've always liked you, Mary. Been attracted to you. But still, I shouldn't have done that. I'm sorry."

"Uh . . . that's okay."

"I really am sorry."

"I know."

"Well, I would love to see you again. If you want to see me again, that is. I promise I won't attack you. I mean it."

I pause. I don't know how to say what I need to say. That I haven't dated in ten years? That the last man I dated before Mike was Ned? That I'm not ready yet? That I may never be?

"Okay, fine," Ned says suddenly. "Whatever you want. Maybe after June you'll change your mind. Does that sound all right to you?"

"Okay. I guess."

"We can be friends until then. Would that be okay with you?"

"Fine."

"God, I hate this talking about feelings. It can be so bloody exhausting."

"So cut it out. Be like me."

He laughs softly. "I'll see you later then, at work."

"Sure." I hang up, feeling somewhat empty. I like him, but I'm not ready for what he wants. And he's a mystery to me, still. Why didn't he tell me about Berkowitz?

Meeeoooow! It's Alice, wanting to be fed. She saunters into the kitchen, tail high.

"You only talk to me when you want something," I say, and follow her in. I pour some allegedly gourmet cat food into her bowl. "You don't call, you don't write."

Alice ignores me; she's heard it all before. I squat down and watch her. She eats with her eyes closed, but still manages to find each little kibble fish. It's her best trick, I decide, stroking her silky back. She'll tolerate my touch until the kibble fish are gone; then she'll return to the windowsill. Her next feeding will be the next time she acknowledges that I pay the rent around here. I'd give her away in a second, to a science lab, if it weren't for Mike. He found her in a trash can and brought her home in the pouring rain, wrapped in his denim jacket. She didn't move the whole time, so Mike thought she was dead.

"If she's dead, why did you bring her home?" I asked, ever the pragmatist.

"I couldn't leave her there, like she was trash," he said. "I'll bury her tomorrow, before school."

He put her in a Converse shoe box and put the shoe box under the bathroom sink. The next morning, Mike found her in the bathtub, staring in wonder at the dripping faucet. He named her Alice in Wonderland; she imprinted him on her cat brain as Mommy. They were crazy about each other.

After Mike died, I got the idea that he would want to see Alice again, at least to say good-bye. I know it sounds crazy, but I drove the animal to the cemetery and made my way through the graves with the bulky cat carrier until I got to the plain gray headstone that says LASSITER. It doesn't say BELOVED HUSBAND on it because I couldn't bear to see that chiseled so finally on his headstone.

I set Alice's carrier down at the foot of Mike's grave and opened the door of the carrier with shaking hands. Out came Alice, sniffing the summer air. I watched, teary-eyed. I didn't know what to expect, but I hoped it would be something magical and profound. It was neither. What happened was that Alice took off, springing between the monuments like a jackrabbit. I shouted for her and gave chase, leaping in my espadrilles over mounds that constituted ANTONELLI and MACARRICCI, by the flying eagle that said TOOHEY and the weeping cherub that marked FERGUSON. Alice kept going and so did I, because the last thing I wanted to do was lose Mike's cat in the frigging cemetery. I caught up with her by the CONLEY mausoleum. She scratched me all the way back to LASSITER.

Brrrnng! The telephone rings loudly, jolting me out of my daydream. I stand up and set my jaw. I'm ready for you, asshole. Star sixty-nine. I run in and pick up the receiver.

"Hello?"

No answer, then *click*, and a dial tone. No static. My heart begins to pound. No static means he's not in the car. He's at home, wherever he lives, lying in bed. Thinking about me. I pound the buttons for star sixty-nine.

I hear one ring, then another. What am I going to say to this guy? There's another ring, then a fourth, and a fifth. He's not answering.

I hang up the phone. This has got to stop. I look around the empty apartment, suddenly aware of my aloneness. I stow the coffee in the freezer and slip out of my T-shirt in the bathroom, away from any windows. I lock the bathroom door before I shower. I'm no dummy; I've seen *Psycho*.

I dress quickly and leave for the office. In the cab, I keep an eye out for the sedan, but it's not in evidence. As soon as I get in, I ask Brent to change my home number.

"Hallelujah," he says.

"Let's have my office number changed, too."

"Now you're talkin'."

"Did I get anything more evil than usual in the Evil mail?"

"No. And no calls from weirdos, either. Except the ones who work here." He hands me a packet of yellow phone messages.

"What is it with these people, they don't sleep?" I look over the messages. Martin, Jameson, a couple of clients, someone named Stephanie Fraser. I hold up the message. "Do I know Stephanie Fraser? Is she at Campbell's?"

"No. That's Stephanie Furst. This one said she met you after your Bitterman argument. She wants you to call back."

"Oh, yeah, I remember her. She thinks Bitter Man hates women. Absurd. He hates everybody." I hand Brent back the messages.

"Did you see the car again last night?"

"No."

"We're on a roll," he says, relieved. He looks good, in a soft rayon shirt.

"New shirt?"

He looks down at it like a little kid. "Jack gave it to me. You like?"

"It's nice. Something about it looks familiar. Let me think. I got it! It's black!"

"Shows how much you know. It's midnight. And yesterday was more of a charcoal."

"Right."

"Get out of my face. I've got filing to do. Now, git!"

"Be that way. I'm going down to see Judy."

"But you have a deposition, remember? Tiziani will be here in an hour."

"Oh, shit! Shit. Shit. Shit." With all that's going on, the dep slipped my mind completely.

"You prepared him last week, didn't you?"

"Right. I gotta go. I'll be back in time." I hand him the messages.

"Did you think any more about the police?" he asks, but I'm off, down Stalling's internal stairwell to Judy's floor.

Judy's office is like a bird's nest. The desk is littered with bits of paper, the bookshelves stuffed with messy books and files. Photos are everywhere. On the wall, there's Kurt, two black Labradors, and Judy's huge family. The Carriers are California's answer to the Von Trapps. They grin from various craggy summits, with heavy ropes, clips, and pulleys hanging from harnesses around their waists. The first time I saw these pictures, I thought the entire family worked for the telephone company.

"Anybody home?"

"Behind the desk," Judy calls out. I find her sitting on the floor in front of an array of trial exhibits. She looks up at me and smiles wearily. "I remember you. I knew you before I became consumed by the price of computer chips in Osaka."

"What are you doing?"

"The *Mitsuko* appeal. You know, the trial that Martin lost last month. The antitrust case."

"The zillion-dollar antitrust case."

She giggles in a naughty way. "I heard that the morning after he lost the trial, the litigation partners dumped a pile of dirty socks in the middle of his desk."

"I don't get it."

"Smell defeat! Smell defeat!" She laughs, then her smile fades. "What's the matter, you don't think that's funny?"

"It's funny."

"You didn't laugh."

I tell her about my dinner with Ned, which I refuse to call a date, and also that he didn't own up to his meeting with Berkowitz. We talk again about the phone calls and the note. She says she suspects Ned because he's so ambitious, or maybe Martin, because he lost the case for Mitsuko and I replaced him on *Harbison's*. Then I remind her of how Delia was fuming at me, and Judy rakes a large hand through a hank of chopped-off hair.

"It could be anyone," she says.

"That's comforting."

"Look. Kurt's sleeping at his studio tonight. Why don't you stay at my house?"

"Why?"

"You'll be safe, genius."

"I have to be able to live in my own apartment, don't I? What am I going to do, spend the rest of my life at your house?"

"It wouldn't be the worst thing. You can cook."

"Oh, sure, we'd be great roommates. I'd give us one week before we killed each other."

She looks hurt. "You always say that, I don't know why. Stay with me for a while. Just until you get your number changed."

"Nah, I'll be okay."

She shakes her head. "So stubborn."

"I appreciate it, though. I do."

"At least answer the phone. I want to be able to reach you."

"You can't. Brent's going to unlist the number, and I don't have the new one yet."

"They won't do it by tonight. I think it takes a day. I'll call you tonight with a signal. I'll let it ring twice and then call right back."

I agree, and promise to buy her two big cookies for her trouble the next time we go to lunch.

"Wow!" she says.

NINE

"Tiziani got here early," Brent says, when I get back upstairs. "I set him up in Conference Room F with coffee and sandwiches for lunch."

"Aren't you the perfect host."

Brent winks. "He's hot."

"I thought you were a one-man man."

He gives me a playful shove and I take off.

Nick Tiziani is the personnel manager at Blake's, a national food manufacturer. He fired his female assistant because she dressed funny. That's the truth, and even though it's a lousy reason to fire someone, it's lawful. However, he also told her to stop dressing like a man and bought her a subscription to *Vogue*. He says he was trying to help; she says it was sex discrimination. A lot depends on how well he tells his story at this dep.

"Mary! *Come sta?*" Tiziani says, when he sees me.

"*Bene. Grazie*, Nick."

He shakes my hand warmly. A suave guy, Nick always smells better than I do. He's dressed head to toe in Gucci, which is part of the reason he's getting sued down to his silk boxers. Clothes are very important to Nick; he's a big proponent of form over substance. The day his funky assistant came in wearing camouflage pants was the last straw, especially because Blake's CEO was visiting from headquarters. Nick fired her on the spot. She's lucky he didn't kill her.

I review the incident with him and teach him the defense witness mantra: Don't volunteer, listen to the question, give me time to object. Don't volunteer, listen to the question, give me time to object. Nick nods pleasantly as I speak, which proves he's not listening to a word I say.

"Nick, you're with me on this, right?"

"Sure, Mary. Piece a cake."

"It's not that easy. You've never been deposed before."

"How hard can it be?"

"Harder than you think. Everything you say is recorded and is admissible in court. They'll use it to rough you up on cross, throw your own words back at you."

"You make it so complicated. It's business, that's all. Her lawyer is a businessman. I am a businessman." He touches a manicured finger to a custom shirt. "I'll explain it to him, we'll see eye to eye. Come to terms."

"Nick. Believe me, this guy is the enemy. He's not going to see it your way. His job is to see it any way *but* your way. Say as little as possible. Remember: Don't volunteer, listen to the question, give me time to object."

"Yeah, yeah, yeah." He fidgets in his chair. "Hey, did you hear this one? What's the difference between a catfish and a lawyer?"

"One is a scum-sucking bottom dweller and the other is a fish."

"You're no fun," he says, pouting.

The deposition is at the offices of Masterson, Moss & Dunbar—an away game. Masterson, Moss is another reason the case is dangerous. A hot-shit firm like that would ordinarily never represent a noncorporate plaintiff, but this plaintiff is the daughter of one of its sharky securities partners. As such, she rates one of the fairest-haired boys, Bob Maher. Maher's on every Young Republicans committee in the tristate area and is more of a sexist than Nick will ever be. But it's not Maher's prick that's in the mousetrap. Not this time, anyway.

Nick and I sit in the reception area at Masterson, which is the oldest law firm in Philadelphia and the largest, at almost three hundred and fifty lawyers. I think of it as the Father firm in the holy trinity because it's so traditional. Somebody has to wave the flag of old-line Philadelphia, and Masterson has pre-empted the field. The decor is early men's club, with bronze sconces and heavy club chairs everywhere. Maps of the city in colonial times adorn its wainscoted walls, wafer-thin oriental carpets blanket its hardwood floors. The place looks like Ralph Lauren heaven. Nick eats it up.

"Classy," he says.

"Prehistoric," I reply.

Soon we're met by Maher himself. A strapping Yale grad, Maher flashes Nick a training-table All-Ivy grin and leads us to a large conference room, which has a glass wall overlooking one of the firm's corridors. He pours Nick a hot cup of fresh coffee and introduces him to the luscious female court reporter, Ginny, no last name. Ginny tells Nick she loves his tie. Nick tells Ginny he loves her scarf. They both laugh. Everything's so chummy, I feel like the new neighbor at a swingers party. I decide that Maher's a fine practitioner of the Seduce-the-Shit-Out-of-'Em approach to deposition taking, and Nick's too turned on to catch on.

Maher begins the questioning with softballs about Nick's personnel history. Nick describes one promotion after another with a braggadocio indigenous to Italian men. I let it run and watch the lawyers scuttle back and forth outside the glass wall. Oblivious to the promenade is a tall, dignified lawyer with wavy silver hair. Legs crossed, he sits in a Windsor chair reading *The Wall Street Journal.* I recognize this as a typical dominance display by an alpha wolf in a corporate law firm. Berkowitz does it too, with less finesse.

"Mr. Tiziani . . . may I call you Nick?" Maher asks.

"Just don't call me late to dinner."

Maher laughs at this joke, ha-ha-ha, as if he's never heard it before. I glance up at the silver wolf. He's looking into the conference room over the top of the wide newspaper. That's unusual. Why would he watch a dep unless he had a specific interest in it? Then it clicks. He must be the plaintiff's father.

"Tell me, Nick, what is your current title at Blake's?"

"I'm Vice President of Personnel. I got the promotion a year ago. A year ago in September. As vice president, I report directly to Chicago. It's a dotted-line relationship with the CEO, as opposed to a straight line. I'm not sure if you're familiar with organizational charts, Bob, and I'd be happy to explain—"

I touch Nick's sleeve gently. "Nick, why don't we just let Bob ask his questions? It'll save time." Don't volunteer, listen to the question, give me time to object. Don't volunteer, listen to the question, give me time to object.

"Oh, sure, Mary. No problem," he replies helpfully. The man hasn't a clue.

The plaintiff's father turns a page of the *Journal* but continues to watch us over its top.

"Thank you, Nick," says Maher. "I'll ask you about that later. Now, as Vice President of Personnel, are you familiar with the federal laws prohibiting sex discrimination in the workplace?"

I ignore the plaintiff's father and lean over. Things are heating up and I want to be in Nick's line of vision during the questioning. Maybe it'll remind him that this is a deposition, not group sex.

"Let the record reflect that defense counsel is blocking my view of the witness," Maher says sharply.

Ginny's fingers move steadily on the black keys of her machine. Everything we say will be on the record. If you can imagine it in black-and-white type like a script, you can fabricate the reality:

"Pardon me. What did you say, Bob?"

"I said you're obstructing my view of the witness."

"I don't know what you mean, Bob."

"I can't see him when you do that."

"I'm sorry."

"There's something about the way you're sitting."

"What? I don't understand."

"Move away from the witness."

"How's this, Bob?" I don't move.

"Not good enough. More to the right."

"This is silly, Bob. Let the record reflect my agreement with counsel for plaintiff that the witness can stay for only three hours today. If we spend much more time discussing my posture, we won't be out of here until seven."

Maher quiets with a scowl.

Nick remembers that he's The Witness, not just-call-me-Nick.

And I sit back and meet the gaze of the lawyer outside, who's plainly glaring at me now over the *Journal*. The eyes of an outraged father. Even from a distance, they seem to drill into me.

"Nick, did there come a time when you met the plaintiff, Donna Reilly?"

"Yes."

"Did you form an impression of her at the time?"

"Objection," I say.

"Why?" Maher demands.

"What's the relevance of his impression of her? And the question is ambiguous. His impression of what?"

"You know full well that relevance isn't a proper objection during deposition. Besides, if the witness thinks the question is unclear, he can say so."

"I'm preserving my objection. And you're right, Bob. If the witness doesn't understand the question, he can say so." I kick Nick in his Gucci loafer.

"I don't understand the question," Nick says.

Suddenly, there's a violent movement outside the conference room. The plaintiff's father has leapt to his feet and thrown the newspaper onto the Kirman. Holy shit. He must have seen me kick Nick, because he looks outraged. Like a football coach when the ref doesn't call clipping.

"All right, Nick, I'll rephrase the question," Maher says, unaware of the scene unfolding behind him.

The lawyer rushes toward the conference room door. My mouth goes dry. What's he going to do, report me to the Disciplinary Board? There's not one of us who hasn't done it—not one.

"Who's that?" Nick asks, pointing through the glass at the charging lawyer.

Maher turns around just as the door bursts open. "Hello, sir!" He pops up but forgets to grin.

The lawyer ignores him. He's taller than I thought, and his patrician features are limned with tiny wrinkles. Anger tinges his face. He looks too angry to report me; he looks angry enough to hit me. He struggles to maintain civility. "I'm loath to interrupt these proceedings, but I thought it an opportune time to meet the opposition. Hello, Miss DiNunzio." He extends a large hand over the conference table.

I'm not sure if he wants to deck me or shake hands. It turns out to be something in between; he squeezes my hand like a used tube of toothpaste.

"That's quite a grip." I withdraw my hand.

He nods curtly. "Court tennis."

"Right." Whatever that is.

"You seem to be having some trouble with your chair, Miss DiNunzio. If it's uncomfortable for you, I can have another brought in." He smiles, but it looks like it's held in place with a mortician's wire.

"I'm fine, thank you."

"If you feel uncomfortable again, feel free to alert young Bob. I'm certain he'll do whatever he can to make you more comfortable. Isn't that right, Bob." It's a command, not a question. The lawyer nods at Maher, who looks confused.

"After all," he continues, "the Masterson firm has always been a great friend to the Stalling firm, and I hear only the best about you, Miss DiNunzio. I understand you're a very fine litigator."

"Thank you."

"You're in my son's class at Stalling, aren't you?"

"Your *son*?"

"Yes. My son. Ned Waters."

TEN

"I'm Nathaniel Waters. You may know that I manage this firm."

"Oh. Yes." Not the plaintiff's father, *Ned's* father!

"I've seen us grow from one hundred lawyers, to one-fifty, to the full complement. I oversaw the opening of our London office. Now we're going to be the first Philadelphia firm in Moscow. Masterson maintains a tradition of excellence, Miss DiNunzio, and of unimpeachable ethics. I'm sure Stalling does the same." He peers at me directly, a menacing version of Ned's green-eyed gaze.

"Of course." No matter what he says, I know he's kicked the Nicks of the world under the table. You don't get where he is without some very pointy shoes. Even if they are made in England.

"Then we're in agreement. I shan't keep you further. It was fine to have met you. Give my regards to Ned, will you. Carry on." He turns on his heel and strides stiffly out the door.

Maher relaxes visibly, and our eyes meet. For a brief moment, we're cubs in the same pack. We become enemies again when Maher takes his seat and the questions begin. "Nick, let me make the question so clear even your lawyer will understand it. The first time you saw Ms. Reilly, did you form an impression of her wearing apparel?"

"Yes."

"What was your impression?"

"I thought she dressed like a slob."

Good for you, Nicky. I almost cheer. For the rest of the deposition, which stretches until the end of the day, I channel the anxiety created by Ned's father into constant objections. Nick cues off me and we work as a team, with him telling his side of the story forcefully and credibly. By the end of the dep, Maher may think that Nick is a stickler about clothes, but he'll be hard pressed to prove he discriminates against women. As we leave Masterson, I congratulate Nick, who tells me I did "a man's job."

I stop short. "Nick, you want some free legal advice?"

"Sure."

"Don't say stuff like that. You got away with it this time, but you might not the next. You know what I mean, Nick? What goes around, comes around."

A hurt look crosses his neat features. "I didn't mean it the way it sounded, Mary."

"Good."

We part company, awkwardly. I thread my way through the crowded street, slightly dazed, wondering why I've just insulted a major client.

It's about time, says the voice, then disappears.

People pour out of office buildings—women with melting makeup, men with unlit cigarettes. They jolt me aside to join the human traffic on the narrow sidewalks, which flows around street vendors like corpuscles through a hardened artery. It's the end of the workday in this weary city, and it occurs to me that I'd better let the rush-hour crowds carry me home before it gets dark, and the car appears.

I mix into the throng for safety but still find myself glancing over my shoulder a lot. I pause before the window of an electronics store and spot an answering machine. Mike hated answering machines, so we never bought one. But some creep is calling me, and Mike is gone. I go in and lay down some plastic for the lady behind the counter.

When I leave with the slim machine in a plastic bag, I expect to feel better, as if I'm doing what I can to protect myself. But I feel exactly the opposite. The purchase makes the threat all too real. I feel scared.

I walk through the square quickly, looking around at the office workers walking tiredly home. At this hour, relatively early for the super-professional crowd, we're talking paralegals, not lawyers. Secretaries, not bosses. Almost all of them are women, the vast underclass of pink-collar workers who keep America word-processed, executive-summaried, and support-staffed. I fall in step with one of the older women. She has a sweet, rounded face and wears a hand-knit sweater. A saleswoman, I think, or a librarian's assistant. We stop together at the edge of the square in front of the Dorchester, waiting for the traffic to give us an even break.

"There should be a light here," she says, slightly annoyed. "Or at least a stop sign."

I scan the cars whizzing by. "I agree."

"They'll kill you to get home five minutes faster."

A Cadillac driver waves us across the street. I lose the saleswoman on Twentieth Street, after the high-rises that demarcate the residential west end of town. I look behind me. The people on the sidewalk look normal. I check back again half a block later, and only two are left. One is a teenage girl with a backpack slung over her shoulder and the other is a flashy woman with lots of shiny shopping bags.

Something catches my eye at the corner of Spruce and Twenty-first. Not the people, the cars. Two white cars are stopped at a light, and after them is a brown one. A brown Cadillac, an older model, somewhat beat-up. An Eldorado or Toronado, one of those.

I squint at the car. Is it the same Cadillac that let me go by in front of the Dorchester?

I can't remember, but try not to leap to conclusions. There are a million Cadillacs in the world, I tell myself, moving quickly to cross.

I turn onto Delancey and can't help but glance back over my shoulder. The Cadillac is coming toward Delancey, cruising slowly. Close up, it looks like the same car.

Chill, as Judy would say. So what if it's the same car? Maybe it's someone looking for a parking space. I used to do it all the time, driving pointlessly around and around the same block. Now I pay a fortune to park in a garage nearby. It's worth every penny.

I stride down Delancey Street, remembering the magazine articles I've read about crime. Don't look like a victim or you'll be one. Stand tall, walk fast. I hoist the plastic bag up and barrel ahead. As I do, I hear the smooth acceleration of a powerful engine coming down the street behind me. I pick up my pace for the half block that's left and check over my shoulder at the corner.

I feel my stomach tighten.

It's the Cadillac, blocked by a station wagon that's trying to wedge itself into a parking space. I catch my breath. I feel like bolting across the street, but there's too much traffic. A limo rolls by, then a clunker and an endless parade of Hondas. I'm only a block from home.

I look back. The Cadillac has freed itself. It's moving forward, speeding to the corner without effort.

I feel panic begin to rise in my throat. "Come on, come on," I say to the traffic. I spot an opening in front of an empty school bus and run for it, my briefcase banging against my thigh. The bus driver protests with a startlingly loud *haaaannk*. I almost drop the briefcase but make it to the other side of the street, breathless.

Run, says the Mike-voice, softly. *Run*.

I glance backward at the top of my street. The traffic screens most of Delancey from view, but glinting at me from between the moving cars is the shimmer of a battered chrome grill. The Cadillac's still there. My heart begins to race. I can't see the driver. The windshield reflects a cloudy sky.

Run. Run. Run for your life.

So I do, a dead run, without looking back. Instantly, I hear the Cadillac gun its engine as it crosses onto my street. I speed up. The Cadillac speeds up. It's almost at my heels as I tear down the street like a madwoman.

Run, run.

The Cadillac's right behind me.

I hear someone screaming and it's me. "No! No! Help!" I keep running until I reach my front door.

Christ! My keys! The answering machine clatters to the sidewalk as I rummage furiously in my bag. Where are my fucking keys?

The Cadillac screeches to a stop behind me, right in front of my door.

"No!" I turn and scream at the car. My back is plastered against the front door, my breast heaving. "You fucking asshole, leave me alone!"

In my fear and panic, I see the driver.

A woman, dark-haired, Hispanic. The Cadillac is loaded with kids. The oldest one, a boy in the back seat, is in hysterics.

I can't quite believe it. I blink at the sight.

A mother and children. She looks upset, but I don't know why, since I'm the one having the coronary. Like my grandfather used to say, my heart attacked me.

The mother leans over an infant in a plastic car seat. "Ah, I scare you," she says, in highly flavored English. "I so sorry. I scare you, poor lady. I no mean."

I almost cry with relief. My briefcase falls to the ground with a leathery slap.

The mother turns to the boy in the back, who's still laughing, and says something to him I can't hear. He leans out of the open window with a smirk. The trace of a mustache covers a prominent lip.

"My mutha says she's sorry she scared you. We're lost. We got off the expressway too soon. She shoulda stayed on. I told her to stay on, but she wouldn't listen." He laughs again. "I told her not to keep after you too, but she wanted to tell you not to be scared. She don't listen to nobody." He points at his temple, and his mother cuffs him lightly on the shoulder. "Get offa me!" he shouts at her, *muy* macho.

They just wanted directions. Christ. I try to recover as they talk again.

The boy leans out of the car. "She wants to know if you're awright, you want to go to the hospital. I told her you don't go to the hospital for this, but she don't listen."

"Tell her thank you for me, will you? I'm fine. Tell her it's okay. It's not her fault."

They talk again, but the mother looks doubtful.

"It's not your fault!" I yell into the car, but she gets distracted by the little girls in the back, fighting over a troll doll. She snatches the troll from them and they begin to wail, identically. They look to be the same age. "Are they twins?"

The mother cups her ear.

"Twins? I'm a twin, too. I have a twin sister."

The mother chatters excitedly to the son and pushes him toward the window. He wrests his arm away and sticks his head out of the car. His expression is pained. "My mutha says that twins are a special blessing from God. You are a special person." Then he rolls his eyes.

I feel my eyes moisten, like an idiot. I want to hug his mother. "Tell her I said thank you. She is a special person, too."

He examines a set of filthy nails. "Great, we're all special. So, you know how to get to the South Street exit?"

"Tell your mother how special she is."

He looks up at me, a wry challenge. "Are you for real?"

I straighten my blazer and pick up my briefcase. "The realest."

He turns from me and shouts at his twin sisters, who are still whimpering. Then he says something to his mother, and she smiles at me happily. He leans back out of the window. "Awright?"

"Thank you. Take a right at the top of the street, then go left on Spruce. Take another right and follow it to Lombard. It'll go right into South Street."

"Got it, babe." He leans back into the car and says something to his mother. The mother waves good-bye. As the Cadillac pulls away, the kid flips me the finger.

I laugh, unaccountably elated. I pick up the answering machine, wondering whether it broke when it fell, but it looks fine. I tuck it under my arm and dig, calmly now, in the bottom of my purse for my keys. I feel giddy, reminded of my father's old joke. Why are your keys always in the last place you look? To which Angie and I would moan, in stereo: Because once you find them, you don't look anymore.

I find my keys and let myself in. I pick up my mail. My heart is even lighter when I find there are no anonymous notes in the mail. I feel like I've gotten a reprieve as I climb the stairs to my door.

But halfway up the staircase, as I thumb through the key ring for my apartment key, I notice that something about the stairwell looks different.

Then I see why.

At the top of the darkening stairway, my apartment door is open.

Wide open.

ELEVEN

I freeze. Did I leave without locking the door this morning? Is that possible?

I feel my senses heighten. I strain to hear something from inside my apartment, but there isn't a sound. The air smells vaguely of cigarettes, but then it always does, since my landlords are smokers. The door is open wide and it looks dark inside. Alice is nowhere in sight. I can't believe this. Someone could be in there, right now. *He* could be in there.

I have to get out and away. I have to call the cops. I will myself into moving. I back slowly down the staircase, easing my back along the wall, my eyes riveted to the door. If he comes out, if anybody comes out, I'll scream like hell. I inch painstakingly downward, trying not to make any noise. The plastic bag rustles slightly as I move, and I curse having bought the answering machine.

My apartment door grows smaller and smaller at the top of the staircase, and I reach the landing. Only a short flight to go. For a fleeting moment I worry about Alice. Would he hurt her? Would he *kill* her? I'm surprised to feel a twinge at the thought; I didn't know I even liked the cat. Still, I'm too frightened to go back. I'm almost at the entrance hall when I hear:

Run.

And I do, bolting out the door, down the pavement, to the pay phone two blocks away. My hands are shaking as I press 911. The woman says they'll have a car there in five minutes.

I walk back and hover at the corner directly across from the top of my street, holding my briefcase, purse, answering machine, and mail.

Five minutes later, there's no police.

Ten minutes later, there's still no police, and I feel like a pack animal.

Half an hour later, the only thing that's changed is that I'm keeping company with Marv, the man who sells tree-height ficus plants on this corner. I've settled into his rickety folding chair to watch the front door to my building. My fear is gone, as is the steely cold taste of panic. Both have been replaced by a low-level tension. Whoever was in my apartment is probably gone by now. I just wonder what he took and what the place looks like. And whether Alice is safe. I squint up at my apartment windows, still dark. The cat isn't on the windowsill.

In exchange for the chair, I had to listen to Marv's life story. He's spent thirty years selling anything that doesn't move—encyclopedias, bronze baby shoes, Amway detergents, and now ficus plants. He told me how he drives a U-Haul down to a Florida nursery where he buys the plants for cheap, then how he brings them up here and sells them for cheap, and how he still makes out like a bandit. The U-Haul is parked in front of his apartment. Each of the ficus trees is chained to its own parking meter. Marv owns this corner. He says, Who better?

"They ain't comin', Mary," he says. "You shoulda told 'em he had a gun. They hear gun, they come. They don't hear gun, they don't come."

"I didn't see a gun. I didn't even see a person." I watch the door across the street, but there's no activity at all. The few passersby don't look inside, which tells me nothing unusual is going on.

"So you say it anyway." He rubs a pitted cheek and looks worriedly at the sky, which is almost dark. "I'm doin' lousy today, I tell you. Can't *give* these plants away today."

I watch the street for the cops. "Maybe I should call them again."

"Won't do you no good. They don't hear gun, they don't come."

"Not even for a burglary?"

"You tell 'em it was a burglary?"

"No, not exactly. I don't know if I was burglarized. I only know the door was open and I didn't leave that way."

He pushes up the brim of a grimy pith helmet, part of his jungle motif. "*That's* what you told 'em?"

I nod.

"Why'd you tell 'em that?"

"Because it's the truth."

He bursts into laughter. "Listen to this kid! Because it's the truth, she says! You're a lawyer, what's the truth to you?" He guffaws. "Mary, you hear the one about the elephant and the tiger?"

I'm in no mood for more lawyer jokes. My chin sinks into my hand as I look down my street.

"Mary?"

"No."

He licks his lips with anticipation. "So this elephant is walkin' along in the jungle and a tiger is walkin' behind him. And every five feet, the elephant, you know, drops a turd. Now the tiger, he's walkin' behind the elephant, and he eats it."

"Jeez, Marv." I wince.

"No, no, listen, it's a good one. So the elephant, he gets disgusted. He turns around to the tiger and he says, 'Yo! Why you eatin' my turds like that?' And the tiger says, 'Because I just ate a lawyer and I want to get the taste out of my mouth.'" Marv bursts into gales of laughter.

I shake my head. "That's disgusting."

"You like that?" he says, delighted. "Wait, wait. I got another one. What's the difference between a porcupine and a Porsche full of lawyers?"

Suddenly, a white police car turns onto my street. The cavalry. "Finally. They're here." I gather up my things and scramble to my feet.

"So they came after all."

The squad car stops in front of my building and a cop climbs out of each front door. One cop is black and one is white; they're both square-jawed enough to be from central casting. It looks like a movie is being filmed in front of my apartment, with a racially balanced cast. But it's not a movie, it's my life. My apartment. My cat. "I gotta go."

"Wait, don't you wanna hear the punch line?"

"I have to go, Marv."

"In a porcupine, the pricks are on the *outside*."

I'm too tense to laugh as I hurry across the street.

"Come back if you need anything!" he calls out.

"Thanks," I call back. I hustle over to the cops, who are standing together like the twin towers. I feel slightly in awe of them, of their authority. They're the good guys. I consider telling them the whole story. About the notes and the car.

"Do you live here?" says the black cop gravely. The nameplate on his broad chest says TARRANT.

"Yes. I'm the one who called. I came home and saw that my apartment door was open. I was too scared to go in."

"Was there any sign of a forced entry?"

"No. But the door was open. I know I didn't leave it that way. I don't know if anybody is up there still. No one's come out since I called you. I've been watching the front door."

"Is there a back door?"

"Not to my apartment. I'm on the third floor."

"No fire escape?"

"No."

"We'll check it out. Do you have a burglar alarm?" Meanwhile, the white cop, named LEWIS, is squinting up at the building. When he looks up, I can see he has braces on his teeth.

"No."

"Is the house yours?"

"No. My landlords are away."

"You live alone?"

"I have a cat."

Tarrant clears his throat. "May I have your key to the front door?"

I dig in my bag again. My father's joke is miles away. With effort, I produce the keys. "This one is to the front door. The next one is the apartment door."

He takes the key ring by the front door key. "We'll check it out. Please stand back and clear the door." He throws a brawny arm in my path and guides me away from the entrance. My stomach begins to churn. In a few minutes, I'll find out what the fuck is going on.

They leave me there and enter the building. One of my neighbors across the way, the one with the Bianchi bike, watches curiously from the window. None of the other neighbors are at the windows. The shades are drawn again in the apartment across from mine. Whoever lives there is never home. A lawyer.

Out of the corner of my eye, I see Marv crossing the street and heading in my direction. I stand away from the building and look up to see if anything's going on in my apartment. The slats in the window blinds are suddenly illuminated. The cops must be in the living room. I bite my lip.

"Did they find anything?" Marv peers up with me at the building.

"They're still up there."

"Don't worry. Anything got taken, you can get replaced. It's only money."

"Except my cat."

"You think they took your cat?"

"No. I'm just worried about her."

"Me, I hate cats."

"Me too."

Suddenly, the window blinds are pulled up and Officer Lewis's silhouette appears in Alice's window. He fusses with the screen and pokes his head out briefly, then replaces it. I crane my neck to see inside the apartment, but I can't see past the cop. He does the same to the other window.

"I wonder what he's doing," I say.

"Seeing how the guy broke in. I heard some guy broke into an apartment on Lombard last week. Climbed right up the front of the building to the third floor. Like a mountain climber. Like Spider-Man."

I look up at the apartment. Two bright windows face the street, glowing from the front of the building like the eyes of a jack-o'-lantern. I wonder how much longer the cops will be. I wonder what they're finding. Suddenly, Alice springs onto her windowsill and does a luxuriant stretch.

"That's Alice! That's my cat!" I can't remember being so happy to see her.

"Cute," Marv says, without enthusiasm. He frowns at the window. "You know, a girl like you, you don't need a cat. You need a dog, for protection. Cats are good for nothing."

Officer Lewis appears in the window behind Alice and picks her up. He makes her do a little wave at me in the window, until she leaps out of his arms.

"Look at that, Marv!"

"Very cute."

A couple of minutes later the cops come out the front door. Lewis is sneezing almost uncontrollably. He runs by, coughing and sneezing, and leaps into the squad car. Officer Tarrant walks over to us, grinning broadly. I can't figure out what's going on.

"Nice cat," he says to me.

"What happened?"

"My partner found out he's allergic."

I look over. The white cop is in the throes of a sneezing fit. "Is he okay?"

"Might have to shoot him." Tarrant laughs, and so does Marv.

"What did you find upstairs?"

"It's fine, ma'am. Everything is absolutely fine. It looks untouched."

"Really?"

"Really."

"No one's there or anything?"

"No."

"It's totally safe?"

"Unless you're allergic to cats." He bends down to peer into the squad car at Lewis, still hacking away.

I can't make sense of this. "But the door was open."

"Come on in with me. We'll take a quick walk through and you tell me if anything is missing." Tarrant opens the front door for me.

"Would you mind going first?"

"Age before beauty, huh?" he says, and walks ahead of me. It all seems so strange; I've never left the door unlocked before. When we reach the door to the apartment, he swings it open wide and we go in.

Everything looks normal. A small living room, with a paisley sofa and a scrubbed-pine coffee table. The TV is in place and the VCR under it. The stereo sits on the shelf. As usual, Alice doesn't even look at me. I reach for her, but she jumps from my arms with a soft thud.

"This how you left it?" Tarrant asks.

"It looks the same."

"Let's check the bedroom." He walks in front of me and flicks on the bedroom light. The bed's unmade, my clothes are piled on top of the computer, and there's a stack of paperbacks beside the bed on the floor. Neat, it's not. But it looks like it always does.

"Take a look at your jewelry box," he says.

I walk to my bureau obediently and look into the open jewelry box. I don't have a lot of jewelry, but there are a few gold chains, a set of pearls, and my gold power earrings for client meetings. "Everything's here."

"You're lucky. You have a lot of expensive things lying around. The TV, the VCR, the computer. You ought to think about a safety deposit box for the jewelry."

"Did you search the whole apartment? I mean, am I alone?"

Tarrant nods. "We even checked under the bed."

I think he intends this as a joke, but it sends a shudder up my spine.

"Like I said, you're lucky, ma'am. I've seen places turned over, cleaned *out*. Next time make sure you lock your door."

"You sure you looked everywhere? I mean, I'm not doubting you, it's just that lately some weird things have been happening to me."

"Like what?"

His eyes are a deep, friendly brown, and his manner is professional. I feel like I can trust him. I take a deep breath and let it rip.

TWELVE

"Wait a minute," Tarrant says. "Did you report any of this?"

"No. If I did, you'd investigate."

"That's the point, isn't it?"

"Well, what would an investigation involve?"

"We'd start with your statement. Then we'd interview anyone you suspect, any witnesses to the incidents with the car."

"There aren't any witnesses."

He purses his lips. "Do you suspect anyone?"

"I think it's someone at my firm."

"I see. What did the note say exactly?"

"It said, *Congratulations on your partnership.*"

He laughs. I see my credibility fall off the table. "That's all it said? Why do you call it a hate note?"

"It was sarcastic, because I—"

"No threats of bodily harm?"

"No."

"A note like that, it could be from a friend of yours, a practical joke."

"But the car doesn't fit, does it?"

Tarrant shakes his head. "No. So come down and file a

report. Bring the note. We'll send it down to the Document Unit. They'll test the paper, analyze the handwriting."

"But I can't file a report."

"Why not?"

"I can't have an investigation of the people at work right now. It'd look terrible. I'd lose my job."

"Our hands are tied unless you do."

"It's out of the question."

He shrugs. "Then my advice is to be cautious. Don't go places alone. If you see the car again, call 911."

"Okay."

"And don't be suspecting every little thing that happens to you, like today. I think you slipped up and forgot to lock the door."

"I don't know. It's not like me."

He nods, a final nod that tells me our conversation is over. "Listen to Uncle Dave. Nine times out of ten, it's a gag. Or an old boyfriend. Some guy you jilted or didn't have time for. They get over it." He claps his hands together. "Now I got to see if my partner is still alive."

"Maybe if I took him something to drink. Water, or a soda."

"I don't usually treat him that nice, but if you want to, it's not a bad idea."

"Good." I head into the kitchen, where the light is already on, and look around briefly before getting a Coke. Nothing has been disturbed. My eyes flit automatically over to the magnetic knife rack. Four steak knives, all accounted for. Plus one lethal-looking chopping knife, Mike's favorite when he played samurai chef. It all looks fine. Maybe I did leave the door open. Maybe I wasn't thinking. I get the Coke and walk downstairs with Tarrant.

Outside, I'm surprised to see Marv still around, leaning on the squad car and talking to Officer Lewis. Lewis's face is covered with hives and his eyes are swollen almost shut.

Tarrant breaks into laughter, staggering backward comically

when he sees his partner. "Oh, man. You look good, Jimmy. What are you doin' Friday night?"

"Come on, Dave. I gotta get to a drugstore before I croak."

Tarrant is laughing too hard even to respond. I hand the Coke to Lewis. "I'm really sorry. Maybe this will help."

He accepts the can miserably. "I can't see it but I can tell it's good."

"Stay cool, Jim. It's not a brew. It's a diet Coke."

"I know that," he scoffs. "Thanks, ma'am."

"Thank you for your help."

They get into the car, with Tarrant driving, and pull away. I'm left standing there with Marv. Even though I'm tired, I'm in no hurry to go back upstairs.

"You musta left the door open," Marv says. He's taken off his pith helmet, and his hair is plastered against his head in a ring.

"I guess. Thanks for the use of the chair."

"Listen, I stuck around 'cause I want to tell you something." He leans over. "You gotta think about protectin' yourself."

"I can't get a dog, Marv. I'm never home."

He looks furtively around. "I'm not talking about a dog. I'm talking about this." He looks down and so do I. In the middle of his calloused palm is a small black gun. It has an embossed black trident on its handle. It looks like a shiny new toy.

"Is that real?"

"It's a Beretta."

"Marv, what are you doing with that? Are you nuts?" I look around wildly. The guy with the Bianchi is gone from the window. So is the Bianchi.

"Shh. Shh. I'm tryin' to tell you somethin'."

"You can't just carry that around in your pocket, for Christ's sake. Is it loaded?"

"Can't drill no holes if it ain't."

I step back. "Jesus, Marv, are you crazy? That's a concealed weapon!"

"It's legal. I got a permit."

"That doesn't mean you can carry it around! Did you have that when you were talking to the cop?"

He smiles slyly. "Right under his nose and he didn't even know it. I'm telling you, Mary, you need one of these. You live by yourself. All you got for protection is that scrawny cat. Wise up." He shoves the gun into my hand.

It terrifies me, just the feel of it. Light and deadly. "Take it back. Get it away from me." I hand it to him, but he pushes it back at me. I feel panicky. "Marv, take it back! It's gonna go off!"

He takes it back, with a chuckle. "Can't go off. It's got a safety." He slips it into his pocket as if it were loose change.

"Marv, why do you have that thing?"

"You think you can run a cash business in this city without a gun? Besides, it's my right. It says it in the United States Constitution. I have the right to bear arms."

"Don't tell me what the Constitution says. The Constitution is talking about the need for an army. It's so the army can have the guns, Marv, not guys who sell plants. You'll get yourself hurt with that thing."

"Oh please."

"You will. I read that. They'll take it from you and use it against you."

"You sure you don't want to borrow it for just one night? If you need to shoot it, you just take the safety off and hold it with two hands, like on *Charlie's Angels*. Like this." He makes a Luger with his fingers.

"No, thanks."

"Sure?"

"I couldn't use it anyway. I couldn't shoot anybody. Now I'm going to bed."

"Yes, you could. If you had to. If somebody was trying to kill you, you sure as hell could."

"See you, Marv."

His thin voice calls after me. "Don't kid yourself, Mary. You'd use it. Every one of us would. Don't kid yourself."

I leave him standing there in the yellow square of light spilling out from my window. A hustler with a toy-sized gun in the pocket of his chinos.

THIRTEEN

I get inside my apartment and check everywhere for notes, for damage, for something missing. For any kind of sign that someone has been here. I find nothing.

I try my best to feel at home. I go around and touch all of my things, rechristening them. I clean up the bedroom. I open a can of Progresso soup. Still, I can't shake the feeling that something is different about the place. I settle down on the living room floor to figure out the directions for the answering machine, but I can't concentrate.

Alice comes over and sniffs the open box. She saw the whole thing. "Did I leave the door open, Alice?"

She ignores me and walks away.

"You can be replaced!" I shout after her.

I sit in the middle of my floor with a mug of lentil soup and look around my empty apartment. I feel edgy and decide to call Judy. She thinks the whole thing is as creepy as I do but convinces me that I left the door unlocked. Everybody makes mistakes, she says, even you. Then she gets worked up about Marv's gun; it takes me ten minutes to persuade her that I wouldn't think of buying one. I hook up the machine and begin screening the calls after that. I pick up when I hear Ned's voice.

"Hey, Mary. I didn't know you had an answering machine."

"It's new."

"You going to use it instead of star sixty-nine?"

"Until my number gets changed."

"I like it, it's cute. You sound like a kid."

"Great. I wanted to sound like a hit man. Hit woman."

He laughs. "Not on your life. So how are you doing? You've been burning up the phone lines."

"Don't ask."

"Anything the matter?"

"Yes, but I'm too tired to talk about it."

"Just give me the headline."

"I thought a car was following me, but it wasn't. I thought someone broke into my apartment, but they didn't. Not a good day."

"Weird."

"Yeah. Now I'm tired. I was just about to go to sleep."

"I should let you go then."

"Oh, I almost forgot. I'm supposed to tell you. Your father sends his regards."

"My father *what*?"

"I was at Masterson. He introduced himself."

"To you? Why?" Ned sounds concerned, almost frightened.

"I don't know. He said he wanted to meet me. I guess you told him that we—"

"I haven't spoken to my father in fifteen years, Mary."

"You haven't? Why not?"

"It's a long story. I'd rather not talk about it over the phone. Can I stop by your office tomorrow?"

I offer a tentative okay and we hang up. None of this makes sense. Why would a grown man sound frightened of his father? Why haven't they spoken in a decade and a half? How does his father know anything about me? I have so many questions lately, and no answers at all. I don't like this feeling, that everything's slipping out of control. I kept it together after Mike died, and it wasn't easy. Now it's all under attack. Threatened at the foundation.

I close the living room blinds and check the dead bolt. I decide to take a hot bubble bath to calm down. I push the ANSWER CALL button on the answering machine and fill the tub. I undress quickly, throwing my clothes into a heap on the bathroom floor. I sink deep into the warm, scented water, artificially blue in imitation of the Caribbean. The box promised that the sapphire currents would wash my troubles away. Don't worry, be happy. I lie still in the tub, listening for any sound in the apartment. The only noise is the crackling of the bubbles as they pop at my earlobes. I try to enjoy high tide, but as soon as I start, the telephone rings. I stiffen and wait for the machine to answer.

The rings stop, and there's a mechanical noise as the tape machine engages. "Mary, this is Timothy Jameson. See me first thing in the morning. You know when I get in." *Click.*

At least it's not *him.*

I relax in the warm, silky water. It feels good, therapeutic. I sink deeper, so the waves lap at my chin. I close my eyes. No problem, mon.

The next time I hear the telephone ring, the water is cool. Barely conscious, I hear the answering machine pick up the call. A woman's voice says, too loudly, "This is Stephanie Fraser. We met in Judge Bitterman's courtroom after your argument. I've been calling your office, but you haven't returned my calls. We just can't sweep this under the rug, Mary. We need to send a message. So please return my call. I know you must be busy, but this is important. Thank you."

Click.

"Go away, Steph. I gave at the office."

But now the water is cold, and I'm awake. How unpleasant. And I have to shave my legs, a task that used to make me feel grown-up but now is merely a pain in the ass. Cranky, I fish under the water for the Dove and soap up the stubble on my legs. I use a new plastic razor, for that extra-close shave. This way I can let it go for three more days. I'm negotiating my ankle bone with concentration when the telephone rings again.

The rings stop and the machine engages.

Silence. No message. No static. It's *him*.

Click.

I feel a sharp pinch at my ankle. A crimson seam crosses the bone. The soap makes it burn.

"Shit!"

I hurl the razor against the tile wall, and it falls to the floor.

That's when I see it: Mike's picture, the little one of his face, in a porcelain heart frame. The only picture of him I haven't packed away. I keep it on my makeup shelf in the bathroom. It's a private place that only I can see, every morning.

But it's not on the makeup shelf tonight. It's on the floor. Shattered.

"No!" I climb out of the bathtub and pick up the frame. It lies in pieces in my hand as I stand dripping on the tile floor. The porcelain has cracked into separate shards, and the glass over Mike's face is a network of tiny slivers.

How did this happen? I don't want to think what I'm thinking.

I check the makeup shelf frantically. A tube of Lancôme foundation. A glass of eye pencils and mascara. A couple of lipsticks and a bottle of contact lens solution. None of the makeup has been disturbed. If it was Alice who knocked over the picture frame, she was pretty choosy.

I look down at my hand. I can't see Mike at all. It's as if a storm cloud has passed over his features.

If someone is trying to hurt me, they sure know how to do it.

FOURTEEN

I take a cab to work at the ungodly hour that Jameson gets in. My nerves feel taut, my stomach queasy. I'm losing weight, but it's not worth it.

I get off the elevator on Jameson's floor, Lust. When I reach his office, his secretary, Stella, tells me he went to the bathroom. I suggest to Stella, my *paisana*, that if Jameson didn't come to work so early, he could take his morning poopie at home like everybody else. This makes Stella laugh, so she tells me a joke too raunchy to repeat. It's for her jokes that Judy calls her The Amazing Stella.

I go into Jameson's office and sit down. The office is vaguely nautical in theme, a place for Jameson to pretend he's the captain of something. For Jameson is short, and has the complex in spades. Suddenly he runs in like a pug off the leash and slams the door behind him. "Well, Mary, I guess what I've been hearing is true."

"What do you mean?"

Jameson remains standing, dipping his fingers into the pockets of a navy blue blazer. "What I am about to tell you is for your own good, Mary. I'm telling it to you because I know you are very interested in becoming a partner here at Stalling."

"What is it?" He's making me even more paranoid than I am already.

"I've been hearing that you're Berkowitz's girl now and that you do your best work only for him."

"But I—"

Jameson holds up a tiny paw, like a doggie pope. "At first, I thought it wasn't true. It didn't sound like the Mary DiNunzio I know. But I got the *Noone* brief yesterday and I was extremely disappointed in it."

"I—"

The paw again. "I know you can do better, Mary, because you have in the past, and for me. But if you think you can make partner in this firm just by keeping Sam Berkowitz happy, you are in error. I should not have to remind you that you have an obligation that runs directly to the client in this matter. *My* client, Noone Pharmaceuticals. Noone is almost as big as SmithKline and growing by leaps and bounds. Noone is not a client I would like to lose. You understand that, don't you?"

I nod, dry-mouthed.

"Good. I thought as much." He plucks the brief from his desk and hands it to me. "Rework this according to my comments, which you'll find in red. Spend time in the library. Get authority for your position. If you can't find the cases, I want your assurance that they don't exist." He makes a note in his day journal to bill the two minutes it took to dress me down. "I need it by the end of the day."

"I can't, Timothy. I have—"

"You'd do it by the end of the day for Sam Berkowitz, so you'll do it by the end of the day for Timothy Jameson. End of discussion."

"Okay . . . I'll postpone some things."

"Fine."

I leave his office, red-faced, with a rose garden abloom on my chest. As I hurry by Stella's desk, she hands me a Styrofoam cup of coffee on a tray. "Don't take it too hard, Mare," she whispers. "He's got no one else to piss on, you know what I mean?"

I escape to my office and collapse into my chair. I feel like crying, and not just because of the brief. My life is going haywire. The center isn't holding. My work is going downhill; I'm forgetting depositions, offending clients. The partners are badmouthing me. Somebody's harassing me, maybe even breaking into my apartment. What goes around comes around.

And it's coming after you, says the voice.

"Mary, you in there?" says someone at the door.

Before I can answer, the door opens a crack and a white paper bag pops through the opening, followed by Ned's handsome face. His expression darkens as he comes in, closing the door behind him. "Mary?"

It's no use, I can't hide it. I feel wretched. It has to show.

"What's the matter?"

Ned looks so concerned and his voice sounds so caring that I lose it. I start to cry and find myself in his arms, which only makes me cry harder. I cry about Mike, who's not coming back, and Jameson's brief, which I can't possibly rewrite in one day, and Angie, who would rather talk to God all day than to her twin. I cry about my apartment, my *home*, which I'll never feel safe in again. I cry like a baby, freely and shamelessly, while Ned holds me close.

In the next moment he's kissing me on my forehead and on my cheeks. It feels so comforting. I hug him back, and he lifts me onto my desk and burrows into my neck. I smell the fresh scent of his aftershave and can't even begin to think about what's happening between us, as I hear my Rolodex tumble off the desk, followed by the splash of a cup of coffee and the creak of my office door.

"Mary! The carpet!" shouts Brent, who looks in, astounded, and slams the door shut with a bang.

It breaks the spell. I push Ned away and wipe the wetness from my eyes. "Jesus. Jesus Christ, Ned. I must be out of my mind."

"Mary, there's nothing wrong with—"

"Yes, there is. I shouldn't be. I can't."

"I want to be close to you, Mary. You need that, I can see it. I used to be just like you, keeping everything in—"

"Please, Ned."

"Tell me what's happening. I can help."

"You want to help? Then stop sending me notes. And stop following me." It's a test. I watch his face for a reaction.

"What are you talking about?"

"Did you break into my apartment?"

"What?" He looks shocked.

"Did you write the note?"

"What note?"

"The note. 'Congratulations on your partnership.' It has to be you. Nobody else makes sense."

He puts up his hands. His mouth goes dry, I can see it. "Wait a minute. Wait a minute. What are you saying? Why would I do something like that to you?"

"Tell the truth, Ned. Have you written me a note or followed me in a car? Like to my parents' house?"

He touches my shoulder. "Why would I do that, Mary?"

"Answer the question."

"No. No, of course not."

I look directly into his green eyes to see whether he's lying, but I'm thrown off by the honest feeling that I find there. The door opens narrowly and Brent slips in. He carries a stack of paper towels and a plastic jug of Palmolive dishwashing liquid. He doesn't look at me or Ned but immediately sets to work sopping up the coffee spill.

"Maybe I'd better go, Mary," Ned says.

"Maybe you'd better!" snaps Brent.

Ned's barely out the door when Brent hits the ceiling. "Mary, are you out of your mind? Have you lost it completely? Have you gone totally fucking loco?" He scrubs the rug so vigorously the detergent lathers up like shaving cream.

"Brent—"

"Fucking on the desk!" He glares up at me, the veins on his slim neck bulging.

"Brent, slow up! We weren't—"

"Do you *know* what they would do if they caught you? If you sneeze without a hankie, they cut off your balls with a cuticle scissors! What do you think they'd do if they caught you *fucking on the desk*? Huh?"

"I would never—"

"I'm sure you're not practicing safe sex!"

"Brent, we didn't—"

"Suicide! Mary, it's suicide! I go to a funeral every weekend! Everyone I know is sick, except for me. And now Jack." He throws down the paper towel.

I feel a chill. "Jack?"

He looks up at me, his eyes full of tears.

My God. Brent is going to lose Jack. My own eyes sting. "Jesus, I'm so sorry." I kneel down and rub his back through his thin black sweater. He returns to cleaning the stain, mechanically.

"I've known for a while, Mary, so it's not sudden, like it was with you and Mike. And you don't have to worry about me. I'm HIV negative. We always practiced safe sex, even from the beginning."

"My God." I hadn't even considered losing Brent. I couldn't lose him too. We've been together for eight years. I don't know what would happen to me.

"It's no joke, Mary. It's real. Anyone can get it, even Magic Johnson, even you. You're playing with fire."

"We didn't do it, Brent."

"You were going to."

"No, I wasn't." I wasn't going that far, but I did feel something for Ned when he kissed me. And I felt something else, a flicker of physical need that I thought had been buried with Mike. It thrilled me; it frightened me. I look down at the stained carpet and Brent does too.

"All that work," he says, "and it's only gone from coffee brown to Palmolive green." He offers me a paper towel and takes one for himself.

I blow my nose. "It looks like Hawaii."

"No. It looks like Placido Domingo." He wipes his eyes and throws an arm around my shoulder. "So tell me, Mare. Why is it always the Catholic girls who are doin' it on the desks?"

"Brent!" I shove him.

"With Waters yet, who writes you poison pen letters. Who follows you around!"

"It's not him."

"He's mind-fucking you, girlfriend. That man is a mind fuck." He gets up and pulls me to my feet.

"I know what I'm doing, Brent."

"Say what?" He bursts into laughter.

I laugh with him, in spite of myself. "All right, maybe I don't. But I don't think Ned's the one. I just don't."

"Oh, really? Well, you'd better be sure about that, because you got another note in this morning's mail."

"No, really?"

"That's what I was coming in to tell you."

From his back pocket, he hands me a piece of white paper. The message is laser-printed in capital letters and reads:

WATCH YOUR STEP, MARY

The envelope, the stamp, everything is the same as last time. My heart sinks. "Who's doing this, Brent? This is so awful."

"You have to call the cops, Mare."

"I talked to them last night."

"Hallelujah! You called them?"

"After someone broke into my apartment. Which they didn't. I hope."

Brent looks crazed. "Mary, what the fuck is going on?"

"I don't know. All I know is that when I got home, the door

was open. Nothing was taken. The apartment was untouched. Except for Mike's picture, which either fell off the shelf—"

"I can't believe this. This is insane! What did the cops say?"

"They think I left the door unlocked. There was no sign of a break-in."

"What do you think?"

"Last night after I saw the picture, I was sure someone was there. Today I'm not so sure."

"You didn't report it?"

"Brent, if I file a report, they'll investigate. The cop told me. They'll interview people at the firm, people I suspect. Which at this point is everyone but you and Judy. Can you imagine that? Even if they interview a handful of people, you don't think that's going to be the kiss of death?"

"They could keep it confidential."

"Sure, like they keep the number of partners confidential. Like they keep the associate reviews confidential. You know better than that—people stand in line to give you the dirt. And as soon as the gossip mill starts up, I look like shit. Either I'm accusing them of something criminal or I'm a hysterical female."

Suddenly, the phone rings. Brent answers it and then hands it to me, mouthing "Martin."

"Hi, Martin." I stare at the note in my hand.

"You're too busy to return my calls?"

"I'm sorry, Martin. I was in a dep until late at Masterson." I read the note again. WATCH YOUR STEP, MARY.

"Bernie Starankovic called. Think you can find the time to call him back?"

"Sure, Martin."

"Capital. Do so."

I hang up slowly and hand the note back to Brent. "Will you keep this somewhere safe, with the other one?"

"Now I'm storing evidence. The cops should have this, not me."

But I'm lost in thought. "You know, what about Martin? He just sounded pissed as hell, and I can see *him* writing notes like this. He's got a motive, because I'm taking his place on *Hart*. If Berkowitz is grooming me to start doing his work . . ."

"You're just guessing, Mary. Only detectives can do detective work. Let them help you, goddamn it! If you don't call them, I will." Brent reaches for the telephone, but I press his hand down onto the receiver. Our hands pile on top of one another, like a dead-serious game of one potato, two potato.

"No, Brent. Wait. It's my career you're playing with. If they investigate, I'm gonna lose my job. I can tell you that right now. As sure as you and I are standing here."

Our eyes meet over the phone. He looks surprised at my urgency. So am I.

"I need this job, Brent. It's what I have now. I started eight years ago, and I want to see it through. It's been a constant. For all the faults in this firm, I know when I come in on Monday morning I'll see you and Judy and The Amazing Stella, and I know where the watercooler is."

"I know that, Mare, we've been together since day one. I love you. You're my friend."

"Then listen to me. I'll make you a deal. After the election, if it's still going on, I'll report it. I'll raise holy hell, I mean it. But not until after the election."

"You don't gamble with stuff like this, Mare."

"My job?"

"Your life."

I give his fist a quick squeeze. "Don't be so dramatic, Brent. This is not *Camille*, Act Three. Nobody's dead."

"Not yet," he says, and his glistening eyes bore into mine. "Not yet."

FIFTEEN

Because of my discussion with Brent, which we resolve by agreeing to disagree, I'm ten minutes late to the Friday morning litigation meeting. Nobody seems to notice except Judy, who looks at me curiously as I take a seat along the wall and put the marked-up *Noone* brief face down in my lap. The meetings are held in Conference Room A, the only conference room large enough to accommodate the whole department. Conference Room A is on the sixth floor, Avarice, but the A doesn't stand for Avarice. At least not officially.

I used to love these meetings, full of war stories about Actual Trials and Real Juries. I loved them even after I realized that their purpose was self-promotion, not self-education. I loved the meetings because this group of litigators—or alligators, as Judy calls us—was my own. I felt I belonged in their swamp. I believed, on faith, that they wouldn't eat me; I was one of their young. But I believe this no longer. I've lost my religion.

I watch the alligators feed voraciously on delicatessen fish, Danish, and bagels. You'd think they haven't eaten in years. I look around the room, seeing them as if for the first time. I scrutinize each freshly shaved or made-up face. Which alligator is sending me these terrible notes? Which one broke into my apartment—or maybe hired someone to do it?

Is it Berkowitz? He starts off the meeting, smoking profusely, telling everyone about the victory before Bitterman, which seems as if it happened a decade ago. He mentions my name in a familiar way and comes dangerously close to giving me some credit. Every head turns in my direction. I hear an undercurrent of snapping jaws.

Is it Jameson? Is his one of the jaws I heard?

Is it Martin? Is he the Guy Who Likes Owls But Hates Me?

Is it Lovell, a semiretired partner who still says Eyetalian?

Is it Ackerman, a supercharged woman partner who hates other women, a bizarre new hybrid in a permanent Man Suit?

There's Ned, looking at me thoughtfully. Not him, I think.

And Judy, whose bright eyes are clear of makeup. Of course not Judy.

Then who? I look at each partner, all thirty of them in the department, racking my brain to see if any one has reason to dislike me. I look at each young associate, a nestful of hatchlings, sixty-two in all. They're free of original sin. At least they look that way.

When the meeting's over, I head straight for the library and grab one of its private study rooms. Each room is soundproof and contains only a desk and a computer. And the doors lock, a feature I hadn't taken advantage of until now. I lock the door and skim the brief for Jameson's bold-red comments.

He finds my sentences TERRIBLE and the central argument INCONSISTENT. Everywhere else he has scribbled CASE CITATION! At the risk of sounding arrogant, I'll tell you there's nothing wrong with this brief. Jameson's going to make me rewrite it just because he can, even though it'll cost Noone as much as a compact car. And I'll do it because I need Jameson's vote.

I flick on the computer and it buzzes to life. I log on to Lexis, a legal research program, and type in a search request for the cases I need. It finds no cases. I reformulate the search request, but still no cases. I change it again and again and finally start to pick up cases from a district court in Arizona. That's what legal research is like—you dig and dig until you strike a line of cases, like a wiggly vein of precious minerals. Then you strip-mine as if it were the mother lode. I'm cheered by my unaccustomed good fortune when someone knocks on the glass window of the door.

It's Brent, carrying a covered salad and a diet Coke. I unlock the door to let him in.

"You vacuum-sealed, Mare?" He sets down my lunch.

"Can you blame me?"

"No, I'm glad of it. Listen, I got them to change your extension. I told them we kept getting calls for Jacoby and Meyers—it was all they had to hear. You'll have a new number by this afternoon. I already sent a letter to the clients."

"Way to go. What about my home number? I'm still getting calls."

"Shit. They wanted your authorization to unlist it, so I wrote a letter from you and faxed it over, okay?"

"Great."

"The only problem is it will take three days to make the change, and weekends don't count. It won't be changed until Wednesday of next week."

"That's not good."

"Did I say I told you so? I must have. I'm just that kind of guy."

"All right, I hear you."

"It's not your fault, it's theirs. The phone company is so much more efficient since they broke it up." Brent rolls his eyes. "What a shame. They used to be my favorite monopoly, after Baltic and Mediterranean."

"You can't make any money on Baltic and Mediterranean."

"I know, but I like the color. Eggplant," he says, in a fake-gay voice. Brent does that sometimes to make the partners laugh. He says, The joke's on them, I *am* what a gay man sounds like. "The good news is, I got you a preferred phone number."

"What's that?"

"You know, where you pick your own four-letter word for the number," he says, with a grin.

"Brent, you didn't."

"Not that, dear. Give me some credit." He pulls a yellow message slip out of his pocket and hands it to me.

I laugh. "546-ARIA?"

"You like?"

"It's cute."

"This way, people will think you got culture."

"Right." I hand him back the slip. "Thanks. For lunch, too. I owe you."

"Forget it. Somebody's got to take care of you, don't they?"

"I got a better idea. Let me buy you dinner tonight."

"Deal. Just don't try to get fresh later." He ruffles the top of my head and is gone.

I lock the door and work through the afternoon, rewriting the brief and adding the new cases. By the time I rush the disk up to Brent to correct my typing, the papers are perfect for the second time. I remember to telephone Starankovic when I get back to my desk. 4:45. He sounds as if he's still sore at the wounds inflicted by Bitter Man and is fighting like Matlock for the one plaintiff he still represents.

"I'm gonna depose the two supervisors in the Northeast store next week, Mr. Grayboyes and Mrs. Breslin," he says. "Then I'm gonna interview each and every one of your staff employees."

"Bernie—"

"If you don't consent to the interviews, I'm gonna file a motion."

"Wait a minute, Bernie." Starankovic knows he has to send a notice to schedule a deposition. He's trying to fuck me, so I fuck back. "No notices, no deps."

"I sent the notices!"

"When? I didn't get them."

"I sent 'em to Martin. I had 'em hand-delivered. I paid extra."

It takes me aback. Martin. "I didn't know about the notices, Bernie. I haven't scheduled the deps. I haven't even called the witnesses."

"That's not my problem."

"Christ! Cooperate, would you?"

"Why should I?"

"Because I'll recommend to Harbison's that they let you do the interviews. Then you won't have to file a motion."

"So?"

"Saves you money."

"Saves *you* money," he retorts.

"You want to go see Bitterman again? Really, Bernie? You need that *acido* in your life?"

There's a short pause. "Okay, Mary. You talk to your client. You schedule the deps. But it's gotta be soon. I want the interviews."

I hang up, with the feeling I've dodged a bullet. But I don't know when the next one is coming, or who's doing the shooting. Why didn't Martin tell me about the notices? What if the note writer is Martin?

Brent brings in the finished copy of the *Noone* brief. After a quick review, I walk it over to Jameson, who has stepped away again. The Amazing Stella says, "That freak spends half his time in the little boy's room."

"That's because he's full of shit," I whisper.

She smirks and beckons me closer with a coral-colored fingernail. "You know what he's doin' in there?"

"What?"

"Whackin' off."

"Stella! Jeez!" I look around to see if anyone is in earshot. The secretaries have gone home, it's after five.

"Mary, you always think everybody's an angel. I'm tellin' youse, he's got a whole drawer full of dirty magazines in his desk. He keeps it locked, but I seen it once. There's sex toys in there, too. Really *weird* toys."

"Sex toys?"

"*Weird* toys," she repeats, with a shudder. Suddenly, she snaps to attention. "Mr. Jameson! Miss DiNunzio was just bringin' this brief to youse."

"*You*, Stella." Jameson all but adds, You ignorant dago.

I try to look at him normally, but the thought of the sex toys almost makes me gag. I have to say something, so I say, "I did manage to find some cases after all. On Lexis."

"Knew you would. I'll look it over later." He scampers past me into his office. He's telling me he didn't really need the brief by the end of the day, he just wanted to make me do tricks.

Weird tricks, I think, and almost shudder myself.

Brent howls at this later, over dinner. We eat at Il Gallo Nero, a restaurant that Brent adores because Riccardo Muti used to eat here. Brent had a heavy crush on Muti. He wore a black armband on his black shirt the day the Maestro left for Milan.

"I knew it! I knew it!" Brent shouts, laughing. "Jameson's in the closet, Mare! He's a closet queen!"

"She didn't say that, Brent." I've had too much chianti and so has he. I don't care, I'm having fun. And Brent has forgotten to nag me about the cops, for which I'm grateful, because I know I'll pay for it in June.

"Yes, she did! She said weird toys. What do you think she meant?"

"I don't know. I'm a good girl."

"Dildos! Nipple pincers! Choke chains! He pretends he's a dog! He fucks rhinos! Oh, no!" We both laugh until the tears flow.

When we leave, Brent puts an arm around my shoulders and we walk up Walnut Street. The asphalt is being repaved to eliminate the potholes, which cover the city streets like mine-fields. Philadelphia being the well-oiled machine that it is, nobody's working on the street even though much of it is blocked to traffic. Cars lurch to avoid the police sawhorses, al-though there isn't much traffic tonight. The new mayor hasn't been real successful in attracting suburbanites to the city on weekends. I can't imagine why. It's a great theater town if you haven't seen *Fiddler*, and there's always that friendly pat-down before you take in a first-run movie.

"Look at this street. What a mess," Brent says. "Here, let me walk on the outside." He do-si-dos around me so he's closer to the curb, then puts his arm back on my shoulder.

"Why did you do that?"

"It's traditional. The man walks on the street side, protect-ing the woman from the carriages, in case they splash mud."

"That's sexist, Brent. And besides, you're gay." I switch places with him, skipping around him so that I'm curbside.

Honk-honk! A truck blares right behind my shoulder.

I jump, startled at the loudness of it. The truck's headlights go by in a double blur. The cars, confused by the roadblocks, are moving in all directions. Suddenly, I feel afraid. I haven't been watching out for the dark car. I start to tell Brent, but he plows into me, laughing, and replaces me at the curb.

"So what if I'm gay?" he says. "I still count!"

At that moment, just as Brent is dancing toward the street, a car jumps the curb in back of him. It bounds up onto the sidewalk and hurtles directly toward him, ramming into his back with a sickening thud.

I can't believe what I'm seeing.

It's the car, the one that's been following me.

"No! Brent!" I shout, but it's too late.

Brent's face freezes in agony and shock as the car lifts him bodily on its grill, like a charging bull gores a matador. His body snaps back against the car and his mouth is a silent scream.

"Stop! No!!" I watch in horror as the car flings Brent's lithe frame up off the sidewalk. He shrieks as his body literally flies through the air and slams into the plate glass window of a bank. The glass shatters with a hideous tinkling sound and rains down on Brent in a deadly sheet. Then the only sound is the clamor of the bank alarm.

And the screech of the murderous car as it digs out onto a chopped-up Walnut Street and busts up a police sawhorse with a splintering *craaaack*.

I whirl around, squinting frantically for a license plate.

There is none.

The car careens crazily up the street and out of sight.

SIXTEEN

The coarse wooden toothpick in Detective Lombardo's mouth wiggles indignantly. "Cheese and crackers! Why do you have to talk that way? I work with cops that have a fifty times better mouth than you." We're sitting in the hospital corridor, waiting for Brent's operation to be over.

"What's the matter with it?"

"It's not nice, for a lady."

"You know, if you'd get as worked up about whoever hit Brent as you do about my language, we'd be in good shape."

"I don't have to get worked up to do my job. I know my job. I'm doin' it." He points at me with his spiral note pad.

"Fine."

"Good."

"Good." We've been arguing like this for hours. Lombardo arrived on the scene after the ambulance got there because I reported the incident as intentional. He asked a lot of questions and wrote the answers down slowly with a stubby pencil, which he seemed to think constituted the sum total of his job. Lombardo played football for Penn State, but I'm beginning to wonder if they gave him a helmet.

Suddenly, his heavy-lidded brown eyes light up. It looks like

Fred Flintstone getting an idea. "Hey, Mary, how about gay-bashing?" Hey, Barn, how about we go bowling?

"You couldn't tell that Brent was gay."

"You can always tell."

"Now what's that supposed to mean?"

"Just what I said."

I feel my eyes well up; I didn't know there were any tears left. "I don't want to hear that, Lombardo. Keep it to yourself, because you don't know what you're talking about. Brent is a great person and so are his friends. Anything else is bigotry."

"Don't get me wrong, I didn't say I don't like gay people." He glances up and down the glistening hallway. "I got a brother, you know, who's a little light in the loafers."

"Christ."

Lombardo leans closer, and I catch a whiff of Brut. "All I'm saying is that you can tell. I knew, with my brother. I knew, right off."

"You knew."

"I knew. It was his eyebrows. Something about his eyebrows." He arches an eyebrow, with effort. "See?"

I look away. I'm glad Jack isn't here for this conversation. I called him the first thing and he arrived in tears. He poured quarters into the pay phone, calling all his friends. They came in a flash and were as loving and supportive a group as I've ever seen. I tried to explain to him about the car, but he was too upset to listen. It doesn't matter how Brent got here, Jack said, only that he gets out. They all went outside a while ago to smoke a cigarette, waiting to hear if they would be going to another funeral this weekend.

"Tom, I'm telling you, the car was meant for me. It's the same car. I'm sure of it."

He frowns at the notes on his pad. "You don't know the color."

"I said it was dark. Navy, black. One of those."

"We don't have the make."

"It's a sedan. An old one. Huge, probably American."

"We don't know if the driver's male or female. You said there was no plate."

"What about the notes? And the calls?"

"I told you, I'll take the notes from you and I'll take your statement about the calls." Lombardo flips the notebook closed and slips it into his back pocket. "Look, Mary, we'll go to the scene, we'll investigate. Christ, the uniforms are already there. They'll talk to the witnesses."

"There weren't any. There were hardly any cars. Nobody stopped."

"So maybe there's a cab still workin'. We'll hear somethin' in a day or two from one of the cars. Meantime the uniforms will scrape some paint off the sawhorse—that might tell us somethin'. Don't look at me like that, Mary. AID's pretty good."

"AID?" The name sounds familiar, but I can't place it.

"Accident Investigation Division. They do all the workup at the scene."

I lean my head against the wall, fighting a wave of nausea. AID. Of course. They investigated Mike's accident. Witness surveys. Scene examination. Analysis of his bicycle shorts for car paint. Even a flyer sent to local auto body shops. Then came the final call, from the Fatal Coordinator Sergeant. Sorry, Mrs. Lassiter, there's nothing else we can do, he said. Oh, yeah? I thought to myself. How about changing your title?

"Where are the notes anyway?" Lombardo asks.

"Brent had them. I'm not sure where they are, probably in his desk."

"You wanna take me there?"

"No. I want to stay here and see what happens to Brent."

Lombardo sucks on his toothpick. "It's not your fault, you know."

I don't reply. My mouth tastes acrid and angry. Of course it's my fault; the driver was trying to kill me. And I didn't listen to Brent and file a report, because I was more concerned about my brilliant career. I feel sick and guilty, and most of all, in the dark and twisted pit of my stomach, I feel a powerful fear. I don't want to lose Brent like I lost Mike.

I close my eyes to the picture forming in my head, the one of the car slamming into Brent's body. It's like a nightmare, a waking nightmare, and one that I had on so many sleepless nights after Mike's death, as I pictured the car slamming into him on his bike. I close my eyes to the horrific visions, trying to squeeze them out. But they bring me to see something, something I hadn't seen before. I sit up in the plastic chair.

"You gotta go to the ladies?" Lombardo asks.

I'm amazed at what I'm thinking. I face Lombardo, but I can't say anything. What if? What if there's a connection between what happened to Mike and what happened to Brent?

"My husband was killed last year by a hit-and-run driver."

"Jesus, Mary, I'm sorry. Jeez, Mary, if I hadda known. Jeez." His beefy face flushes with embarrassment.

"What I'm saying is maybe it's connected to what happened to Brent. Brent was hit by a hit-and-run driver too."

Lombardo takes the toothpick out of his mouth.

I struggle to make my argument, to find the right words. My brain is tired, so tired, and I can't think fast enough. "Tom, couldn't it be the same driver? Let's say someone is very angry at me, hates me for some reason. They even kill my husband, hit him with a car. They write me hate notes, they call me, they stalk me. They break into my apartment, they break my husband's picture—"

"Yo, wait a minute—"

"Let me finish. Then, almost a year later, about the same time they killed my husband, they try to kill me. The same way, even. But they hit Brent by accident. Right before it happened we were dancing around on the curb."

"What did they rule your husband's death?"

"An accident. He was riding his bike by the river. It was an accident, that's what we all thought at the time."

"Why do you think it wasn't?"

"Because of what happened to Brent, Tom! The same thing!"

Lombardo blinks, dully. "He wasn't on a bike, was he?" He pops his toothpick back into his mouth and reaches for his notebook.

I grab his hand. "No, Brent wasn't on a bike. He was walking."

"You said it's the same thing. It's not the same thing."

"But it is. They were both hit by a car. A hit-and-run."

"It's not the same thing. One is on a bike and the other is walking."

"All right, it's not the exact same thing."

"You can say the exact same, you can say the same. It's not the same thing." Flustered, Lombardo smooths down his nylon windbreaker.

I feel like screaming. "But they're both hit—"

"There are other differences."

"What?"

"Different time of day. Different place. With the construction on Walnut, it was probably an accident."

"But it makes sense!"

Lombardo looks at me gravely, like I'm crazed from my recent widowhood. "Mary, you're upset. Let me take care of—"

"For Christ's sake, will you fucking *think!*"

"That's it! Stop talkin' like that!" He jabs the air between us with his toothpick. A nurse, walking by, looks back with concern.

Suddenly, the double doors to the operating room swing open and the surgeon, an older man, walks out. I stand up, and Lombardo surprises me by taking my arm. I search the doctor's eyes for a sign about Brent, but there is none. He tugs down his green half-mask and walks over to us, heaving a sigh.

The sigh, I recognize. The sigh, I know. It happened just this way the last time. Oh, no.

"I'm sorry. We did everything. The injuries were extensive. There were massive chest and skull fractures. The carotid artery was severed. There was just too much bleeding."

Oh, no. Just what they said with Mike. Chest injury. Skull fracture. Brain lacerations. The medical mumbo-jumbo that provides the background noise for the worst news of your life.

"We fought very hard. So did your husband," he says.

My husband. Not my husband. Oh, no.

"It wasn't her husband," says Lombardo. "It was her secretary. A male secretary."

"I'm sorry," the doctor says awkwardly. "Well, your secretary fought very hard. I'm very sorry."

I nod and feel Lombardo's solid grip on my arm. He leads me to the elevator, and we leave the hospital. Jack and his friends, smoking nervously at the hospital entrance, take one look at us and know Brent is dead. I go over to Jack, but he breaks down and his friends close around him. They sob openly, this pale group of too-thin gay men. The two security guards exchange glances, but there's no compassion there.

Lombardo leads me to his squad car and drives to my apartment. Neither of us says anything on the ride home. I leave Brent at the hospital, just like I left Mike at the hospital. My husband, not my husband. I hear the voice, faint and far away, from within:

I tried to warn you, but you wouldn't listen. I tried, it says, and then deserts me.

"Mary?"

It's Lombardo, opening the car door for me. He helps me out of the car and walks me up to my apartment. "You're gonna be okay, you'll see. Just get some rest."

"Would you look inside my apartment? Just to make sure?"

"Sure. Sure." I hand Lombardo the key and he walks in. He finds the light switch and I hear the floors of my apartment groan, unaccustomed to such a heavy tread. In a minute he's back at the door. "Everything's okay. There's nobody here."

"Thanks."

"I'll do some checkin' about your husband. When AID investigates, they make a report. Those guys are real thorough."

I nod. Lombardo gives my shoulder a squeeze and climbs down the stairs. Cautiously, I go into the apartment. Alice sits on the windowsill, her hidden body making a hump in the tangled blinds. I walk over to the window and peek through the blinds.

The car that killed Brent isn't on the street. I watch Lombardo's squad car pull away from the curb. When I turn around, the red light on the answering machine is flashing. I pound the PLAYBACK button with a clenched fist.

The first message is silence, then *click*.

Fuck you! Fuck you! I scream in my head.

The second message is Ned. "Are you out there gallivanting around? Call me. I'm Cooooool." There's the sound of mechanical laughter, then *click*.

It has to be him. It just has to.

He's trying to mind-fuck you, Brent says.

He's too cool, Judy says.

Nine times out of ten, it's an old boyfriend, says Officer Tarrant.

I check my watch. It's 4 A.M.

I'm going crazy.

I'm going to see Ned.

Watch your step, Mary.

SEVENTEEN

I run to Ned's house without stopping, driven by a force and a strength I can't control. I reach his door in no time and pound on it with my fist. *Boom-boom-boom*, right next to the brass house number, 2355. Its jagged edge rips the side of my hand. *Boom!* Blood runs out, but I don't feel it.

Open the fucking door, Cool.

Boom-boom-boom! My blood stains the number.

The door opens. It's him in sweatpants and a T-shirt that says ANDOVER. He rubs his eyes and smiles sleepily. "Mary, this is a pleasant surprise."

So cool.

I push him back into the house and slam into the middle of his big fat ANDOVER, bloodying it. "Where the fuck were you tonight, Cool?"

He looks astonished, his eyes wide. "Mary?"

I grit my teeth and shove him again. "Where were you tonight?" I advance on him, and he steps backward. "Answer the question, Cool! Why is it you never answer the fucking question?"

"Mary, what is—"

"Tell me!" I smack him across the face. My blood sears a

perfect cheekbone. His hand flies to his face, and he edges against the stairwell.

"I . . . was here!"

"Doing what?" I smack him again, so hard the blood from my hand spatters in a tiny fan across his T-shirt.

"Mary, stop it!"

"You killed Brent! And Mike!" I start to slap him again, but he catches my wrist in midair.

"Mary, no!" He wrenches my arms together.

"You did it! You!" I scream, kicking and clawing at his arms and legs. I can't believe what's happening, that I'm struggling in his arms, that I'm raging. He wrestles me to the floor, pinning me there, pressing my wrists back into the rug.

"Stop it now!" he cries out.

"You! You!" I hear myself, shouting over and over, then the huff of my own panting. I can't seem to catch my breath. I feel I'm coming out of a fit.

"Stop it, Mary!" he shouts.

"You!"

"No!"

"Cool!"

"Ned—my name is Ned! I'm not Cool, I don't know who that is. I don't know what you're talking about. I would never hurt you, you know that!"

"Let go of my wrists!"

"Not until you're calm."

I look up at him, on top of me, looking down. His face is barely visible in the half-light. Flecks of blood mingle with his freckles; the two are hard to distinguish. I can make out his eyes, his green eyes, oddly bright and feral. His eyes are full of pain. He's not the killer, he can't be. He's hurting for me, I see it there, in his animal eyes. "Brent's dead," I whisper.

"Your secretary?"

"A car hit him. It wasn't an accident."

"My God. And you think I did it?" He shakes his head in

disbelief. "Never, Mary. Never." Still straddling me, he releases my wrists.

I don't move, I can't. I feel utterly drained, shaken to the core. I want to surrender myself to the force out there that wants to hurt me, wants to punish me for what I've done. It should have been me it claimed. Not Brent, and not Mike. "It's because of me."

"No, Mary." He leans down, supporting himself on his arms, and kisses me softly.

Without thinking about it, merely responding, as a child to the breast, I kiss him back. He kisses me again, so carefully, trying to reach me. He strokes my hair as we kiss, and eases himself on top of me. I feel like I want to lose myself in him, to heal somehow this great gaping hole that's been rent in my heart by losing Mike and now Brent. I want him to love me, to fill me up inside. I don't want to be alone anymore. I want the pain to stop.

All I can feel are his kisses, deep and sweet. And his hands, stroking my hair, then cradling me, so gently. His touch feels wonderful, my skin is hungry for it. I haven't been touched like this in so long, and it feels so good that I go toward it. I feel my body surge to him as he lifts me easily to the couch and strips down my pantyhose and panties. He pulls up my skirt, and I can feel the cool leather of the couch under me and the weight of his hips parting my legs. He keeps kissing me, as I feel him, probing me slowly and purposefully with his fingers.

It's what I want, and what terrifies me, too.

He enters me gently and I gasp, taking him in all at once. I can't say anything, though I hear his whispered words in my ear, because he's moving inside me. I can hardly catch my breath. All I can do is grab his back and hold on. And I do, clinging to him there. Suspended somewhere between heaven and hell.

EIGHTEEN

I wake up with my cheek on Ned's chest and his arms linked loosely around me. His freckled skin feels cool, and his chest, almost hairless, looks smooth and perfect. I move slowly, not wanting to wake him, and let my eyes wander over the four walls of his bedroom, which are almost as familiar by now as my own. The walls are covered with a seemingly endless series of sailing photographs, taken at locales I've heard about but never seen. Wellfleet. Bar Harbor. Newport.

I turn over as carefully, and rest my head on the meaty part of Ned's forearm. It brings me eye level with the desk of a very hard-working lawyer. Legal pads are neatly piled there, as are photocopied cases, highlighted with pink and yellow marker. A coffee can holds a bunch of sharpened pencils. There's a file box of index cards, with homemade dividers starting with AP-PEALABILITY and going straight through to ZENITH CASE (EV-IDENTIARY ISSUES). Next to the card file is a photo of a boat that Ned sails on weekends on the Schuylkill.

I pull the sheet up to my shoulders and hug it to my breast. I figure it's midmorning, judging from the bright sun in the window. It must be Sunday. I know it's not Saturday, because I spent much of Saturday in tears, telling Ned all about Brent.

He listened patiently and kindly. He kept me in aspirin and water and even went to my apartment to fetch some clean clothes. I called Jack on Saturday too, but he was too miserable to talk. He gave the phone to a friend, who told me there would be a memorial service for Brent on Sunday night.

Saturday evening Ned and I ate Raisin Bran for dinner and went back to bed. We slept like spoons until the middle of the night, when I felt him stirring. I remember him fumbling gently behind me. I reached for him, but he felt cold and slick.

"It's a condom," he whispered. "I'm crazy about you, but I'm not crazy."

Then I turned over to face him, half asleep and half awake. We made love again, slowly and quietly in the still darkness, and I felt as far away from everything as I've ever felt. It was time-out-of-time for us both, I think. Just the two of us, moving there together. Moving into each other.

We slept until dawn, when Ned disappeared downstairs into the kitchen to get us breakfast. He returned with a *Hammond's World Atlas* heaped with American cheese, white bread, and a plastic bottle of seltzer water. We talked while we ate. Then I called my mother and told her the news about Brent. She insisted on coming to the memorial service, to pay her respects to Brent's family. I didn't tell her Brent had been estranged from his family since the day he told them he was gay. Nor did I tell her I'd been standing next to Brent when he was killed.

My eyes fall on Ned's answering machine. There are no messages showing, which means Judy didn't call back while we were asleep. I called her from the hospital as soon as it happened, but she wasn't home. It seemed odd, because I remember her telling me that Kurt would be in New York for the weekend and she'd be free. I even tried reaching her up there, with no luck. I left a bunch of messages on her machine at home and also on the voice mail at work. I asked her to call me at Ned's but didn't say why.

It feels wrong that Judy doesn't know yet. I get out of bed to call her from the downstairs phone, so I don't wake Ned. I look back at him; he's sound asleep. I ease my bare feet onto a cotton dhurrie rug and tiptoe out of the room. I stop in the bathroom first. The room is immaculate; the man is either compulsively neat or has a lot of penance to do. The sink sparkles, and there's no toothpaste glommed onto its sides like in my sink. In fact, there's nothing sitting on the rim of the sink at all—no razor, aftershave, or toothpaste. Where does he keep it all? I look up at the medicine cabinet. Its mirror reflects a very nosy woman.

No. It's none of my business.

I rinse off my face with some warm water, but there's no soap in sight. I check the shower stall, but there's none there either. Where is the fucking soap? I decide not to make a Fourth Amendment issue of it and open the medicine cabinet.

What I find inside startles me.

Pills. Lots of pills. In brown plastic bottles and clear ones, too. I recognize none of their names. Imipramine. Nortriptyline. Nardil. I pick up one of the bottles as quietly as possible and read its label quickly.

NED WATERS—ONE TABLET AT BEDTIME— HALCION

Halcion. It sounds familiar. I remember something about George Bush being on it for jet lag. I replace the bottle and pick up another.

NED WATERS—ONE CAPSULE EVERY MORNING—PROZAC

Prozac, I've heard of. An antidepressant. A controversial antidepressant. Isn't Prozac the one that makes people do crazy things? As I replace the bottle, the capsules inside it rattle slightly. What is all this stuff? Why is Ned taking Prozac?

"Mary? Where are you?" Ned calls out, from inside the bedroom.

I close the medicine chest hastily and grab an oxford shirt from the doorknob. I slip it on and pad into the bedroom.

"There you are," he says with a lazy grin. He turns over and extends a hand to me. I walk over, and he pulls me to a sitting position on the bed. I study his face. His eyes are a little puffy from sleep, but he looks like himself. Is he on Prozac now? Is it time for his next dose?

"Do I look that bad?" He sits up and smooths his ruffled hair with a flat hand.

"No. You look fine."

He flops back down, making a snow angel in the white sheets. "Good. I feel fine. I feel better than fine. I feel happy!" He grabs my hand and kisses the inside of it. "All because of you."

Yesterday I would have been touched by the sentiment, but now I question it. Why this sudden exuberance? Is it a side effect of the Prozac, or the reason he's on it in the first place? What are those other pills he's taking?

"Hey, you're supposed to say something nice back to me." He pouts in an exaggerated way.

"Why is it that when handsome men make faces they still look handsome?"

"I don't know, you'll have to ask a handsome man. But not dressed like that. Now gimme back my shirt." He pulls me to him and flips me over with ease. In a flash I've tumbled to the messy comforter, and he's above me.

"Hey! How'd you do that?"

"I wrestled in school." He kisses me suddenly, with feeling. I find myself responding, though with less ardor than before. I can't stop thinking about what's in the medicine chest. Maybe I don't know him as well as I thought. I pull away.

"I have to call Judy."

"She hasn't called?" he asks with a frown.

"No."

He sits back on his haunches and pulls me up easily by my hand. "If you don't reach her, we can go down to her house and look around. Doesn't she live in town?"

"Yes. Olde City."

"That's easy enough. My car's downstairs."

"You park on the street?"

"No, this house has a garage."

"Let me try her again."

Ned rubs his eyes and stretches. "I'm awake. You hungry, sweetheart? You want anything?"

"Maybe. After I call her."

He touches my cheek, gently. "How are you doing?"

"I feel better today. More normal."

"Good. It's gonna be tough telling Judy, isn't it? You three were pretty close."

I nod.

"I'll go take a shower and give you some privacy, okay?"

"Thanks."

"You want to come with me? Think of all the water we'd save." He leans over and gives me a kiss. I can feel the urgency behind it, his need for more, but I keep thinking of the row of bottles. I feel myself tense up. Ned feels it too. "Is something the matter?"

I don't know what to say. I want to be straight with him, but I shouldn't have gone into the medicine cabinet. None of it is my business, even the fact that he's taking medication. "Uh, it's nothing."

"It doesn't look like nothing. It doesn't feel like nothing." He releases me and looks me in the eye. "You having regrets?"

"No."

"What then?"

"It's none of my business."

"You're sleeping with me. If it's about me, it's your business." He cocks his head slightly.

"Well, then." I clear my throat.

"That bad, huh?"

It's hard to face him. His eyes are so bright, and they smile when he does, showing the barest trace of crow's feet. I love crow's feet. On other people. "Okay, here's my confession. I wanted to wash my face, and I couldn't find the soap. So I went in the medicine chest. I'm sorry, but I couldn't help seeing."

His face is a blank. "Seeing what?"

I look at him; he seems so earnest. I don't want to hurt him. He's been nothing but good to me.

"My Clearasil?"

"No. The bottles. The pills."

"Ohhhhh," he says, with a slow sigh, deflating on the spot.

"It doesn't matter to me. It's not that I hold it against you or anything. It's just that . . ."

His green eyes flicker with hurt. "Just that what?"

"I was surprised, I guess. You seem so fine to me, Ned, you really do. But then I open up the medicine chest and there's a Rite-Aid in there. What do you need those pills for? You're fine. Aren't you?"

"What if I wasn't? Then you leave?"

A fair question. I'm not sure I know the answer.

"Forget it, Mary. You want to understand, right?"

"Right."

"Well, once I did need those meds. All of them. But I don't need them anymore. I'm better now. Over it. If you look at the bottles, the dates are years old."

"Okay." I feel relieved. What I've been seeing are his real emotions, not some drug-induced elation.

He draws the comforter around his waist. "You want to hear the whole story?"

"Yes."

"I don't know where to begin. Wait a minute." He screws up his face in thought. "Once upon a time, I was very depressed. I didn't even know it, in the beginning. I'd been depressed for so long, I thought it was my personality. I was never really able to stay close to anyone, especially a woman. That's why I was so reserved on our first date. I was too busy figuring out how to act."

"You *were* kind of quiet."

"Nicely put," he says, with a weak smile. "I spent most of my adult life being kind of quiet. All it got me was alone—and gossiped about. Then I hit bottom, a couple of years ago, at work. Nothing interested me. I had no energy for anything, even sailing. I could hardly get out of bed to start the day. I started missing work. I don't know if you noticed." He glances at me.

"Not really."

"No one did, except my secretary. She thought I was a tomcat." He laughs, ironically. "I was a mess. I just lost it. Lost my way. A nervous breakdown, my mother called it, but that's a dumb term. Technically, I had a major depressive episode, according to the DSM. That's closer to it."

"DSM?"

"Diagnostic something-or-other Manual. You want to read all about me? I used to know my page number, but I forget now." He gets up as if to leave the room, but I grab his hand.

"Forget the book. Tell me the story."

He settles back down. "Where was I? Oh, yes. God, I feel like I'm on Sally Jessy."

"Sally Jessy?"

"Morning TV. A big hit with depressed people." He smiles. "Anyway, to make a long story short, it was my mother who got me help. Drove into town, pulled me out of bed, and stuck me in the car. She did the job. She got me to a shrink, Dr. Kate. Little Dr. Kate. You'd like her." He laughs softly and seems to warm up.

"Yeah?"

"She's great. Pretty. Tough. Like you." Suddenly his eyes

look strained. "I would have killed myself if it hadn't been for her, I know it. I thought about it enough. All the time, in fact." He looks at me, seeming to check my reaction.

I hope my face doesn't show the shock I feel.

"The first session, I sat there on this IKEA couch she has, and the first thing out of her mouth is, 'No wonder you're depressed, you smell like shit.'" He laughs.

"That's not very nice."

"I didn't need very nice. I needed a kick in the pants. I needed to understand myself and my family. I went into therapy with her. Every day. Sometimes twice a day, at lunch and after work. She started me on meds, which ones I don't remember, but they didn't help. We tried a few others until we got to Prozac—it was new at the time. It worked well—and Halcion, to help me sleep. I could never sleep. Christ, I was a mess." A strand of silky hair falls over his face, and he brushes it away quickly.

"It sounds hard."

"It was. But it was a while ago, and I lived through it. I've thought about throwing the meds away, but they remind me of where I was. Of how far I've come. Kate says I'm supposed to be proud of that. Make an affirmation, every morning." He rolls his eyes. "Can you see it? Me, facing a mirror, saying to myself, 'I'm proud of you, Ned. I'm proud of you, Ned.'" He bursts into laughter. "I don't think so."

"I'm proud of you, Ned."

He laughs. "I'm proud of you, Mary."

"No, I mean it. I *am* proud of you."

"Yeah?"

"Yeah."

"So you're not going to pack?"

I shake my head. It's hard to speak. I feel so much for him.

His green eyes narrow like a cat's in the sun. "Even though I'm not as cool as you thought?"

"You're cooler than I thought."

"Oh, therapy is cool, huh?"

"Yeah. It's the nineties. Decade of the Democrats."

"Right." He laughs. "Then you won't mind that I still see Kate."

"You do?"

"Three times a week, at lunchtime. Her office is like home now, only better. I always hated my house. My father's house, I should say."

"What's the story with your father? You were going to tell me."

"He's a tyrant. He thinks he's God. He ran our house like he runs Masterson. Produce or you're out of here!" Ned's tone turns suddenly angry. Beneath the anger I can hear the hurt.

"Is that why you haven't talked to him in so long?"

"I haven't talked to him since the day I had to keep him from strangling my mother. For changing a seating arrangement without his permission."

"My God."

"Nice guy, huh?"

"Did that happen a lot? That he'd be violent, I mean."

"I was away at school, so I didn't see it. I knew it was happening, though." He leans back on his hands. "Denial is a funny thing. You're in this place where you know but you don't know. You're keeping secrets from yourself. I think that's what my trust fund's for. He screwed me up, but at least he gave me the means to figure out how." He laughs, but it sounds empty this time.

"Why do you think your father wanted to meet me?"

"I bet he knows we went out the other night. I think he keeps tabs on me."

I sit up straight, slowly. I remember the look on his father's face when he stormed into the glass-walled conference room, his fury barely held in check. It's not hard to believe that he'd be violent with his wife. Or even that he could kill. "You mean he follows you? Or has you followed?"

Ned looks stricken as he makes the connection. "What are you saying? You think he killed Brent? You think he's trying to kill *you*?"

"Do you?"

"Why would he?"

"So that you can make partner at Stalling. To assure your position."

"No. No, I can't imagine that. It's inconceivable. Uh-uh." He shakes his head.

"But you said he keeps tabs on you."

"Not that way. I think he hears things, finds out the gossip. I don't think he follows me around. No way."

"Are you sure, Ned? If you're not, we should give his name to the police."

"Mary, he's my father, for Christ's sake. Let me talk to him first."

"You want to? After fifteen years?"

"Yes. Just give me a couple of days and I'll talk to him. If I have any suspicions at all, we'll call the cops. I'm not going to take any chances with your safety, you know that."

The telephone rings suddenly. Ned reaches past me to the night table and picks it up. "Hello? Sure, Judy. She's right here." He covers the receiver with his hand. "I'll take that shower."

I nod, and he hands me the phone. As he gets up, the comforter falls away. He walks to the closet without a second thought to his nakedness. A man thing.

Judy starts talking before I even have the phone to my ear. "Mary, what's the matter? What are you doing at Ned's?"

"I've been trying to reach you since Friday night. Where were you?"

Ned takes his bathrobe from a hook on his closet door and leaves the bedroom.

"It's a long story," she says. "My brother was going to Princeton, and I had to . . . forget it. What's going on with you? What are you doing at Ned's, of all places? I just got your messages."

"It's bad news, Judy. Very bad." I swallow hard.

"What?"

"Is Kurt around? Are you alone?" From the bathroom, I hear the metallic scrape of the shower curtain on its rod and the sound of water turned on.

"He's in New York, but he should be home any minute. Why are you at Ned's—in the *morning?*"

"I'll explain later. Judy, listen."

I take a deep breath. I have to tell her about Brent. It reminds me of when I had to tell her about Mike. My parents had called her from the hospital, but she wasn't home. I reached her later with the news. It was awful. I could barely speak; she could barely speak. She practically moved into my apartment. Judy, more than anyone, got me through the funeral.

"Mary? What's going on?"

I tell her the whole story, and that I think it was the same car that's been following me. All she says, over and over, is, "Oh, my God. Oh, my God." Her voice sounds faint and tinny on the other end of the line.

"Do you think he suffered?" she asks finally.

I remember Brent's face and the agonized expression on it when the car plowed into him. There's no reason to tell Judy that. "I don't know."

"Poor Brent. Poor, poor Brent. Oh, my God."

The water shuts off in the shower. I hear Ned banging around in the bathroom.

"What are you doing at Ned's?"

"I came here. I thought he did it."

"So why are you still there? Brent is killed and you're at Ned's?"

"It's not him, Judy."

"I can't believe you. What are you doing?"

I hear Ned scrubbing his teeth, humming to himself tunelessly.

"He's been wonderful to me, Judy. He—"

"You're fucking Ned Waters? Mary, is that what you're doing?" She sounds angry.

"It's not like—"

"You're in danger, Mary! We don't know anything about him. He has every reason to try and hurt you."

Ned switches off the water in the bathroom, and I hear him walking toward the bedroom. His off-key hum has segued into an off-key march. *H.M.S. Pinafore*, as sung by a coyote.

"He'd never do that, Judy."

"But Mary!"

Ned appears in the doorway to the bedroom, bundled up in a thick terry robe. His wet hair is spiky and uncombed; his beard is slightly stubbly. He balls up a damp towel and shoots it at a wicker hamper across the room. It goes in, barely, and he grins at me.

"Don't worry, Jude. I'm fine."

"Is he right there? You can't talk, can you."

"Not exactly."

"I think you should get out of there."

"I'm fine, Jude. You can call here if you need to. Whenever you need to."

Ned sits down on the bed behind me. I feel his hands on my back, still warm from the shower.

"But what if it's him?" Judy says.

"I'm fine. I really am."

Ned massages my shoulders, pressing into them from behind. His touch is firm, insistent. I can feel the tightness in my muscles begin to disappear.

"You're making a big mistake, Mary."

"Believe me, I'm okay."

He applies more pressure, and his fingers knead the top of my shoulders. I move my neck from side to side, and it loosens up.

"We'll talk tonight. Look for me before the service."

"Good. Take care." I hang up. I wish she wouldn't worry about me with Ned. My shoulders are warm and tingly underneath his hands.

"How does that feel?" Ned asks softly.

"Terrific."

"So Judy's worried about you."

"Uh-huh."

"She thinks I'm the bad guy."

"Honestly, yes."

"I thought so."

"I'll talk to her."

"Therapy 101. You can't control what people think."

"Lawyering 101. Yes, you can."

He laughs. "Close your eyes, sweetheart."

I close my eyes and concentrate on the gentle kneading motion of his fingers on my shoulders.

"Let your head relax. Let it fall forward."

So I do, like a rag doll, as his hands work their way to my neck. He takes it slow, inch by inch. It reminds me of the way he made love to me, in the darkness. He didn't rush anything. He felt it, that's why.

"Everything's gonna be all right, Mary," he says quietly.

I almost believe him.

NINETEEN

That evening, I'm sitting between my parents and Ned at Brent's memorial service. It's at the Philadelphia Art Alliance, an elegant old building on Rittenhouse Square, not six blocks from where Brent was killed. Some of Brent's friends put flowers on the sidewalk in front of the bank today, and his death was all over the news. They called it a "hit-and-run accident," which to me is a contradiction in terms. But it doesn't matter what the TV says. The only thing that matters is what the police say. I wonder if Lombardo will be here tonight.

I look around at the crowd, which appears to be growing larger by the minute, but I don't see Lombardo. The service is full of friends from the nonintersecting circles of Brent's life. There are his gay friends, the biggest group by far, as well as his fellow voice students, and a contingent from Stalling. Judy's here with Kurt, and so are most of the secretaries from the office, sitting together in a teary clump that includes Delia, Annie Zirilli, and Stella. Even Stalling's personnel manager is here, the one who gave Brent such a hard time about the tray. She eyes the gay men with contempt. Her expression says, I knew it.

Watching her, I remember what Brent said just last week.

When I die, I want my ashes ground into the carpet at Stalling & Webb. He wasn't kidding.

I look down at the program with his picture on the front. A smiling face in a black shirt, surrounded by a skinny black border. This should not be. He's not supposed to die; he's too young to be inside a skinny black border. He would have said, What's wrong with this picture?

My mother touches my hand, and I give hers a perfunctory squeeze. I don't want to feel anything tonight. I want to be numb.

The eulogies begin, and Brent's voice coach is the first to speak. She's a bosomy brunette, middle-aged and wearing lipstick that's theatrically red. Brent once described her to me as robust; actually he said robusty. But she doesn't look robust tonight: She looks broken. Her speaking voice, which has a remarkable timbre, sounds so grief-stricken I can't bear to listen. I look around the room and spot Lombardo, sitting alone on one of the folding chairs against the wall. His hair is slicked down with water and he wears an ill-fitting black raincoat. He looks like an overgrown altar boy, not somebody smart enough to catch Brent's killer. And maybe Mike's.

"He had a fine voice, mind you," the singing coach is saying. Her head is held high, her posture almost a dancer's. "But Brent was never ambitious in music. He never entered any of the competitions I told him to, even when I got him the forms. He refused to do it. 'I won't go on *Star Search*, Margaret,' he said to me. '*Dance Fever*, maybe. But *Star Search*, never.'"

There's laughter at this, and quiet sniffles.

"Brent studied because he loved music with all his heart. He sang because he loved to sing. It was an end in itself for him. I used to try to instill that in all my students, but I stopped after I met Brent. That was the lesson Brent taught me. You can't teach joy." She faces the audience in a dignified way, then steps away from the podium.

There is utter silence.

I try not to think about what she said.

Two young men appear on the dais. One is almost emaciated, obviously very sick, and is being physically supported by the other. Both wear red ribbons, which on them means more than it does on all the Shannen Dohertys put together.

I know I cannot hear this.

I screen it all out.

I go somewhere else in my mind.

I think about what Judy said before the service started. How she apologized for being sharp with me on the phone. How she really doesn't trust Ned. Nothing I said could change her mind. It was the closest we've come to a fight, and at the end she backed off. Her nerves were frayed, she said. I look over at her, weeping quietly, with Kurt at her side. She loved Brent too. That's why she's acting so crazy.

The eulogies are almost over, and someone's introducing the final speaker.

Mr. Samuel Berkowitz.

I look up in amazement.

Sure enough, it *is* Berkowitz, lumbering up to the flower-filled podium in a dark suit. He adjusts a microphone barely camouflaged by Easter lilies and clears his throat. "I didn't know Brent Polk very well, but as I listen to you all here today, I wish I had. What I do know about Brent is that he was an intelligent young man, a fine secretary, and a good and loyal friend to many people. Also, that he broke every rule my stuffy old law firm holds dear."

There's laughter at this, and renewed sniffles. I smile myself, and feel so proud of Berkowitz for being here. He has more class than any of them put together. I squeeze Ned's hand, but he's not smiling. Neither are my parents; they look somber and upset. They must be thinking of Mike. They hardly knew Brent.

"In addition, I would like to announce a donation in Brent's name, which has been authorized by my partners at Stalling and Webb. Tomorrow we give ten thousand dollars on Brent Polk's behalf to Pennsylvanians Against Drunk Driving. It is our sincere hope that we can help prevent what happened to Brent from happening to other fine young men and women. Thank you." Applause breaks out as Berkowitz steps down and disappears into the crowd.

"What are they talking about?" I whisper to Ned, over the din.

"I don't know." He looks grim.

"Drunk driver, my ass!"

My mother nudges me. Don't talk in church, says the nudge.

I wheel around and look at Lombardo. His dull eyes warn me to relax. Drunk driver? I mouth to him.

He puts a finger to his lips.

Christ! I can barely contain myself. Brent is murdered in cold blood, and they're going to say it was drunk driving? It's all I can do after the service not to pound directly over to him, but I have to take care of my parents first. Ned and I help them down the steps of the Art Alliance and wait with them for a cab. My mother's eyes are smudged and teary behind her glasses; my father looks crestfallen.

"I don't like that man from your office, Maria," she says. "The big one. You know which one I mean? The big one?"

"Yes, Ma."

"No. I don't like that man at all." She shakes her head, and her heavy glasses slip down.

"Why not, Mrs. DiNunzio?" Ned asks, with a faint smile.

She holds up a finger, mysteriously. "Thin lips. You can't even find the man's lips. Like pencil lines, they are."

"Ma. His lips aren't thin. It's just your eyes."

"Don't be fresh, I saw them. He's got the thin lips. Mark my words."

Ned seems amused by this. "He's the boss, Mrs. DiNunzio."

She drills her index finger into the hand-stitched lapel of Ned's coat. "I don't care who he is. I don't like him."

"Don't give the kids no trouble, Vita," says my father. "They got enough trouble right now. A world of trouble."

"I'm not giving them trouble, Matty. I'm taking care of Maria!" People leaving the service look over, startled at the loudness of her voice. "That's what mothers are for! That's a mother's job, Matty."

A yellow cab stops at the light, and I wave it down.

"Look at Maria, Veet," says my father, momentarily cheered. "Just like a big city girl." My mother looks at me proudly. I've hailed a cab, *mirabile dictu.*

"Please, guys. Don't embarrass me in front of Ned, okay? I'm trying to make a good impression."

My father smiles, and my mother gives me a shove. "You. Always with the jokes."

The cab pulls up and Ned opens the door for them. I lean down and give them both a quick kiss. Ned helps my father into the dark cab, but my mother is tougher to shake. She grabs me by my coat and whispers, "Call me. I want to talk to you about this young man."

"Okay, I'll call you."

She whispers loudly into my ear. "It's good to see you with someone. You're too young to put yourself up on the shelf."

"Ma . . ."

She looks at Ned sternly. "You take good care of my daughter. Or you answer to me!"

"I will," he says, surprised.

"Time to go, Ma." I fight the urge to push her into the cab.

"We love you, doll," says my father, as my mother gets in.

"Love you too," I say, closing the heavy door with relief. I feel like I've tucked them into bed. I wave, and the cab pulls away.

Ned gives me a hug. "They're wonderful," he says happily.

"The Flying DiNunzios. They're something, aren't they?"

"You're lucky, you know."

"I know, but let's not get into it now. Help me find Lombardo." I squint at the crowd coming out of the building's narrow front doors.

"I don't know what he looks like."

"Fred Flintstone."

Judy comes out with Kurt, who has managed to find a suit jacket for the occasion. She waves good-bye over the sea of people. I wave back.

Ned points over at the far edge of the crowd. "Is that him?"

"Yes!" Sure enough, it's Lombardo. I flag him down and he finally spots me. Even from a distance, his expression tells me he wishes he hadn't.

"Don't get upset, Mary."

"I'm already upset. I feel like I want to break his face." I plunge into the crowd of people, with Ned beside me. Lombardo threads his way toward us, and we meet in the middle.

"Drunk driver, Lombardo?" I say to him. "You have to be kidding!"

Lombardo looks around nervously. "Mary, settle down."

"That's almost as absurd as gay-basher!"

Lombardo takes me aside, and Ned follows. "Look, Mary, it's just a preliminary finding, we haven't stopped the investigation. You said the car was driving crazy when it left the sidewalk. It crashed into the sawhorse. We know it was driving crazy to go up on the—"

"Bullshit!"

"Mary, don't play cop. I'm the cop."

One of the gay men in the crowd glances back. On his short leather jacket is a pink button that says ACT UP; they tangled with the police at a demonstration last year. There's no love lost between the two groups. Lombardo says, "Let's take it out of here."

We regroup at the entrance to the Barclay Hotel, next to the Art Alliance. The canvas awning snaps in the swirling winds around Rittenhouse Square. "Aren't you gonna introduce me to your friend?" Lombardo asks.

"I'm Ned Waters, Detective Lombardo." Ned extends a hand, but Lombardo hesitates before he shakes it. He's remembering that Ned's is one of the names I gave him in the hospital as a suspect.

"He's okay, Tom," I say.

Lombardo looks from me to Ned. Whatever he's thinking, he decides not to say it. "Mary, I followed up on what you told me about your husband. I looked up the AID file on his accident. I even talked to one of the men who investigated. Your husband was hit on the West River Drive, going out of town, at that first curve."

"I know that."

"It's almost a blind curve, Mary. I went out and checked it myself. I found out your husband's not the only bicycle rider to be killed at the same spot. There was an architect, three months ago."

"I read about him. He was only twenty-six."

"Your husband and the architect were killed at about the same time—Sunday morning, bright and early. Probably by someone who'd been out partyin' the night before and was drivin' home to the subs."

"But—"

"Wait a minute." Lombardo pulls out his notebook and flips through it in the light coming from the hotel. "Wait. Here we go. A doctor was killed there too. An internist, who lived in Mount Airy. The guy was fifty-eight. Two years ago, the same curve. Now Brent was hit at a whole 'nother time and place. So I—"

"Isn't that a distinction without a difference?" Ned asks.

Lombardo looks up from his little book. "What?"

"Does it really make a difference that one is in the morning and one is at night? Just because they happen at different times and places doesn't mean it can't be the same person."

"Listen, Mr. Waters, I've been a detective a little longer than you."

"I understand that."

"My gut tells me it ain't the same guy." He turns to me. "I ran down your lead, Mary. I treated it serious, because I admit it looks strange, the two incidents bein' so close together like that. But I gotta go on what makes the most sense, and it's not homicide. I see two accidents, both involving booze. It's too bad that one of them was your husband and the other was your secretary, but it's just one of those coincidences. At least that's what I think so far."

"But, Tom, the license plate."

"Half the cars in this city got no plate. The crackheads take 'em off to sell; the thieves take 'em off for the registration stickers. Look, the way I see it, the guy who killed Brent jumped the curb, trying to avoid the construction. AID told me they had two fender-benders on Walnut Street the same day, all on account of the construction."

"Then why did he drive away?"

"Happens a lot, Mary. More than you think. Somebody's drinkin' a little too much, especially on a Friday night, and before they know it—*boom*—they're up on the sidewalk. They're juiced, they panic. We usually catch up with 'em in a couple of months. Some of 'em even come clean from a guilty conscience. That's what happened with the architect." He pauses and returns the notebook to his back pocket. "AID don't have that many open fatals, you know. The doctor, a kid in a crosswalk in the Northeast, and your husband. He's one of three."

I feel numb again. Mike's a fatal. An open fatal.

"What about the calls?" Ned asks testily.

"You get any more over the weekend, Mary?"

"I don't know. I haven't been home yet."

"And what about the notes?" Ned says.

Lombardo glares at him. "I'll come by and get 'em from Mary. I'll look 'em over and send 'em to the Document Unit, but I don't think they have anything to do with Brent. They don't sound like the kinda notes you see with a killer."

"What do you mean?"

"The notes don't say 'I'm gonna kill you,' 'I'm gonna mess you up,' 'You ain't gonna live another day,' like that. That's the kind of notes you get from a freak who kills. A freak with *cipollines*. You know what that means, buddy?"

"Educate me, Detective Lombardo."

I know what it means, little onions. But the connotation is—

"Balls!"

"Tom, Ned, please."

Lombardo hunches to replace his raincoat. "I want to see the notes, Mary, but I gotta tell you, I think they're from some weak sister who's got a thing for you. Could be someone you used to know, could be someone you know now. It could even be somebody you don't know at all, like a guy in the mailroom at work. Some jerk with a crush. That's the pattern, especially with ladies like yourself, career girls. Their name's in the paper, they're on this committee, that committee. You on committees like that?"

"Some."

"This kind of guy isn't a fighter, he's a lover. He's at home, swoonin' over your picture, tryin' to get up the nerve to talk to you. So don't worry. Call me tomorrow and we'll set up a time." Lombardo's attention is suddenly diverted by Delia, who appears out of the darkness, followed by Berkowitz.

"Thomas!" Berkowitz says heartily, grabbing Lombardo's hand and pumping it. "Thanks for all you've done."

"It's nothin', Sam." Lombardo can't tear his eyes off of Delia.

"Mary," Berkowitz says, "I'm sorry about your secretary."

"Thank you."

"Why don't you take a couple days off? I'll cover your desk."

Delia purses her glossy pink lips.

I'm surprised by the offer. Covering someone's desk is strictly associate work. "Uh, thanks. I'll see."

"You let me know if you need me, Mary. It's your call."

"Sure."

Berkowitz turns to go. "Thomas, thanks again."

"No problem."

Berkowitz strides off, his heavy trenchcoat flapping, and pauses to light a cigarette in a cupped hand. The flame from the lighter illuminates the contours of his face and Delia's.

Lombardo jerks his head in Berkowitz's direction. "He's an all right guy, for a big shot. He thinks the notes are nothin' too, Mary."

"You told him?"

"Sure, we talked a coupla times over the weekend. He was very interested in the investigation."

"Let's go, Mary." Ned squeezes my arm.

I feel tired, suddenly. I'm getting nowhere with Lombardo, I can see that. I know I'm right; I can just feel it. It all makes sense, but there's nothing I can do about it tonight. Wearily, I give in. "Okay."

"Call me, Mary," Lombardo says.

I nod, and Ned steers me home. Neither of us says anything on the short walk to my apartment. I don't know what's on his mind, but my thoughts are muffled by a thick blanket of fatigue and sorrow. As we get closer to my building, I feel a distance between Ned and me. I want to be alone with my memories of Brent, and of Mike. I'm in mourning, and it's déjà vu all over again. We reach the door to my building, near where Ned kissed me for the first time. A lot has happened since that first kiss. Brent was alive then.

"You want to pick up some clothes, Mary?"

"Actually, I think I should get some sleep tonight."

"You mean you want to stay here? By yourself?" He frowns, causing his freckles to converge at the bridge of his nose.

I nod.

"I'm worried, honey. I don't know what's going on, and I have no confidence in that detective. I don't think you're safe."

"Maybe I can call Judy or something."

"You don't want me to stay?" He looks confused.

"Ned, it's not that it wasn't wonderful . . ."

His green eyes harden. "Oh, is that it? Was it wonderful for you? Because it was wonderful for me too."

"That's not what I meant."

"I got to you this weekend, Mary. I know I did. So don't pull away from me, not now."

"I'm not, but we're only a part of what happened this weekend. I keep thinking about Brent."

"Okay," he says quickly. "Okay. I'm sorry."

"I just want to be alone for a while."

"But call me, will you? Call me if you need anything, no matter how late it is. Call me."

"Okay."

"Lock the door."

"Okay."

"Eat your vegetables. And wear your muffler."

"Thanks." I give him a quick kiss and let myself into the front door of my building. I wave to him through the leaded glass in the outer door, and I think he waves back, but I can't see him clearly. The bumpy glass transforms his silhouette into a wavy shadow.

I gather the mail and check each letter as I stack it up. I never thought I would be relieved to see a pile of junk mail addressed to Dee Nunzone, but I am. I climb up to my floor, regretting that I didn't ask Ned to check the apartment. I reach the door, which still says LASSITER-DiNUNZIO, and peek vainly through the peephole. I take a deep breath and unlock the door slowly. I open it a bit, then wider. The apartment is dark. I snap on the light with a finger and stick my head in the door. It looks just the way I left it. And it's silent. No ringing telephone. No other sound. I walk slowly inside, then shut and lock the door behind me.

"Alice?" The window blinds rustle slightly. She's on the windowsill. I walk nervously into the kitchen, refill Alice's bowl, and take Mike's samurai knife from the rack. I head into the bedroom, brandishing the knife. I figure I must look scary; I'm scaring myself. The bedroom looks absolutely normal. I take a deep breath and look under the bed. Dustballs as big as sagebrush, mounds of pink Kleenex, and a tortoiseshell barrette I'd been looking for. I grab the barrette and put it on my bed.

I leave the bedroom and walk into the bathroom. The makeup shelf, which I leave in a secret configuration now—moisturizer, foundation, eye pencil, lipstick—is still in its secret configuration. And the smell of the ripe cat box confirms that at least one other thing remains undisturbed.

I relax slightly and return to the living room.

"Alice?"

The window blinds move in reply, but Alice doesn't leave her post.

"He's not coming back, Alice," I say. I'm not sure whether I mean Mike or Brent, but Alice doesn't ask for a clarification.

I fall into a chair with my killer knife and close my eyes.

TWENTY

The next sound I hear is the ear-splitting buzz of my downstairs doorbell. I glance at my watch. It's 10:00. I must have
fallen asleep. Groggy, I get up and press the intercom button,
still holding the chef's knife. "Who is it?"

"Little pig, little pig, let me come in," shouts a strong voice.
Judy's.

"Hold on." I buzz her in and she arrives in seconds, having
taken the stairs two by two, like she always does. She bangs
into the apartment wearing a reinforced backpack and toting
a rolled-up sleeping bag. She gasps when she sees the knife.
"What the hell is that for?" she asks.

"Bad guys. Are you terrified?"

"Of you?"

"Yes, of me. Of me and my big no-joke knife." I wave it
around and she backs away.

"Watch it with that thing."

"You ought to see what this knife can do to a piece of celery.
It's not a pretty sight."

"Is this what we've come to? You running around with a
machete?" She kicks the door closed with the back of her run-

ning shoe and tosses the sleeping bag onto the floor, where it rolls into the couch. Alice arches her back.

"Who are you, Nanook of the North?"

"Are you okay?"

"Yeah."

Her eyes narrow. "Yeah?"

"Okay as I can be."

"I thought so," Judy says, frowning like a doctor confirming a child's case of tonsillitis. "I brought something to make us feel better." She swings the backpack off her shoulder and tugs its zipper open, walking into the kitchen. I follow her in and watch her unpack a bag of sugar, two sticks of butter, and a cellophane pack of chocolate chips.

"You left Kurt to come here and bake stuff?" I stick the knife back onto the rack.

"Not exactly. Your new boyfriend called and said you needed protection. You did use protection, didn't you?"

I feel terrible all of a sudden. It reminds me of Brent. I flash on him that day in my office, cleaning up the coffee stain. He was so worried about me.

"What's the matter?" Judy asks, alarmed.

"Brent, Judy. Brent." I feel myself sag and Judy gathers me up in her strong arms. I burrow into her fuzzy Patagonia pullover, with its fresh soapy smell, and start to cry.

"I know, Mare," she says, her voice sounding unusually small. "He was a good man. He loved you." She hugs me closer, and I try not to feel funny about the fact that we're two women hugging breast to breast. In fact, Judy's squeezing me so tightly that I stumble backward, to the sound of a loud *reeaow!*

We both jump. I've crunched Alice's tail underfoot. She hisses at me fiercely.

Judy laughs, wiping her eyes. "Fuck the cookies. Let's bake Alice."

I laugh too, for a long time, and it feels good, a release. We take turns drying our eyes with a roll of paper towels that has tiny daisies marching along its border. Afterward, feeling shaky and sober, we look at each other. Judy's lips are a wavy line. "This must be how you felt after Mike, huh?" she says, leaning against the kitchen counter.

Mike. His voice is gone now, and it was the last of him. I nod.

"You came back to work so soon. I never knew how you did it."

"I had to. When something like that happens, you have to do the next thing."

"The next thing?"

"Right. Whatever's next. You go and do it. Then you do what comes next after that. File a brief. Bake cookies."

Judy smiles weakly.

I point to the base cabinet. "The cookbook's inside. You want coffee?"

"Thanks." Judy yanks her pullover off over her head, revealing one of Kurt's V-neck undershirts, and settles down on the pine floor of the kitchen. She tugs my *Joy of Cooking* from the shelf and opens the thick book, idly twisting the red ribbons glued to its spine. "What is this, the wartime edition? You should throw this thing out."

"I can't." I scoop some dry coffee into the coffeemaker. "It reminds me of a missal."

"A what?"

"Forget it." Judy was raised without a religion, which is why she has so much faith.

"So, are you in love?"

I watch the coffee dribble into the glass pot. It takes forever.

"Mary? You in love?" She looks up at me expectantly. With her shaggy haircut, there on the floor, she reminds me of a sheepdog waiting for a Milk-Bone.

"I'm in confusion."

"Tell me what's going on or I'll make the German Honey Bars."

I retrieve two mugs from the cabinet and pour us both some coffee. I take mine with extra cream and extra sugar; she takes hers black. "I don't know where to start."

"Start with his German Honey Bar." She pats the floor beside her.

"You want to sit on the floor?" I hand her the coffee.

"You had sex on the floor, didn't you?"

I sit down with a sigh. The kitchen is so cramped our shoes touch in the middle—Ferragamo meets New Balance. I wrap my hands around my own toasty mug.

"Your Honor," she says, "please instruct the witness to answer the question." She looks happy again, bugging me to say the unsayable.

"What question?"

"Did you do it on the floor?"

I wince.

"It's okay to talk about sex, Mary. You're a grown-up now, and there are no commandments within a five-mile radius. So. On the couch?"

"Judith."

"That counts as a yes on the couch."

"You're relentless."

"All right. Forget it. You're in confusion. Are you in danger?" She stops smiling.

"From Ned? No."

"You sure?"

I tell Judy all about Ned, his therapy and his father. She listens carefully, sipping her coffee. When I'm done, she sets her mug down on the floor and leans forward intently. Uneven bangs shade her eyes from the Chinese paper lamp overhead.

"You want to know what I think?"

I bite my lip. Judy's a certifiably smart person; she was number one at Boalt. If she says it, it carries weight.

"I think Brent was murdered, and I think there *is* some connection between Brent and Mike. It's too coincidental."

"So I'm not crazy."

"No. But listen to this. I think you've been analyzing this all wrong. Forget for a minute that you think the car was aiming at you, that's just an assumption. The only facts we have are that Mike's been killed and Brent's been killed. So reason backward from that. Assume that the killer did what he intended to do—kill the two men closest to you. He wasn't after you, he was after them."

"You think?"

She yanks a hand through lemony hair. "We've been reading the notes as threats to you, but what if it's someone who's just trying to get close to you? To communicate with you the only way he can? Not someone who hates you, someone who loves you. Someone who wants you all to himself."

My gut tightens as she speaks. She's close to what Lombardo was saying after the memorial service, and I forgot to mention it to her. But it doesn't square, not entirely. "A note that says 'watch your step'? It sounds like a threat to me."

"Or a warning. Particularly since almost the next night, the man you're with gets hit by a car."

"But that assumes the killer knew I'd be out with Brent, and he couldn't have. We didn't plan to go out to dinner, I offered to take him out after I finished a brief for Jameson."

"Jameson? Yuck."

I'm reminded of the weird toys in Jameson's desk, and how Brent had laughed and laughed. I tell her what Stella said. It doesn't seem funny now.

"I don't think it's Jameson," she says, shaking her head. "He's too much of a wuss. I don't think it's Ned's father either, even though he wanted to meet you that day. He could have found out that you were in Ned's class from Martindale-Hubbell."

"But Ned said he keeps tabs on him."

"That doesn't mean he has him—or you—followed. Maybe he asked around. People know you. You've been in practice for eight years in this city. You went to Penn Law, you even went to Penn undergrad."

"Maybe."

"You know, you're resisting the most obvious conclusion, Mary, and the most logical. It's Ned."

"It can't be." I shake my head.

"Look at the facts—there's a pattern here. You date Ned in law school, then you pick up with Mike. You marry Mike, and he's killed by a hit-and-run. You begin dating Ned again, and a couple of nights later Brent's killed by a hit-and-run. Don't you think that's strange?"

"It's strange, but it doesn't mean anything."

"Why doesn't it? Ned even sends you a warning after you have dinner with him—watch your step. Read it as a threat to keep you away from other men, even Brent. Look, Ned didn't know Brent was gay. You remember the rumors that you and Brent were having an affair?"

"That was ridiculous."

"I know that, but Ned doesn't. Plus he admits he's been interested in you since law school. That's weird, Mare."

"Not necessarily. He said he'd been depressed. He's had a lot of problems."

"Which way does that cut? So he's hardly the picture of mental stability."

"I'm surprised at you, to hold that against him. He was depressed. He got help. I give him credit for that, don't you?"

"That's not the point. The man has a history of serious mental illness. I'm glad he dealt with it, but that's the fact. I mean, depressed or not, he hasn't dated anyone since law school. Pining away for you? Doesn't that strike you as obsessional? Almost sick?"

"He never said that, Judy. We didn't discuss other women. You know, if you knew him, you wouldn't say these things. He's beautiful, really."

But she doesn't seem to be listening. "Look, I don't blame you for not wanting to believe me, but think like a lawyer. Imagine that you're the client. What advice would you give?" Her azure gaze is forceful, and it angers me.

"You don't like him, Judy. You never have. He cares for me, he makes me happy. I would think you'd want that for me, for Christ's sake." My tone sounds bitter; my chest is a knot. I can't remember ever fighting with her this way. "What's happening to us, Jude?"

"I don't know." She leans back against the wall, wounded and hurt. She's my best friend; she's trying to help me.

"I'm sorry," I say. "It's hard."

She flicks her hair back, dry-eyed. "I know. I'm sorry too." We fall silent a minute.

"You know, Mary, you asked me once if I ever worry. Well, I do. About you. I used to worry about your emotional health, after Mike died, but now we're at the point where I'm worried about your life. It scares me that something could happen to you. It makes me very . . . bitchy. Bossy. I'm sorry for that."

"Jude—"

"But that doesn't mean I'm letting you off the hook. I can't watch you walk into the lion's mouth. So I'm asking you, for me. For my sake. Follow your head and not your heart. Err on the side of caution. Cut him loose."

I feel an ache in my chest. "He said he didn't do it."

"No shit, Sherlock."

I shoot her a look.

"I'm sorry, that was unkind." She thinks a minute. "Here's an idea. Don't see him for a week. We'll know a lot more in just a week. Maybe Lombardo will find out something; maybe you'll get another note. Seven days, that's all."

Easy for her to say. I feel like I need him now. I remember the weekend together, how sweet he was, and how open with me. He made love to me, he held me. He said things, things that thrilled me. Things it hurts to remember now. Tears come to my eyes; I blink them back. "You're tough, Jude."

"The stakes are high, Mary. I want to win."

And either way, I lose. Because the ache inside me is telling me something, and it's too strong to be something else.

I'm in love.

TWENTY-ONE

I feel like everyone's watching me the next morning when I get off the elevator and walk to my desk. The secretaries in my area gaze at me bathetically, to them I'm the Young Widow Times Two. A partner glances back at me, wondering whether my billable hours will fall off. A messenger pushing a mail cart hurries by with a sideways glance. His look says, The broad must be some kind of jinx.

Why are they thinking about me? Why aren't they thinking about Brent?

I feel shaky, disoriented. Nothing seems familiar here, least of all Brent's desk. There's a blotter with floral edges where there used to be a friendly clutter of wind-up toys and a rubberband gun. Brent's mug—WHAT DO I LOOK LIKE, AN IN-FORMATION BOOTH?—is gone. A calendar with fuzzy kittens has replaced a portrait of Luciano Pavarotti. The air smells like nothing at all; I can't believe I miss the tang of Obsession. What I miss is Brent. He deserved a long and happy life. He deserved to be singing his heart out somewhere, for the sheer joy of it.

Somebody's grandmother is sitting in Brent's chair. She introduces herself as Miss Pershing and refuses to call me anything but Miss DiNunzio. Her dull gray hair is pulled back into a French twist, and she wears a pink Fair Isle sweater held together at the top by a gold-plated chain. She's been a secretary in the Estates Department for thirty years. She brings me coffee on a tray.

It makes me want to cry.

I close my door and stare at the pile of mail on my desk. Without Brent, it's not organized into Good and Evil and totters precariously to the left. Mixed in with the thick case summaries and fuck-you letters are batches of envelopes in somber pastel shades. I remember them from before. Sympathy cards, dispensing a generic sentiment in every cursive iteration imaginable: *My thoughts/feelings are with you/your loved ones at this time of difficulty/of sorrow. May you have the comfort/solace of your loved ones/faith in God at this time.*

I can't bring myself to read any of the mail, especially the sympathy cards. They're only a comfort to people who don't know anyone who died.

I poke at a pink card on the top of the mail, and the tower topples over. It fans out across my desk, revealing at its center a bulky manila envelope bearing my name scrawled in pen.

Odd.

Miss Pershing's sheared the top off the envelope, and so neatly that there's barely any tearing. I open it. Inside is a piece of blue notepaper which says FROM THE DESK OF JACKIE O at the top and reads:

> Mary—
>   *I cleaned out Brent's desk. Thank you for everything, and for being so good to Brent. You may need this.*
>   Love, Jack

Stuck in the envelope is Brent's rubber-band gun. I smile, and am trying not to cry, when I remember the notes.

The notes! Brent kept them for me. Where are they?

I ransack my desk, but they're not there. I rush out to Miss Pershing's desk, and she watches, aghast, as I slam through the drawers. They're all empty except for typing paper and Stalling letterhead.

Where are the notes? Brent would have put them someplace safe. He took care of me.

I run back to my office and call Jack, but he's not at home. I leave a message, asking him to call back. I feel panicked. It doesn't make sense that Jack would take them, but maybe he'll know where they are. I still have my hand on the telephone receiver when it rings, jangling in my palm.

"DiNunzio?" barks Starankovic. His voice has a Monday-morning-I'm-refreshed punch to it. "You changed your number? I had to go through the switchboard."

"I'm sorry—"

"When are the interviews?"

I cringe. I'd totally forgotten. "My secretary—"

"Don't blame it on him, DiNunzio. Set 'em up today or I file the motion."

"Bernie—"

Click.

I hang up the phone by the pile of disordered mail. I should straighten it up. It's the Next Thing to do and I should do it. Dictate, return phone calls, back-fuck. I pick up an envelope, a white hand-delivery from Thomas, Main & Chandler, the third firm in the holy trinity. It must be a response to a motion I filed last week. Last week, when Brent was telling me to call the cops.

What did the Mike-voice say? *I tried. I tried.*

I put the envelope back down, feeling empty inside. Hollow. Aching. Exactly how I felt after Mike died, and how I was beginning not to feel before Brent was killed. I let the leaden sensation leech into my bones, into my soul. A little white pillowcase of a soul that turned black the instant of my birth, and even blacker when the men I love were killed on my account.

Suddenly, someone is clearing his throat directly above me. I look up into the bland visage of Martin H. Chatham IV.

"How do you tolerate it?" he says, with as much emotion as I've ever heard from him.

"Stand what?"

"That blasted clock!" Martin sits down in one of the Stalling-issue chairs in front of my desk and crosses his legs.

I look over my shoulder. 9:15. "You get used to it. Sort of."

"I don't see how. But you'll be vacating this office after June, *n'est-ce pas?* When we make our new litigation partners." His tone is oh-so-controlled, but I'm in no mood to fence.

"I hope so."

"Come on, Mary. We both know you're on track."

"I am? I guess I haven't thought about it lately."

Martin's face changes, as if he's remembered his manners. "Yes. Of course. I'm sorry about your secretary."

"Thank you."

"Damn drunk drivers. It's a terrible way to go."

I flash on the car as it explodes into Brent's body. And Mike's. I feel stunned.

Martin tosses some papers onto my desk. "Here are a couple of deposition notices in *Harbison's*. They're for the two supervisors, Breslin and Grayboyes."

I should call him on it, but I feel upset, off balance. I bear down and say the Next Thing. "I talked to Starankovic. It's taken care of."

He looks mildly surprised. "Did you postpone them?"

"Yes. Starankovic wants to take some employee interviews. I told him I'd think about it."

"I know you. You won't let him do that."

"I won't?"

"You? Voluntarily expose your employees to interviews with the enemy, without benefit of counsel? So that they can say anything? It goes against all those hot-blooded instincts of yours, even if there is precedent for it."

"He's going to file a motion if we don't consent."

"Bah! Is the man a glutton for punishment?" Martin can always tap into the our-team-kicked-ass mentality that flows like blood at Stalling.

"He might win it. Even if he doesn't, it'll cost Harbison's more to fight the motion than it will to let him do the interviews."

"Money's no object, Mary, when it's the client's."

I don't bother forcing a smile.

"By the by, I understand you'll be handling the new age case for Harbison's. The plaintiff's named Hart, right?" He gets up, tugging at suspenders needlepointed with flying owls.

"Right."

"Sam wasn't sure you were ready, but I told him it was time we gave you a case of your own. If you need a hand, let me know. I'll keep it to myself," he says with a wink.

He's about to leave when Ned suddenly sticks his head in the doorway. His jacket is off and one hand is hidden behind his back. "Mary?" he says, in the split second before he spots Martin.

"Young Waters!" Martin booms. "What brings you up to this neck of the woods?"

"I thought I'd stop in to see Mary." Ned beams at me from the doorway. His smile says, We're lovers now.

I can't help but return the smile. I feel it too. Bonded to him invisibly, by virtue of the fact that he's been that close. When there's not many who have.

Martin tugs at Ned's shirtsleeve like an insistent child. "Haven't seen much of you lately at the club."

"No. I haven't been there."

"Working hard or hardly working?"

"I just haven't had a chance to sail much yet this spring."

"Too bad. I got out on Sunday. Had a beautiful day, a beau-

tiful day. You're welcome along anytime. Alida would love another lesson," he says, with measurable warmth. His hand
rests on Ned's shoulder. "She's darn good for a sixteen-year-
old, don't you agree?"

"She's good," Ned says.

Martin turns to me. "Waters here taught Alida more in one
afternoon than that school in Annapolis did all last summer."
He slaps Ned on the back. "How about this Sunday, my man?
What are you doing this weekend? Why don't you head over
for brunch? We'll spend all afternoon on the water. What do
you say?"

"Uh, I'm busy." Ned flashes me a grin. His eyes are bright,
and his look is undisguised. "I have big plans."

Martin looks from Ned to me. His smile fades slowly. "Do
my eyes deceive me?"

"It depends on what they're telling you," Ned says, with a
laugh.

"Ned—" I'm not sure how to finish the sentence. I don't
want Ned telling Martin about us. Not when I'm about to
break us up, at least temporarily.

"What?" Ned asks, smiling. "Don't you want to tell the
world? I do."

Martin looks back and forth between us again. "Say it ain't
so, Joe," he says.

I'm not sure I like Martin's tone. Neither does Ned, who
bristles. "Something wrong, Martin?"

"With you and DiNunzio?" Martin asks. "Of course not.
I'm surprised, that's all."

"So am I," Ned answers lightly. "She's the best thing that
ever happened to me."

I shoot Ned a warning glance.

Martin pats Ned's shoulder. "Don't take offense, Waters."

"None taken," Ned says abruptly, brushing past Martin to
me. "Now if you'll excuse us." He whips his hand out from

behind his back, but it's covered by a gray wool jacket. The jacket conceals something huge, almost as big as his arm.

Martin clears his throat behind Ned. "Well. It looks like you won't be needing me."

"I can handle it from here," Ned calls back, and Martin closes the door. Ned beams at me. "Guess what the bulge is. And it's not that I'm happy to see you, even though I am happy to see you."

"You didn't have to do anything."

"I know that. Now guess. It's in disguise." He wiggles the jacket, and it makes a crinkling sound.

"A really big muffin?"

"You're half right." He snaps the jacket off with a magician's flourish. Underneath is a full bouquet of rich red roses, wrapped in cellophane. "Ta-da!"

"Jeez, Ned!"

He hands the bouquet to me and kisses me on the cheek. "These are for you, sweetheart."

I take the crinkly bouquet and feel myself blushing. The flowers are beautiful. The man is charming. I am in love. How am I supposed to give this up? How am I supposed to hurt him?

"Do you like them?" he asks worriedly.

"They're lovely." I avoid his eye.

Suddenly, he takes my face in his hands and gives me a long, deep kiss. I return it over the sweet smell of the flowers, feeling touched and confused at the same time.

"I missed you last night. I really did." He kisses me again, but I pull away.

"You sent Judy."

"To take care of you. But she's no substitute, right?"

I nod. The roses are a cardinal red, and the underside of each petal has a dense and velvety texture. There are twelve in all. They must have cost a fortune.

"I did get you a muffin, by the way." He wrestles with the pocket of his suit jacket and pulls out a crumpled white bag the size of a hardball. "Blueberry." He shakes it beside his ear like a light bulb. "It's in three hundred and fifty-seven pieces at this point. Sorry about that." He sets it down on my desk.

"Thank you."

"You still don't look happy. Was Martin giving you a hard time?"

"Uh, yeah. First he holds back on the two deposition notices, the ones I told you about. Then he tells me he's the one who told Berkowitz to give me the *Hart* case, not the other way around. I think he's trying to save face."

"How do you know?"

"How do I know what?"

"That Martin wasn't the one to suggest it to Berkowitz?"

"That's not what Berkowitz said. Implied, anyway."

Ned looks skeptical. "Maybe Berkowitz wasn't telling the truth. Maybe it was Martin who suggested you get the case."

"I don't understand. Why would Martin champion my cause, Ned? You saw him just now."

"That was because he wants to fix me up with his daughter. It wasn't directed at you."

"No?"

"No. I'd take Martin over Berkowitz any day."

"I'd take Berkowitz over Martin any day."

We regard each other over the flowers. We seem to be lined up on opposing sides of a class war. It breaks the mood— which is a godsend, for what I have to do.

"Is this our first fight?" he asks, with a sad smile.

"Ned—"

"Then I have something to say." He grabs the flowers and puts them on the desk. Then he walks over to me and takes me in his arms. "I'm sorry."

I can smell his aftershave, familiar to me now, and feel the heavy cotton of his shirt. "Ned—"

"You don't need a hard time from me this morning, do you?" He hugs me tighter, rocking a little, and I feel myself relax into the comfort of his arms. My hands slip easily around the small of his back. He wears no undershirt, which I love, and his shirt is slightly damp from the walk to work.

"The notes are missing, Ned."

He kisses my hair. "No, they're not. I have them."

I pull away from him. "You have the notes, Ned? *You?*"

"Not with me. I put them in my safe at home, behind the picture of that old Lightning, at Wellfleet."

"Where did you get them?"

"The notes? I went to the office after the memorial service."

"Why?"

"I had work to do, honey. I was going to work the weekend, but we spent it in bed, remember? I stopped by your office and found them on top of your desk with a note."

"But why were you even on this floor? Your office is on—"

"I don't know. I just was."

"Why did you go in my office?"

"On impulse, I guess. I wanted to be around something of yours. Look at your handwriting, you know. It was goony." He laughs nervously. "What's with all the questions?"

Fear rises in my throat. He has no reason to be on my floor, no right to come into my office. I imagine him rooting through my desk in the glow of the clock. I hope Judy isn't right about him, but I can't take any more chances. I steel myself. "Ned, I can't see you for a while."

"What?" He looks shocked.

"I want you to bring the notes to the office as soon as you can. Maybe you should go home at lunch."

"What are you saying? What about us?"

"I'm . . . not ready for us. Not yet. Not now."

"Wait a minute, what's happening?" His voice breaks. "Mary, I love you!"

He hadn't said that, not once the whole weekend, though I

wondered how deep his feelings went. Now I know, if he's telling the truth. *I love you.* The words reach out and grab me by the heart. I want so much for it not to be him, but I'm afraid Judy's right. And now I'm afraid of him. "I need time."

"Time? Time for what?"

"To think. I want the notes back."

He grabs my arms. "Mary, I love you. I'll get you the notes. I was only trying to help. I didn't think they should be left out like that, where anybody could pick them up."

I can't look at him. "Ned, please."

He releases me suddenly. "I get it. You think it's me, don't you? You suspect me." His tone is bitter.

"I don't know what I think."

"You think it's me. You think I'm trying to kill you. I can't believe this." He throws up his hands in disgust. "We spent the weekend together, Mary. I told you things I never told anybody else in the world!"

He falls silent suddenly. I look at him, and his face is full of anger.

"That's why, isn't it?" he asks quietly. "Because of what I told you. I was depressed, so now you have me pegged for a psycho killer. Oh, this is beautiful. This is really beautiful. Tell me again how proud you are of me, Mary."

"That's not it. I just need time, Ned."

"Fine. You just got it." He stalks to the door but stops there, his back to me. "Whoever it is, they'll still be after you. And I won't be around to keep you safe."

I feel sick inside. He hurts so much, and it hurts to see him go.

"Is this really what you want?" he asks, without turning around.

I close my eyes. "Yes."

"So be it." The next sound is the harsh *ca-chunk* of the door as it closes.

When I open my eyes, I'm alone. I cross my arms and try to keep it together, looking around my office at the books and the files and the diplomas. They're so cold, fungible. They could belong to anybody, and they do. Every lawyer here has the same rust-colored accordion files, the same framed diplomas from the same handful of schools. My eyes fall on the roses, so out of place in this cold little office with the clock staring in. 10:36.

I feel like I have to regroup, to sort out everything that's been happening. I need to think things out in a safe place, but I can't remember the last time I felt safe. In Mike's arms. Another time.

In church, as a child.

In church, what a thought. I haven't been to church in ages and had lapsed way before that. But I always felt safe in church as a little girl. Protected, watched over. The idea grows on me as I stand, frozen, facing the clock.

I think of the church I grew up in, Our Lady of Perpetual Help. I was a believer then. A believer in a God who watched over us all, the cyclists and the gay secretaries. A believer in the goodness of all men, even partners, and lovers too. A believer in our fraternity with animals, including cats who won't rub against your leg no matter what.

I grab my blazer from behind the door and stop by Miss Pershing's desk. "Miss Pershing, I'll be out of the office for a couple of hours."

"Oh?" She takes off her glasses and places them carefully on her shallow chest, where they dangle on a lorgnette. "Where shall I say you are, Miss DiNunzio?"

"You shouldn't say, but the answer is, in church."

For the first time, Miss Pershing smiles at me.

I hail a cab outside our building. The cabbie, an old man with greasy white hair, stabs out his cigarette and flips down the flag on the meter. "Where to?"

"Our Lady of Perpetual Help. Ninth and Wolf."

"Lawyers go to church?" A final puff of smoke bursts from his mouth.

"Only when they have to."

He chuckles thickly, and it ends in a coughing spasm. We take off in silence, except for the crackling of the radio. The cab swings onto Broad Street, which bisects the city at City Hall and runs straight to South Philly. Broad Street is congested, as usual. We stop in the cool shadow cast by a skyscraper and then lurch into the bright light of the sun. I crank open the window, watching us pass through light and dark, listening to the old cabbie swear at the traffic, and trying to remember the last time I was in church.

Bless me, Father, for I have sinned. It's been 3,492,972 weeks since my last confession. The Jurassic Period. When I did everything the nuns told me to, so I wouldn't get my knuckles rapped, and memorized the Baltimore Catechism. I made my First Holy Communion at age seven, during which the priest put a wafer onto my tongue that he said was the body of Jesus Christ. I didn't swallow it until right before they took my picture, and my baby face is beatific in the photo. I'd swallowed my slice of Our Savior and was overjoyed that this cannibalistic act had not sent lightning zigzagging to my head.

"Shit!" The cabbie bangs on the steering wheel, foiled in his attempt to run a traffic light. Sunlight blazes into the old cab, illuminating its dusty interior and heating its duct-taped seat covers. "You think they'd time these goddamn lights, like on Chestnut Street. But no, that would make too much sense."

I nod, half listening. As soon as the light changes, the cabbie guns the motor and we leap forward into the tall shadow cast by the Fidelity Building. Its darkness comes as a relief and seems to quiet even the irritable driver.

As a child, I used to look at my communion picture on top of our boxy television. I wanted to be as good as the little girl in my picture, she of the praying hands and the lacquered corkscrews. But I wasn't her. I knew it inside. The church told me so. They taught me that Jesus Christ suffered on the cross and died because of me. All because of me. Blood dripped from his crown of thorns and flowed in rivulets from rough bolts hammered clear through his wrists and insteps. His agony was all my fault. I felt so sorry, as a little girl, and so ashamed. Of myself.

"Hey, asshole!" shouts the cabbie, hanging out the window. "Move that shitwagon! I'm tryin' to make a living here!" The cab bucks violently in the shade. I grab for the yellowed hand strap just as we burst free of the snarled traffic into the light.

And in my religious life, what happened next was calamitous. I grew up. It was Luke who said that whoever does not accept the kingdom of God like a child will not enter it, and I stopped being a child. I stopped accepting on faith and started to doubt. Then I started to question, which brought the heavens, in the form of school administration, crashing down upon my head. I took biological issue with the Resurrection and was suspended for three days.

Light and dark, light and dark.

That's when it started, the split between me and the church. And me and my twin. For as I began to turn away from the light, Angie began to embrace it. I resented the church, for making me feel so terrible about myself as a child and for dividing Angie and me. In time, I stopped going to mass altogether, and my parents didn't force the issue. The three of them went every Sunday, while I stayed home with the Eagles pregame show. They prayed for my soul. I prayed for the Eagles.

"Do you remember Roman Gabriel?" I say to the cabbie. We're almost there.

He looks into the rearview mirror with rheumy eyes. "Sure. Quarterback for the Birds. We got him from the Rams."

"Do you remember when?"

He squints, in thought. "'Seventy-three, I think. Yeah, in 'seventy-three."

So long ago. I can't do the math in my head.

"What a fruit he was," says the cabbie. "We shoulda kept Liske."

Bless me, Father, for I have sinned. I can't remember a thing about my last confession.

And I can't forget a thing about my abortion.

TWENTY-TWO

It was so long ago.

I never told anyone, not even Mike. I intended to tell him, but changed my mind when we found out he couldn't have kids. It would have made it worse. I know it did for me.

"This it?" says the cabbie, pulling up in front of the red-brick fortress on the corner of Ninth and Wolf. He ducks down to see it better. "It don't look like a church. What'd you say it was? Our Lady of Perpetual—"

"Motion." I get out of the cab and throw him a ten-dollar bill, with no tip. "Here. This is from a fruit I know."

"Crazy broad," he mutters. The cab lurches off.

I glance around to see if I've been followed, but the street is quiet. I turn and confront my church. From the outside, there is no way to tell what type of building it is. The windows are bricked in and the heavy oak doors are squared off at the top. But for the black sign that says the times of the masses in tiny white numbers, you would think that OLPH is a Mafia front. Except that the Mafia front is across the street.

In contrast to the bleakness of the church is the grassy lot beside it, a sheltered grotto for the statue of the Virgin Mary, Our Lady of Perpetual Help herself. I remember thinking that the grotto was a miraculous place, a baby's blanket of perfect green grass tucked away from the city sidewalks. Gazing benignly over the grass, high above the electric trolley cars, was the slim, robed figure of the Virgin, tall as a spire in white marble, with her hands outstretched in welcome. I felt peaceful there as a child.

I have the same feeling today. The statue looks the same, and so does the grass. It's verdant and thick; it looks newly mown and raked. Tulips dip their heavy heads at the statue's pedestal. No one's around, so I sit on the bench in front of it, completing my Catholic impersonation. I'm eye level with the pedestal's inscription, but don't have to look at the Roman-carved letters to know what they say. I remember:

VIRGIN MARY
MARIAN YEAR 1954
GIFT OF MR. AND MRS. RAFAELLO D. SABATINI

Mr. and Mrs. Rafaello D. Sabatini owned the Mafia front across the street, but who cared? They were good Catholics, they supported the church and the school. That was all that mattered.

At the statue's feet are plastic bouquets of red roses, Mary's flower, and along her hem are the lipsticked kisses of the insanely faithful. Rosaries dangle from her inanimate fingers, and she wears a crown made of glitter pasted onto cardboard, as if by a child. A little girl, no doubt, for little girls love the Virgin. Was I a little girl like that once? I feel a stab of pain. What does Mary think of Mary now, since her abortion?

I squint up at Mary's eyes, there at the top of the tall statue. She doesn't answer me but gazes straight ahead. She's innocent, the Eternal Virgin. Her conception, unlike mine, was Immaculate. She knows nothing of couplings that happen to Catholic girls who are on the third date of their life, with

Bobby Mancuso from Latin Club. Who, despite his braces, is terribly cute and plays varsity basketball. Who takes her to McDonald's and then, in his Corvair, kisses her hotly, ignoring her protestations. Who doesn't rape her exactly, but who complains that he's in intense pain from something called blue balls, which means either that his balls are turning blue because the blood to them is cut off, or there's too much blood getting to them. She's confused about the physiology of the blue balls but understands clearly that his pain is all because of her.

His agony is all her fault.

Which makes her sorry, so sorry.

He says if she would just let him touch between her legs, just let him do what he wanted, his pain would be relieved and his balls wouldn't be blue anymore. And before she knows it, her new plaid kilt is up and he is inside her. It's over so fast, and the whole thing is so painful and strange, so impossibly *strange,* that she's really not sure she's not a virgin Mary anymore. Until she gets home and finds the spots on her flowered Carter's. Red splotches, shaped like infernal stars, among the delicate pink blossoms. Then she's pregnant and decides to have an abortion.

No one knew. Not even Angie, and especially not Angie. I was terrified. I was ashamed. I had committed a mortal sin and would burn in eternal fire unless I repented. But the only way to repent was to confess my sin to God and to my parents, who would die from the shock. I felt trapped between commandments: THOU SHALT NOT KILL and HONOR THY FATHER AND THY MOTHER.

Not only that, but both Angie and I had been awarded scholarships to Penn, which was my only hope of going to college. Would the university extend mine until my baby—and Bobby's, who ignored me from that day forward—was born? Of course not. Even if they did, how would I support a child?

My mother couldn't; her piecework sewing barely bought my uniform and books. My father couldn't; he was already on disability.

I had no choice.

I found Planned Parenthood in the Yellow Pages and took the bus to center city one Saturday morning, with an Etienne Aigner wallet full of confirmation money. The abortion would cost the $150 earmarked for a white ten-speed, but I was putting away childish things. Of necessity.

When I got to the clinic, I filled out some forms, on which I lied about my age and changed my name. I told them I was Jane Hathaway, after Nancy Kulp in *The Beverly Hillbillies,* because she seemed like such a classy lady. Then I was taken to see a counselor, a black woman named Adelaide Huckaby, who wore an African dashiki. Her nappy hair was close-cropped, revealing a marvelously round head, and her eyes were a dark brown, like her skin. We talked for a long time, and she gave me a warm hug when I cried. "You want to think about it some more?" she asked. "You can change your mind, even now."

I said no.

Adelaide came with me into what they called the Procedure Room, and we waited for the doctor together. I was lying flat on a skinny and unforgiving table in a hospital gown, with my knees supported from underneath. On the ceiling was a circle of fluorescent light. I tried not to think of it as an all-seeing eye, looking down on me from above, witnessing everything in mute horror.

"I see you get those blotches on your chest," Adelaide said softly. "My sister gets 'em too. Only you can't see 'em so well on her."

I smiled.

"It's all right, baby. Everything's gonna be all right."

Then the doctor came in. He wore granny glasses and gave me a brief hello before he disappeared behind the white tent covering my knees. Adelaide took my hand and held it. She seemed to know I needed a hand to hold on to, and hers was strong and generous. While the doctor worked away, Adelaide described the procedure for me, her voice quietly resonant.

"Now he's inserting the speculum, so you'll feel some coldness. You know what a speculum is, baby?"

I shook my head, no.

"That's what your doctor uses during a pelvic exam, the same instrument, to hold the walls of the vagina apart."

I had never had a pelvic exam. This was, in effect, my first trip to the gynecologist. I didn't tell Adelaide that. I was supposed to be nineteen and was already feeling bad about lying.

"Now he's going to give you two shots, into your cervix, to relax the muscle."

"Needles?"

"Don't worry. In about two minutes you'll feel two tiny little pinches, not too bad."

Adelaide was as good as her word. One. Two. Like little pinpricks.

"Now we're comin' up on the part of the procedure where the doctor's going to dilate you. He's gonna use two rods, one small and one large, to open up your cervix. This is gonna be a little uncomfortable for you, honey, and I want you to hold my hand good and tight. It's gonna feel like cramps, just like the kind you get on your period."

"I don't get cramps."

"Not even the first day?"

I shook my head, no, feeling embarrassed. At that age, I felt inferior because I didn't get menstrual cramps, which kept Angie and my classmates popping blue Midols in French class. Real women got cramps.

"Well," she said, "you're a lucky girl."

I had never thought of it that way. Suddenly, I felt a violent squeeze around my lower abdomen, then another. I bit my lip, closing my eyes to the luminous cyclops in the ceiling. The pain came again and again, bringing tears to my eyes. I held on to Adelaide, and she to me, saying, "Just a couple more minutes. Hold on to my hand, honey."

Then it stopped. No more pain, no more cramping. Adelaide explained about the curette while the doctor scraped the baby off the insides of my uterus. I felt nothing.

It was over when the scraping was done. The doctor left the room, saying a quick good-bye. Adelaide stood over me, smoothing my hair back from my face like my own mother would have. She looked so happy and relieved I felt like I had graduated from something.

"Adelaide, I have to tell you something. My name—"

"Hush, baby," she said, smiling down at me. "You think I don't watch television?"

She helped me to a recovery room. I had to leave her and was led to a chair near eight other patients. Some of them were having cookies and juice, others were resting in their seats. I stayed there awhile, leaning my head back into the cushions, feeling a mixture of relief and sadness. In time, another counselor came by and roused me. She had an intense medical-student look about her, and she told me in a technical fashion about the pads and the bleeding and the follow-up and the product of the pregnancy.

When I got home, I mumbled something about the flu and crawled into bed with my stuffed Snoopy. I felt raw inside, achy. I stayed in bed through dinner, fake-sleeping when Angie came in at night. I just lay there, bleeding secretly into a pad attached to a strappy sanitary belt. Thinking about how I went in full and came out empty.

The product of the pregnancy.

I knew it was a baby; I didn't kid myself about that. But for me, that wasn't the end of the question. We killed in war; we killed in self-defense. Sometimes killing was murder and sometimes it wasn't. I was confused. I felt that what I did was right, even though I felt just as certainly that it was wrong. My church, being a lot smarter than I, exhibited no such ambivalence. It had all the answers from the get-go, so I knew my family's prayers for me were lost for good. They would disappear on the way to heaven like the smoky trail of an altar candle.

I look up at Our Lady of Perpetual Help, searching in vain for her eyes. If anyone could understand, Mary could. She had also sacrificed her child. She had no choice either.

"Are you all right, miss?" asks a voice.

I look up, with a shock. An old man is peering into my face, not ten inches from my nose. He looks worried, and I realize, to my surprise, that I've been crying. I wipe my cheek with a hand.

"Here you go," he says. He tucks a broom under his arm and offers me a folded red bandanna from the pocket of his baggy pants. "Take it."

"No, thanks. I'm fine."

"Here." Before I can stop him, he puts the bandanna up to my nose. It smells like fabric softener. "Give 'er a blow. A good hard blow."

"Are you serious?"

"Go for it."

So for a minute I forget that I'm over ten years old, a lawyer and a sinner to boot, and let the church janitor blow my nose.

"Good for you!" He folds up the bandanna and tucks it back into his pocket. He's cute, with a wizened face and sparse tufts of white Bozo hair at each temple. His nose is small and blunted at its tip, as if by a common spade. A safety pin holds his bifocals together, but his blue eyes are sharp behind the glasses. "You got troubles?"

"I'm okay."

He eases himself onto the bench, leaning on the wiggly broom for support. "That why you're cryin'? 'Cause you're okay?"

"I don't know. I don't even know why I came here."

"For help. That's why people come, for help."

"You think the church can help?"

"Sure. It's helped me all my life—God has. He's guided me." The old man leans back and smiles. His teeth are too perfect. Dentures, like my father.

"You believe."

"Of course." He looks at the statue, his back making a tiny hunch. "When was your last confession?" It sounds odd, coming from him.

"Are you a janitor?"

"Are you?"

"I'm a lawyer."

"I'm a priest! Ha!" He cackles happily, banging his broom on the ground. "Gotcha, didn't I?"

I laugh. "That's not fair, Father."

"No, it isn't, is it? I'm undercover, like in *Miami Vice*." His eyes smile with delight.

I turn away from his bright eyes, confounded by his ruse and his warmth. I don't remember priests being like this when I was little. They were distant, and disapproving.

"I'm Father Cassiotti. I'm too old to do the masses, Father Napole does that. I assist him. I help however I can. I hear confessions. I tend the Virgin."

I don't say anything. I'm not sure what to say. I look at my navy blue pumps planted in the grass.

"See my Darwin tulips? They're doing just fine. The hyacinths should be up any day now. They're always slow in coming. They need some coaxing, but I don't push it. They come up when they're ready. I just wait."

I stare at my shoes.

"I'm good at waiting."

I can almost hear the smile in his voice. My heart wells up. He's a good man, a kind man. He's the best of the church, of what's right about the church. I take a deep breath. "Where were you when I was a teenager?"

Into my ear, he whispers, "Waukegan."

I burst into laughter.

"Exiled," he says, without rancor. "And where were you when you were a teenager?"

"Here."

"You went to school at OLPH? So, a long time ago, you were a good Catholic. Tell me, are we gonna get you back?"

"I don't think you want me back, Father."

"Of course we do! God loves us all. He forgives us all."

"Not me. Not this." I look up at the Virgin, but she won't look at me.

He slaps his knee. "Let's make a reconciliation! Right now."

"Confession? Here?"

"Why not?"

"There's no confessional. I can see you."

"Silly! Why do we have to sit in a telephone booth! In Waukegan, I performed many confessions face-to-face, although I'll admit I've never done one outdoors." He chuckles. "You don't need a booth for a confession, my dear. All you need is to examine your conscience. If you resolve not to sin in the future, confess, and accept your penance, you've reconciled yourself with God."

I search the eyes behind the bifocals. He makes it sound so easy, but I know it isn't. There are bodies on my back, big ones and little ones, and despite the kindness in his eyes, I understand that they're mine to bear. I can't confess, not to his blue eyes, not in the yellow sunshine, not before the white Virgin on the green grass. The colors are too dense here, like a child's box of crayons, and too painfully pretty. "God won't forgive me, Father."

"I'm sure that God already has, my dear. But I don't think you have forgiven yourself."

Suddenly, we're interrupted by a flock of apoplectic *mammarellas* in flowered housedresses. "Father Cassiotti! Father Cassiotti! Thank God we found you! The church door is locked, and the mass is in fifteen minutes! We can't get in!"

Their agitation rattles him. His hands shake as he reaches into his pocket and pulls out a jingling ring of keys. "My goodness, I'm sorry, ladies." He looks at me worriedly. "I have to go open the church. Will you excuse me?"

"I should be going anyway." I rise to my feet, uncertainly.

"No, please. Stay here. Please."

"Father, your flowers look so good!" chirps one of the women, grabbing Father Cassiotti by the elbow. "Look at them, Conchetta. So pretty!"

"It's a sin!" adds a second, taking his other arm.

They surge forward like a rugby team, pound for pound outweighing the little priest, and engulf him in their enthusiasm. They sweep him to the church like a winning coach, and all I can see of him is his bony hand in the air, bearing its janitor's key ring. I shout good-bye, and the key ring jingles back.

I decide to walk back to the office. It'll clear my head, and it would be impossible to find a cab down here anyway. I realize that Father Cassiotti is right: I have to forgive myself. But I don't know how, even so many years later. I head north toward the center of the city, leaving behind the blocks that measure my girlhood.

Once out of the neighborhood, I feel nervous again. The sun is white-hot, unseasonably so, and leaves me exposed on the bare sidewalks. My walk picks up to a run, and before I know it I'm hustling through the city blocks. I glance around for the dark sedan but keep moving, jogging past babies in strollers and teenagers hanging out on the corner.

I'm slowed by the busy lunchtime crowd at Pat's, a popular cheese-steak stand across from a playground. I thread my way through the crowd; a couple of the men in line look at me curiously. My armholes are wet underneath my blazer and blotches itch on my chest. I'm about to cross the street, still going north, when I see the figures.

About fifty feet away, at the edge of the basketball court, two big men are arguing. A crowd of basketball players and truants collects around the pair. Even at this distance, something about the men looks familiar.

I freeze when I recognize them.

It's Detective Lombardo. And Berkowitz.

TWENTY-THREE

I duck behind a minivan parked on Federal Street and watch them through its sooty windows. The argument escalates as Berkowitz gestures wildly, almost out of control. Suddenly, he drives his fist into Lombardo's cheek. Blood pours from the detective's nose. He cups it in pain, staggering backward.

Berkowitz eyes the crowd uneasily, then stalks off the court. The onlookers applaud as he climbs into his black Mercedes sedan, parked illegally at the curb, and drives away. Lombardo shuffles off in the opposite direction, cradling his nose. The crowd boos loudly. "Pussy!" they shout. "Hit 'em back, you dumb fuck!"

I draw a breath. It feels like the first one in five minutes. What the hell is going on? What are they doing, having a fight in the middle of South Philly? I remember what Lombardo said after the memorial service—that Berkowitz was very interested in the investigation. Is the investigation what they were fighting about? What else could it be, if not something having to do with Brent's death? And maybe even Mike's?

I'm scared, and Father Cassiotti's no help now. Apparently, neither are the police. I consider busting into Lombardo's office and demanding an explanation, or busting into Berkowitz's office and demanding an explanation, but who am I kidding? I'm not a gunslinger; I'm in way over my head. My first thought is to run, to get the hell out of Dodge, but where can I go? The only person I know who lives out of the city is Angie.

Angie!

In the convent, near Baltimore. The idea appeals to me immediately. I'll bang on the convent doors, pound them until they let me in. I'll say it's a family emergency, which it is, and they'll open the doors. They have to, they're a convent. What could be safer than a convent?

I look around for a phone and spot one back at Pat's. I walk over to it, trying not to break into a dead run in front of the noisy crowd of office workers and construction jocks. Almost as soon as I pick up the greasy receiver, a rangy black basketball player gets in line behind me to use it. Behind him comes a mailman. I reach Judy and tell her what I saw, shouting into the receiver over the crowd noise.

"He *punched* him?" Judy says. "What are they doing down there anyway? What are *you* doing down there?"

The basketball player makes a pleading face for the phone, and I give him a one-minute sign.

"I'm leaving the city, Judy. For the night, anyway."

"Where are you going?"

I can barely hear her. I put a finger in my free ear. "I was going to get the notes from Ned after lunch, but I can't. Will you call him and get them?"

"*Ned* has the notes? I was wondering where they were!"

"Keep them someplace safe, okay?"

The basketball player folds his hands in mock prayer.

"Judy, I have to go, somebody wants to use the phone. He's begging already."

"But where are you going to stay tonight? You can stay with me, you know that."

An old man in a mesh cap that says OLD FART gets in line for the phone behind the mailman.

"Thanks, but I got a better idea. Call you tomorrow." I hang up.

"Thanks a lot," the ballplayer says, tucking the basketball under his arm. "I got to call my girl. We had a fight, you know what I'm sayin'?"

"I think so."

I push through the crowd, looking for a cab. One should be around soon; Pat's is like a magnet. My blotches announce themselves with a vengeance. I worry about running into Lombardo, Berkowitz, or whoever's following me. My head is spinning. I spot a yellow cab and jump in, slumping down all the way in the seat. Partly from exhaustion, partly from fear.

The cab driver is a streetwise manchild in a backwards Phillies cap. He eyes me warily over his shoulder. "Look, lady, I don't want no trouble in my cab."

"There won't be. Please, I have to go to a garage at Twenty-second and Pine. My car's there. Can we just go?"

He shakes his head. "You don't look like the type to be running from the cops, but you're sure runnin' from somethin'."

"I am. I'm running from . . . my boyfriend. We had a fight."

He breaks into a knowing grin. "Man trouble."

I nod. "We have to get out of here. Fast."

"You got it, gorgeous." He flips down the flag and guns the motor. He runs two lights as he zips up Twenty-second Street. At the same time, he manages to give me unsolicited advice on my love life, delivered to a rapper's beat: Gotta make 'em beg for it, gotta make 'em want it, gotta make 'em show respect. We're at the garage by the time he shifts into, "Gotta shop around."

"Right. Listen, would you do me a favor, please? Just wait here for two minutes until you see me drive out?"

"Ain't no way he coulda followed me, lady. I was bookin'."

I hand him a tip the size of the fare.

"All right!" he says appreciatively.

"It's a green BMW."

"A BMW? I like it! Which one, the 325 or the 535?"

"The 2002, from before you were born. It's lime green, you can't miss it." I get out of the cab.

"You gotta pick and choose, remember that now."

In ten minutes, I'm making my way through the western part of the city to the Schuylkill Expressway. I almost have an accident from driving with one eye on the rearview mirror. No one appears to be following me, and when I pull onto the expressway I begin to breathe easier. The traffic is light, and I switch lanes a couple of times to see if anyone behind me does the same. It takes only a minute for me to realize that everybody else is switching lanes in a similarly haphazard way.

Which looks normal.

I hit warp speed in the car Mike lovingly called the Snotmobile and bust through the city limits like I'm breaking the sound barrier. After a time I satisfy myself that no one's on my tail, and I feel freer, safer. Like I'm not trapped anymore, by the city and by whoever's after me there. I roll down the window and snap on the radio. I recognize the husky bass voice as George Michael's, in the middle of "Father Figure." I love that song. I turn it louder.

I remember going to visit Angie, singing along to the radio while Mike drove this car. My parents trailed us in their Oldsmobile, which meant we pulled over every ten minutes for them to catch up. It didn't bother Mike that my father poked along so. Nothing really fazed him, he was like Judy that way. He loved life, truly. He let it wash over him.

I swing the peppy BMW onto Route 1 heading south, serenaded by Prince. Route 1, the old Baltimore Pike, is more direct to the convent than I-95. If I don't get lost, I'll be there by nightfall.

Angie entered the convent just after we graduated from Penn. I majored in English, she in religion. "What kind of job will you get with that major?" I asked when she chose it, but she answered with a shrug. When she finally told us, my parents were delighted, but I was appalled. I screamed at her, told her she was throwing her life away. My mother begged me to stop, my father merely shook. I ran from the house. My last look back was at Angie. She sat there, impassive behind her coffee, dead calm at the vortex of a familial hurricane.

The traffic on Route 1 moves swiftly, fluidly. I catch barely a light. A woman I don't recognize sings a ballad. My thoughts turn to the convent.

Angie's first year as a novitiate was my first year as a law student. She wasn't allowed visitors, telephone calls, or even mail. It was to be a test of her commitment to a religious life, and we heard nothing from her. I felt an almost unendurable loss, as if she were held hostage by religious fanatics, which was my take on the situation anyway. Outside the cloister, life went on. My mother's eyes deteriorated, my father gained twenty pounds. I made law review and learned to trust men again. With Mike's help.

The sad song ends abruptly, in silence.

Which was the worst thing about Angie's life in the cloister. Her vow of silence. How could they silence Angie, who was so full of talk, of ideas? I remembered the nights we gossiped in our room, the whispered jokes in class, the shouted jeers on the walk home. So much talk, so much language. English and Italian at home, French in school, Latin at mass. No more.

The traffic thins out, the stoplights are fewer. Madonna comes on, *thumpa thumpa thumpa*, and I turn off the radio with a satisfying *click*. I hate Madonna; she's even more confused about Catholicism than I am. I barrel through the rural stretches south of Media, past dairy cows and old barns. The odor of manure wafts through the air. I step on the gas.

After Angie's first year, we were permitted to see her. The visits—four a year—were held in a small room called the Parlor, and there was a wooden screen between us, almost like the lattice in a garden trellis. I wasn't able to touch her, and there was no privacy; the room was filled with the equally excited families of the other nuns. I found the visits an exercise in frustration. I couldn't talk to Angie about anything that mattered, couldn't reach her in any meaningful way at all, so the garden trellis might as well have been made of concrete. All I could do was watch us grow apart. Over the years, her face thinned out and her demeanor grew subdued. By the time she became a professed sister five years later, I felt I hardly knew her at all. I hugged her then, after the mass, and cried most of the way home.

I speed by farm after farm, and all I see for a long time are cows and billboards. WELCOME TO MARYLAND, says the sign when I cross the border. I wind slowly through Harford County, with its quaint farms and not-so-quaint trailer parks. The sun sets off to my left, behind a Bob's Big Boy. The car rumbles along quietly; my mind is a blank. The exit for the convent comes up. I twist the car off the highway, into a suburb near the convent. I forget the name of the town, but I recognize the landmarks. A housing development of fake English mews, then a housing development of fake French chateaux.

My anticipation sours slightly. I grow apprehensive. What if they won't let me stay? What if Angie's angry at me for coming? A hard ball begins to form in my chest. It seems to calcify as I drive by a diner where Mike and I ate lunch after he met Angie for the first time. I remember that lunch.

"I understand why you miss her so much," Mike said, fiddling with the top of a red squeeze bottle of ketchup. "It would mean a lot to me if she could be at our wedding."

"Our wedding?"

"Our wedding." He grinned and slid the ketchup bottle toward me. On the red cone of its lid hung a small diamond solitaire.

That was Mike's proposal, and I accepted, but Mike didn't get his wish. Angie wasn't allowed out of the cloister to go to his wedding.

They did let her go to his funeral, however.

TWENTY-FOUR

I walk alongside the convent's high stone wall until I find the front gate. It's an ancient iron gate, painted in a color impossible to determine in the twilight: forest green, maybe, or black. I can't see through the gate—it's opaque and reaches at least ten feet high, culminating in a crucifix. Of course.

Boom! Boom! I bang on the gate. Its bubbled paint flakes off. *Boom! Boom! Boom!*

Silence.

"Is anybody there? Can anybody let me in?"

More silence.

Boom! "Please, it's an emergency! Please!"

"Wait a minute," says a thin female voice on the other side. I hear the metallic clatter of a barrel latch being retracted, and the door opens a crack. One blue eye peers out from behind a rimless spectacle. I catch a glimpse of a white veil—a novitiate—whose face comes happily to life when she sees me. "You look exactly like one of my sisters!"

"Really?"

"Yes! Sister Angela Charles."

Her sister. I'll never get used to this. "Angela's my twin. I'm

Mary DiNunzio. I need to see her. It's a . . . family emergency."

The novitiate looks alarmed. "Oh, my. Well. Good thing I was out here. Come in, please." She yanks on the iron gate, grunting with effort. I push on the gate from the outside, but even with both of us laboring, it'll only open enough to let me through sideways. "Sorry about that," she says, with an easy laugh.

"That's okay. I appreciate your letting me in."

"No problem. Follow me. I'll tell Mother you're here." She bounces ahead of me, up a flagstone path that winds through the grass to the convent. Over a hundred years old, the convent's made of Brandywine granite and covered with lush ivy. If it weren't holding my twin sister captive, I'd say it was beautiful. The roof is terracotta tile, like the rooftops of Florence, and the arched windows are a stained glass that seems to glow with deep colors, radiating light from within on this dusky evening.

As we approach the front door, unmarked except for the Sacred Heart at its keystone, I can hear the nuns singing in the chapel. Their voices, forty in all, carry in the still night, floating over the lawn. One of the voices belongs to Angie. An alto, like me.

"In we go," says the novitiate, as she opens the carved oak door.

It's the smell that hits me first, the smell of holy water. It's a faint and sweet scent, vaguely like rosewater. The novitiate's breath smells of it too, and I wonder how this is so, or if I'm imagining it. I hear the singing, louder now that I'm inside, and we pass the closed chapel doors, over which is stenciled:

CHAPEL
DEDICATED TO ST. JOSEPH
RECOLLECTION

Angie is inside.

The novitiate leads me to the parlor. Above the door it says:

PARLOR
DEDICATED TO ST. L. GONZAGA
DISCRETION, MODESTY

The novitiate flicks on a lamp, which barely illuminates the room. "Please wait a minute while I tell Mother that you're here," she says.

"Thank you."

She closes the door, leaving me alone. The parlor looks larger now that it's empty, but it still evokes frustration in me. I sit among the vacant wooden chairs on the civilian side of the trellis, wondering how many twin sisters have sat here in the past century and if any of them felt like I do. The order used to be much more isolated, and Angie says there's talk of moving to a remote location in the Adirondacks. That's so far away I'd never get to see her. It makes me feel sick inside.

"Miss DiNunzio?" says the novitiate, back at the threshold. The singing intensifies with the open door. "Come with me. Mother is waiting to see you in her cabinet."

"Cabinet?"

"Office. Cabinet is the French term, but we still use it."

"Force of habit, huh?"

She smiles.

"I got a million of 'em."

I follow her down the bare, narrow hallway. The hardwood floors shine even in the dim light. The novitiate pads ahead softly; I clatter obscenely in my pumps. I look around the pale walls, reading the writing stenciled in black letters at the top. I HAVE A SAVIOR AND I TRUST IN HIM. I KNOW NOTHING SWEETER THAN TO MORTIFY AND CONQUER SELF. WALK BEFORE ME AND BE PERFECT.

The hallway ends in a white door, and the singing stops suddenly. This is the door that encloses the cloistered area. I live on the outside of it; Angie lives on the inside. Over the jamb it says:

GIVE GLORY TO THE LORD OF LORDS AND HIS
MERCY ENDURETH FOREVER.

It should say: POINT OF NO RETURN.

We pass through the door in silence. I take in everything as we go by, trying to imagine what Angie's daily life is like. We enter another hallway, also clean and spare, and come to a door on the left, over which is stenciled:

SUPERIORESS'S CABINET
DEDICATED TO OUR HOLY MOTHER
LONGANIMITY

"What does that mean?" I ask the novitiate. "Longan . . ."

"It's a toughie, isn't it? Longanimity. It means forbearance. This is your stop. Mother will be along in a minute. You can have a seat in her office."

"Thank you."

"Sure thing," she says and pads off.

I sit down in a hard mission chair across from a desk so clean it could be for sale. The office is empty and bare, except for a two-tier set of bookshelves and an old black rotary phone. The tinny fixture in the ceiling casts a dim pool of light over the desktop. My chest tightens around the ball at its core. I can't shake the feeling that I'm back in school, waiting in the principal's office to answer for some sin. Like an abortion.

Suddenly, with a *whoosh* of her thick habit, the Mother Superior enters the office. She's tall, bone-thin, and at least seventy-five years old. There are deep wrinkles etched into her face, which contrast with the starchy smoothness of her guimpe, the cloth covering her neck and shoulders. A heavy sterling crucifix swings from a pin in her habit. "Ah, yes, Miss

DiNunzio," she says. "You look more like Sister Angela Charles every day."

I rise and smile. It occurs to me that this is a variant of pop-up-and-grin. "I'm sorry to barge in, but I need to see my sister. It's a family emergency."

"So I understand. I have sent for Sister Angela." The tall nun sits down, very erect, in a wooden chair. "Please, sit." She waves me into the chair with a bony hand.

There's a soft rapping at the door. "Come in," says the Mother Superior. The door opens, and it's Angie.

"Angie!" I blurt out happily. At the sight of her, the hardness in my chest breaks up, like ice floes on the prow of a tanker.

Angie looks guarded. "Yes, Mother?"

"Sister Angela, I understand there is an emergency."

Angie's eyes widen with fear as she turns to me. "Pop? Is it Pop?"

"No, Angie. Not Pop. They're both fine."

Her shoulders relax visibly. She steps into the room and closes the door quietly behind her. "What's the matter?"

I glance at the Mother Superior. "Is it possible for me to speak with my sister alone?"

The Mother Superior purses her lips, which are so thin that they're merely a vertical wrinkle. I wonder fleetingly if my mother ever noticed them. "As you know, we frown upon in-terruptions of this sort."

Suddenly Angie finds her voice, earnest and just a touch de-fiant. "I'm sure it's important, Mother, or my sister wouldn't have come."

"It's true." The story tumbles out, vaguely crazed. "I think someone is stalking me, I'm not sure who. They killed my sec-retary."

"Mary, no!" exclaims Angie.

The Mother Superior blinks in surprise; her crow's feet deepen. "Have you called the police?"

"I think the police are involved somehow. I really need to talk to Angie—and stay the night. Just tonight—please?"

Angie looks nervously from me to the Mother Superior.

"Considering your circumstances, you're welcome to do so, although I'm not sure it will alleviate your plight in the long run. I will return to Chapel and will expect you in due course, Sister Angela."

"Thank you, Mother," says Angie. She bows her head as the Mother Superior passes out through the door.

"Thank you," I say. As soon as she closes the door, I rush over to Angie. She hugs me back and I cling to her, not wanting to let go. I feel whole again. "I missed you!" I say into a mouthful of lightweight wool.

"What's going on, Mary?"

I tell her everything, in fits and starts. She listens. She touches my face. She's worried for me. She loves me still. I feel happy, and so safe. When I'm finished, she leaves and tells me she'll be right back.

But the next time the door opens, it's the Mother Superior. "Come with me, please, Miss DiNunzio," she says. She reaches into the desk for a flashlight. The oak drawer closes with a harsh sliding sound.

"Where's my sister?"

"She's completing her prayers. I'm sure you'll be in them tonight. Please follow me quietly. We have a room for you in the retreatants' area. The rest of the convent is fast asleep." She flicks on the flashlight, pointing it toward the floor, and leaves the room.

I follow her into the corridor, feeling like a kid late to a scary movie. The lights seem even dimmer than they were before, but I realize it's just gotten darker outside. We walk down one bare corridor after the next, past closed door after closed door. Over each is a stenciled description:

WORK ROOM
DEDICATED TO ST. JOSEPH
SILENCE

KITCHEN
DEDICATED TO ST. MARTIN
RECOLLECTION

REFECTORY
DEDICATED TO ST. BERNARD
MORTIFICATION

ASSISTANT'S OFFICE
DEDICATED TO OUR LADY
RETIREMENT

The Mother Superior moves quickly for a woman her age, sweeping from side to side like a whisk broom. I hustle to keep up with her as we climb a creaky staircase and walk past a series of doors that have no descriptions above them. They stretch down a long corridor as it veers off to the left. Beside each door hangs a clothes brush on a hook. "What are these rooms?" I ask.

"The sisters' cells," says the Mother Superior, without looking back.

I wonder which one is Angie's but decide not to ask. At the top of the wall it says, YOU CANNOT BE A SPOUSE OF JESUS CHRIST BUT INASMUCH AS YOU CRUCIFY YOUR INCLINATIONS, YOUR JUDGMENT, AND YOUR WILL TO CONFORM YOURSELVES TO HIS TEACHINGS. I stumble, reading the long inscription.

"Watch your step," says the Mother Superior. I gasp. *Watch your step, Mary.*

She whirls around on her heel. "Are you all right? Did you trip?"

"No. Uh, I'm fine."

"You're safe here, dear. You have nothing to worry about tonight." She strides past a library and an infirmary, both dedicated to saints I've never heard of, as well as virtues I have. She stops before a door and opens it. In the half-light I see a single bed and a spindly night table. "It's not the Sheraton, but it's not meant to be," she says, with a slight smile.

"Thank you. I really am grateful."

"Don't be too grateful, we rise at five. Sleep well." She leaves and shuts the door behind her.

It plunges me into pitch blackness. I can't see the bed in the dark. I wait for my eyes to adjust, but they don't. I stumble in the darkness, then find the bed's thin coverlet with my hands. I crawl onto the mattress, feeling safe and exhausted, and drift into sleep.

The next thing I know, my shoulder's being touched. I look up, blinking in the gloom. There's a shadow standing over me. Suddenly, a hand covers my mouth.

"It's me, you idiot." Angie removes her hand.

"Jesus, you scared me!"

"Shhh! Whisper. I'm supposed to be asleep." Angie flicks on a flashlight and sets it down like a lamp on the night table. She's still dressed in her habit, and her silver crucifix catches the light.

"Do you sleep in that getup?" I whisper hoarsely.

"I had Hours."

"What's that?"

"Nighttime prayers. I had from three to four o'clock."

"You mean you wake up in the middle of the night to pray?"

"We pray all night, in shifts."

"Are you serious?" Something in me snaps at the thought of these poor women—my twin included—praying all night long for a world that doesn't even know they exist. "What's the point of that? It makes no sense."

"Shhh!"

"It's crazy! It's just plain crazy, don't you see that?"

"Mary, whisper!"

"Why should I? You're an adult and I'm an adult and it's a free country. Why can't I talk to my own twin?"

"Mary, please. If you don't whisper, I'll leave." She looks grave, and her mouth puckers slightly. I know that pucker. My mother's, when she means business.

"All right, I'll whisper. Just tell me what kind of place this is. They don't let you talk. They don't let you out. They barely let you see your family. And these sayings on the walls, it's like a cult! They cut you off from the world and they brainwash you."

"Mary, please. Do we have to fight?"

"It's not a fight, it's a discussion. Can't we just discuss it? I'm whispering!"

She sighs. "It's not a cult, Mary. It's a different way of life. A contemplative way of life. A religious life. It's just as valid as the way you live."

"But it's a lie. A fiction. They pretend they're your family, but they're not. She's not your mother and they're not your sisters."

"You sound jealous."

"I am, I admit it! Mea culpa, sister. Mea culpa—*Sister*." Angie looks hurt.

"I'm sorry, but this makes me nuts! I'm your sister, your twin. I know you, Angie, like I know myself. And I agree with you. This is a perfectly valid way to live, but not for you." I search her round brown eyes, identical to mine. We're mirror images as we face one another in the tight cell.

"I'm here for a reason," she whispers. "You just can't accept that."

"Maybe if I understood it, I could accept it."

"You won't try."

"Give me a chance. I'm smarter than I look. What's the reason?"

"To serve God. To live a spiritual life."

"I don't believe you."

Angie averts her eyes but doesn't say anything.

"I believe it from the others, but not from you."

Still she says nothing.

"Why don't you talk? You hate silence. You love to talk."

She lifts her head abruptly. "No, Mary, *you* love to talk."

"So do you!"

"No." She points at me. "I am not you. We look the same. We sound the same. But *I am not you*." Her lips tremble.

"I know that, Angie."

"You do? Are you sure?"

"Sure I'm sure."

"What makes you so sure? What? How do you know?" She doesn't pause for my answer but says softly, "As kids, we dressed the same. We wore our hair the same. We had the same favorite sandwich—bologna with mustard on white. We got duplicate presents on our birthday and at Christmas. We went to the same schools. We sat next to each other in the same classes, all our lives."

"So?"

"So who are you, Mary? And who am I?" Angie's tone is almost desperate. "Where do you end and I begin?"

My heart fairly breaks with the revelation. "Is *that* what this is about?"

"I need to think. I need to find out."

"But it's been so long, Angie! The prime of your life! Can't you find out on the outside?"

"I tried to, but I couldn't." She shakes her head sadly. "I couldn't as long as you were around, and Mom and Pop. And I love you all. I want you all to be happy." She shudders with the force of a hoarse sob.

I feel an anguish so deep it hurts. Now that I understand what she's asking, I know the convent is no answer. And I know because I've asked the same question. I have to get her out, to convince her. I prepare to make the most important oral argument of my life. For the life of my sister.

"Angie, I didn't know who I was either, until I *lived*. Graduated. Met Mike, lost Mike. I got knocked around and twisted every which way. Things happened to me I've never told you about. Bad things, good things, too. Those things helped me find out who I am. They made me who I am. It's life, Angie. You don't figure it out before you live it. It takes living it to figure it out."

She's crying softly, but she's listening.

"Angie, you don't have to hide yourself to find yourself!"

Suddenly the door bursts open. It's the Mother Superior, whose slash of a mouth sets grimly when she discovers Angie. "Sister Angela. To Lauds."

Angie springs from my embrace and backs away.

"Angie!" I shout, my arms empty.

But Angie runs from me, and the sound of her footfalls disappears into silence.

TWENTY-FIVE

I dress before dawn in the quiet little cell. The shadows are a purple-gray, but now at least I can see around me. Not that there's much to see. There's no stenciling on the wall, and the night table is bare on top. The bed looks like a child's bunk bed, maybe donated from one of the families, and the white coverlet that felt so scratchy last night has fuzzy tufts of cotton scattered over it. Behind the table is a rectangular window. I slip into my shoes and look outside.

I think it's the back yard of the convent, but I can't orient myself. I know I've never seen it before. Huge oak trees climb to my window and even higher; some of them look a century old. Their thick branches block the view of what's beneath them, but if I tilt my head I can see down below: a grouping of white crosses, set in rows. There are about fifty of them, white as bleached bones. It takes me a minute to realize what I'm seeing.

A cemetery.

I never thought about that. I never knew. Of course, it makes sense. The nuns who live here are buried here, in rows of crosses, like at Verdun, or Arlington.

Will Angie be buried here? I can't quite believe it. Even in death, would she stay here? I draw away from the window.

There's a soft knock at the door. "Mary, are you awake?" whispers a voice. Angie's.

I cross to the door and open it.

Angie's face looks pale, almost pasty against the raven-colored habit. There are dark circles under her eyes; I know they match mine. "You didn't sleep either, huh?" I ask.

She puts a finger to her lips. "Mother says we may take a short walk together before you go," she whispers. "Follow me."

So I do. She leads me down hallway after hallway, like the Mother Superior did last night. I have to admit that the convent looks better in the daylight. The hardwood floors that seemed dark last night are in fact a golden honey tone, a high-quality pine, and they reflect the morning light. The walls are pure white, without a scuff mark on them. The sayings seem less bizarre too, once you get over the shock of phrases like MORTIFICATION OF THE FLESH in ten-inch letters. But I keep thinking of the cemetery in the back. Tucked away, like a secret.

We head down a flight of spiral stairs that appears to be at a corner of the convent. I don't remember going up them last night. They're narrow and there's no rail, so I run my hand along the wall as we wind down them like a nautilus shell. Angie holds a tiny door for me at the bottom. I have to stoop to pass through it.

And then we're in paradise. The door opens onto a lush garden, with a skinny brick path outlining it in the shape of a heart. The path's border is marked by low-lying plants with rich olive-colored leaves, thriving even in the shade of the pin oaks. A row of flowers grows behind the row of plants, dotting the perimeter with blossoms of pink, yellow, and white. Behind them are rosebushes, one after another, just beginning to bud. The effect is something like an old-fashioned floral valentine.

"Wow!" I say.

Angie pushes the door closed in a businesslike way and moves aside a stack of clay pots. "Thank you."

"You did this?"

She blushes. "I shouldn't take all the credit." She steps into the garden and stands at the point of the heart. "I designed it."

I follow her. "When? How? What do we know about gardens? We're city kids."

She smiles, and her face relaxes. "Which question do you want me to answer first?"

"Pick one."

"Well, I designed it about five years ago. Mother felt we needed a garden, a place for quiet contemplation. The shape, obviously, is the Sacred Heart."

"Obviously."

Angie glances back at me. "You haven't forgotten everything, have you?"

"I've tried, Lord knows I've tried."

She suppresses a smile. "Let's take a walk. There's a bench at the top where we can sit down." She leads me up the path, slipping both hands into the sleeves of her habit, like the nuns did at school.

"So tell me how you did this. It's wonderful."

"It wasn't hard. We have a library here. I read about the types of flowers. Perennials. Annuals. What grows in shade, what doesn't." Angie looks up at the sky. "I think we'll get some sun today. Good."

"You can get out the sun reflector like you used to."

She stops on the path and shakes her head. "I can't believe we actually did that. A sun reflector, of all things. With only baby oil for protection. What were we thinking?"

"We were thinking we wanted to look good. What all teenage girls think. Burn off those zits."

"Stop." She bumps me with her shoulder. "Look here. These are my favorites." She nods in the direction of a group of white flowers. The stems stand about two feet high and are covered with what appears to be soft white bells. They nod gracefully in the slight breeze.

"They're beautiful. What are they?"

She bends over and cups a dimpled bell in her fingertips. "Campanula. Bellflower. Aren't they lovely? They need some sun, but they don't like too much. Most of the varieties bloom in the summer. I have those on the north side of the heart. But this little baby, this is an early version. Aren't you, sweetie?" she coos comically into the upturned face of the flower.

"The vow of silence doesn't extend to flowers, huh?"

"Why do you think they grow so well?" Angie says, and we both laugh.

"That's the first time you ever made a joke about this place, you know."

She straightens up. "Don't start, Mary."

"All right, all right."

"Come on, let's go. We don't have much time." She walks briskly toward a weathered wooden bench. She seems more energetic than when she first met me this morning.

"You love this garden, don't you?"

"Yes." She sits down on the bench. "Step into my office," she says.

I sit down obediently.

"Look over there." She points to the right of the bench, where mounds of trailing green vines make a glossy carpet. "You know what that is?"

"Free parking?"

"No, wise guy. I planted it in our honor. It's Italian bell-flower."

"I love it. Goombah foliage."

She looks over at the vines. "They're hard to grow. They're like you, stubborn. I couldn't get them to come up last year. But they're lovely when they do. I saw them in a picture." Her gaze is suddenly far away.

"What do they look like?"

"Little stars. Little bell-shaped stars. They call them Star-of-Bethlehem." She keeps looking far away. I wonder what she's looking at, what she's thinking about. I follow her gaze over the garden, past the statue of some saint. I can't see anything after that, except the wrought-iron crucifix on top of the gate.

"Remember when we used to read each other's minds?" I ask her.

She doesn't answer.

"What are you looking at, Ange?"

"The other side."

"The other side of what?"

"The other side of the rose garden. On the other side is our new gazebo. Have you seen it?" She squints, as if she were trying to see through the roses.

"No."

"It's lovely. It's made from the lightest wood, a blond color. Inside are statues of the Sacred Heart and the Immaculate Heart, both hand carved in Italy. Hand painted, too. The statues gave me the idea for the garden." She pauses a minute. "The statues are in the middle of the floor, and there's a skylight over the top. When the sun shines in, the whole room glows. The light inside is remarkable. It's full." Angie looks at me. Her eyes are bright. "Do you understand what I mean, that light can be *full?* Can you see that?"

I swallow hard. "You're never going to leave this place, are you?"

Angie smiles. "You're not a very good listener, you know that?"

"I'm a lawyer. We don't get paid to listen. We get paid to talk."

"But no one's paying you now."

"No, no, you're right. No one's paying me now." It's my turn to look past the roses.

"So. I was up last night, thinking about what you said and

other things." She folds her hands neatly in her lap. She seems tense again.

"I didn't mean to upset you, hurt you. It's just that I don't want you here, Angie. I saw the cemetery out back. I don't want you here then and I don't want you here now."

"I understand that."

"I really think—"

"I know what you think. You want me to go out there." She nods over the garden to the gate beyond.

"Right."

"Because you think it's better than here. Than this lovely place." Her brown eyes move over the bright flowers of the garden.

"Not that it's better. Just that it's real. It's the real world, and you have to deal with it. You can't just ignore it. Run away from it."

"No? Why not?"

"What do you mean why not?"

"Why not?"

"Because you have to live in it. Because you learn by dealing with it, by coping with it. We're strong, Angie. Mom and Pop raised us that way. They taught us that we can deal with whatever comes our way. I know you can resolve what you have to on the outside. I just know it."

"Do you think it's important for me to do that?"

"More than important. Vital."

She pauses. "Is it important for you to do that?"

I shrug. "Sure."

"I see. Well, then, may I ask you a question?"

"Shoot."

"Why are you here?"

I look at her. She looks back. My eyes narrow, then hers. Identically.

"What?" I ask.

"Why are you here?"

"I don't know what you mean."

"It's fairly obvious, isn't it? If what you're saying is true, then why are you here? Why did you run to the convent, from the vast and wonderful outside world?"

I have no answer for this. It doesn't seem like a fair question.

"You tell me there are dangerous people out there, stalking you. They send you notes. They enter your apartment when you're not there. They might have *killed* your secretary. Your *husband*." Her pained look flickers across her face. "You believe these things to be true."

"I do."

"So leaving aside the question of why anybody in her right mind would ever choose such a place as that over such a place as this, why was your first impulse to come here? Not even to call somebody else in the police department, somebody other than this Lombardo. But to come to a convent."

"I didn't come to a convent, Angie, I came to you. If you were in Camden, I would have gone to Camden."

"But what can *I* do? I'm a nun. I have no money, no power, no resources. I don't own a single thing, not even this garden. How can I help you?"

"By seeing me. By listening to me." I rub my forehead. "I don't get it. Why are you saying this?"

"I saw you. I listened to you. Now it's the next morning and you have to leave. You have to go beyond the walls, into the world of wonderful and terrifying things. Into *your* world, where two people close to you have been killed. And what are you going to do? What are you going to do?"

I look at her, suddenly crushed, and not understanding why.

"You see, Mary, this is very hard for me." She folds her hands again in her lap. "Because I have to let you go out there, into the world you love so much, into the world you ran from. I have to let you go. But I don't see you reaching within yourself to deal with this situation, one that threatens your very life."

I look at her wide-eyed.

"How am I supposed to let you go out there, when all I can do is pray to God to protect you and I don't see you doing anything at all to protect yourself?" Her lips look parched, her expression pained. "You said we could handle anything, and I've always thought that of you, though not of myself. Can you handle this?"

"I . . . don't know."

She looks away, quiet for a minute. "You're right about one thing. You know that light I was telling you about? That I said was full?"

"Yes."

"Well, I never will leave it. I can't. It's inside me. In here." She touches her chest with a slim hand. "Do you understand?"

I nod, yes, but she isn't watching.

"It has a kind of substance to it, it's tangible to me. It guides me, and I follow it like a river. It's what I dip into when I need to know the answer. For me, it's my faith in God." Angie turns to me. "What is inside of you, Mary?"

I shake my head. "I don't know."

"Think."

"Ever since Mike—"

She holds up a finger. "No. No. No man can give it to you. Not Mike, and not this other man. No one else can give it to you. It's inside you. It's there already."

"You think?"

"I know. Isn't that what you told me last night?"

"I guess so."

"See? I listen," she says, with a smile.

Suddenly, the chapel bells peal loudly, *bong, bong, bong*, in some indeterminant hymn. Angie turns toward the sound. "I have to go." She looks worriedly back at me. "Do you see what I'm trying to tell you?"

"Yes."

She begins to rise. "I have to let you go now, and I have to know you'll be all right if I do. I was never worried about you before, Mary, but now I am. I prayed all night for you, prayed to God to keep you safe." Her eyes are brimming with tears.

I stand up and hug her tight. "Read my mind," I whisper into her habit.

"I know. You love me," she says, her voice choked.

"Right. Want me to read your mind?"

"No." She hugs me tighter.

"You love me too."

The chapel bells fall silent as suddenly as they commenced. She braces me by the shoulders. Her wet eyes search my face.

"I'll be okay, Ange."

"You swear?"

"On a stack of Bibles."

She laughs and wipes a cheek on her sleeve. "Swear on something else. Something *you* believe in."

I give her a quick hug. "Have faith. Now go."

"Do you know how to get out of here?"

"Do you?"

Angie rolls her eyes. "I have to go. The gate's over that way. Take care of yourself."

"I will."

She kisses my cheek, then runs off toward the convent. Midway down the garden path, she gathers her skirt into her hands so she can run faster.

"Way to go!" I call after her.

She looks back with a sly smile. Then off she runs, with her veil flying and her black wool leggings churning away.

TWENTY-SIX

Clouds of steam billow around me. The water superheats my skin. My blood pumps faster; my thoughts flow like quicksilver. I'm taking a steaming hot shower in Stalling's locker room on the second floor, Anger.

How perfect.

I'm angry at myself, for rolling over like a puppy for whatever devil is out there, trying to hurt me. But no longer.

Angie was right. I preached to her to face life, but when I got scared, I ran too. But like Brent says, that was then and this is now. I had an epiphany as I drove back to the city, hurtling into a cloudless dawn on a Route 1 empty of travelers. I found my river, but its source sure as hell isn't my faith in God. And it doesn't flow with holy water, but with something closer to bile, at least right now. Whatever it is that drives me, it's why I became a lawyer in the first place. Every day on my job I fuck back professionally for Stalling's clients, and I like it. Well, I've decided it's time to start fucking back for myself. I'm not going to run for my life anymore, I'm going to fight for it.

I twist off the water and step dripping out of the shower. I towel off and slip into a white linen dress that I keep in my locker. I dry my hair quickly, ignoring the blotches aflame on my chest. I unlock the locker room door and head for my office.

The big clock stares at me. 7:56. I stare right back. Lying abandoned on my desk is Ned's bouquet of roses. They're wilted, but still holding their perfume. I take a deep breath and toss them into the wastebasket. I try not to look back as I pick up the telephone receiver and punch in the numbers from the Rolodex. It turns out that Detective Lombardo answers his own phone.

"How's your nose this morning, Lombardo?"

"Who is this?"

"Mary DiNunzio, remember me? The crazy widow? The one you tried to convince it's all in her head? I saw Berkowitz clean your clock, Lombardo, and I want to know why."

"Mary, jeez. It's not . . . you gotta ask Sam, I can't say any more."

"Bullshit."

"It's confidential."

"What about this investigation could possibly be confidential from me? Brent was my friend. Mike was my husband."

"Let me get my jacket off, okay? I just got in. Christ, you're worse than that Amazon you sent over."

"Amazon?"

"Your friend Carrier. She came in here last night and read me the riot act. What is it, you both on the rag?"

My blood boils over. "You got a house, Lombardo? A car? You like your job? Your pension?"

"What?"

"So how come you didn't investigate this matter when I first made a report?"

"What are you talkin' about, Mary? You never made a report!"

"The hell I didn't, you must've lost it. So it's your word against mine. Which would you believe—that the young widow is a filthy liar or that a city employee lost a form? Please. It's not even close."

"You would—"

"My memory is crystal clear. I came down to the station. We met. I told you about the car that was following me and my secretary. The next day he's dead, hit by the same car I warned you about. You ever been sued, Lombardo?"

"What's this all—"

"You were negligent, pal. You denied me my civil rights. I'm gonna take your shitty little house and your car. I'll garnish every paycheck you ever get."

"Don't you threaten me!"

"I'll make your life a living hell. I know how to do it, you understand? It's my job. I'm a lawyer."

"Now wait a minute—"

"Brent was gay, maybe that's why you didn't investigate. You can always tell, that's what you said. And something else, something about your brother being 'light in the loafers.' I love that colloquial stuff. It'll look so good in the complaint. It lends realism, don't you agree?"

"You're crazy!"

"A line like that, could be the newspapers will pick it up. In fact, why leave it to chance? I'll send them a copy of the complaint—maybe ten copies, to play it safe."

"I don't have to listen to this."

"Yes, you do. You do have to listen, Lombardo, and you will if you're smart. What I need from you is protection. Low-profile confidential protection from whoever's trying to hurt me. I want you to do your job, so I can do mine. I want you to watch me at Stalling—"

"Now how am I gonna do that?" he explodes. "They'd recognize me. I couldn't pass for a lawyer!"

"Put somebody else on the inside. You figure it out."

"You're safe at work. Everyone's around."

"Waters is here, Lombardo. If he's the one—"

"Oh, this is rich! Change your mind about your boyfriend?"

"I'm taking no chances. You have to watch me here."

"No way. I'll cover you on the outside, but that's it! I'll put my buddy on Waters—on the outside. You call me on the beeper when you leave and when you go in. You work only during business hours, when everyone's around. Your Amazon friend, you stay with her. After work, you go straight home. You got it? For three days."

"Two weeks."

"Four days."

"Ten days."

"Seven," Lombardo says, finally. "That's it. That's all I'm doing. I'll be damned if I'll put a tail on every nervous Nellie in this city! *Goddamned!*"

"Did you just cuss? In front of a lady?"

"I gotta go. I got a real job to do."

"Not so fast. I need something else."

"Jesus."

"Information. Those files you told me about, the ones on Mike and Brent. Where are they now?"

"AID has 'em. I shipped 'em back. But you can't get 'em."

"Why not? They should be public record."

"Not when the investigations are open. They're not gonna give you an open file. Brent has all my notes, all the investigation notes, what leads they're following—"

"That's why I want it."

"You can't get it."

"I appreciate the vote of confidence."

"Seven days, Mary. That's it."

"And this is confidential, Lombardo. That we talked, that I'm investigating the files. All of it. I don't want Berkowitz or anybody else at this firm to know about it. Understand?"

"I have better things to do."

"Thank you. And have a happy day."

Lombardo hangs up with a bang.

I hang up and exhale. So far, so good. While I'm still on a roll, I pick up the receiver and punch in four numbers.

"Mr. Berkowitz's office," Delia says.

"Hi, Delia, it's Mary. Is he in yet?"

She hesitates. "Come on up."

I bound up the stairs to Pride. Delia isn't at her desk when I stalk to Berkowitz's office, but the door is open slightly. I grit my teeth and burst in. And come face to face with the Honorable Morton A. Weinstein, the Honorable William A. Bitterman, and the Honorable Jeremy M. Van Houten, all of whom are sitting directly across from Berkowitz and looking rather startled.

"Oh . . . my Oh."

"Mary! Why don't you come in and meet some of the hardworking members of the Rules Committee?" Berkowitz says heartily, as if I were expected. The three judges rise to their feet. In fact, they're popping up and grinning, for me.

Bitter Man, the closest, grasps my hand with clammy fingers. "I know Miz DiNunzio, Sam. She was my research assistant on that article I published on federal court jurisdiction. I believe I sent you a reprint. It was in the *Yale Law Journal*."

Berkowitz nods sagely. "I remember, Bill." He has no idea what Bitter Man is talking about.

"In fact, I bet I know more about Miz DiNunzio than you do," Bitter Man says.

"Oh, really?"

"I know she's an alto, for example. Quite a good alto at that. Am I right, Miz DiNunzio? An alto?" Bitter Man's puffy lips break into a cynical smile.

I nod. You asshole.

"You mean like in singing?" Berkowitz asks. "How do you know that, Bill?"

My chest erupts into prickly blotches.

"I don't know if I should say, Sam. Should it remain our little secret, Miz DiNunzio?"

Einstein steps in to save me, his distaste for Bitter Man evident. "Don't let Brother Bitterman get to you, Ms. DiNunzio. We can dress him up, but we can't take him out. You and I met just the other day, didn't we? On the *Hart* case?" He clasps my hand warmly.

"Yes, Your Honor."

"You made a nice point in a tough spot."

Berkowitz places a heavy arm around my shoulders. His pinstriped jacket reeks of cigarette smoke. "I'm not surprised, Morton. Mary is one of our finest young lawyers."

I try to edge away from Berkowitz, blushing deeply. It erupts at my hairline and rushes straight down my chest, like lava down a volcano. I feel awkward and confused. I want to fuck back at him, but he's co-opting the shit out of me. Anger is almost elbowed out of the way by Pride.

"Have you met Judge Van Houten, Mary?" Berkowitz says, giving my shoulders another squeeze. "He was appointed to the bench last year to replace Judge Marston."

"I'm the rookie," quips Van Houten, shaking my hand with a self-assured grin. His features are small and even, and his hair is as smooth and tawny as butterscotch. Good-looking, if you go for those Ken types. Judy calls him Golden Rod, because the scuttlebutt is that he gets around. Now I see why. "We were just discussing the issue of note-taking by jurors," he says. "It's the sort of thing that gets the academics all excited."

"At least something does," says Berkowitz, with a loud laugh. He slaps me on the back so hard I expect my contacts to take flight. Golden Rod thinks this is a real hoot too.

Einstein looks at them with tolerance over his little half-glasses. "You see, Mary, we conducted a survey to determine the bar's view on the practice of note-taking by jurors. Unfortunately, we're having a tough time coming up with a conclusion, because the findings were so diverse."

"What a surprise," Bitter Man says.

Einstein ignores him. "We have a meeting with the chief

judge at noon today, so we should have learned something by then."

"We learned one thing, right, gentlemen? Next time—don't ask!" Berkowitz explodes into laughter and so does Golden Rod.

Bitter Man shifts uncomfortably in his chair. "Miz DiNunzio, why don't you share with us your view of the practice? Do you think jurors should be permitted to take notes during trial?"

The question catches me off guard. "I . . . uh . . ."

Einstein scoffs. "Come on, Bill, you're not going to cross-examine her, are you? Court's adjourned, for God's sake."

I look stupidly from Bitter Man to Einstein, waiting to see if I'm to perform. There's so much tension between them, I don't want to take sides.

"Now, Morton, don't underestimate the woman," Berkowitz says. "I'm sure she has an opinion. Don't you, Mary?"

The three judges look at me expectantly. I do have an opinion, but it might not be the right opinion, which is Berkowitz's. A week ago I would have avoided the question, but that was before I became the New Me. Now I say what I really think, possibly committing career hara-kiri:

"I think they shouldn't. It distracts them. Their job is to hear the evidence and the testimony, then do a sort of rough justice."

Einstein smiles.

Golden Rod smiles.

And, most importantly, Berkowitz smiles.

Yes!

"They don't know shit from Shinola," mutters Bitter Man.

"That's my girl!" Berkowitz says. "We report that Mary Di-Nunzio thinks jurors should not be permitted to take notes during trial. Now we can get on to more important subjects."

"Like golf," says Golden Rod. They all laugh, except for Bitter Man.

I seize the moment to back toward the door. "It was a pleasure seeing all of you. I'd better get back to my office."

"Back to the yoke, eh?" says Golden Rod. "Just slip it on and go plodding around in a circle."

Berkowitz laughs. "Watch it, Jeremy. We don't want an insurrection. See you later, Mary."

"Sounds good," I say casually, like I'm not at the man's beck and call. I close the door and allow the mask to slip. I feel disgusted at myself. I was bought off too easily. And I still don't know why Berkowitz was meeting with Lombardo, much less why he slugged him.

Delia's not at her desk when I leave, and I'm sure it's no accident. She would want to evade my very important question: Why did you set me up? I wonder about this on the way to the elevator, swimming upstream against the lawyers and secretaries flooding into Stalling to start the day. I stop down on Judy's floor before I go back to my office.

Judy's in the middle of her Zen-like brief-writing ritual. The trial record, marked with yellow Post-Its, is stacked on her left, Xerox copies of cases are stacked on her right, and a lone legal pad occupies the middle of a newly immaculate desk. Judy slams down her thick pencil when she sees me. "Mary, I was worried about you! Everybody was worried about you. Where'd you go last night?"

"Angie's convent." I flop into the chair facing her desk.

"Christ!"

"Exactly."

"Tell me about it." She leans forward, but I wave her off.

"Did you get the notes from Ned?" I ignore the pang when I say his name.

"Yepper. I saw Lombardo, too."

"So I heard." We trade Lombardo stories. She applauds after mine.

"You got protection! What a good idea!"

"I know. You're smarter than I am, why didn't you think of it?"

She smiles. "You'd still better stick with me when you're in the office, like Lombardo said."

"That shouldn't be too hard. We're together all the time anyway."

"Right. So how are you going to get the files?"

"I can't subpoena them until I start suit, and I can't start suit yet because Lombardo won't protect me."

"Start suit? Who are you gonna sue?"

"The police department. Maybe the city."

"Are you serious? For what?"

"I haven't figured it out yet. It doesn't matter. The complaint will be one page of civil rights bullshit, I only need it to be able to get the files. I'll withdraw it as soon as I do."

She nods. "Quite a plan."

"And that's only Plan B, the fallback. Plan A is me going down to AID and convincing them to give me the files. As the widow. I'll get the documents sooner that way, if they'll go for it."

"What do you think you'll find in the files?"

"The killer, ultimately. But for starters I want to see what similarities there are between Brent's case and Mike's. I'm going to try to get the other two files on open fatals too. Who knows what will turn up? It's like any other case."

"And you're the client."

"No. Brent is. And Mike."

She looks concerned. "Are you going to be able to do this? Emotionally, I mean?"

"If you're asking me do I look forward to reading those files, the answer is no. But I have to."

"Okay," Judy says, with a sigh. "Let me know what AID says on the phone, okay? I'll go down with you. We can go through the files together."

"Thanks, but you look busy enough. Very industrious, with the clean desk and all. What are you working on?"

She picks up her pencil. "The *Mitsuko* brief. If this argument's accepted, it'll make new law in the Third Circuit." Judy tells me about her argument with the degree of detail that most people reserve for their children or their dreams the night before. She loves the law. I guess it's her river.

Later, as I climb the busy stairwell to my office, what Judy said begins to sink in. I can't imagine sitting at my desk reading the police file on Mike's death or Brent's. Open fatals, my husband and my friend. I'm kidding myself that it's just like any other case. It's harder than any other case, but it's also more important. I'll call AID when I get back to my office. Maybe I can get a meeting this morning.

But when I reach Gluttony, Miss Pershing is pacing in front of her desk in an absolute panic. "My goodness, where have you been? You didn't come back yesterday the whole day, and you didn't call! I left messages on your machine. I even tried your parents, but they didn't know where you were. Now they're waiting upstairs in the reception area for the deposition!"

"Who is? What deposition?"

"Your parents, they're waiting."

"My parents are upstairs?"

"They're very worried. They wanted to see you the moment you arrived. And Mr. Hart! He's upstairs with his lawyer now."

"Hart is here for his deposition? Oh, Christ." I didn't notice a deposition in *Hart* for today. I didn't see a notice in the pleadings index, so I assume that nobody at Masterson noticed a dep, either. Maybe the notice got lost when the file was sent to Stalling. Or maybe somebody deliberately took it out.

"Miss DiNunzio, they're waiting. All of them." Miss Pershing's thin fingers dance along the edge of her chin.

I steady her by her Olive Oyl shoulders. "Here's what I need you to do, Miss Pershing. Get us a conference room and have Catering Services set us up for breakfast. Then call Legal Court Reporters, the number's on the Rolodex. Ask them to send over Pete if he's available. Pete Benesante, got that?"

"Benesante." She's so nervous she's quivering, and it makes her look vulnerable. Her job is all she has. She's me in thirty years.

"After you do that, take the Harts to the conference room for me. Tell them I'll be right there. I have to see my parents first. Okay?"

She nods.

"Are they having a shit fit?"

She colors slightly.

"Excuse me. My parents. How are they?"

"They're fine. They're very nice people. Lovely people. They invited me over for coffee this Saturday. They said perhaps you'd be free as well."

"Maybe, Miss Pershing. But right now we have to get moving. Welcome to litigation. This is called a fire drill."

She looks nervous again.

"Don't worry. Everything's going to be all right."

"It's in God's hands." She walks unsteadily out the door, chanting Benesante, Benesante, Benesante, like a Latin prayer.

I go through my drawer for the thin *Hart* file and page through it quickly. As I remembered, the only papers in it are the complaint and some scribbled notes from the lawyer at Masterson who represented Harbison's. I've seen the notes before, on the way to the pretrial conference with Einstein. They're practically indecipherable, written in a shaky hand. I can make out sentences here and there—what I told Einstein about Hart's rudeness to company employees—but most of it's a mess.

Who took these notes? Who did we steal this case from, anyway? I flip through the notes, three pages long. On the last page is a notation: 5/10 CON OUT/FS 1.0 NSW. I recognize it as a billing code. Stalling's is almost identical. The notation means that on May 10, the Masterson lawyer had a conference out of the office with Franklin Stapleton, Harbison's CEO. Their conference lasted an hour. The Masterson lawyer must be NSW.

NSW. Nathaniel Waters?

Ned's father.

TWENTY-SEVEN

"Everything's ready, Miss DiNunzio," says Miss Pershing, practically hyperventilating in the doorway to my office. "You have Conference Room C. Mr. Benesante's on his way."

"Thank you, Miss Pershing." I stare at the notation. Is NSW Ned's father? It would make sense, because only a megapartner would get an hour's audience with Stapleton. Even Berkowitz has never met Stapleton. He deals with Harbison's through the GC.

"Also, there's someone on the telephone." She frowns at the message slip. "It's a Miss Krytiatow . . . Miss Krytiatows. . . ." She looks up, exasperated. "Her first name is Lu Ann."

"I don't know her, Miss Pershing. Take her number. I'll get back to her when I can."

"All right. I'll be back at my desk if you need anything." She turns to go.

"Miss Pershing, the Harts, remember?"

Her hand flutters to her mouth. "Oh, my. I forgot. I'm so sorry."

"No problem. Just take them to the conference room and tell them I'll be there."

"You mean, *stall* them. Like Jessica Fletcher." She winks at me.

"Jessica who?"

"Jessica Fletcher, on *Murder, She Wrote*. She's a sleuth!" Miss Pershing's eyes light up.

"You got it. Like Jessica Fletcher."

"Right-o."

"In fact, I have a favor to ask you. Something I need to have done while I'm in the dep. The kind of favor a sleuth would like."

"Now this is my cup of tea," she says, brightening.

"Get a district court subpoena from my form files. Then call up the Accident Investigation Division—they're a part of the Philadelphia police. Don't tell them who you are. Get some information about who's in charge of their records on open investigations for fatal accidents. Put that name on two of the subpoenas. My guess is that it's the Fatal Coordinator Sergeant, but I'm not sure. Just don't tell them why."

"Got it," she says, with another wink, and hobbles off.

I return to the file and read the notation again. 5/10 CON OUT/FS 1.0 NSW. If NSW is Ned's father, does that explain why the deposition notice is missing? Did he tamper with the file to make me look bad in comparison to Ned? Is Ned's father the note writer? The killer?

I slap the file closed and tuck it under my arm. I head up the stairs slowly enough to give Miss Pershing time to get the Harts out of the reception area. My parents must have been worried sick. I wonder if they got hold of Angie and how much she told them. It had to be the whole story for them to come here. They've only been to Stalling once, when I was first hired. My father got lost on the way to the bathroom.

The Harts are gone when I reach the reception area. A CEO type, his lawyer, and his lawyer's bag carrier are engaged in a whispered confab at one end of a glass coffee table, leaning over slick copies of *Forbes*, *Time*, and *Town and Country*. At the other end of the table is the redoubtable team of Vita and Matthew DiNunzio. They sit together in their heavy car coats, a worsted mountain of concerned parenthood, slumping badly in the soft whiter-than-white sectional furniture. I know what my mother is thinking: This sofa, it cost a fortune, and it has no support.

"Maria!" shouts my father, with joy. He stands up, arms outstretched. "Maria! Doll!"

Every head in the place turns. The CEO and his lawyer break off their expensive conversation. The bag carrier stifles a laugh. Two young associates, running by with files, look back curiously. Stalling's veteran receptionist, Mrs. Littleton of the purple hair, just beams. I wonder if she's invited to coffee too.

I cross to greet my parents before my father shouts again. "Ma. Pop. Are you guys okay?"

They reach for me and envelop me in their scratchy coats. They smell like home, a closed-up odor of marinara and mothballs. It's crazy, all hell is breaking loose in my life, but I'm happy to see them. I hope Angie didn't tell them everything. I don't know how much more they can take, particularly my father.

"Maria, what happened? Where were you?" says my mother, half moaning. Her pancake makeup looks extra heavy, which signifies that she's come downtown. "We were so worried!"

"We called Angie," my father chimes in. "She said you went to see her. Are you in trouble, honey?"

The CEO leans closer to his lawyer and continues his conversation. The bag carrier has nothing to do but watch us, which he does. I don't like the way he looks at my parents, with a mixture of incredulity and amusement. What's the matter? I want to say. You never seen Italians before?

"Pop, I'm not in trouble. Everything's—"

"What?" He nudges my mother, agitated. "What did she say, Vita?"

"She said she's not in trouble, but I don't believe her," my mother shouts. "Look at her eyes, Matty. Look at her eyes." She grabs for my chin, but I intercept her deftly, having had some practice with this.

I look over her shoulder at the smirking lawyer. "Come with me. Let's get out of here." I take her by one hand and him by the other and walk them out of the reception area. We gather in front of one of the conference rooms, away from the elevator bank. I stand very close to my father, so I don't have to yell too loudly. "Listen to me. Everything is fine. I am fine."

"Then why did you go see Angie?" my mother asks, blinking defiantly behind her thick glasses.

"What did Angie say?"

"Hah! You think I was born yesterday? You tell me why you went, then I tell you what she said."

"What?" asks my father.

I hug him close and talk directly into his ear. "I went to see Angie. I was worried about something, but now it's fine. I'm fine. I'm sorry if I made you worry."

"Angie said you were lonely."

"That's right, Pop. I was lonely. I was worried about her, missing her. Everything's okay now. But I have to get back to work. I have a deposition. I have to go take it."

"You givin' us the bum's rush?"

"I have to, Pop. I can't help it."

"Something's wrong, Matty. I can see it in the child's eyes. Ever since she was little, she can't hide her eyes." My mother trembles, agitated.

I touch her shoulder. "Ma. I promise you, I'm fine. If my eyes look funny, it's because I'm about to lose my job." I press the button to get them an elevator.

"No. We're not leaving until this is settled."

"What, Vita?"

"We're not leaving until my daughter tells me what is going on. And that's final!"

My father winces. "Veet, she has to do her job."

I nod. "Right. Pop's right. I have to do my job." The elevator arrives. I step inside and press the HOLD button. "Ma, please. I have to work. I have to go, they're waiting for me. There's nothing to worry about. I'm sorry I upset you, I really am."

My father shuffles into the elevator, but my mother merely folds her arms. It's easier to move the Mummers up Broad Street than it is to move my mother one inch. Especially when she folds her arms like that.

The elevator starts to buzz loudly. The noise reverberates in the elevator. Even my father covers his ears.

"Ma, please."

"Vita, please."

She wags a finger at me, her knuckle as knobby as the knot on an oak tree. "I don't like this. I don't like this at all."

"Ma, I'm fine."

The elevator buzzes madly.

She takes two reluctant steps into the elevator. I release the button and the buzzing stops abruptly. "Don't worry, Ma. I love you both." I jump out of the elevator.

"We love you," says my father. The doors close on my mother's scowl.

When I turn around, the bag carrier is standing alone in the elevator bank. He's wearing a three-piece suit and a smirk I would love to smack off.

"You look familiar to me," he says casually. "Did you go to Harvard?"

"No. I'm too stupid." I start to walk past him, but he touches my arm.

"You look like somebody I knew on law review there, in 1986. I was editor in chief that year."

"Editor in chief, huh?"

"Editor in chief."

I lean in close to him. "Let me tell you something. I saw the way you carried that bag, and I must say I've never seen a man carry a bag as well as you did. In fact, it takes an editor in chief to carry a bag that well." I chuck him one in the padded shoulder. "Keep up the good work."

I take off and head for the stairs.

Fucking back. It's getting to be fun.

I run up the stairs to the conference room, mentally switching gears on the way. I have a job to do. I have to ask Hart every question I can think of, and I have only this one shot before trial. I have to find out everything he has to support his case so I can get a defense ready. And I have to find out what the hell is going on with Ned's father and my files.

I slip inside the conference room. It smells of fresh coffee and virgin legal pads. Pete's already there, setting up his stenography machine. He gives me a professional nonpartisan-type nod. We both know this is bullshit. He's my reporter and it will be my record. He'll make me sound like Clarence Darrow before he's done, with none of the uhs, hums, and ers that I come out with in real life.

The Harts stand together at the coffee tray. I reach for Hank's hand. "Hello, Hank."

"Hi, Mary," Hank says. "I assumed the dep would be here, since you replaced Masterson as defense counsel." He looks like an English schoolboy in a plaid bow tie, which is slightly askew.

"Right. I should have called you, but I was out yesterday."

"I know, I tried to confirm."

"I'm sorry. By the way, when did you get the Notice of Deposition? I don't seem to have a copy in my pleadings index."

He thinks a minute. "We got it when Masterson filed the answer, I think. No, we got it with the other stuff."

"Other stuff?"

234 LISA SCOTTOLINE: THE FIRST TWO NOVELS

"You know, the discovery. Interrogatories and document requests. We answered them two weeks ago. You've seen them, haven't you?"

"No, actually. Maybe they got lost when the file was transferred to us." Discovery. Of course, the written questions that Hart would have to answer and the papers he'd have to produce. Without those papers, I'm crippled for today. "Hank, would you mind if I borrowed your copy of the discovery for the deposition?"

"Not at all." He sets his shiny briefcase on the table and opens it up. Anybody else would have denied having the documents and exploited my disadvantage, but Hank hands me a thick packet of paper. Candy from a baby. I'm almost too ashamed to take it. Almost.

"Thanks, Hank."

"The documents we produced are on the bottom," he says helpfully.

"Great." I take the papers, but there's too much to read now. I'll do it over the lunch break, and wing it this morning. But why are the papers missing from the file in the first place? Who did this to me? "Who handled this case at Masterson, Hank? I forget. Was it—"

"Nathaniel Waters," booms a deep voice, speaking for the first time. It's Hart the Elder. "They pulled out their big gun."

NSW *is* Ned's father. Jesus H. Christ.

"Mary, this is my father, Henry Hart," Hank says.

"Hello, Mr. Hart." I extend a hand, but he ignores it. I withdraw it quickly, as Hank looks uncomfortably at me. Hart the Elder won't even meet my eye and yanks a chair out from under the table. He's an attractive man, tanned and trim. There's almost no gray in his hair; I wonder if he dyes it. It would be consistent, for he seems vain, in a European-tailored suit and a light pink shirt. I can see why he was an executive at Harbison's and can also imagine him being rude to employees, because he's breathing fire at me.

Two hours later, it's a full-fledged conflagration, and I've taken Saint Joan's place at the stake. I started out with only the most reasonable questions, mainly about his early years at Harbison's, but Hart fought me on each one. His son never objected. He couldn't get a word in edgewise.

"Mr. Hart, has anyone from Harbison's ever made a statement to you regarding your age?"

"Mrs. DiNunzio, you know full well they have."

"The purpose of this deposition is to find out your version of the facts, Mr. Hart. Now please answer the question."

"My version? It's the truth."

"Look, Mr. Hart, this is your chance to tell your side of the story. Why don't you do so?"

"It's not a story."

I grit my teeth. "Mr. Benesante, would you please read back the question?"

Pete picks up the tape and translates its machine-made abbreviations to Hart. "Mr. Hart, has anyone from Harbison's ever made a statement to you regarding your age?"

"Do you understand the question, Mr. Hart?" I ask.

"English is my mother tongue, Mrs. DiNunzio."

"Then answer it, please."

"Yes, they have."

"How many such statements have been made to you, sir?"

"Three."

"Do you remember when the first such statement was made?"

"Sure. It's a day that will live in infamy, if I have any say in the matter."

"When was the statement made?"

"February seventh, 1990."

"Who made the statement?"

"Frank Stapleton."

"Would that be Franklin Stapleton, the chief executive officer of Harbison's?"

"None other."

"Was there anyone else present when he made this statement?"

"You think they're dumb enough to have a witness there?"

"I take it your answer is no, Mr. Hart?"

"You take it right, Mrs. DiNunzio."

I sip some ice-cold coffee. "Where was the statement made?"

"In Frank's office."

"Do you recall the statement, Mr. Hart?"

"I'll never forget it."

"What was the statement, Mr. Hart?"

"Mr. Stapleton said to me, 'Henry, face it. You're not getting any younger, and it's time for you to retire. You can't teach an old dog new tricks, you know.' "

Pow! It's a fireball.

Soon it blazes out of control. Hart goes on to testify with certainty about the two other statements, each one referring to his age as it relates to his employment. Clearly unlawful, and each statement was made by Stapleton himself, so it's directly chargeable to Harbison's. *Pow! Pow!*

"Mr. Hart, do you have any documents regarding these alleged statements by Mr. Stapleton?"

"I most certainly do."

Pow!

"What might those documents be?"

"They might be notes."

"Have you brought them to this deposition?"

"Yes. My son gave them to you already."

"They're the ones at the bottom of the pile, Mary," Hank says.

"Excuse me a minute." I flip through the pages until I reach a set of documents on Harbison's letterhead. They're neatly typed and laser-printed, in capital letters. I pull them out and hold them up. "Are these the ones, Hank?"

Hank squints across the conference table. "Yes. That's them."

"Bear with me a minute, gentlemen." I arrange my face into a mask of scholarly calm as I read the notes. Frolicking across the top of each page is a conga line of ecstatic nuts and bolts, ending in the tagline HARBISON'S THE HARDWARE PEOPLE. On each page are verbatim accounts of Hart's conversations with Stapleton, which appear to have been made right after the conversations.

God help me.

The notes will be admissible at trial. They'll prove the truth of every word Hart says. The jury will rise up like an avenging angel. They'll take millions from Harbison's; it'll be the biggest age discrimination verdict in Pennsylvania history. *Kaboom!* The conflagration explodes into a city-wide five-alarmer. And the flames, crackling in my ears, are eating me alive.

Pete cracks his knuckles loudly. "Can we break for lunch now, Mary? My fingers are killing me."

"Sure."

"An hour okay?"

"Fine."

The Harts leave with Pete, who gives me a quick smile before he goes. He's never asked for a break before. I've had him on deps with no break all day. He was trying to save me. He knew I was tumbling into the inferno.

He's Catholic too.

TWENTY-EIGHT

I plunge my hot face into a golden basin of cool water in the ladies' room, half expecting to hear a hissing sound. Then I towel off and head back to the conference room to read over Hart's notes. They're bad, but I decide not to think about how very bad they are. I have to find out more about them and find out anything else he has. Fuck back, in overdrive.

I'm almost finished reading the stack of documents, which luckily contain no more surprises, when the telephone rings. It's Miss Pershing. "Miss DiNunzio, I'm sorry to interrupt you, but I have this Lu Ann on the line again. She's very anxious to talk to you. She says it's about Mr. Hart's deposition."

Who can this be? I take the call. "This is Mary DiNunzio."

"You're the lawyer for Harbison's, aren't you, miss?" says a young woman. She sounds upset. "Because I heard you're a lady lawyer, and I heard Henry's getting his deposition today."

"I represent the company, Lu Ann. Do you work for Harbison's?"

"Let me just ask you is the judge there?"

"There's no judge at a deposition, Lu Ann."

"Who's there? The jury?" Her voice grows tremulous. I can't

place her flat accent. Maybe it's from Kensington, a working-class section of the city.

"No. Just relax, I think you're confused. A deposition is between—"

"Did he say anything about me? 'Cause if he does, you tell them I said it's not true! If my Kevin hears it, if anybody on that jury says anything, or it gets in the newspapers, he'll beat the shit out of me! Me and my kids both! So you just tell him that! If he loves me, you tell him to shut the fuck up!" The phone goes dead.

Stunned, I hang up the receiver. My conversation with Lu Ann is over, but my conversation with the devil is just beginning. I didn't think I believed in the devil, but I can't ignore the fact that I hear his hot whisper at my ear in the stillness of Conference Room C, on Lust.

So Hart's been playing hide the kielbasa with a Polish girl from Kensington. Let the jury in on that, Mare, and you win.

I can't. It wouldn't even be admissible.

Then ask Hart about Lu Ann right now. Take him through her phone call, expose the little shit. He'll pack up his lawsuit and go home. You can win this case today, Mary. It's yours for the asking.

I can't do that. It's not fair. It has nothing to do with the case.

You can and you should. A quick victory would clinch your partnership, Mare. No more worrying, no more vote-counting, no more headaches. Relief from pain, isn't that what you want? Peace. You could buy a house. Get your life back on track.

I can't do it. His son is right here.

So what? You're Harbison's lawyer, you should be representing its interests, not Little Hank's. You're supposed to use every weapon in the arsenal to win, even the MAC-10s. Especially the MAC-10s.

I'm damned if I do and damned if I don't.

There's no time to decide, because the door opens and the

Harts enter. Though the elder Hart doesn't smile, Hank's spirits are high. Undoubtedly, he'd advised his father to take notes of his conversations with Stapleton and is expecting a settlement offer after the dep. He's been planning this victory since his graduation and thinks that its sweet moment is at hand.

That's what he thinks, whispers the devil.

I take my seat in front of the notes, and Pete comes in.

Congratulations on your partnership, Mary. It's your choice.

Pete sits down behind the stenography machine. "You ready?"

I nod, but I'm not. I can't decide what to do. I look down at the notes and ask a couple of stupid questions about them. All the time, the devil pours poison in my ear, tempting me, taunting me. I look at Hank, sitting so proudly at his father's side. If I ask about Lu Ann, what will his cherubic face look like? What will happen at home that night, with his mother? And Lu Ann, will this Kevin—

Save it, Mary! You've represented worse. You've done worse. You and I know that, don't we? Mary and Bobby, sittin' in a tree, K-I-S-S-I-N-G. First comes love . . .

"Mr. Hart, were you ever rude to Harbison's employees?"

"I don't understand the question."

See, he deserves it. Give it to him. Right between the legs.

"What part of the question didn't you understand, Mr. Hart?"

"Any of it, Mrs. DiNunzio."

"Then let me change it slightly. Have you ever been reprimanded by anyone at Harbison's for being rude to its employees?"

"I have never been rude to anyone at Harbison's."

"That's not my question, Mr. Hart. My question is, Have you ever been reprimanded by anyone at Harbison's for being rude to its employees?"

"No."

"Has anyone at Harbison's ever told you that they thought you were rude to company employees?"

"Yes."

God, I hate this man. I should do it, I should.

Sure you should. But will you?

"And who told you this?"

"Frank Stapleton."

A break for me. If Hart admits that Stapleton talked to him about his rudeness, I can prove that Harbison's had a business motive to demote him. That makes it a "mixed motive" case under the law—a tough defense for me to win, but it's the best I've got.

Hank makes a note on his legal pad.

Just breathe the little slut's name.

"How many times did Mr. Stapleton discuss this subject with you?"

"I wouldn't call it a discussion. That would be making too much of it, and I'm not about to let you do that."

"Fine. How many times did Mr. Stapleton make a statement to you about rudeness?"

"Only once."

"Was anyone else present when he made this statement?"

"No."

"Where did it take place?"

"On the golf course. Ninth hole." At this he smirks.

Hank makes another notation.

"What did Mr. Stapleton say about the subject?"

"It was just a comment between friends. Former friends, I should say."

"What did Mr. Stapleton say, Mr. Hart?"

"Just that sometimes I could be a little hard on the staff. That's all."

"Are you sure that's all you can recall?"

"Yes."

"What did you say in reply?"

"Nice drive." Hart glances at Pete to see if he appreciates the joke. Pete's face is stony.

"Mr. Hart, what did you say to Mr. Stapleton in reply?"

"Nothing. That was the end of it."

"Are you sure?"

"Sure as God made little green apples."

"Did you make any notes of any kind regarding this conversation?"

"On the golf course? With those sawed-off pencils?" Hart rolls his eyes.

"Anywhere at all."

"Why would I? It wasn't important enough."

"Is that a no, Mr. Hart?"

"Yes, it's a no, Mrs. DiNunzio."

I need more detail to sell this to the jury. "Mr. Hart, was there a specific incident Mr. Stapleton referred to when he discussed this with you?"

"No."

"Do you know what occasioned this discussion with you?"

"You'd have to ask him."

"I take it that's a no, Mr. Hart?"

"You're getting pretty good at this, Mrs. DiNunzio."

How long are you going to eat his shit?

"Mr. Hart, did Mr. Stapleton refer to any employee in particular during this conversation?"

"Just the kitchen help."

"Kitchen help?"

"The people who work in the company cafeteria. The Jell-O slingers in the hairnets."

"Anyone in particular?"

"Lu Ann, I think he said her name was."

Whoa, baby. That's a surprise.

Whoa, baby, is right, mocks the devil. He sounds less surprised.

Hank writes the name on his pad, then looks at me, expectantly, innocently, for the next question.

His father's sneer betrays nothing as he awaits the next question.

Pete waits too, his long fingers poised in midair over the black keys.

Do-it-do-it-do-it-do-it-do-it! screeches the devil.

It's out of my mouth before I can stop it.

It's the little voice inside me talking. The Mike-voice, chirping up. It hasn't deserted me after all. It's still with me, and it says, "I have no further questions."

It's over. Everybody packs up and shakes hands, except for Hart. "See you in court," he says, with a braying laugh. The derisive sound is echoed by a more distant infernal laughter.

Get thee behind me, Satan!

I wonder if I'm losing my mind. I gather up the file and practically flee the conference room.

Outside, the firm is alive with commerce and industry. Secretaries fly to the mailroom to get out that last letter. Associates beg another draft out of Word Processing. Partners rush to review briefs before they're filed, the better to leave their distinctive mark on it, like a poodle does a hydrant. Everyone's following the Stalling commandment THOU SHALT WAIT UNTIL THE LAST MINUTE, THEN GO CRAZY. The life signs at Stalling ground me, and I don't hear the devil anymore. By the time I reach Gluttony, I'm feeling normal, almost good, for the first time in a long time.

"Miss DiNunzio, here I am!" It's Miss Pershing, looking up at me from the bottom of the stairs. Her rubber pocketbook's slung over her wrist, and she's holding an Agatha Christie paperback. Secretaries flow around her to get to the stairwell, following the first in a set of counter-commandments, THOU SHALT BOLT AT FIVE O'CLOCK. Miss Pershing's too single-minded to notice the activity around her, like an aged pointer who's found her quarry.

"Miss Pershing, step over here." I take her by the elbow and she does a mincing side step out of the path of travel. The Amazing Stella sashays behind her, making the crazy sign at her forehead, but I don't laugh.

Miss Pershing looks suspiciously at the secretaries passing by. "I got that information you wanted." She leans toward me; her soft breath smells like Altoids. "You know which information I mean? *The* information."

"*The* information, Miss Pershing?"

"*The* information. The *police* information."

"Oh. Thank you."

"The papers are on your desk. Your theory is confirmed."

"My theory? You mean about who—"

"Yes."

"Good. Thank you. I appreciate it."

"That's all right. It's my job."

I suppress a smile. "Well, thank you, just the same."

"Also, Mr. Starankovic telephoned. He said—"

"Starankovic? Oh, fuck!"

Her eyes flare open.

"I'm sorry, Miss Pershing."

"No need to apologize, Miss DiNunzio. I'm getting used to it."

"Thanks."

"Mr. Starankovic said you didn't call him back about the interviews, so he had to file a motion. I put the papers on your desk. I hope this doesn't mean you need me to stay late tonight, because I can't. I have my book club tonight."

"Agatha Christie, right?"

She nods happily.

"It's okay, Miss Pershing. I don't need you to stay."

"Well, then, nighty-night," she says, and smiles. She's about to turn toward the elevator when Martin comes charging out of nowhere and knocks her over.

"My!" she yelps. She falls backward into my arms.

Martin runs down the stairs, elbowing everyone aside frantically, with a sheaf of curly faxes in his hand.

"Are you all right, Miss P.?" I set her back onto her feet, like Dorothy did the scarecrow. She seems more embarrassed than anything else.

"Goodness!"

I look down the stairs after Martin, but he's long gone. He didn't even look back. He knocked down an old woman and didn't even look back. What kind of a man does that? A hit-and-run. I shudder, involuntarily.

"Wasn't that the young man who likes owls?" asks Miss Pershing.

"Martin H. Chatham IV."

"What bad manners!" She produces a flowery handkerchief from the sleeve of her sweater and dabs at her forehead. The handkerchief must be scented, for the air is suddenly redolent of lilac.

"Let me walk you to the elevator, Miss P." I offer her my arm and we hobble to the elevator together. I tuck her in, in front of the secretaries with the neon eyeshadow and the black miniskirts. She gives me a game wave with her pocketbook as the doors close.

Martin.

I wonder where he was the night Brent was killed. I wonder what kind of car he drives, where he lives. If he lives in town, it makes it more likely that it's him, since it would be easier for him to follow me. But I think he lives in the suburbs somewhere, on the Main Line. I decide to do a little research.

I head into my office and find Stalling's pig book on the shelf. It has photos of all the lawyers in the firm, with their degrees and home addresses. I flip through the first couple of pages to Martin's name. Under his head shot, which makes him look almost animate, it says Dartmouth College, B.A.

1969; Yale Law School, J.D. 1972. His home address is "Rondelay II" in Bryn Mawr. The Main Line, of course. Even the houses have Roman numerals after their names.

Damn. Who else could be jealous of me? Jameson. I wonder where he lives.

I page to the J's and find his picture. He looks like Atom Ant, only smug. He went to Penn too, graduating from the undergraduate school in 1970 and the law school in 1974. His home address is on Pine Street in Society Hill. A city dweller; I didn't know that. And the houses down there—the new ones—have built-in garages. I make a mental note to ask Judy if she knows what kind of car he drives. Kurt would remember if he'd seen it at a firm party. He's always working on old cars; he uses them in his sculpture. His last show was called Body Parts. I passed.

I flip the pages forward to look Ned up. Ned Waters, it says, underneath a picture of him that almost takes my breath away. His eyes, his face. His smile. God, he's beautiful. I think of him in bed, during the night, arousing me despite my slumber. It's hard to believe he's the killer, but Judy made sense. At least for now. I snap the book closed. The end.

I'm about to reshelve it when I remember. Berkowitz. Everybody knows where he lives, he custom-built the house two years ago in Gladwyne, one of Philadelphia's ritziest suburbs. The house is a palace, with a pool and a tennis court. But Gladwyne isn't that far from the city, just ten minutes up the West River Drive.

The West River Drive. Where Mike was killed.

I thumb quickly to Berkowitz's page. His meaty face takes up the entire picture frame. I skim over the schools. Drexel University, Temple Law School. City schools for smart kids with no money. I stop short when I reach his home address— or addresses, because to my surprise, there are two. One is in Gladwyne, like I thought. But the other is an apartment in the Rittenhouse, a new high-rise condo on Rittenhouse Square.

Rittenhouse Square. Where Brent was killed. Right near my apartment. So Berkowitz had access to both sites. He could have hit Mike and disappeared up the West River Drive to Gladwyne, or hit Brent and headed home to the Rittenhouse.

Berkowitz? Could it really be him?

Wait. I know he has a Mercedes, and it wasn't a Mercedes that hit Brent. But what if he has another car, an old car, that he keeps in town? The Rittenhouse has its own parking in the basement garage.

Christ. Berkowitz. Maybe Brent was right about him all along; he never did like him. Neither does my mother. Thin lips. I slip the book back onto the shelf.

I check the clock behind me. The huge golden dial glows brightly: 6:20. The sky looks too dark for six o'clock, as if a thunderstorm's coming. On my desk are the subpoenas. Miss Pershing has typed in the name of the Fatal Coordinator Sergeant, and the address looks right. SUBPOENA DUCES TECUM. It's one of the older forms, which I prefer. They look positively terroristic. I peel off the yellow Post-It that Miss Pershing has signed, Secret Agent Secretary. She's cute, but I don't want to like her. I miss Brent.

It's too late, but I punch in the number for AID and listen to their telephone ring and ring. I decide to go down tomorrow, first thing. Fuck the appointment. I'm the wife, for Christ's sake. And the lawyer.

I hang up the telephone and flop into my chair. I look at the pile of mail on my desk. It's not like I don't have other things to do. There's a mountain of mail, including the expected motion from Starankovic. I open the envelope and read through the motion papers. They're not bad, an improvement over the crap he usually files. At least he didn't request oral argument, so I don't have to sing to Bitter Man again.

I look through the pile of phone messages on my desk, and there's one from Jameson. FILE THE BRIEF HE SAYS! Miss Pershing has written, with a little daisy in the exclamation point.

I thumb through the rest of the pile. Judy, Judy, my mother, Stephanie Fraser again, the rest are clients that will have to wait. None are from Ned. Be careful what you wish, you might get it.

I turn to the mail. My heart begins to pound. On top is a plain white business envelope, with my name laser-printed in capital letters. But there's no Stalling address. And no stamp or postmark. It came through the interoffice mail, from somebody at Stalling. I pick up the envelope. My hand begins to shake slightly.

Berkowitz. Martin. Jameson. Ned. Not Ned's father, because it came interoffice.

I tear open the envelope.

I LOVE YOU, MARY

Ned. It has to be. I feel a sharp pain. How could I have been so thoroughly duped? I close my eyes.

When I open them, Berkowitz is standing in the doorway.

TWENTY-NINE

Berkowitz lurches into my office as if he owns it. I'm struck by his size, intimidated by his power. For the first time, his presence alone seems menacing, and I understand why a lot of people don't like him.

"Mary had a little lamb," he says. "Nice place you got here."

"It looks just like everybody else's." I slip the note and the subpoenas under my mail.

"Except for the view, of course."

"Right." I glance back at the clock, luminous against the darkening sky. Storm clouds gather behind the clock tower.

Berkowitz leans against the file cabinet by the bookshelves. "Must be a weird feeling, having that thing over your shoulder. Like you're being watched all the time."

The comment sends a chill down my spine. He knows about the notes. What is this, a game? I say nothing.

"I don't think I would like that."

"The feeling or the clock?"

"Both. Either." He snorts out a little laugh.

"I don't like the feeling. The clock I can live with."

He doesn't reply, but his eyes scan my diplomas, my desk,

and the other file cabinet. His expression is unreadable. "You don't have any pictures."

"No."

"Why not?"

"I don't know."

"But you have family. In South Philly."

"Yes." I flash on the car barreling by me down my parents' street. "How did you know that?"

"Your accent. It's a dead giveaway." He pauses before *Black's Law Dictionary* and runs a thick finger along its binding. I can't gauge his mood, I don't know him well enough. He seems distracted. Tense. "Do you ever use this thing?"

"No."

"Then why do you have it?"

"My parents gave it to me." The detail makes me feel exposed to him, increasing my nervousness. I tell myself to relax. I handled Lombardo, I can handle him. "Did you have an office like this when you were an associate?"

"When I started out, we were in the Fidelity Building on Broad Street. All the windows opened." He laughs, abruptly, and slaps his breast pocket. "Do you smoke?"

"No."

"Shit."

"Sorry."

"So." He leans against the file cabinet. "Mind if I close the door?"

I feel my chest flush. "Uh . . . why?"

He cocks his head. "Now why do you think, Mary, Mary?" Suddenly he grabs the door and slams it shut. "Alone at last," he says, with a dry chuckle.

I find myself rising, involuntarily. I scan my desk for a pair of scissors or a letter opener. Nothing's there except a stapler and a dictaphone. I have no protection. I back up and feel the cold window at my back.

"Aren't you standing kind of close to the window, Mary?"
I glance over my shoulder. The clock face glows fiercely at me through a thunderstorm. We're forty stories up, in a tower of black mirrors that flexes and groans in high winds. I tell myself to stay cool. "Why don't you just tell me what you're doing down here, Sam?"

His eyebrow arches in surprise. "Enough with the small talk, is that the idea?"

"Exactly."

"Fine. Two reasons. One: I'm having a reception for the Rules Committee tomorrow night in Conference Room A. Eight o'clock. The litigation partners and the district court judges are invited. You should be there."

"What?" I don't understand.

"There's a reception tomorrow night, and I want you there. Conference Room A. Eight o'clock."

"Me, at a partners' reception?"

Berkowitz looks at me like I'm crazy. "Yes, you. Do you go to receptions, Mary, Mary?"

"Yes." I relax slightly.

"Bring Carrier. You two are pals, aren't you?"

"Yes. We are." I breathe easier and step away from the window. I hear a thunderclap outside and step even farther away from the window.

"Good." He fingers his breast pocket again. "Well. Okay. Two: This goddamned thing with Tom Lombardo. I got a call today. He said you saw what happened."

"I did."

"Well, forget you did."

"What?"

"Forget about it."

"I'm just supposed to forget—"

"Yes. That's an order." His tone is gruff.

I'm beginning to understand what he's saying. "I get it—it's a deal. You want to trade off my partnership and Judy's for my forgetting about what happened with Lombardo? And maybe to Brent?"

"Mary, it's none of your fucking *business!*" he explodes, out of nowhere. With his face suddenly florid, he looks like a devil. But I fight the devils now and win. Fuck back, even when you're fucking with the devil himself.

"Don't you scream at me!" I lean toward him. We're almost nose to nose over the desk. Berkowitz, the King of Fucking Back, and me, a pretender to the throne.

Suddenly, he breaks into a sheepish smile. The redness in his face vanishes. "That's what my wife always says."

"You ought to listen."

He laughs loudly. "Lombardo's right. You got balls."

"No, I don't. So what was it about?"

"Would you believe me if I told you it's not your concern?"

"You mean not to worry my pretty little head?"

"Okay. Down, girl." He looks amused but still tense. Whatever it is, it's driving him nuts. "All right, it's about Delia. She's got her hand in the till. She's taken a hundred thou over five years."

"You're kidding."

"Wish I were." His face falls, he shakes his head. "I thought it was somebody in Accounting, maybe that asshole bean counter we let push us around. I didn't think it was her. It never even occurred to me it was her. I asked Lombardo to track it down for me, but I didn't want to believe him."

"So you hit him?"

He looks pained. "Hey, you know, it hurts. She betrayed me after I took good care of her. I loved that kid."

I meet his eye. Was Brent right about them?

"Don't give me that look. I know everybody says I'm running around with her. I let 'em think it. Fact is, she's my best friend's kid, her father was my sparring partner. He and I were like this." He holds up two tight fingers in a gesture I haven't seen in ages.

"For real?"

"For real. I'm her godfather. The first Jewish godfather in history."

I laugh, with relief. Part of the puzzle falls into place. "Is that why she's so mad lately?"

"Oh, yeah, Delia's mad at the world; she must've seen it coming. She won't even talk to me, even though I convinced the policy committee not to prosecute her. All she lost was her job, and we got a payment schedule worked out. She throws in one, I throw in ten. Can I drive a bargain or what?"

"You do okay."

He slaps his breast pocket again for a cigarette. "Anyway, she left this morning. Now I have no secretary. Got a good one I can steal?"

I think of Miss Pershing. "No."

"So. We all better here, Mary, Queen of Scots?"

"All better."

"Okay, I gotta go. I don't have to tell you not to mention this, do I?"

"Nope."

"Tomorrow night," he calls out, as he opens the door and walks out.

I collapse into my chair, hugely relieved. Tired. Drained. So the fight I saw wasn't about Brent after all, and Berkowitz isn't having an affair with Delia. I wonder what Brent would say to that revelation, but Brent isn't here. I miss him. And I think I know who killed him.

My eyes fall on the note, sticking out from underneath the mail. Ned, my lover. My love. I feel heartsick and scared. He must be crazy, really crazy. Maybe that stuff he told me about the Prozac was just a story; I never did go back and check the dates on the bottles. Is the man I slept with really capable of killing Brent? And Mike, a year earlier? Maybe, if he's obsessed with me like Judy says. And am I safe from him, or will he turn on me now that I've rejected him?

I check the clock. 7:02. Too late for me to be alone in the office. Rain falls in sheets on City Hall; I feel the building sway slightly. I lock the note in my middle drawer and leave for Judy's office.

But I forget all about it when I see her.

THIRTY

"I'm fired," Judy says flatly.

"What?!"

"I fucked up." Her eyes are red-rimmed and puffy, as if she's been crying hard. She slouches in her chair. Her chin sags into a sturdy hand.

"What happened?" I sit down.

"The *Mitsuko* brief is in the hopper. The Supremes reversed a similar argument in a case decided yesterday. I didn't even know the case was up on appeal, because I hadn't checked the cites yet. Great, huh? A first-year mistake." Her jowl wrinkles into her hand like a basset hound's. "I'm not paying attention lately."

"Oh, Jude. How'd you catch it?"

"Guess."

I flash on Martin, banging into Miss Pershing on the way downstairs. "Martin?"

"Nope. Guess again."

"Not the client."

"Yes, the client. Certainly, the client. Who better to catch you in the biggest blunder of your career than the client? The GC faxed us a copy of the Supreme Court decision after we faxed him a draft of my brief. Don't you just love faxes? You can find out you fucked up when you're still in mid-fuckup. That's what I call technology!"

I groan. That must be why Martin had the faxes.

"Wait. That's not all. The Third Circuit brief is due in two days. I have forty-eight hours to produce a winning brief or I'm fired."

"Who said that, Martin? He can't do that!"

"No? I've pissed off a house client and embarrassed the firm. Mitsuko's appeal is in jeopardy—it's their legal right, not ours." She rakes her fingers through her hair, and it sticks up in funny places, making her look demented. "It was such a stupid mistake, I should resign."

"You'd better not. We can rewrite the brief."

"We?"

"We. I help. We do it together."

"You can't help, Mary. You don't know the record."

"I don't need to, you do. Besides, what you need is a new legal argument. A new angle."

She smiles wanly. "I appreciate it, but it's hopeless. I've thought about every argument. This was the best."

"Jude! Where's that pioneering western spirit? The Oregon Trail? The Louisiana Purchase? The Missouri Compromise?"

"Stop trying to cheer me up. And your geography sucks."

"Listen, I beat the devil today. I can do anything!"

"You're crazy. We don't have time."

"We have all night. It's pouring outside and I have to stick with you anyway. You're my bodyguard."

"Give it up, Mary."

"No. Tell me why we lost *Mitsuko*, besides the fact that Martin has no business being in front of a jury unless they all went to Choate."

"Mary, it's no use."

"Tell me, Judith Carrier!"

"Aaargh," she growls, in frustration. "Okay. I think the jury just didn't understand the case. There were too many facts. Too much financial data. The legal issues were too abstract—"

"Were the jurors allowed to take notes?"

"Yes. Judge Rasmussen always lets—"

"Yes!" I have an idea. I tell it to Judy and she loves it instantly, realizing that even if it goes down in flames, it'll be a blaze of glory.

She calls Kurt and makes two pots of coffee, one for her and one for me. I call Lombardo and give him the night off, but he doesn't even thank me. We lock ourselves in a study room in the library and burn up the Lexis hookup. After a couple of hours, we lock ourselves in a war room on Gluttony and start drafting. We send out for Chinese food twice, once at eight o'clock and again at ten o'clock. We order lo mein both times. After our second dinner, Stalling's decrepit security guard, whom Judy calls Mack Sennett, knocks on the door.

"You girls okay in there?" he asks, in a Ronald Reagan voice.

"We're fine now," I call back. "But keep checking."

"Roger wilco," he says.

Judy changes his nickname to Roger Wilco. I re-check the lock on the door.

At midnight, we persuade Roger Wilco to be our lookout while we stage a giddy raid on Catering Services for potato chips, chocolate cupcakes, and more coffee. Judy tries to snort the Coffeemate, and we think this is wildly funny. The coffee sobers us up and we draft until dawn in the locked war room. Finally, at the end of the night, we put the draft on Miss Pershing's desk, because she gets in earlier than Judy's secretary. We shower in the locked locker room, me for the second day in a row. When we get out of the shower, we realize we have no clean clothes.

"Let's just switch clothes," Judy says.

"What?"

"At least it's a change."

I pop Judy's tent of a peasant dress over my head. It billows to my ankles like a parachute. When I emerge from the embroidered hole in its top, Judy is still wrapped in a towel, holding up my tailored white dress.

"Do you need a bra with this dress?" she asks.

"Of course."

"I don't have a bra."

"What do you mean you don't have a bra?"

"I never wear a bra."

"You don't wear a bra to work? At Stalling and Webb? That's a federal offense!"

"You can't tell, my breasts are so small. You want to see?"

"No! Jesus Christ, will you cover up?"

"We're both women, Mary." She teases me by starting to unwrap the towel.

"I know that. That's why." I unhook my bra and slip it out through the wide sleeves of the smock. "Here, take mine. It's one size fits all. Nobody can tell if I'm wearing one in this dress."

"The bra off your back? What a pal!"

While Judy slips into the bra, I go over to the mirror and try to do something with my limp hair. A project for St. Rita of Cascia, Saint of the Impossible.

"Well, what do you think?" Judy asks.

I turn around. The dress, which is boxy on me, is too small for Judy, and it hugs each curve of her body. She looks dynamite. "Sell it, baby."

She gives the hem a final tug. "Can it, baby."

After we're ready, we troop out to see if Miss Pershing has arrived. She's closing up her clear plastic umbrella when I spot her, in jelly boots and a cellophane rain bonnet, at the secretaries' closet.

"Good morning, Miss Pershing."

She looks me over and smiles sweetly. "You look very pretty today, Miss DiNunzio. Very feminine."

Judy slaps a hearty hand on my shoulder. "Doesn't she though? I helped her pick out that dress."

I give Judy a look. "Thank you, Miss Pershing. How was your book club last night?"

"Wonderful. Next week is Mary Higgins Clark."

"Sounds great. Now I have to warn you, today is going to be a tough day, because Judy and I are working on an appellate brief. We need to finish it by the end of today. It's on your desk, so could you start on it right away? We don't have time to deal with Word Processing."

"What about that other matter? The one we discussed yesterday." She meets my eye significantly.

"It will have to wait, Miss P."

"Got it!" She squares her shoulders.

"Call me as soon as you finish each page. I'll come get it. Meantime, please hold my calls. And don't tell anyone where I am, especially Ned Waters. We have to rewrite the whole day, because the brief has to be filed tomorrow."

"Not to worry." And she's off, marching to her desk in her rain helmet and jelly boots.

THIRTY-ONE

We christen it the Shit from Shinola Brief and work on it all day in the war room. We run through draft after draft and eat everything that Catering Services carts up to us. We're alternately dizzy, nauseated, euphoric, and cranky. By the end of the day, we have a terrible case of indigestion and a terrific brief. We place the final draft on Martin's desk. His office is dark, and the empty eyes of the owls follow us as we leave. "I hate those fucking owls," I say to Judy.

"They're the only friends he has."

My fatigue is catching up with me. "Think he'll like the brief?"

Judy nods happily. "He has to. It's brilliant. Thanks to you."

"No."

"Yes. You, Mary." She gives me a playful push, which sends me crashing into the wall.

"What do you eat for breakfast?" I ask, as she skips ahead.

Back at the conference room, we pull up identical swivel chairs. I collapse into mine while Judy plays in hers, spinning in a circle. Miss Pershing appears in the doorway and steals a glance at Judy, going around and around. "Miss DiNunzio, aren't you ladies through for the day?"

"No, we have a reception to go to upstairs."

"Wheeeeeeee!" says Judy.

"I would think you'd be too tired for a reception. You both worked so hard."

"We are, at least I am. But we have to go."

"We must, we must! We must increase our bust!" Judy sings, spinning. Miss Pershing looks away.

"Miss Pershing, thank you for everything you did today. I appreciate it very much, and so does my co-counsel the lunatic."

Judy stops spinning and grins, gaps on display. "God, I'm dizzy." She holds her forehead. "Miss Pershing, I want to thank you for putting up with us, especially Mary. She can be so difficult when she's under pressure."

"I don't know, I haven't found that to be the case." She smiles warmly.

"Thank you, Miss P."

"I noticed you didn't send out the . . . messages we discussed." Miss Pershing looks nervously in Judy's direction.

"It's all right, Miss Pershing. Judy knows about the subpoenas."

She seems disappointed. "Oh. Well. Why didn't you mail them? Was something wrong with the way I filled them out?"

"No, they were fine, but I'm going to wait on them."

"Well then," Miss Pershing says. "Nighty-night, girls."

"Nighty-night," I say.

Judy's eyes widen comically. "Nighty-night?"

"Say nighty-night to Miss Pershing, Judy."

But Judy's in hysterics, and Miss Pershing is long gone.

Before we leave for the reception on Avarice, we go to the locker room to freshen up. Judy offers me my clothes back, but I decline. I'm starting to like her artsy smock, and even my own bralessness. It makes me feel looser, freer. I splash water on my face to bring me back to life. Holy water, I think crazily. "Look, Jude, I'm reborn."

"You're not reborn, you're exhausted." She taps the soap dispenser. "You've been up for two days, kid. Remember your call to Lombardo? That was yesterday morning."

I rinse my face with warm water. I think of Lombardo, then Berkowitz, and finally Ned. My heart turns bitter. "You know, you were right. It was Ned who sent the notes. I can't believe it, but I think he killed Brent. And maybe even Mike." I twist off the taps with a sigh.

Judy looks surprised. "How do you know?"

"I got another note. A love note, this time. It has to be from him. It came in the interoffice mail." I bury my face in a nubby hand towel. Maybe I'll never come out.

"Stay with me tonight. Kurt's at the studio."

I throw the towel at the hamper. It misses, but I don't bother to retrieve it. "Thanks, but I don't need to. I'm safe now. No more subpoenas, no more lawsuit. I'll call Lombardo after the reception and have him question Ned."

"What if you can't find Lombardo? You're not going home."

"Alice hasn't eaten in days. She'll starve."

"So what's your point?"

We finish up, and take the elevator to Avarice. Roger Wilco greets us when we get off and waves us grandly into Conference Room A. I hardly recognize it; it's been transformed. A string quartet plays Vivaldi in a corner. Lights glow softly on dimmer switches I never knew existed, and tuxedoed waiters pass through the crowd. The horseshoe table, covered with a pristine linen tablecloth, is laden with silver trays of jumbo shrimp, fresh fruit, and crudités. It looks like an expense account version of the Last Supper.

"Christ Almighty," I say, under my breath.

"They're just men," Judy whispers.

But the men are another story. The room reeks of their power. The apostles on the Rules Committee are here, along with a full complement of judges from the district court. I spot

Chief Judge Helfer with Einstein, being fawned over by Golden Rod and a flotilla of Stalling alligators. The Honorable Jacob A. Vanek, who practically made the law in my field, yuks it up with Berkowitz and the Honorable John T. Shales, who's rumored to be the next choice for the Supremes. The Honorable Mark C. Grossman and the Honorable Al Martinez, newly appointed from the counties, talk earnestly with Martin, who listens and listens. Bitter Man hovers over the jumbo shrimp like a blimp at the Superbowl.

"I have a job to do," Judy says, and edges into the crowd.

I float over to the bar and watch Judy mingle with Einstein and Golden Rod. She's perfect for the job, which is to collect affidavits for the Shit from Shinola Brief. Our main argument is that the jurors' note-taking contributed to their confusion about the evidence and caused a defective verdict. The record supports the argument; the jurors returned from their deliberations six times with questions from their notes. There're no cases to support our argument, but that's where the affidavits come in. That's the beauty part.

I watch Judy as she strikes up a conversation with Einstein, wherein she'll get him to tell her what a lousy idea it is for jurors to take notes. Then she'll speak to as many other judges as she can, parlaying Einstein's opinion into a consensus. Later, we'll write affidavits saying that the consensus is that jurors should not be permitted to take notes, and we'll file the affidavits with the brief. They're not a part of the trial record, but the Third Circuit isn't afraid to make new law. If it disapproves of note-taking by jurors, as the intellects like Einstein do, it'll find a way to give Mitsuko a new trial. And Judy her job back.

I raise my champagne in a silent toast to the Shit from Shinola Brief and then to Martin, who'll file it because his back is to the wall. I take deep gulps from the fizzy drink, toasting Judy and Berkowitz. The champagne is gone too soon. I grab another from a passing waiter. It goes straight to my head. I feel dizzy and happy. I ask the bartender for a third and drink a toast to Ned, whom I loved and lost, then to Brent and to my beloved Mike. I begin to understand the expression "feeling no pain."

"Don't drink that too fast now," says the young bartender, handing me a refill. Even though his face is blurry, I see that he's a parking valet from the basement garage, disguised in a tux.

"You can't fool me, I know who you really are. Anthony from the garage, right?"

He laughs. "I can't fool you, Miss Dee."

"Doing double-duty, huh?"

"I got a choice, Miss Dee. I can look at pretty ladies or I can park a bunch of big cars. It's a no-brainer."

"We're traveling incognito, Anthony."

"In what, Miss Dee?"

Suddenly, there's a deep voice beside me, murmuring almost in my ear. I look over and it's Golden Rod, glass in hand. He looks blurry too, even though he's standing very close. "What did you say, Judge Gold . . . Van Houten?" Hearing the sloppiness of my own words, I set down my glass.

"I said, that's a very nice dress."

"Thank you."

"It's a peasant dress, isn't it? Did you get it in Mexico, or someplace else more exciting than Philadelphia?"

"There is no place more exciting than Philadelphia, Judge."

He laughs and traces the gathered edge of the dress with an index finger. "I like the embroidery at the top."

Dumbly, I watch his finger touch my chest, just above my bare breasts. "You shouldn't do that. I'm Mike's wife, and I'm not wearing a bra," I blurt out.

Golden Rod looks stunned. Simultaneously, I realize that I'm too drunk to be here. I look around the room for Judy, but it's out of kilter. All I see are cockeyed three-piece suits. I mumble a good-bye to the startled judge and make my way to the door.

But my escape route is blocked. Bitter Man's standing right in front of the door, talking to Jameson. The mountain talking to the molehill. I walk as steadily as I can toward them. "Excuse me," I say slowly. It's an effort to talk. My head is spinning.

"Miz DiNunzio," says Bitter Man. He holds a plate with a mound of shrimp carcasses on the side. "I'm surprised to see you here."

Jameson tips forward on his toes. "You shouldn't be, Judge Bitterman. Mary's our star. Her rise in the past year has been positively meteoric." His voice is full of undisguised jealousy. He must be drunker than I am.

"I really should go, Timothy."

"Don't be so antisocial, Mary." Jameson reaches out and grabs my arm roughly. "Tell Judge Bitterman how you're going to make partner this June. Tell him how your mentor is going to ram you down our throats."

"Timothy, I don't know what—"

He squeezes my arm. "Isn't that a nice word, Judge Bitterman? Mentor. It could mean anything, couldn't it? Teacher. Friend. Confidant. Counselor. Do you know the origin of the word *mentor*, Judge?"

For once, Bitter Man is speechless. He shakes his head.

"Mentor was the friend of Odysseus, to whom the hero entrusted the education of his son, Telemachus. Isn't that interesting? Did you know that Mary has a very special mentor too? A very powerful mentor. Sam Berkowitz is Mary's mentor. He takes very good care of Mary. Right, Mary?"

"Timothy, stop it." I try to wrest my arm away, but Jameson's grip is surprisingly strong.

"What do you think, Judge? Do you think it's Mary's sharp analytical skills that Mr. Berkowitz so admires? Or do you think it's her superb writing ability? *I* had both of those things, Judge, but our fearless leader did everything he could to block *my* partnership. So tell me, what do you think she's got that I haven't?"

Bitter Man looks from me to Jameson.

"You know, don't you, Judge? You're a brilliant man, but I'll give you a hint anyway. Mary's a merry widow. A *very* merry widow."

Bitter Man's mouth drops open.

I can't believe what Jameson's saying. It's outrageous. "I worked to get where I am, Timothy."

Jameson yanks me to his side. "I know you did, Mary. A big, strong man like Berkowitz, I bet you take quite a pounding—"

"Fuck you!" I shout at Jameson. I wrench my arm free.

Bitter Man's eyes narrow. His face is red, inflamed with anger. "Mary, you didn't!"

I can't take the fury from his face, I couldn't convince him in a million years. I feel dizzy and faint. Heads turn behind Bitter Man, looking at us. I have to get out. I lunge for the door and run to the stairwell. I stagger down it in tears, leaning heavily on the brass banister past Lust and Envy. By the time I reach Gluttony, I'm feeling sick. From embarrassment. From alcohol. From sleep deprivation. I collapse into my chair, and my head falls forward onto a cool pillow of stacked-up mail.

THIRTY-TWO

He is seething.

His lips are moving, though I can't hear what he's shouting at me. He's shaking, he's so infuriated. His face, almost womanish in its softness, is twisted by rage.

We are alone, he and I. It's dusk, and his office is empty and dim. The secretaries have gone home, as have the others. The room is cold; he keeps the thermostat low. He has to set an example, he says.

There are photos of him, with other men who set examples. Richard Nixon. Chief Justice William Rehnquist. Clarence Thomas. Beside the photos are bookshelves filled with books, lots of books, all about the law. Legal philosophy, legal writing, legal analysis. One book after another, in perfect order. And rows and rows of golden federal casebooks, their black volume numbers floating eerily in the half-light: 361, 362, and 363. He has an entire set all to himself. He is a man of importance, a legal scholar.

But he is so angry. Raging, quite nearly out of control. I've never seen him this angry. I've never seen anyone as angry as Judge Bitterman on the day I quit.

Why is he so mad? I did one article, that was all we agreed to, I say to him. I don't have time to do another.

You used to have time! he shouts.

I don't anymore. Things have changed.

It's a young man, isn't it?

I don't answer him. It's none of his business. I am in love, though, with Mike.

Miz DiNunzio, let me quote you one of the most profound legal thinkers there was. The law is a jealous mistress, and requires a long and constant courtship. It is not to be won by trifling favors but by lavish homage. The quotation is Professor Story's, Miz DiNunzio, not mine. A jealous mistress. It means you can't have it both ways. It's your young man or the law. You have to choose.

I already have, I say to him.

That's when it dawns on me, half in a dream and half out of it. I know why Bitter Man was so angry. His speech about the law being jealous was bullshit. He was hiding behind the law, using it as a smokescreen. I didn't see through it then, but I do now. It was Bitter Man who was jealous, crazy jealous, of Mike. It's almost inconceivable, but it makes sense.

I awake with a start.

Bitter Man is standing over me, stroking my hair with a peaceful smile. "Hello, Mary," he says softly.

"Judge?"

"You are so precious to me, my dear." His cheeks look like they're about to burst with happiness, like an overfed baby.

I look around, panicky. My office door is closed. Everyone's at the reception, three floors above.

His swollen underbelly presses against my chair. "I've cared for you ever since the first day you came to work for me. Do you remember?"

I'm too stunned to answer.

"We spent the whole year together, you and I. I watched you

grow, watched you learn. I know I was hard on you at times, but it was for your own good. I was your mentor then, wasn't I, Mary? I was the only one." His voice is unnaturally high.

I nod mechanically. My gorge rises at his touch.

"I tried to forget about you for many years, after you left me, but I couldn't. No other woman would do. Imagine how happy I was when a case of yours finally got assigned to me. I could barely wait until the day of oral argument. It was your first argument, wasn't it, Mary? I could tell. I thought, She has so much more to learn, and there's so much more I can teach her. She still needs me."

Oh no. I won that motion, and Mike was there, watching me with his class. Mike.

"I got the *Harbison's* case a year later almost to the day. As if fate had planned it. I scheduled argument just to see you before me, and you looked so professional in your dark blue suit. As soon as I entered the courtroom, you jumped up and smiled at me in the prettiest way. That's when I knew you felt the same way I did. After all this time."

Of course. I won that motion too. Then came the first note: CONGRATULATIONS ON YOUR PARTNERSHIP, MARY. Bitter Man knew the win would help me make partner. Why didn't I think of him? I squeeze my eyes shut.

"I was silly to make you sing. Forgive me, but I wanted to test your love. And the other day in Sam's office, when I asked for your opinion, I was just giving you a chance to shine. But you seemed upset with me, so I sent you another note. I put it in Sam's box after our noon meeting. Did you get my note, Mary? I was worried you wouldn't get it."

My heart is pounding. My chest is flushed with blood.

"A penny for your thoughts." His hand reaches under my chin and he wrenches my face up to him. His eyes, almost engulfed by the flesh around them, look out of control.

Suddenly, the door to my office bursts open and Judy

bounds in. "Mary, what happened?" she says. "I heard that Jameson—"

"Close the door!" Bitter Man shouts. He steps away from me and whips a silver revolver from his jacket, pointing it at Judy. She looks wildly from me to him. "What the—"

"I said close the door! And lock it!"

Judy obeys quickly, staring at the gun in fear.

"Who is this woman, Mary?" Bitter Man's hammy hands train the gun expertly at Judy's chest. There's a metallic click as he cocks the trigger.

My heart leaps up at the sound. "No!" I shout.

Bitter Man looks at me sharply, a silent reprimand.

I swallow hard. "Please don't hurt her, Bill. She's my best friend. My dearest friend. Please don't."

Judy nods emphatically, her eyes wide.

Bitter Man eases off the trigger. "Your best friend? Good. We'll need her. She'll be our witness."

"Yes, that's right," I say evenly. "Now let her go, Bill. She has to go home now."

"She can't go, she's the witness. For our wedding. I'm performing it tonight. Get up, Mary!"

"Wedding?"

"There's no time to waste. I know the truth now. I have to get you away from the Jew. That blustering fool, he's no lawyer. He's nothing but a horse trader. So get up!"

I don't move. I can't.

"Get up, you whore!" He swings the gun crazily over to me.

I can barely breathe. The gun is two inches from my forehead. It's a dull silver color, like a shark, and bigger than I thought. Bigger than Marv's gun. The end of the barrel points directly at me, a lethal black circle.

"Get up!" His shout reverberates in the tiny office. Suddenly, he shoves the gun against my forehead.

I hear Judy gasp.

The cold metal digs into my skin. I feel paralyzed in my chair, terrified to move an inch. I will myself to speak. "Bill, please. Let's talk—"

"There's no time for talk." He pushes the gun into my head.

My gut tightens. "I don't understand. I need you to . . . teach me."

"What?"

"I don't understand you, your feelings."

"My feelings?" he says, testy.

"Yes. About me."

"We don't have time for this, Mary. What about my feelings? Be precise!"

"Do you really love me? I'm not—"

"Of course I love you, of course I do." His head shakes slightly. The gun barrel jiggles against my forehead.

"I wasn't sure, Bill. I didn't know . . . how you felt. You never told me."

"Well, I do love you. I love you more than any of them."

"But how can I trust your love, when you—"

"Trust my love!" he roars. "Trust my love! I've risked everything for you. It's all been for you. All of it!"

I catch my breath. I can hear the blood throbbing in my ears. "What have you done for me, Bill?"

"I killed him! Your husband, the schoolteacher. He took you away from me, away from the law. He brought those brats into my courtroom. So ignorant. They *clapped*, by God. In *my* courtroom!"

My heart stops. Mike. I hear myself moan.

"He didn't deserve you, Mary. He couldn't offer you what I can. He taught spelling, for God's sake, to small children. He knew nothing about the law. Nothing!"

"Did you kill my secretary, Bill?" I can barely utter the words.

"He had his arm around you. I thought he was your date from the night before. The one you had dinner with. The one who kissed you at your doorstep. He had no right!"

I close my eyes. Brent. A mistake. "So you followed me in the car. And called me."

"I had to."

"Why? Why did you have to?"

"To be near you. And to check up on you, I admit it. I had to make sure you were working hard, applying yourself. You get distracted by men, Mary, we both know this. I couldn't let it happen again. You have a brilliant career ahead of you. I'll teach you everything I know. You'll write, publish. You're going to be one of the best!"

The gun barrel bores into my temple.

"Now do you see how much I care for you? Now do you understand?"

The office is dead quiet. Judy is frozen in front of the door, her eyes full of horror.

"I see now . . . that you've done a lot for me, Bill. But if you really love me, you'll give me the gun. That will prove you really love me."

"I'm not stupid, Mary," he says coldly.

"But how can I believe you love me when you're threatening to kill me? It's not . . . logical, Bill. It doesn't stand to reason. You taught me that, how important it was to test—"

"Why is it so hot in here? Why?" Bitter Man looks angrily around the room. "They keep it too hot!"

The gun moves on my head. I try to squeeze back my fear. "As soon as you give me the gun, we can be married. But I won't go as your prisoner. I'll go freely. As your wife."

"No, no. This is all wrong." Tears begin to gather in his eyes, but he shakes them off. "All wrong. I need the gun. I can't give it to you."

"I'll be your wife, Bill. Finally and forever. Think of it."

"It's not going to work." He starts to sob. "You want *him* now. You don't want me anymore. You betrayed me." He drills the gun into my forehead, shoving me backward with it. I feel panic rising in my throat, almost choking me. "No, I didn't, Bill. It wasn't true, what Jameson said. I want you. I'll work hard, I'll make you proud of me. We'll be the best, Bill. The two of us."

Bitter Man starts to whisper furiously, incomprehensibly, to himself. Tears stream down his face. I look over at Judy, who looks terrified. The judge is a madman, and he's falling apart like a demented Humpty Dumpty. "Bill, give me the gun. I want to be the best. I can't do it without you. I need you!"

"Mary," he says, crying. "Mary." It's the only understandable word he utters; the rest are whispered ravings. His eyes are so tear-filled he can't see. He moves to wipe them on his sleeve and the gun drops away slightly from my temple.

It's my only chance. And Judy's.

I reach for the barrel and yank the gun away from him with all my might. It comes free in my hand.

Bitter Man looks at me in shock, then in fury. "Mary, what are you doing!" His eyes are like glittering slits.

"Get back! Get away from me!" I scream. I point the heavy gun at him and rise to my feet, weak-kneed. I hold the gun with two hands, like Marv said.

"I'll get help!" Judy shouts. She opens the door and runs out. As fast as she is, two stairs at a time, it'll take her just minutes to get to Avarice and back to Gluttony.

"Back up, Judge!"

"You can't be serious," he says, in a voice suddenly dark with malevolence. His tears have stopped completely, as have his mutterings.

"Get back!" I aim the gun higher, right at his eyes. "Now!" He backs up against the bookcase, sneering at me.

"Stay there! I mean it!" I lock my arms out straight. The gun wobbles slightly as I grip its grooved wooden handle.

"You would never hurt me."

"Stay back!" I try to hold the gun still. There's engraving on its steel barrel. S&W .357 MAGNUM. Jesus, it's terrifying to have something like that in your hand. To hold something that packs so much power. It can kill in the blink of an eye. *I* could kill in the blink of an eye. The realization hits me with as much impact as any bullet. There are no witnesses. I could get away with murder.

"You couldn't hurt me. You love me."

"No. I love Mike."

Bitter Man flinches. "The teacher? Forget him, he was dog shit. That's why I killed him. He died like a dog, too. Road kill." He laughs softly.

I can't hear this. I look down the barrel of the gun. At the end is an orange sight. I line it up with the small American flag that is Bitter Man's tie tack. My hand shakes slightly, but it's easier to aim the gun than I thought.

"He was nothing. Insignificant. Weak. If you had seen his face—"

"Stop it!" I use the flag like a bull's-eye. I focus on it and breathe deeply. Once, then again. An absolute calm comes over me. Bitter Man is three feet away, a large target. I have the weapon, I can use it. He killed two innocent men, men I loved. They didn't deserve to die. He does, and I can kill him. All I have to do is pull the trigger. The ultimate in fucking back.

"He whimpered like—"

"Shut up!" I spit at him, in a voice I've never heard before. I have a split second before Judy gets back.

"Mary—"

"Shut up, I said! Shut up!" I look down the barrel at his expression of contempt and disgust. I ease the trigger just a fraction. The hammer, with its corrugated pad, falls back ever so slightly. There's the loud, metallic click I heard before as the chamber rotates a millimeter. It's all very mechanical. A very handsome killing machine, precision engineered in the United States of America. If I pull the trigger a fraction of an inch more, Messrs. Smith and Wesson will kill Bitter Man for me. I don't even have to do it myself.

I raise the gun and get the flag in my sight. And then my hand isn't shaking anymore.

"Give me one good reason," I say to him.

THIRTY-THREE

That's when I hear the voice. I recognize it suddenly. I know now who it is.

I thought it was Mike's voice, but it's not him at all. And it's not the devil's voice, or an angel's either. It's my soul's own voice, gamely trying to climb out of the hole I've been digging for it steadily, daily, since the hour of my birth.

It's me, trying to save my own soul.

Thou shalt not kill.

But I have killed. And I want to now. So much.

Spare him. Redeem yourself.

Redeem yourself. It resonates inside me, at the core.

Redemption.

I can't change the past, but I can make the future. I know what it cost me to kill before. This time I have a choice. I choose no.

I release the trigger. The hammer snaps forward with a final click.

At the same moment, a terrified Judy appears at the doorway, followed by Berkowitz, Einstein, Golden Rod, and a crowd of appalled judges. In the instant that I look back, Bitter

Man hurls himself into my arms. "Give me that gun!" he roars.

His weight sends me crashing back onto my desk. I feel his hands scrambling at my breast for the weapon. Suddenly, the gun goes off, with an earsplitting report. I hear myself scream. The force of the explosion reverberates in my ears and vibrates up my arm. For a minute I'm not sure who's been hit.

One look at Bitter Man tells me the answer. His face is twisted in pain and surprise. He falls slowly backward, then slumps heavily to the floor. His shirt, in tatters, is black with smoke; his tie is shorn into two ragged halves. A crimson bud appears over his heart, then bursts into full vermillion bloom as he lies, contorted, on the carpet. The air stinks of fire and smoke.

Berkowitz rushes over to Bitter Man, stretched out on the floor, his blood staining the carpet. "Jesus," Berkowitz says, looking up at me. "He's dead."

The judges, all of them assembled, look at me in disbelief. In shock. In revulsion.

I freeze at the judgment in their eyes. I'm stunned, shaking, in shock. I want to explain, but I can't. All I can do is look back at them. It's Judgment Day. I knew it was coming. It was just a question of time.

"Jesus, Mary!" Berkowitz cries out. He takes the revolver from me and gathers me up in his arms. I feel an enormous weight in my chest, the wrench of my heart breaking. I start to cry, first in great hiccups, then out of control. I'm not crying for Bitter Man. I'm crying for Mike and for Brent.

That night, after a chastened Lombardo has come and gone, Berkowitz drives me home himself. I feel utterly drained as I sit in the gleaming Mercedes-Benz, with its odor of fine leather and stale cigarettes. Berkowitz opens the car door for me and offers to walk me upstairs, but I turn him down. There's no need. I'm safe now. No more telephone calls, no more notes. My empty apartment is my own again.

The door closes behind me, and I lean against it in the dark. I stand there for the longest time, thinking of Mike, who brought me from fear into love, using only his patience and his heart. I can't believe he's gone; it's so awful that he died, and in so much pain. I feel newly grief-stricken; it makes me wonder if I ever let myself truly mourn him. Maybe I did the Next Thing too soon.

My thoughts run to Brent, who was so innocent. A wonderful friend, a loving man. His voice coach was right; he was full of joy. He's gone now, cut down by the same man, mistakenly. Somehow that makes it much worse.

Bitter Man. He was bitter and evil for a reason no one can ever fathom. The devil, truly. Their deaths were his doing. It was his fault, not mine. Now he's gone too. That much is my doing, that much I'm responsible for. No more.

Soon I'm crying, sobbing hard, and I can't seem to make it stop. I feel overwhelmed by grief; it brings me to my knees in front of the closed door. I can't believe that Mike is gone, that Brent is gone. That I'll never see either of them again.

I wish I could stop crying, but I can't, and soon I hear a loud *boom boom boom* against the door. Only it's not someone else pounding on the door.

It's my own skull.

THIRTY-FOUR

FEDERAL ATTRACTION! screams the three-inch headline in the morning edition of *The Philadelphia Daily News*.

FEDERAL JUDGE ATTACKS WOMAN LAWYER: D.A. FINDS SELF-DEFENSE, reads the smaller headline in *The Philadelphia Inquirer*, its calmer sister publication.

I don't read the newspaper accounts, don't even want to see them. I just want to know if Berkowitz kept my name out of the papers, so I can practice law again in this city. Someday.

"I don't see it anywhere," Ned says, skimming the articles at my kitchen table. His tie is tucked carefully into a white oxford shirt. He stopped by on the way to work to see how I was, bearing blueberry muffins. He didn't try to hug or kiss me. He seemed to sense that I needed the distance.

"Good."

"You should take your time going back to work, Mary." The muffins lie crumbled on the plate between us.

"I will, this time."

"I'll take care of your desk. Don't worry about a thing."

"Thanks. I'll return the favor."

Ned smiles mysteriously.

"What?"

"I'm not telling you now. You've had enough surprises." He folds up the newspaper and sets it down on the table.

"Tell me, Ned."

"Actually, it's a good surprise. You really want to hear it?" His green eyes shine.

"Sure."

"I'm leaving the firm. As soon as you come back."

"What?" It's so unexpected, it draws me out of myself for a minute.

"There's no future for me there. I'm not going to make partner."

"How do you know that?"

"Berkowitz told me."

Now I'm totally confounded. I sit up in the chair.

"He told me one day in his office, when I went in to ask him how many partners they were making."

I remember, the conversation he materially omitted at dinner that night.

"Berkowitz told me I wasn't going to be one of them, no matter how many they made."

"Why?" I feel hurt for him.

"He said I didn't have what it takes. The fire in the belly. The *cipollines*, I think he meant." He smiles crookedly.

"That's ridiculous."

"No, it's not. He's right, Mary. I didn't realize it until he said it, but he's right. I don't have the heart for it. I don't even like being a lawyer. I was only doing it to prove something to my father."

I don't know what to say. Silence comes between us.

"I did talk to him, you know," he says.

"Your father?"

"Yes. I told you I would. I called you about it, but you weren't returning my calls." He winces slightly.

"Ned—"

"That's okay, you explained it. With the last note, even I

would have suspected me. Anyway, my father never had you followed, but he did do a lot of research on you. He searched your name in Lexis and pulled all the cases you worked on."

"Why?"

"To see what the competition was like. To size up my chances of making partner. That's why he watched you at your dep."

"Jesus."

"He researched Judy, too, and me. He said he wanted to know what I was working on. I guess it never occurred to him to pick up the phone." He picks idly at a blueberry crumb.

"Did he say anything about tampering with files?"

"No. I don't think he'd do that, he'd think it was unethical. Wife-beating is okay, but tampering with case files, no."

"How was it, seeing him again?"

"He looks older. His hair is all silver."

"Are you two going to—"

"No, we're not going to be pals, if that's your question. We'll talk from time to time, but that's it. Nothing's changed but his hair, I can see that. I asked him if he wanted to go into therapy with me. That went over real big." He smiles, but it's sour.

"So what are you going to do now? For a job?"

Ned pops a blueberry into his mouth. "I don't know yet. Teach law, teach sailing. Get married, stay home with the kids. All ten of them. What do you say?"

"Am I supposed to answer that?"

"I drive a Miata, what more do you want?"

"A continuance."

"Just like a lawyer, DiNunzio. Just like a lawyer." He laughs loudly, throwing his head back. He looks happy and free.

"So do I get it?"

"Motion granted," he says.

And Alice, who has been sitting under the kitchen table, rubs up against his leg.

THIRTY-FIVE

It's June 28, the first anniversary of Mike's death.

I cruise up the smooth asphalt road that leads to the pink magnolia tree. I think of it as Mike's tree, even though it shelters at least sixty other graves. They fan out from the trunk of the magnolia in concentric circles, ring upon ring of headstones.

I pull over at the side of the road, where I always park. I cut the ignition, and the air-conditioning shuts down with a wheeze. Outside the car, the air is damp and sweet. The radio called for thundershowers this afternoon, and I believe it. The air is so wet you know the bottom's got to tear open, like a tissue holding water.

The cemetery is silent. The only sounds are the cars rushing by on the distant expressway and the intermittent quarreling of the squirrels. I make my way to Mike's grave. Only a year ago, it was on the outermost ring, but now it's somewhere toward the middle. More graves are being added, more people are passing on. Like the rings of the magnolia tree itself, it's just time moving on, life moving on.

Death moving on, too.

I walk past the monuments with names I don't recognize

until I reach the ones I do. I feel as if I know these people. They're Mike's neighbors in a way, and they seem like a good lot. ANTONELLI has a new DAD sign; his family is very attentive to him. LORENZ's grave is bare, though her monument bears its chipper epitaph: ALWAYS KIND, GENEROUS, AND CHEERFUL. I love Mrs. Lorenz, how could you not?

I pass BARSON, which stands alone, off to the right. It's a child's grave, and its pink marble headstone has a picture of a ballerina etched into it. There's a Barbie doll there today, sitting straight-legged in tiny spike heels. I can never bring myself to look at BARSON for long and hurry by it to MARTIN. Something's always going on at MARTIN. It's a hubbub of activity, for a final resting place. Today I note that the showy Martin family has added yet another bush to the border that surrounds their mother's monument. I wonder about these people. I don't understand how they can bring themselves to garden on top of someone they loved.

I reach Mike's monument and brush away the curly magnolia petals that have fallen on its bumpy top. I pick a candy wrapper off his grave, like I used to pick cat hair off his sweaters. Just because I'm not planting shrubs on his head doesn't mean I don't care how he looks. I bunch up the debris in my hand and sit down, facing his monument.

LASSITER, MICHAEL A.

It's a simple granite monument, but so striking. Or maybe I feel that way because it's Mike's name cut into the granite with such finality and clarity, and I hadn't expected to see his name on a gravestone. Not yet. Not when I can still remember doodling on a legal pad during our engagement.

Mrs. Mary Lassiter.

Mrs. Mary DiNunzio Lassiter.

Mary DiNunzio-Lassiter.

I eventually stuck with my own name, but I confess to a politically incorrect thrill when the mail came addressed to Mrs. Michael Lassiter. Because that's who I was inside, wholly his.

I still am.

I've learned that you don't stop loving someone just because they die. And you don't stop loving someone who's dead just because you start loving someone else. I know this violates the natural law that two things can't occupy the same place at the same time, but that's never been true of the human heart anyway.

I breathe a deep sigh and close my eyes.

"Look!" squeals a child's voice at my ear. "Look what I have!"

I look over and find myself face to face with a blue-eyed toddler in a white pinafore. In her dimpled arms is a wreath of scarlet roses and a couple of miniature American flags. Plainly, the child has gone shopping on the graves. "You have a lot of stuff."

"I have a lot of stuff!" says the little girl. "I found it! That's okay!" She jumps up and down and a flag falls to the ground. "Uh-oh, flag."

A woman in a prim linen suit rushes up and takes the child by the arm. "I'm sorry that she bothered you," she says, flustered. "Lily, wherever did you get those things?"

Lily struggles to reach the fallen flag. "Flag, Mommy. Flag."

"She's no bother. She's sweet." I pick up the flag and hand it to Lily.

"Tank you," Lily says, quite distinctly.

"Where do you suppose these things belong? I'd hate to put them on the wrong . . . places."

"The flags go with those soldiers, in the bronze flag holders. The VFW gives them the flag holders, I think. That one over there, HAWLEY, he was in Vietnam."

"Oh, dear. Poor man." She turns around worriedly. "Where do you think the wreath goes?"

I take a look at it. I have no idea where it belongs. "I'll take the wreath."

"Thank you. I'm so sorry." She hands it to me gratefully and hoists Lily to her hip. "Can you make sure I find the soldiers?"

"Sure. Just look for the flag holders."

Lily howls with frustration as her mother drops the flags into the flag holders at MACARRICI, WAINWRIGHT, and HAWLEY. I give her the thumbs up.

I stand and examine the wreath. The roses are a velvety red, fastened to the circular frame with green wire. There's even a little green tripod to make the wreath stand up. I take it and set it at the head of Mike's grave, right under LASSITER.

On its white satin sash, it says in gold script:

BELOVED HUSBAND

I look at it for a long time.

It looks good.

THIRTY-SIX

A month later, I'm in my new office at Stalling & Webb. On the wall hangs an antique quilt that I bought in Lancaster County, from the Amish. It's called a friendship quilt and has the names of the quilters and their best friends sewn onto spools of a dozen bright colors. The other day I read all the names. Emma Miller, from Nappanee, Indiana. Katie Yoder, of Brinton, Ohio. Sarah Helmuth, from Kokomo, Indiana. I like to think about these women, whose lives were so different from my own but who valued each other so much. That much we have in common, and it ties me to them.

I'm thinking about this as Judy sits on the other side of my new desk, an Irish farm table that cost Stalling more than an Irish farm. She sports the latest example of Kurt's handiwork, a spiky haircut that looks like Jean Seberg's. If only by accident, the cut brings out the richness of her blue eyes and the curve of a strong cheekbone. She looks beautiful in it, especially when she laughs. She's a good woman; I feel blessed in knowing her. In having her in my life.

"Why are you looking at me like that, Mary?" she asks, with an amused frown.

I try to swallow the lump in my throat. How can I say *I love you?* Her eyes meet mine, and for once she doesn't bug me to say the unsayable. She knows it anyway. She wasn't number one for nothing.

"So what do you think?" Judy asks, with a grin. She gestures to the mound of filthy men's socks in the middle of my costly rustic desk. "I bet they expect you to wash them."

I clear my throat. "I think it's a good sign. They're treating me as shitty as they treat each other."

She smiles. "So you only lost fifty grand. Not too bad."

"Play money."

"Pin money."

"Mad money." I laugh. "You know, it was a lot less than Hart asked for. They must not have liked him. Particularly the forewoman, from Ambler. She could tell he was a pig." I'm smelling defeat, but it doesn't hurt half as much as I thought it would. I think this is called perspective, but I'm not sure. I never had it before.

"They should have taken notes, then you'd have grounds for appeal." She giggles.

"Right. We're zero for two, since we lost *Mitsuko*. We have to be the only lawyers chastised as a team by the Third Circuit and in record time. What did they say again?"

She straightens up and tries to look judicial. "I quote—'A bald attempt by a duo of overzealous counsel to circumvent the Federal Rules of Appellate Procedure by the deliberate inclusion of affidavits not of record.'"

"They can't take a joke."

"Bingo."

We both laugh. "So we lost two, Jude. We're doin' good."

"But we're partners now. We can screw up with impunity."

"You know, it doesn't matter that we lost *Mitsuko*. The Shit from Shinola Brief was a thing of beauty. Martin had to admit it, even though he was too gutless to sign it." I shift on the needlepointed chair that Martin is lending me; every morning I have to stick my butt into a nest of tiny owlets.

"True. And even though you lost your trial, the case went in well, it really did. You handled Hart on cross, too. Didn't ask too much, stopped at just the right time."

"Tell me again how good my closing was. I like it when you say it was good, damn good."

"Your closing was good, Mary. Damn good!" Judy shakes her wiggy little haircut.

"You don't say!"

Her blue eyes glitter. "You know, you and I could be two halves of a very tough whole."

"You want to get married?"

She grins, gap-toothed. "In a way."

Finally I realize what she's driving at. "You serious?"

"Yepper. You could do the trial work and I could do the paperwork. We could make a go of it, run a first-class little spin-off. A boutique practice, everyone calls it now."

"Wait a minute, Judy. We'd get some referral work from Stalling, but I'd worry about where the business would come from."

"You'd worry anyway. It's in you and it's gots to come out. We'll start out small, for sure, but I don't need half the money I make here. Do you?"

"Not really. I don't have time to spend it."

"Me neither. Even with the catalogs, there's only so much damage you can do. Except for Victoria's Secret."

"Hah! What do you buy from them? You don't even wear a bra. In our new firm you'd have to wear a bra. I won't stand for—"

Judy throws a black sock at me, but I duck. "Joke all you want, but it's a good idea. You could do discrimination work, but plaintiff's side. Think about it. Do well *and* do good."

"Work for the angels, huh?" The thought strikes a chord.

"There you go! You've represented defendants for years. You can anticipate every move, right?"

"Maybe."

"So you want to do it? Let's do it. Let's just fucking *do* it!" Judy says, brimming with excitement. The woman can go from zero to sixty in two minutes. "We don't need Stalling, Mare, we're just two more mouths to feed here. We apprenticed for eight years, it's our time now. Let's go! Onward and upward!"

I look at her. She feels none of the doubt that I do. Judy loves a challenge. She climbs mountains for fun. "You think it's that easy?"

"Yes."

I squint at her, and she grins.

Who better to jump across an abyss with than someone who climbs mountains? says the voice.

I smile, reluctantly at first, but then it grows into laughter of its own momentum. It feels like my heart opening up. "Okay. Okay. Okay!"

"Okay!" Judy launches herself into the air, arms stretched up high, and dances around my bookshelves. "She said okay!"

I can't stop smiling. "What should we call ourselves?"

She shakes her butt in a circle. "DiNunzio and Carrier! If not that, Bert and Ernie!"

"No, it has to be girls! Lucy and Ethel?"

"Thelma and Louise!"

"Forget them, they die in the end. Wait, we forgot one thing. We gotta take Miss P, agreed?"

"Of course. We need someone to wish us nighty-night."

Suddenly, Miss Pershing appears at the door, interrupting our party. "Speak of the devil," I say, as Judy boogies by and takes her for a spin.

"Ohh!" she yips. "My, my!"

"Unhand that secretary," I say, since I'm not sure Miss P's into the lambada.

"Aw," Judy says.

Her cheeks flushed, Miss Pershing smooths her hair needlessly into its twist. "Sakes alive. Well, my goodness. That was . . . exciting."

Judy curtseys. "Thank you, Miss P."

Miss Pershing looks slightly confused. "Miss DiNunzio, I thought I heard your voice, but I'm surprised to see you here."

"You didn't think I'd come in today, after I smelled defeat at the hands of that mean old jury?"

"No, it's not that. But didn't I just see you upstairs?"

"No. I haven't been upstairs at all."

Her back to Miss Pershing, Judy makes a face that says: Miss Pershing's rope has come unclipped.

"That's strange," she mutters, shaking her head. "I could swear I just saw you sitting in the reception area." She hobbles away, befuddled. I have a sharp sense of déjà vu. I see my mother, who would walk away exactly like Miss Pershing just did, when I used to pretend to be Angie. All of a sudden, it clicks. I jump out of my chair and fly out the door.

"Mary?" says Judy, after me.

"Be right back, pardner!"

And I'm gone, leaping up the stairs, two by two, until I reach the reception area. I see her, sitting by herself on a white sofa that has no support. She looks just like me, except that she has a pixie haircut. And a suitcase.

She rises to her feet when she sees me. "Hello, beautiful," she says.

ACKNOWLEDGMENTS

I think it was Chekhov or Tolstoy, one or the other, who said something about someone being the most extraordinary ordinary person he'd ever met. Such people exist, I know, because I'm friends with them, and I met many others in researching and writing this novel. In fact, I know so many of them by now that I'm quite sure they constitute the world's sum total, and I worry that you are fresh out of luck.

The first such person is my agent, Linda Hayes of Columbia Literary Associates. It was Kermit the Frog—I'm on firmer ground here—who said something about the wonderful things that can happen when one whole person believes in you. Linda was the first one whole person (not related to me by blood or affection) to believe in me. She nurtured me, and this book, as if she had given birth to both of us. Linda is truly extraordinary. I am forever in her debt.

And she's a great judge of character. She introduced me to Carolyn Marino, another extraordinary ordinary person, who became my editor at HarperCollins. Carolyn believed too, and I thank her for that. Also, while she appreciated what worked in the novel, she knew how to improve it. That she managed to tell me so, and for me still to find the editorial process so much fun, is a tribute to her grace, intelligence, and sensitivity.

Thanks, too, to Chassie West, for her enormously valuable (and fun-to-read) suggestions.

I also met a number of extraordinary ordinary people in researching the book. There were good Catholics, mountain climbers, a priest, women's health care providers, officers of my local police department and the Philadelphia Police Department, an ex-nun, an order of cloistered nuns, and Eileen at the Dusty Rhoads Gun Shop, who knows more about revolvers than anyone should. These people answered every question I had, carefully and without once checking their watches, and all I was to them was some lady with a legal pad. Thank you.

Finally, all my love and thanks to my family, the first whole people who believed, and to my daughter. To my very supportive friends—extraordinary ordinary people all—Rachel Kull, Judith Hill, Susan White, Laura Henrich, Franca Palumbo, and Jerry Hoffman. Special thanks to Fayne Landes and Sandy Steingard for the psychiatric consults (not mine, my character's), to Liz Savitt, whose enormous energy and bravery got me writing in the first place, and to Marsha Klein, who helped me find a smidgen of bravery in myself.

FINAL
APPEAL

To all my parents, and to Kiki

ONE

At times like this I realize I'm too old to be starting over, working with law clerks. I own pantyhose with more mileage than
these kids, and better judgment. For example, two of the
clerks, Ben Safer and Artie Weiss, are bickering as we speak;
never mind that they're making a scene in an otherwise quiet
appellate courtroom, in front of the most expensive members
of the Philadelphia bar.

"No arguing in the courtroom," I tell them, in the same tone
I use on my six-year-old. Not that it works with her either.

"He started it, Grace," Ben says in a firm stage whisper,
standing before the bank of leather chairs against the wall.
"He told me he'd save me a seat and he didn't. Now there's no
seats left."

"Will you move, geek? You're blocking my sun," Artie says,
not bothering to look up from the sports page. He rarely
overexerts himself; he's sauntered through life to date, relying
on his golden-boy good looks, native intelligence, and uncanny
jump shot. He throws one strong leg over the other and turns
the page, confident he'll win this argument even if it runs into
overtime. Artie, in short, is a winner.

But so is Ben in his own way; he was number two at Chicago

Law School, meat grinder of the Midwest. "You told me you'd save me a seat, Weiss," he says, "so you owe me one. Yours. Get up."

"Eat me," Artie says, loud enough to distract the lawyers conferring at the counsel table like a bouquet of bald spots. They'd give him a dirty look if he were anyone else, but because he works for the chief judge they flash capped smiles; you never know which clerk's got your case on his desk.

"Get up. Now, Weiss."

"Separate, you two," I say. "Ben, go sit in the back. Argument's going to start any minute."

"Out of the question. I won't sit in public seating. He said he'd save me a seat, he owes me a seat."

"It's not a contract, Ben," I advise him. For free.

"I understand that. But he should be the one who moves, not me." He straightens the knot on his tie, already at tourniquet tension; between the squeeze on his neck and the one on his sphincter, the kid's twisted shut at both ends like a skinny piece of saltwater taffy. "I have a case being argued."

"So do I, jizzbag," Artie says, flipping the page.

I like Artie, but the problem with the Artie Weisses of the world is they have no limits. "Artie, did you tell him you'd save him a seat?"

"Why would I do that? Then I'd have to sit next to him." He gives Ben the finger behind the tent of newspaper.

I draw the line. "Artie, put your finger away."

"Ooooh, spank me, Grace. Spank me hard. Pull my wittle pants down and throw me over your gorgeous knees."

"You couldn't handle it, big guy."

"Try me." He leans over with a broad grin.

"I mean it, Artie. You're on notice." He doesn't know I haven't had sex since my marriage ended three years ago. Nobody's in the market for a single mother, even a decent-looking one with improved brown hair, authentic blue eyes, and a body that's staying the course, at least as we speak.

"Come on, sugar," Artie says, nuzzling my shoulder. "Live the dream."

"Cut it out."

"You read the book, now see the movie."

I turn toward Ben to avoid laughing; it's not good to laugh when you're setting limits. "Ben, you know he's not going to move. The judges will be out any minute. Go find a seat in the back."

Ben scans the back row where the courthouse groupies sit; it's a lineup that includes retired men, the truly lunatic, even the homeless. Ben, looking them over, makes no effort to hide his disdain; you'd think he'd been asked to skinny-dip in the Ganges. He turns to me, vaguely desperate. "Let me have your seat, Grace. I'll take notes for you."

"No."

"But my notes are like transcripts. I used to sell them at school."

"I can take my own notes, thank you." Ten years as a trial lawyer, I can handle taking notes; taking notes is mostly what I do now as the assistant to the chief judge. I take notes while real lawyers argue, then I go to the library and draft an opinion that real lawyers cite in their next argument. But I'm not complaining. I took this job because it was part-time and I'm not as good a juggler as Joan Lunden, Paula Zahn, and other circus performers.

"How about you, Sarah?" Ben asks the third law clerk, Sarah Whittemore, sitting on my other side. "You don't have a case this morning. You can sit in the back."

Fat chance. Sarah smooths a strand of cool blond hair away from her face, revealing a nose so diminutive it's a wonder she gets any oxygen at all. "Sorry, I need this seat," she says.

I could have told him that. Sarah wants to represent the downtrodden, not mingle with them.

A paneled door opens near the dais and the court crier, a compact man with a competent air, begins a last-minute check on the microphones at the dais and podium. Ben glances at the back row with dismay. "I can't sit back there with those people. One of them has a plastic hat on, for God's sake."

Artie looks over the top of his paper. "A plastic hat? Where?"

"There." Ben jerks his thumb toward a bearded man sporting a crinkled cellophane rain bonnet and a black raincoat buttoned to the neck. The man's collar is flipped up, ready for monsoon season, but it's not raining in the courtroom today.

"It's Shake and Bake! He came!" Artie says. His face lights up and he waves at the man with his newspaper. "Go sit with him, Safer, he's all right."

"You know that guy, Artie?" I ask, sitting straighter to get a better look. The bearded man grins in a loopy way at the massive gold seal of the United States courts mounted behind the dais, his grubby face tilted to the disk like a black-eyed Susan to the sun.

"Sure. He hangs out at the Y, plays ball with me and Armen. You oughta see his spin move, it's awesome when he's not zoned out. I told him to stop by and see the judge on the bench."

Ben's dark eyes widen. "You *invited* that kook to oral argument? How could you do that?"

I don't say it, but for the first time I agree with Ben. I am becoming a geek, a superannuated geek.

"Why shouldn't he come to court?" Artie says. "It's a free country. He's got rights." He stands up and signals wildly, as ill-mannered as a golden retriever puppy; Artie's the pick of the litter out of Harvard, where they evidently do not teach common sense.

The lawyers in the first three rows of the courtroom crane their necks at him, and I tug at the rough khaki of his sport coat. "Artie, don't embarrass me," I say.

Sarah leans over. "Artie, you're crazier than he is. Sit down."

"He's not crazy," Artie says, still signaling.

"He's wearing Saran Wrap," I point out.

"He always does. It's Shake and Bake, man. You gotta love it."

"Fine," Ben says. "You like him so much, *you* go sit with him."

"Don't mind if I do. Party on, Safer." Artie claps Ben on the back and walks toward the back row.

"Please rise!" shouts the crier, standing behind a desk at the side of the dais. "The Honorable Judges of the United States Court of Appeals for the Third Circuit."

A concealed door to the left of the dais swings open, and the judges parade out, resplendent in their swishing black robes. The federal courts decide appeals in three-judge panels, inviting comparison to the three wise men or the three stooges, depending on whether you win or lose. First comes the Honorable Phillip Galanter, tall, thin, and Aryan, with slack jowls like Ed Meese used to have and blond hair thinning to gray. He's followed by a wizened senior judge, the Honorable Morris Townsend, shuffling slowly along, and finally the Very Honorable and Terribly Handsome Chief Judge Armen Gregorian, my boss.

"Armen looks good up there, doesn't he?" Sarah says, crossing her legs under the skirt of her sleek slate-gray suit.

He sure as hell does. Towering over the two of them, Armen grins down at the crowd in an easy way. His complexion is tinged with olive; his oversized teeth remind me of an exotic JFK. There are precious few perks in working for the judicial branch, and a boss who looks like a sultan is one of them. I lean near Sarah's perfumed neck and whisper, "I got first dibs."

"In your dreams."

"But you're too young for him."

She smirks. "Too young? Is there such a thing?"

"Bitch." I elbow her in the ovary.

"Oyez! Oyez!" calls the crier. "All persons having business with the United States Court of Appeals for the Third Circuit are admonished to draw near and give their attention, for this court is now in session. God save the United States and this honorable court. Be seated, please."

The panel sits down and the first appeal begins. Ben takes notes on the argument by the appellant's lawyer, who had his civil case dismissed by the district court ten floors below us. The young lawyer has been granted ten minutes without questions from the judges to present his argument, but he's blowing them fast. Armen's forehead wrinkles with concern; he wants to cut to the chase, but this poor guy can't get out of the garage.

"A Third Circuit virgin," Ben says, with the superior snicker of someone who has never done it. I fail to see the humor. I know what it's like to stand before a judge when the words you memorized don't seem to come and the ones that do roll down backward through your gullet and tumble out your butt.

"I guess my time is up," the lawyer says, obviously relieved to see the Christmas light on the podium blink from yellow to red. He thinks the hard part's over, but he's dead wrong. The light turns green again. *Go!*

"Who wants the first question?" Armen says, looking over his colleagues on the panel. He flicks a silky black forelock out of his eyes; he always needs a haircut, it's part of his sex appeal. "Judge Galanter?"

"Counsel," Judge Galanter says quickly, "your appeal concerns the Racketeer Influenced and Corrupt Organizations Act, RICO, but I wonder if you understand why the statute at issue was enacted by Congress."

"It was passed because of organized crime, Your Honor."

"The statute was aimed at extortionists, murderers, and loan sharks. The typical organized criminals, correct?"

The young lawyer looks puzzled. "Yes, Judge Galanter."

"It prohibits a pattern of racketeering activity, the so-called predicate acts, does it not?"

"Yes, sir."

Armen shifts in his high-backed chair.

"But your client isn't suing mobsters under RICO, is he, counsel?" Galanter says.

"With all due respect, Your Honor, I think this appeal presents a matter of national importance. It involves the manipulation of—"

"Flower peddlers, isn't that right, counsel? Not mobsters, not extortionists, not killers. Florists. The ad says, *Nothing but the Best for Your Wedding or Bar Mitzvah.*" He chuckles, as does the gallery. They have to, he's an Article III judge, as in Article III of the Constitution; if you don't laugh, the FBI shows up at your door.

"Yes, the defendants are floral vendors."

Galanter's thin lips part in an approximation of a smile and he arches an eyebrow so blond it's almost invisible. "Floral vendors? Is that a term of art, counsel?"

The gallery laughs again.

"Florists," the lawyer concedes.

"Thank you. Now, carnations are the bulk of your client's business, is that correct?" Galanter flips through the appendix with assurance and reads aloud. " 'Pink ones, red ones, even the sprayed ones,' according to your client's affidavit. Although I see sweetheart roses did well in February." He pauses to look significantly at Judge Townsend, but Townsend's eyes are closed; God knows which way he'll go on this case. He thinks people enter his dreams to have sex with him, so it's impossible to tell right now if he's pondering RICO law or watching lesbians frolic.

"They're a group of florists. A *network* of florists."

"Oh, I see, a *ring* of florists. Do you think Congress intended even a *ring* of florists to be covered by this racketeering statute?"

Armen hunches over his microphone. "Counsel, does it really matter what they sell?"

"Go get 'em, boss," I say under my breath.

"Sir?" says the lawyer. He grabs the side of the podium like a kid stowed away on a sinking ship.

"It wouldn't make sense to have a rule of law that turned on the occupation of the defendant, would it?"

"No, sir," says the lawyer, shaking his head.

Armen leans forward, his eyes dark as Turkish coffee. "In fact, after what the Supreme Court said in *Scheidler,* even a group of abortion protestors can be subject to RICO, isn't that right, Mr. Noble?"

Galanter glances over at Armen like a jockey on a Thoroughbred. "But Chief Justice Rehnquist made clear in *Scheidler* that there was a pattern of extortion, of federal crimes. Where's the federal crimes with the floral conspiracy? Florists wielding pruning shears? Gimme that money or I snip the orchid?" Galanter shudders comically and the gallery laughs on cue.

"But they do threaten society," the lawyer says, fumbling for the rigging. "Mr. Canavan signed a contract, and they didn't send him any orders. They intended to drive Canavan Flowers into bankruptcy. It was part of a plan."

"Your client did file for Chapter Eleven protection, didn't he?" Armen says.

Suddenly Judge Townsend emits a noisy snort that sounds like an ancient steamboat chugging to life. Armen and Galanter look over as Judge Townsend's heavy-lidded eyes creak open. "If I may, I have a question," he says, smacking his dry lips.

"Go right ahead," Armen says. Galanter forces a well-bred smile.

"Thank you, Chief Judge Gregorian," Judge Townsend says. He nods graciously. "Now, counselor, why are you letting my colleagues badger you?"

The smile on Galanter's face freezes in place. The gallery laughs uncertainly.

"Sir?" the lawyer says.

Judge Townsend snorts again and lists gently to the starboard side. "As I see it, the question with this new statute is always the same."

Ben whispers, "New? RICO was passed in the seventies."

"The question is always, How is this case different from a case of garden-variety fraud? How is it different from other injuries to one's business, which we decide under the common law?"

Judge Townsend waves his wrinkled hand in the air; it cuts a jagged swath. "In other words, have you got some precedent for us? A case to hang your hat on?"

The lawyer reads his notes. "Wait a minute, Your Honor."

Judge Townsend blinks once, then again. Galanter smooths back the few hairs he has left. The lawyers in the gallery glance at one another. They're all thinking the same thing: Nobody tells the Third Circuit to wait a minute. The answers are supposed to roll off your tongue. The case is supposed to be at your fingertips. Better you should pee on the counsel table.

"Way to go, Einstein," Ben says.

"I know I have the case somewhere," says the attorney, nervously riffling through his legal pad. He should be nervous; the circuit court is the last stop before the Supreme Court, which takes fewer appeals each year. It's all those speaking engagements.

"Armen's upset," Sarah whispers, and I follow her eyes. Armen is looking down, worried about the appeal. The only sound in the tense courtroom is a frantic rustling as the lawyer ransacks the podium. A yellow page sails to the rich navy carpet.

The silence seems to intensify.

Galanter glares at the lawyer's bent head.

A sound shatters the silence—*tickticktickticktickticktick*—from the back of the courtroom.

The back rows of the gallery turn around. The sound is loud, unmistakable.

Tickticktickticktickticktick.

Row after row looks back in disbelief, then in alarm.

Tickticktickticktickticktick.

"It's a bomb!" one of the lawyers shouts.

"A bomb!" yells an older lawyer. "No!"

Tickticktickticktickticktick.

The crowded courtroom bursts into chaos. The gallery surges to its feet in confusion and fear. Lawyers grab their briefcases and files. People slam into each other in panic, trying to escape to the exit doors.

"No!" someone shouts. "Stay calm!"

I look wildly toward the back row where Artie was sitting. I can't see him at all. The mob at the back is pushing and shouting.

Tickticktickticktickticktick.

Ben and other law clerks run for the judges' exit next to the dais. My heart begins to thunder. Time is slowed, stretched out.

"Artie's back there!" I shout.

Sarah grabs my arm. "Armen!"

I look back at the dais. Armen stands at the center, shielding his eyes from the overhead lights, squinting into the back row. Judge Townsend is stalled at his chair.

Galanter snatches Armen's gavel and pounds it on the dais: *boom boom boom!* "Order! Order, I say!" he bellows, red-faced. He slams the chief judge's gavel again and again. "Order!"

"Oh, my God," Armen says, when he realizes what's happening. "It can't be."

TWO

"Are you saying it was Shake and Bake?" I ask, incredulous.

"Yes. I'm busted. Totally," Artie says. He flops into his chair in the small law library that serves as the clerks' office, having been grilled behind closed doors by Armen and an assortment of bureaucrats. "It took the poor guy an hour to stop crying. He was worried he got Armen in trouble, can you believe that?"

"Yes," Ben says, typing nimbly at his computer keyboard.

"I don't get it," I say. "Did he have a bomb?"

"No. He had a shot clock."

"A what?"

"Actually, he *was* the shot clock."

"I still don't get it."

"Neither do I," Sarah says.

"I do, but I don't care," Ben says, gulping down his third cup of coffee. He gets in at seven and guzzles the stuff like a thirsty vampire. "The whole thing's absurd."

"No, it isn't," Artie says. "Not if you think like Shake and Bake."

"Like a paranoid schizophrenic?" I say.

"Look, Shake and Bake was watching the argument. He

knew the lawyer had to answer a question and he thought time was running out, like in basketball. He figured the guy had twenty-four seconds to shoot. It got all crossed up in his head."

I try not to laugh. "So he starts ticking."

"Yeah, with his mouth. He was counting off the time." Artie yanks the knot on his cotton tie from side to side to loosen it.

"That's ridiculous," Sarah says.

"Not to a paranoid schizophrenic who loves basketball," I say, a quick study.

"Right, Grace." Artie nods and tosses the tie on the briefs scattered across his desk.

"Told you. Absurd," Ben says, tapping away.

"Is he really schizophrenic?" Sarah leans over the Diet Coke and soft pretzel that constitute her breakfast. These kids eat trash; it gives me the heebie-jeebies.

"I don't think so," Artie says, unbuttoning the collar of his work shirt. "He's like a little kid. Harmless."

I smile. I own a little kid. They're not harmless.

"Why do you say he's harmless?" Sarah asks. "He's obviously not."

"Come on, Sar. He's fine. Shake and Bake can't even do his laundry. You think he can blow up a building?"

"I do, Weiss," says a dry voice at the door to the clerks' office. It's Eletha Staples, the judge's Secretary for Life, a willowy, elegant black woman. Prone to drama, Eletha pauses dramatically in the doorway.

"Yo," Artie says.

"Right, bro. Yo." Eletha rolls her eyes as she walks into the room, trailing expensive perfume. Her glossy hair is pulled back into a neat bun at the nape of a slim neck. In her trim camel suit she looks more like a judge than a secretary, and the day black women get to be federal appellate judges, she'll be mistaken for one. "Who you invitin' next, Charlie Manson?"

"That's not funny, El."

Eletha stops in the center of the office and puts a hand on

her hip; a quintet of clawlike polka-dotted fingernails stand out on her otherwise classy look. "It's not funny, bro?"

"No."

"It's not funny when you invite a *crazy man* to court? It's not funny that some *nut boy* endangers Armen's life? Endangers the lives of us *all*?"

Artie fiddles glumly with his Magic 8 Ball, one of the many toys on his desk. "He'd never hurt any of us, he idolizes Armen. And he's not a nut boy."

"He ticks, Artie," I remind him.

Eletha looks crazed, but she crazes easily. "What are you tellin' me, he's not a nut? The man thinks he's a friggin' Timex! Why they let him in the courthouse I'll never know."

"They have to," Sarah says. "He has a right to access. It's in the Constitution."

"The hell it is," Ben says, without looking away from his monitor.

"He's not a nut." Artie pouts.

Eletha puts a hand to her chest and begins Lamaze breathing to calm herself. I first saw this routine three months ago when she had to interview me for my job, because Armen had gotten stuck in Washington. After she calmed down, we spent an hour swapping ex-husband stories. I touch her arm. "El, keep breathing. Don't push, it's too soon."

She looks down at me, her face suddenly grave. "That's not the worst of it. Did you hear?"

"Hear what?"

"They filed the appeal in the death penalty case this morning. *Hightower*. The death warrant expires in a week." Her words hang in the air for a moment.

"Oh, no." I sink deeper into the leather chair next to Artie's desk. I better not get this case. I'm a working mother now; I have enough guilt for an entire hemisphere.

"A week?" Ben says, shaking his neat head. "Of course Hightower waited until the last minute. Wait till the bitter end to file and hope the warrant expires. It's a game with them."

Sarah looks over sharply. "It's only his first appeal."

"Fine. Let's make it his last."

"Ben, he even tried to kill himself. He thought he deserved to die."

"He did."

Eletha's soft brown eyes linger on Ben's face, but her thoughts are clearly elsewhere. "This case is gonna be a real bitch. The law clerk's gonna be up all night, Armen's gonna be up all night, and I'll be up all night. Last time, I didn't tell Malcolm why." Malcolm is Eletha's son, whose picture she keeps on her desk; he's an intelligent-looking boy with lightish skin and glasses. "Some things kids don't have to know."

I wonder how I'd tell Maddie. What would I say? Honey, Mommy works for a man who decides whether another man should live or die. No, Mommy's boss is not God, he just looks like him.

"Has Armen served on many death panels?" Sarah asks.

Eletha rubs her forehead. "Too many."

"Three," Ben says. "All dissents. The proverbial voice in the wilderness."

Eletha glances at him. "They were from Delaware, I think. None from Jersey. And we haven't executed in Pennsylvania since I don't know when."

"About thirty years." Ben pops the SAVE button with an index finger. "Elmo Smith, for the rape-murder of a Catholic high school girl. But I can't recall the method." He pauses just a nanosecond, his mind working as rapidly as the microprocessor. "Pennsylvania executes by lethal injection now, but then—"

"Christ, what difference does it make?" Sarah says, making tea on the spare desk. "Move to Texas, you can watch it on pay-per-view."

Ben snaps his fingers. "Electrocution, that's right!"

"Death penalty for twenty, Alex," Artie says, and Eletha starts to breathe in and out, in and out.

"The death penalty is revenge masquerading as justice," Sarah says, unwilling to let the grisly subject go. I like Sarah but am coming to understand that not letting anything go is an avocation of hers. It served her well last November; she worked on Armen's wife's campaign for the Senate, in which the feminist lawyer came from behind to win by a turned-up nose.

"When we talk about justice," Ben says, "we shirk thinking in legal terms."

"I'm impressed, Ben. Did you make that up all by yourself?"

"No. Oliver Wendell Holmes said it."

Sarah looks nonplussed.

"Played for the Knicks," Artie says. He launches the Magic 8 Ball on an imaginary trajectory through that great basketball hoop in the sky, that one all men can find when they don't have a real ball. The air guitar principle.

"It's irrelevant what happens at this level anyway," Ben says. "It's going up to the Court."

"And what'll that do to your chances, Safer?" Artie says.

Ben hits a key but says nothing.

"Chances for what?" I say.

"Didn't you know, Grace? Ben is waiting for a phone call from Justice Scalia. He's this close to a Supreme Court clerkship." Artie squints at his forefinger and thumb, held a half-inch apart. "Maybe even *this* close, am I right, Ben? *This* close?" He makes his fingers touch.

"Ask the 8 Ball," Sarah says.

"The 8 Ball! Excellent!" Artie shakes the ball and turns it upside down to read it. "Oh, my God, Ben," he says in mock horror. " '*Better not tell you now.*' Very mysterious."

I look at Ben, reading his monitor screen. "Ben, did you really get an interview with Scalia?"

"Yes," Ben replies, without looking away from the monitor.

"But Grace, Ben has a big problem," Artie says ominously. "If Armen decides *Hightower* and the guy don't fry, we got trouble. Big trouble, right, Ben?"

Ben types away. "Of course not, Weiss. I still have the credentials."

"You mean like clerking for Armen the Armenian? Husband of Senator Susan, another flamer?" Artie winks slyly at Sarah, and she smiles back. I wonder if they're sleeping together, and how Sarah squares it with her lust for Armen. Not to mention her alleged allegiance to Armen's wife.

"The chief has sent clerks to the Court," Ben says. "He's very well regarded by the Justices."

"By the *conservative* Justices?"

"Depends on what you mean by conservative."

"Anybody not on life support."

Ben's mouth twitches, and I can tell Artie's hit a nerve. I hold up my hand like a traffic cop. "That's enough outta you, Weiss. Don't make me come over there."

"Who else is on the panel in *Hightower*?" Sarah says.

Eletha looks at a piece of paper in her hands. She doesn't notice Ben reading the paper upside down, but I do; Ben spends more time reading upside down than right side up. "Here it is. Gregorian, Robbins, and Galanter."

"Awesome!" Artie says. "That means Hightower walks. Armen writes the opinion, Robbins joins it, and Galanter pounds sand. Two to one."

Sarah looks less certain. "Galanter's a Federalist, but Robbins can go either way on this one."

"What's a Federalist?" I ask.

"Fascists. Nazis."

"Republicans with boners," Artie adds.

Ben clears his throat. "It's a conservative organization, Grace. Of which I was an officer in law school, as a matter of fact."

Suddenly, the door to Armen's office opens and men talk in low, governmental tones as Armen walks them to the main door of chambers. Artie strains to listen and Ben inhales what's left of his coffee. Eletha turns around just in time to catch Bernice.

"Roarf! Roarf!" Bernice, a huge Bernese mountain dog, bounds through the door. Yes, Armen brings his shaggy black doggie to work, all hundred pounds of her. He's the chief judge, so who's gonna tell him he can't? Me? You? *"Roarf!"*

"No! Don't jump up!" Eletha barks back. The sharp noise stops Bernice in her tracks. Her bushy black tail, white at the tip, switches back and forth; she sneezes with the vigor of a Clydesdale.

"Sit, Bernice. Sit!" Armen says, coming up behind the dog.

Bernice wiggles her wavy hindquarters in response. Her eyes roll around in a white mask that ends in rust-colored markings on her muzzle. Bushy rust eyebrows give her a permanently confused look; appearances are not always deceiving.

"She never sits, Armen," Eletha says. "I don't know why you even bother."

"She used to, she just forgets," Armen says. "Right, girl?" He scratches the plume of raggy hair behind Bernice's ears and looks at Artie. "So, Weiss, you shitting bricks?"

Artie sets the 8 Ball down. "Enough to build a house, coach. I'm really sorry."

"Can't you grovel better than that? I'm disappointed."

"*Really* sorry, coach. I am not worthy." Artie bends over and touches his forehead to the briefs on his desk. "It'll never happen again," he says, his voice muffled.

Armen smiles. "Good enough. Shake and Bake can come to the games, but he has to stay away from the courthouse. If he doesn't, the marshals will shoot him on sight. Plus I got you out of jail free, so you owe me a beer."

Artie looks up, relieved. "After the game next week. At Keeton's."

"Fine." Armen's gaze falls on the papers in Eletha's hands and his smile fades. "Is that *Hightower?*"

"Yes."

He takes the papers and begins to read the first page. His brow wrinkles deeply; I notice that the dark wells under his eyes look even darker today. He's given to occasional black moods; something will set him off and he'll brood for a day. It makes you want to comfort him. In bed.

"Chief," Ben says, "the defendant killed two sisters."

Armen seems not to hear him. His broad shoulders slump slightly as he reads.

"One was a little girl and one was a teenager, very popular in the town."

Armen looks up from the memo and his eyes find me. "It's yours, lady," he says.

I hear myself suck wind. "Mine?"

"You're Grace Rossi, right? It's got your name all over it."

"Me, on a death penalty case? But I'm part-time."

"I'll give you time off later, and don't whine."

"But I don't want to get involved," I whine.

He half smiles. "Get involved. Somebody's life is at stake."

"But why me?"

"I need a lawyer on this one."

Sarah freezes as she looks at Armen. I can almost hear the squeak of a hinge as her perfect mouth drops open.

THREE

Empty coffee cups dot the surface of Armen's conference table, along with sheaves of curly faxes, photocopied cases, and trial transcripts from the *Hightower* record. We worked straight through dinner and into the night, reading cases and talking through the opinion. Then Armen began to tap out an outline on his laptop and I picked up the habeas petition to check our facts.

It says that Thomas Hightower was seventeen when he cut school to go drinking with a fast crowd, which got him drunk and dared him to kiss the prettiest girl in school. Hightower went to her farm, where he found Sherri Gilpin in the shed. He asked her out, and she laughed at him.

"Date a nigger?" she said. Allegedly.

In a drunken rage, Hightower slapped her and she fell off balance, cracking her skull against a tractor. He tried to give her CPR, at which point her little sister Sally came in and began to cry. Hightower says he panicked. He couldn't leave witnesses; it would have killed his mother. So he throttled the child, then, full of shame, he got back into his car and drove himself into a tree. Enter the Commonwealth of Pennsylvania, which saved his life, reserving for itself the honor of putting him on trial. For death.

Hightower couldn't afford a lawyer, not that one in the small coal-mining town would represent him anyway. The county judge appointed a kid barely out of night law school to the case, and the jury convicted Hightower of capital murder. During the sentencing hearing, where the jury decides life or death, Hightower's lawyer argued from the wrong death penalty statute, one that had been ruled unconstitutional three years earlier by the Pennsylvania Supreme Court. Somehow he had missed that.

The obsolete death statute, the only one presented to this predominantly white jury, said nothing about the fact that a jury could consider Hightower's youth, his diminished capacity because of alcohol, his lack of a prior criminal record, and the remorse that he demonstrated by his suicide attempt as "mitigating circumstances" in deciding whether to impose the death penalty. The jury took only fifteen minutes to reach its decision. Death.

I set the papers down and look out the huge windows that make up the fourth wall of the office. It's the dead of night. Orangey streetlamps stretch toward the Delaware River in ribbons. White lights dot the suspension cables on the Ben Franklin Bridge. Traffic signals blink on and off: red, yellow, green. The lights remind me of jewels, twinkling in the black night. I watch them shimmer outside the window and turn the legal issues over in my mind.

The question is whether Hightower's lawyer was so ineffective that the trial was unfair. Strictly as a legal matter, Hightower probably deserves a new trial; what he deserves as a matter of justice is another matter. This is why I practiced commercial litigation. It has nothing to do with life or death; the questions are black and white, and the right answer is always green.

"Well," Armen says to himself. "Well, well, well." He stops

typing and reads the last page of his draft. The office is quiet now that Bernice has stopped snoring. I feel like we're the only people awake, high in the night sky over the twinkly city.

"Well what?"

"I think we're going to save this kid's life. What do you think?"

The question takes me aback. "I don't know. I don't think of it that way."

"I do." He smiles wearily, wrinkling the crows' feet that make him look older than he is. "I wouldn't stop if I didn't think so."

"Was that your goal?"

"It had to be. His lawyer was incompetent. Anybody else would have gotten him life in prison, instead he's scheduled to die. They set him up." He leans back in the chair. Fatigue has stripped something from him: his defenses, maybe, or the professional distance between us. He seems open to me in a way he hasn't before.

"I didn't think of it as saving his life. I thought of it as a legal issue."

"I know that, Grace. That's why I wanted you on this case. You narrowed your focus to the legalities, divorced yourself from the morality of the thing."

It stings. "Do you fault me? It's a legal question, not a moral one."

"Really? Who said?"

"Holmes."

"Fuck Holmes," he says, stretching luxuriously in a blue oxford shirt. His shirtsleeves are bunched at his elbows; his tie is loose. He's so close I can pick up a trace of his aftershave. "It's both those things, Grace, law *and* morality. You can't separate law from justice. You shouldn't want to."

"But then it's your view of justice, and that varies from judge to judge."

"I can live with that, it's in my job description. Judges are supposed to judge. When I read the Eighth Amendment, I think the framers were telling us that government should not torture and kill. That's the ultimate evil, isn't it, and it's impossible to check." His face darkens.

"I don't understand," I say, but I do in part. Armen's culture is written all over his olive-skinned features, as well as his chambers: the framed documents in a squiggly alphabet on the walls, the picture of Mount Ararat over his desk chair, the oddly ornate lamp bases and brocaded pillows.

"It started piecemeal with the Armenians," he says, leaning forward. "Our right to speak our own language was taken away. Then our right to worship as Christians. By 1915, they had taken our lives. We were starved, hanged, tortured. Beaten to death, most of us, with that." He points at a rough-hewn wooden cudgel mounted over the bookshelf.

"I didn't know."

"Not many do. Half my people were killed. Half a million of us, wiped out by the Turkish government. All my family, except for my mother." A flicker of pain furrows his brow.

"I'm sorry."

He shakes it off. "The point is, government cannot kill its own citizens, not with my help. I know Hightower did a terrible thing. He killed, but I won't kill *him* to prove it's wrong. He should be locked up forever so he never hurts another child. He will be, if I have any say in it." He seems to catch himself in mid-lecture; then his expression softens. "So thank you, for getting involved."

"Did I have a choice?"

"No." He relaxes in the leather chair. "You are involved, you know," he says quietly.

I see the city lights glowing softly behind him and feel, more than I can understand, that we aren't talking about the case anymore. "I don't know—"

"Yes, you do. I'm involved too, Grace. Very involved, as a matter of fact."

I can't believe what I'm hearing. I feel my heart start to pound softly. "We can't do anything about it."

"Yes, we can. Give me your hand." He holds out his hand to me.

I look at it, suspended between us, at once a question and an answer. This situation is supposed to be black and white, but it doesn't feel that way inside.

"Stop thinking. Take it."

So I do, and it feels strong and warm. He pulls me in to him, as naturally as if we've done this a million times before, and in a second I feel myself in his arms and his kiss, gentle on my mouth. Suddenly I hear a noise outside the office and push myself away from his chest. "Did you hear that?"

"What?"

"There was a noise. Maybe the door?"

"Everything's all right," he says. He kisses me again and shifts his weight up underneath me but I press him away.

"Wait. Stop. We can't."

"Why not?"

There are rules, aren't there? "You're married, for starters."

He smooths my hair back from my forehead and looks everywhere on my face. "Not anymore," he says. "My marriage is over."

It's a shock. "What? How?"

"It was over a long time ago. Susan asked me to stay with her until the election was over, and I did. She's coming in the morning to sign the papers. We file tomorrow."

"For divorce?"

"Yes."

"I can't believe it."

"It's true." He touches my face. "So you're not in love? Have I been reading you wrong?"

So much for hiding my emotions. "I don't know. I mean, I think about you, but it's been so long."

"How long?"

"Too long to admit."

"That's long enough, don't you think," he says, kissing me deeply. Before I can object I find myself responding, and then I don't want to object anymore. I lose myself in his kiss, in his warmth. His hands find their way to my breasts, caressing them as we kiss, arousing me. He begins to unfasten the buttons of my blouse, and I feel a skittishness rise, a sort of shame.

"You sure no one's out there, in the office?" I say.

"No one." He undoes the button above my breasts, exposing the string of pearls inside my blouse. I stop his hand and his eyes meet mine, uncomprehending. "I won't hurt you, Grace," he says softly. "Let me. Let me love you a little."

"But I—"

"Shhh. I dream about this, about doing this with you."

"Armen—"

"Let me. You have to." He smiles and moves my hands away, placing each one on the armrests of the heavy chair. "Keep your hands there. We're going to take this slow."

I feel myself breathing hard, excited and scared. "We can't do this, not here."

"Hush." He unfastens the next button, then the next. "Look at yourself, you're so beautiful."

I look down and see a flash of pearls tumbling between my breasts. The scalloped cup of a bra. My skirt hiked way up, past the opaque ivory at the top of my pantyhose. I can't stand it, being undone like this. I look away, out the window. I expect to see the night sky, but the wall of plate glass reflects a dark-haired man and a lighter-haired woman astride him.

Strangely, it's easier to bear this way, like in a mirror. I can watch it as if it were happening to someone else.

"It's all right now," he whispers.

I watch him slip the silk blouse from my shoulders, freeing one arm and the other, then reaching around and unhooking my bra. I feel my breath stop as he tugs my bra down slowly, as if he's unveiling something precious and pure. He takes a breast in each hand and teases the nipples, and I feel an exquisite tingle as each one contracts under his thumbs. I encircle his head, this head of too-long hair that I know so well, and he burrows happily between my breasts, nuzzling one and then the other.

I hear myself moan and wrap my legs more tightly around him. He responds, rocking me against the hardness growing in his lap, sucking at one nipple and then the other. I feel wetness where he's suckled and then a slight chill as he suddenly lifts me up and lays me gently back on his arms across the table. My legs lock around his waist and my hands reach for the edge of the table. My pearls fall to the side, the *Hightower* papers flutter to the floor, and God knows what else slides off the desk.

Poised over me, he stops suddenly. "You're not looking at me. Look at me, Grace."

I watch him in the reflection. I can't do what he's asking.

He turns my face to his, and his expression mingles concern and pleasure. "Why won't you look at me?"

"Is your marriage really over?"

"Yes."

"You swear it?"

"On my life." He bends over and kisses me gently, pressing between my legs. "Now let it go, Grace. Let go."

I close my eyes as my body responds to him. And then my heart.

FOUR

The ringing of a telephone shatters a deep, lovely slumber. I hear it, half in and half out of sleep, not sure whether it's real.

PPPRRRRRRINNNGGG!

I open my eyes a crack and peer at the clock. Its digital numbers read 7:26 A.M.; I've been asleep for two hours. I have four whole minutes left. The phone call is a bad dream.

PPPRRRINNNGGG!

It's real, not a dream. Who the hell could be calling at this hour? Then I remember: Armen. I feel a rush of warmth and stumble to my bureau, cursing the fact that I don't have an extension close to the bed like everybody else in America. I wish I could just roll over and hear his voice.

"Honey?" says the voice on the line. It's not Armen, it's my mother. "Are you up?"

"Of course not. You know how late I got in, you were babysitting. What do you want?"

"I've been watching the TV news." I picture her parked in front of her ancient Zenith, with a glass mug of coffee in one hand and a skinny cigarette in the other.

"Mom, it's seven-thirty. Did you call to chat?" I flop backward onto my quilt.

"I have news."

I'm sure. You would not believe the things my mother considers news. Liz Taylor gained weight. Liz Taylor lost weight. "What, Ma?"

"Your boss, Judge Gregorian? He committed suicide this morning."

I sit bolt upright, as if I've been electrocuted. I can't speak.

"They found him at his townhouse in Society Hill. I didn't know he lived in Society Hill. They said his house is on the National Register of Historic Places."

I'm stunned.

"He was at his desk, reading papers in that death penalty case."

"How—"

"He shot himself."

No. I close my eyes to the mental picture forming like cancer in my brain.

"There was no suicide note," she continues. "They called somebody named Judge Galanter, who lives in Rosemont. This Galanter gets to be chief judge now, eh?"

I shake my head. There must be some mistake. "My God," is all I can say.

"Judge Galanter says the court will continue with its operations as before."

I think of Galanter, taking over. Then Armen, dead. This can't be happening.

"Galanter said the *Hightower* case will be reassigned to another judge. Wasn't that the case you stayed late on?"

"Who found him?"

"His wife, when she got in from Washington. She's the one who called the police."

"Susan found him? Did she say anything? Did they interview her?"

Her response is an abrupt laugh; I imagine a puff of smoke erupting from her mouth. "She's holding a press conference this morning."

Susan. A press conference. What is going on? Why would Armen do such a thing? I close my eyes, breathing him in, feeling him still. Just hours ago, he was with me. Inside me.

"Are you there?" my mother asks.

I want to say, I'm not sure.

I'm not sure where I am at all.

FIVE

I pack Maddie off to school in record time and barrel down the expressway into Center City, rattling in my VW station wagon past far more able cars. KYW news radio confirms over and over that Armen committed suicide. I swallow the pain welling up inside and tromp on the gas.

I can't get to the courthouse doors because of the press, newly arrived to feast on the news. Reporters are everywhere, the TV newspeople waiting around in apricot-colored pancake. Cameramen thread black cables through a group of demonstrators, also new to the scene. There must be forty pickets, walking in a silent circle, saying nothing. I look up at their signs, screaming for justice against a searing blue sky: HIGHTOWER.

But I have to get inside.

"Would you like one?" asks an older man in a checked short-sleeved shirt. He holds a pink flyer in a hand missing a thumb; his face is weatherbeaten like a farmer's. "It tells about my daughters."

"Your daughters?" I look up in surprise.

He nods. "Do you have children?"

"Yes. A daughter."

"How old?"

"Six." I don't want to talk to him. I can't think about *Hightower* now. I want to get inside.

"Does she like Barney?"

"No, she likes Madeline. The doll."

The deep creases at his eyes soften into laugh lines. "My little one, Sally? She liked dolls. She had a Barbie, and Barbie's sister, too. What was the name of that sister doll?" He looks down at a pair of shiny brown shoes and scratches his head between grayish slats of hair. "My wife would know," he says, his voice trailing off.

"Skipper."

"Right!" He laughs thickly, a smoker. "That's right. Skipper. Skipper, that's the one."

I seize the moment. "Well, I should go."

"Sure thing. You hafta get to work." He thrusts the flyer into my hand. On it is a black-and-white photograph of two pretty girls sitting on a split wooden rail. The typed caption says SHERRI AND SALLY GILPIN. I glance at it, stunned for a second. I knew the way they died, but I didn't know the way they lived. The younger one, Sally, has a meandering part in her hair like Maddie's, a giveaway that she hated to have her hair brushed. I can't take my eyes from the little girl; she was strangled, the life choked out of her. What did Armen say last night? *We saved a life.*

"You better go, we don't want you to get fired on our account," says the man. "God bless you now."

I nod, rattled, and make my way through the crowd with difficulty. Several of the women in line look at me: solid, sturdy women, their faces plain, without makeup. I avoid them and push open the heavy glass doors to the bustling courthouse lobby. I slip the flyer into my purse and flash a laminated court ID at the marshals at the security desk in front of the elevator bank. Two minutes later, I plow through the heavy door to chambers.

Eletha is sitting at her desk, staring at a blue monitor with a stick-figure rendering of a courthouse made by one of the programmer's kids. Underneath the picture it says: ORDER IN THE COURT! WELCOME TO THE THIRD CIRCUIT COURT WORD PROCESSING SYSTEM! The door closes behind me, but Eletha doesn't seem to hear it.

"El?"

She swivels slowly in her chair. Her eyes are puffy, and she rises unsteadily when she sees me. "Grace."

I go over to her, and she almost collapses into my arms, her bony frame caving in like a rickety house. "It's okay, Eletha. It's gonna be okay," I say, feeling just the opposite.

I rub her back, and her body shakes with high-pitched, wrenching cries. "No, no, no," is all she says, over and over, and I hold her steady through her weeping. I feel oddly remote in the face of her obvious grief, and realize with a chill I'm acting like my mother did when my father disappeared; nothing has changed, pass the salt.

I ease Eletha into her chair and snatch her some tissues from a flowered box. "Here you go."

"This is terrible. Just terrible. Armen, God." She presses the Kleenex into her watery eyes.

"I know."

"I can't believe it."

Neither can I. I don't say anything.

"I was going to call you when I came in, but I couldn't." Her eyes brim over again.

"It's okay now."

"Susan called me. This morning. Then the police. Then Galanter. God, how I hate that man!"

"It was Susan who found Armen, right?"

"She came in from Washington and there he was."

"When did she come in, right before dawn?"

"I guess. I don't know." She blows her nose loudly.

"Who told Galanter?"

"I don't know, why?"

"I don't understand. I was with Armen until five."

"So you two worked late."

"Right." I avoid her eye; Eletha left at two o'clock. Then I think of the noise I heard, or thought I heard. What time was that? "Eletha, last night after you left, did you come back to the office?"

"No, why?"

"When I was with Armen, I thought I heard somebody out here."

"Who?"

"I don't know."

"Didn't they come into Armen's office?"

"No. Not that I saw."

She shakes her head; she's not wearing any makeup today. "The clerk's office, the staff attorneys, they got work to do on a death penalty case. Maybe it was one of them, dropping off papers."

Just then the chambers door opens and in walk Sarah and Artie. They both look like they've been crying; I recognize Sarah's anguished expression as the one I saw in the mirror this morning. She breaks away from Artie and storms into the room.

"Is Ben here?" she shouts, pounding past us to the law clerks' office, her short cardigan flying. "Where the fuck is Ben?"

"I don't know," I say. "Eletha, do you?"

"He hasn't called."

Sarah punches the doorjamb with a clenched fist. "Damn it! I want to see him, the little prick!"

"Sar, stop," Artie says. He walks numbly over to Eletha and puts his arm around her. "It's not going to bring Armen back."

Sarah strides to the phone on Eletha's desk and punches in seven numbers without looking at anyone. "I've been calling that asshole all morning. Pick it up, you little prick!"

"Relax, Sarah," I say.

Her blue eyes turn cold. "What do you mean, relax?" She slams down the phone.

"Look, we're all hurting."

"Ben's not, he caused it. He pressured Armen about *Hightower* so he could get that fucking clerkship. He even showed him that newspaper article, the one about victim's rights. He knew it would bother Armen. He didn't care how much."

"You're talkin' crazy," Eletha says, between sniffles.

Sarah looks from her to me. "Grace, you saw him last night. Was he upset?"

"No," I say, wanting to change the subject. "I thought I heard a noise—"

"What?" Sarah says. "What kind of noise?"

"I don't know, a noise. Like someone was here, outside his office. Maybe around three o'clock or later."

"Did you see anyone?"

"No."

"So what if you heard a noise?"

"Nothing," I say. "Unless it was you or Artie. Was it?"

Artie snorts. "At three? We were asleep." Then he catches himself. "Oh, shit."

Sarah glares at him. "Nice move, Weiss."

So it's true about them. I don't understand Sarah; sleeping with Artie, but crazy about Armen. And Artie and Armen are so close. *Were* so close.

"Oh, what's the difference now?" Artie says. "I don't care if everybody knows, it's not like we're doing anything wrong." He looks at me and Eletha, his eyes full of pain. "I love her, okay? We fuck like bunnies, okay? Is that okay with you?"

"Sure," I say. Eletha nods uncertainly.

"See, Sar, the world didn't end."

Sarah ignores him and presses REDIAL. "The important thing is to find Ben."

I walk away from the tense group. I want to see Armen's

office before they do. Alone. I stop in the doorway, bracing myself. Still, I feel a sharp pang at the sight. My gaze wanders over the exotic brocade, the strange-looking documents, and the Armenian books in their paper dust jackets, frayed at the top. The place smells of him still; I can almost feel his presence. I can't believe he would kill himself. Why didn't I know? Why didn't I see it coming?

I enter the room and finger the papers on the conference table. Everything is the way I remember it, except that some of the *Hightower* papers are gone, the ones he was working on at home. The cases are scattered over the table; the laptop is at the edge. Even the dog hairs on the prayer rug are the same. It reminds me of Bernice. Where was she last night when he killed himself? Where was I, sound asleep?

Suddenly I hear a commotion in the outer office, then shouting. I rush to the door and see Artie shove Ben up against the wall, rattling a group portrait of the appeals court.

"Artie, stop it!" I shout, but Eletha's already on the spot. She steps in front of Ben, shielding him with her body.

"He deserves it!" Artie says, his chest heaving in a thick sweatshirt. He stands over Ben, who begins to *kack-kack-kack* in his old man cough, rubbing his head where it hit the wall.

"Back off!" Eletha says, in a voice resonant with authority. A sense of order returns for a moment; Eletha is in charge and we are in chambers. The king is dead, long live the queen. Then it passes.

"Where have you been?" Sarah shouts at Ben, who struggles to his feet, hiding almost comically behind Eletha.

"Go to hell, Sarah. I pulled an all-nighter, so I slept in. Do I need your permission?"

"You worked all night? On what?"

"*Germantown Savings*. I wanted to finish it."

"You didn't hear the phone?"

"No."

"The fuck you didn't!" Sarah looks like she's about to pick

up where Artie left off and Eletha wilts between them, her strength spent.

"Okay, Sarah," I say, "cool it. You want to talk to Ben, do it when you're calmer."

Her eyes flash with anger. "Playing Mommy again?"

"Yes, it comes naturally. Now go to your room. Time out until the press conference." I point to the clerk's office.

"Press conference?" Eletha says. "Who's givin' a press conference?"

I check the clock above the chambers door. "Susan is, in fifteen minutes."

Eletha's eyes threaten to tear up again. "How can she? Before Armen's body is even cold."

"It's not like it's so easy for her," Sarah says defensively, "but she feels the need to explain. The public has the right to know."

I feel my heart beat faster. "She's going to explain why he committed suicide?"

"That's what she told me on the phone."

"It's his business, not the public's," Ben says, smoothing his tie.

Eletha looks as surprised as I do. "But how does she know? There was no note."

"She's his *wife*, Eletha," Sarah says.

His wife. The word digs at me inside. If he hadn't died, they'd have filed for divorce. Today.

We gather around the old plastic television in the law clerks' office, watching Senator Susan Waterman take her place at the podium. I suppress a twinge of jealousy and scan her face for a clue about what she's going to say. Her stoic expression reveals nothing. She looks like a wan version of her academic image; her straight dark-blond hair, unfashionably long, is swept into a loose top-knot, and her small, even features are pale, a telegenic contrast to the inky blackness of a knit suit.

"Ladies and gentlemen," she says. She glances up from the podium, unaffected by the barrage of electronic flashes. "My husband, Chief Judge Armen Gregorian of the Third Circuit Court of Appeals, died this morning by his own hand, here in Philadelphia. He loved this city, even though it had not always been kind to him. Even though the press had not always been kind to him, and especially of late." She glares collectively at the press, which dubbed the fierce expression "Susan's stare" during her campaign.

"They're all pricks," Sarah says, but even she sounds spent.

Susan takes a sip of water. "My husband did not leave a note to explain his actions, but it is no mystery to me. Some are already saying he did it because of the press's criticism of his liberal views, but I assure you that was not the reason. Armen was made of sterner stuff." She manages a tight smile at the crowded room, having reprimanded and absolved them in one blow.

"I've heard others say it was because of the death penalty case he had to decide, and the stress and strain it may have caused him. It would break anyone, but not Armen Gregorian. He *was* made of sterner stuff." She lifts her head higher, in tacit tribute. Eletha, in the chair next to me, squeezes my hand.

"On the surface, my husband had everything to live for," Susan says. "He was the chief judge, and we had a wonderful, happy marriage that was a solid source of comfort and support to us both."

What is she saying? They were on the brink of divorce.

"But my husband was Armenian. The genocide of the Armenian people is called the forgotten genocide. Most of his family was murdered. His mother survived, only to commit suicide herself. This month—April—is when Armenians remember their tragic history." She looks around the room. "Like the Holocaust survivors who later died by their own hand, my husband was a victim of hate. Let us pause for a moment of silence to remember Armen Gregorian and to remember that the power of hate can destroy us if we do not fight against it." The camera lingers on her bowed head.

Sarah begins to sob, and Artie hugs her close.

I lean back in my chair, as if pressed there by a gigantic weight. Armen told me about the genocide, though he didn't tell me about his mother. But still, would he commit suicide because of it? That night? The genocide was on his mind, but so was *Hightower*. And me. I feel like crying, but the tears won't come.

Neither will Ben's. He looks knowingly at Sarah and Artie, cuddled together.

His dark eyes are bone dry.

SIX

Judge Galanter's breath carries the harsh tang of Binaca. Cigar smoke clings to the fine wool of his double-breasted suit. His movements are deliberate and his speech formal, as if he were trying to control each syllable. I know as sure as he's standing before us, flushed slightly in front of Armen's desk, that Galanter has been drinking. It evokes another memory of my father, flitting like a ghost across my mind.

"You law clerks can stay on for a week or two," he says.

"We hadn't even thought about it," Artie snaps from the doorway.

"I'll attribute that crack to your extreme emotional distress, Mr. Weiss."

Artie looks away from Galanter, out the window. The courthouse flag flies at half mast, flapping in the wind that gusts off the Delaware River.

"Finish up the cases you're working on. Draft the bench memos as before and hand them in to me. Argued cases will have to be reargued." Galanter slides a gleaming Mont Blanc from his breast pocket and makes a check in a leather Filofax he's holding like a missal. I can imagine what it says.

Things to do: Take over. Before noon.

"Next order of business. The office will have to be packed up. How much time will you need, Eletha?"

Eletha sits at the end of the conference table, fuming. "I would have to talk to Susan about that," she says, crossing her slender arms across her chest.

"Senator Waterman? Already spoke with her. She said it's up to you. Box the stuff and ship it to the house, she'll go through it there. How long will it take you? I have to plan my own move."

"You mean you're takin' this office?" Eletha asks.

Galanter jerks his chin upward, as if the folds of his turkey neck were pinched in his collar. "Of course, it's the chief judge's. I'd like to be in in two weeks. By the way, I understand the staff attorneys need an extra secretary, so there's room for you there. Talk to Peter about that." He makes another check in his Filofax, and Eletha breathes in and out, in and out.

"Judge," I say. "I was wondering—"

"Of course. I forgot about you. They may need an extra staff attorney downstairs. You should apply. Part-time will be a problem, you'll have to step up to a normal work week."

"No. I wanted to ask about *Hightower*."

He purses his thin lips. "I've reassigned it. The death warrant expires Monday, but we'll have it decided well in advance."

"Who was it reassigned to?"

"That information is strictly need-to-know. Did I mention the memorial service?" He shoots a questioning look at Ben, who's standing against the bookshelves. Ben shakes his head discreetly.

"Not a high priority," Artie says.

Galanter points at Artie with his pen. "Don't test me, young man. I've just about had it with your lack of respect."

"Respect?" Artie explodes. "Who are you to talk about respect? Armen just died and you can't wait to take his office. Can't wait!"

"Artie," Sarah says nervously.

"Listen, you," Galanter says, raising his voice. "This court has to maintain operations. We have a public trust."

"Fuck you!" Artie shouts, almost in tears. He storms out of the room into his office and slams the door.

"I've never seen such conduct in a law clerk! Ever!" Galanter says.

"Judge Galanter." I start talking, almost reflexively. "Artie and Armen were close. This is hard for him. For us all." I hear an involuntary catch in my voice, but Galanter's gaze is fixed in the direction of the clerks' office. I feel a shiver of fear inside, from somewhere deep, but press it away. "You were saying, Judge, about the memorial service?"

Galanter looks down at me, still lost in his own anger. "What did you say?"

"The memorial service."

"The memorial service? Oh, yes." He exhales sharply, regaining control, and returns the pen to his breast pocket. "Memorial service. The day after tomorrow, Thursday. In the ceremonial courtroom. The time's not fixed yet."

"Have you heard about the funeral arrangements?"

"No idea. Senator Waterman said she'd call about that. Eletha, get me that memo I sent you."

Eletha doesn't move a muscle. "Memo? What memo, Judge?"

Galanter hasn't drunk enough to miss the challenge in her manner. He tilts his head ever so slightly. "The one about the new sitting schedule. I sent it this morning, on E-mail."

"I was busy this morning."

"So was I. Get it now," he says, staccato.

Eletha leaves the room. In a second she's slamming her desk drawers unnecessarily.

Galanter hands me some papers from his book. "Xerox these for me and come right back."

I take the papers and leave the office. When I open the door to the hallway, Eletha's giving the finger to the wall.

I read the papers on the way to the Xerox machine. It's a complete sitting schedule, with Armen's initials crossed out next to his cases and a new judge's written in. All of Armen's cases, reassigned so fast it'd make your head spin.

READY TO COPY, the photocopier says. I open the heavy lid, slap the paper onto the glass, and hit the button. The light from the machine rolls calcium white across my face.

Suicide? I don't understand. They were going to file for divorce, if what Armen said was true. I feel a pang of doubt; would Armen lie? Of course not. Afterward we talked for a long time, holding each other on the couch. He was an honest man, a wonderful man.

READY TO COPY. I hit the button. You don't kill yourself just because you're Armenian. Armen was a survivor. And he hated guns, was against keeping them in the house. Where did he get the gun?

READY TO COPY, says the machine again, but I'm not ready to copy. So much has happened. We found and lost each other in one night. I stare at the glass over the shadowy innards of the machine; all I see is my own confused reflection. What was that noise last night, and does it matter?

I turn around and look down the hall, but it's empty. There are only two occupied judges' chambers on this whole floor, ours and Galanter's; the rest are vacant, the chambers of judges who sit nearer their homes in Wilmington and northern New Jersey. Only eleven people work on the entire floor.

Now it's ten.

A boxy file cabinet sits against the wall next to the judges' elevator. A few paces to the left is the door to the law clerks' office. To the right, down the hall, are Galanter's chambers.

Everything looks perfectly normal.

I step away from the machine and peer at the government-spec brown carpet. There's nothing on the rug, no trace of any-thing. I straighten up, feeling stupid. What am I looking for, muddy footprints? Clothing fibers? What am I thinking? I shake my head and turn back to the Xerox machine.

ADD PAPER, it says. The words blink red, like the old pinball machines that go tilt.

Damn it. Why am I the only one who refills this thing? I look in the cabinet next to the machine for a ream of paper, but it's empty except for the torn wrapper. The law clerks never pick up after themselves. I slam the cabinet door and walk down the hallway back to chambers.

Bbbzzzzzz goes the security camera, as I tramp angrily by.

Then it hits me. I do an about-face and look up at the camera. It's black and boxy, and looks back at me like a me-chanical vulture perched above the judges' elevator.

The camera's on all the time, monitored by the federal mar-shals. It saw everything that happened in the hall last night and probably recorded it, like at ATM machines.

It knows if anyone came into chambers and saw Armen and me together. And it knows who they are.

SEVEN

His breast pocket bears a plastic plate that says R. ARRINGTON over the shiny five-star badge of the marshal service. His frame is brawny in its official blue blazer, and his dark skin is slightly pitted up close. "Lunchtime!" I say to him, making an over-stuffed tuna hoagie do the cha-cha with a chilly bottle of Snapple lemonade. "All this can be yours."

He does not look impressed. "No can do, Grace."

The hoagie and the lemonade jump up and down in frustration. "All I want is two minutes. I look at the monitors, then I'm outta there."

"There's twenty monitors, Grace," he says, sighing deeply. Maryellen, the cashier in the building's snack shop, cocks her head in our direction. She may be blind, but she's not deaf. I decide to be more quiet.

"Come on, Ray. You said only one monitor shows our hallway. How long can it take to look at a monitor?"

He folds his thick arms. "Maybe if you tell me why this matters."

I glance at the jurors behind us buying newspapers, gum, and fountain soda. The ice machine spits chunks into a tall paper cup, and a juror plays mix-and-match to find the right size lid. He'll never find it; I never can, and I have a J.D. "Let's just say I want to check security."

"Come clean, Rossi."

I consider this. Ray is one of the few marshals who liked Armen; he's also one of the few African Americans, which I suspect is no coincidence. "Tell you what. Get me in. If it pays off, I'll tell you why."

"What am I supposed to tell the marshals?"

"What marshals? You're the marshal."

"I'm a CSO, technically. A court security officer. I mean the marshals watching the monitors."

"Tell 'em I'm checking security, that I'm the administrative law clerk to the chief judge."

"Grace." His somber expression reminds me of something I'd rather not dwell on. Armen is gone.

"Forget it, I'll tell them something. I'll handle it. Just get me in, I'll owe you. Big-time."

Suddenly he snaps his fingers. "I know what you can do for me."

"Anything."

"You can introduce me to your fine friend, the lovely Eletha Staples."

"Eletha? Don't you know her?"

"I've been workin' here as long as she has, but she won't give me the time of day. She seein' anybody?"

I think of Leon, Eletha's boyfriend, who gives her nothing but grief. "No."

"Hot dog!" He rubs his hands together; it makes a dry sound. "Lunch. I'll start with lunch, take it nice and easy. Can you set it up?"

"Deal." I set the tuna hoagie and Snapple on the counter in front of Maryellen. At the last minute, Ray tosses in two packs of chocolate Tastykakes.

"What are you having today, Grace?" Maryellen says. Her cloudy eyes veer wildly around the room.

"Thanksgiving dinner," I say to her, and she laughs.

After we leave the snack bar, Ray leads me through a labyrinth of hallways to the core of a secured part of the courthouse. It would have been impossible to find this myself, and when I reach the barred entrance I understand why.

It's a prison.

Sixteen floors from where I work, in the same building. It gives me the creeps. The sign on the barred door says: ONLY COUNSEL MAY VISIT PRISONERS.

We head down another hall, past a room with a number of empty desks in it, and open a door onto a small room, brightly lit by a ceiling of fluorescents. A wall of TV screens dominates the room, giving it a futuristic feel. There must be twenty-five black-and-white TV screens here, trained everywhere throughout the courthouse.

The monitors in the left bank flash on the stairwells at each floor of the building, and the large screens in the middle offer an ever-changing peek into the courtrooms. In 12-A there's a young woman crying on the witness stand. In 13-A an older man is being sentenced. In 14-A a little boy is testifying.

"It's like a soap opera, huh, Worrell?" Ray says amiably to the stony-faced marshal watching the screens. He's a stocky middle-aged man in a black T-shirt that says UNITED STATES MARSHAL SERVICE. It looks more like a get-up for Hell's Angels, but I do not remark this aloud.

"Ugh," the man says, his attention focused on the TV pictures of prison cells on the far right. Each cell is numbered and occupied by a man in street clothes, probably awaiting trial. They sit slumped or asleep in their cells; one is a black teenager in an oversized sweatshirt, just a kid. I think of Hightower.

"This is Grace Rossi, Worrell. She's a lawyer, works for the appeals court. She wants to see—"

"I want to see the monitors," I say with faux authority. "It's a security check for the new chief judge."

Worrell begins to laugh at one of the prisoners, a Muslim crouched over in prayer. "Say it loud, brother. You're gonna need it." Ray looks sideways at the monitor.

"Where's the screen for the eighteenth floor?" I ask.

"That one." He points to one of the screens. The bottom of the screen reads 16-B. In the high-resolution picture, a young secretary pauses to tug up her slip. Worrell chuckles. "They forget Big Brother's watching."

Of course they forget; I did. So did whoever came into our chambers, if anyone. I watch the picture flicker to 17-B. It's a view of the hallway outside the judges' elevator on the seventeenth floor. On the wall hangs a fake parchment copy of the Constitution. Our floor is next.

"Yeow!" Ray hoots as soon as the scene changes. Eletha is photocopying at the Xerox machine, her back to the camera. Her skirt clings softly to her curves, and with her back turned you can't see how haggard she looks today. "Now ain't that pretty?" he says, in a tone men usually reserve for touchdown passes and vintage Corvettes.

Worrell grunts. "She's all right."

Ray gives him a solid shove. "Listen to you, 'She's *all right*.' Shit, man! She's more than all right, she's *fine*. And she's mine, all mine. Right, Grace? Grace?"

"Right," I say, preoccupied by the scene on the TV screen, which shows Eletha walking down the hall and into chambers. Bingo. The camera would have seen whoever came into chambers last night, wherever they came from. "Where's the tape?"

Worrell looks at me blankly. "What tape?"

"The tape. The tape of what the camera saw last night."

"We don't tape."

"What?"

"There's no tape, lady."

"I don't understand." I look at Ray for confirmation.

"I coulda told you that, Grace," he says.

I don't believe this. "At the MAC machine they tape. Even in the Seven-Eleven they tape."

"Seven-Eleven's got the money. This is the U.S. government. You're lucky we got the goddamn judges."

Ray looks embarrassed. "Downstairs we tape. The monitors at the security desk, they tape the stairwell and the judges' garage. Just not here."

"But somebody watches the monitors at night, don't they?"

Worrell leans back in the creaky chair, plainly amused. "Guess again."

"Maybe we should go," Ray says.

"Hold on. There's no night shift?" I hear myself sounding like an outraged customer.

"We got a fella walks around the halls," Worrell says, "but that's it. One marshal. The government don't have the money for somebody to watch TV all night." His face slackens as he returns to the screens.

"All right. Who was the marshal last night, walking the halls?"

"McLean, I think."

"McLean? Is he the big one with the mustache?" The Mutt of the Mutt-and-Jeff marshals I see in the mornings.

Worrell nods. "Don't you guys got some work to do?"

"Let's go, Grace," Ray says.

"Sure. Thanks," I say, disappointed. So much for the short answer. We start toward the door but Worrell erupts into raucous laughter.

"Holy shit, what a case this one is."

Ray glances at the monitor, then scowls. "I'd love a piece of that guy. He's not crazy, he knows just what he's doin'. Jerkin' us around."

I look back. One of the prisoners is smack in the middle of cell seven, standing on his head. "Jesus."

"What a country," Worrell says. "That jerk's gettin' a nice bed for the night, and you know who's gonna pay for it? You and me. The taxpayers. For him they got the money. For us, no. You talk to your boss about that, okay, lady?"

But I don't answer. I recognize the man in the cell. "Ray, let's go."

EIGHT

"Shake and Bake is in jail?" Artie says, shocked. "Show me where, Grace."

"You can't visit him."

"What do you mean I can't visit him?"

Eletha looks over wearily, dead on her feet against the bookcase in the law clerks' office. "That lunatic is the last thing you should be worried about today."

"Grace," Sarah calls from her desk, "what were you doing in the security office?"

"I wanted to see the cameras."

"What cameras?"

"You know, the ones in the hallways. I wanted to see who's on the other side."

"Why?"

"I was curious. I wanted to know if they saw anything peculiar."

"Is this about the noise?" Sarah asks.

Ben looks up from the newspaper accounts of Armen's death. "What noise?"

"I heard a noise last night, so I wanted to see the tapes, only—"

"Tapes?" Sarah asks. "You mean of what they see in the cameras?" She flushes slightly, and I play a hunch I didn't even know I had.

"Yes. They tape everything, for security reasons. Like at Seven-Eleven."

"They do?"

"Sure." I look at Eletha. "Right, El? They tape from those cameras."

"If you say so," Eletha says, playing along. "They keep the tapes?"

Thanks, El. "Yep, in a vault. They said they'd show me tomorrow."

Ben presses a button on his computer keyboard. The modem sings a computer song as he logs on to Lexis, the legal research database. "Surprised the government has the money."

"Safer, what the fuck are you doing?" Artie asks. "Are you working? *Today?*"

"I'm going on Nexis, that okay with you?"

"What's Nexis?" Eletha asks, as Sarah suddenly busies herself making a full-fledged tea ceremony out of a single bag of Constant Comment. She has to be the one I heard last night, and she should never play poker.

"Anybody gonna answer me? What's Nexis?" Eletha plops into a chair like a much heavier woman. Her chin falls into her hand. "Forget it. Who gives a shit?"

"Nexis is a database of newspapers," I say. "It has magazines, newspapers, wire services. Everything."

"How do you like that?" Ben says, in his own world as he reads his computer screen. "We're under HOTTOP. *Hightower* and the Chief."

"Christ, Safer!" Artie says.

"I need a translation," Eletha says.

"HOTTOP stands for hot topics in the news," I say, the words sour in my mouth. Without thinking twice, I cross to Ben's computer and press the power switch to OFF. The powerful unit crackles in protest, then fizzles out. "Show some respect, Ben. A man is dead." I feel a wrenching inside my chest and turn my back on Ben's surprised expression.

"Way to go, Grace!" Artie says, bursting into applause.

"She's right," Eletha says. She stands up and smooths out her skirt. "I don't even know what we're still doin' here. We should all go home. The packing can wait."

"I can't believe he's gone," Sarah says, standing at the coffeemaker. The only sound is the hot water spurting into the glass pot. Sarah removes the pot a little too soon and the last drops dance across the searing griddle like St. Vitus.

"Let's not get maudlin, please," Ben says.

Artie looks as if he's about to snap, then his brow knits in alarm. "Wait a minute. Grace, does Shake and Bake know about Armen?"

"I have no idea."

"Oh, fuck. I have to get in to see him. There's no telling what he'll do when he hears. Where's the prison?"

"On the second floor, but they won't let you in."

"The hell they won't. He has a right to counsel, doesn't he? I'm counsel." Artie bounds over to the coat rack and tears Ben's jacket from a wooden hanger, leaving it swinging.

"That's my best jacket, Weiss," Ben says.

"I know, dude. Thanks." He yanks the jacket over his chest. "Sar, lend me your briefcase."

"You really want to do this?" Sarah hands him a flowered canvas briefcase but Artie pushes it back at her.

"Give me a pad instead. Where'd you say they're taking him, Grace?"

"Courtroom Fourteen-A, before Katzmann. They're trying to charge him with trespassing on federal property."

Artie shakes his head. "I tell ya, these kids today, in and out of trouble. Where did I go wrong, Mom?"

"Don't ask me, pal."

"I gave him everything. Summers in Montauk, winters in

Miami Beach." He gives the jacket a reckless tug and Ben flinches.

"Will you at least take it easy?" Ben says.

Eletha covers her eyes. "I didn't see this. This is not happening."

"How do I look, Mom?" Artie says to me. He sticks out his arms, and the sleeves ride up to his elbows. "Hot?"

"Smokin'."

"Excellent." He sticks a legal pad under his arm and runs out of the clerks' office. I hear the heavy pounding of his feet as he heads for the outer door. My eyes meet Sarah's, but she looks down into her steaming mug of tea.

"You okay, Sar?" I ask her. Flush her out. Isn't that what detectives do?

"Sure." She takes a quick sip of tea, avoiding my gaze. "Who's *Hightower* been reassigned to, Ben?" she asks.

"What makes you think I know?"

"You know Galanter's clerks. The buzz-cut boys."

The telephone rings at Eletha's desk. "Shit," she says. "Thing's been ringing all day." Before I can offer to get it, she kicks off her heels and is padding to her desk.

Ben flicks on the power switch, animating the machine. "Grace, hate me if you must, but I'm logging on again."

"Tell us who got *Hightower*, Safer," Sarah says, but I hold up my hand.

"Sarah, think a minute. Who's even more conservative than Galanter?"

"Adolf Hitler."

"On our court, I mean."

"Judge Foudy."

"Right. And Galanter would pick somebody to vote with him, now that Armen's gone. He'd want to stack the deck. Change the result."

She blinks. "Could he do that?"

"Sure. He's the chief judge. In an emergency, he picks the panels."

Ben pounds the keys. "I neither confirm nor deny."

He doesn't have to, I know it. Galanter has shifted the majority to himself, blocking Hightower in. No matter which way Robbins goes, it'll be two votes to one for death. Poor Armen; he didn't save Hightower's life after all. I stand up, wanting suddenly to be alone.

"Look at this item," Ben says, his voice tinged with sarcasm. "What a nice gesture from Senator Susan, and how like a Democrat."

"What?" Sarah says, and I stop at the doorway.

"From the *Washington Post*. Says here that Susan tried to donate Bernice to a group called Service Dogs for the Handicapped. I can almost hear the wheelchairs plowing into each other, can't you?" He laughs so hard he coughs: *kack-kack-kack.*

"Very funny," Sarah says.

"Bernice is gone?" I say, surprised to feel a twinge inside.

"Gone but not forgotten," Ben says, recovering enough to hit another key. "They didn't want her, evidently. They only take puppies."

"So where is she?" I ask from the doorway, only half wanting to know.

Ben hits the key again. "It doesn't say."

"I know," Eletha says. She walks into the room, waving a yellow Post-it on her finger. "They just called."

"Who did?"

She holds the paper in front of my face. On it is a phone number I don't recognize. "I voted for Susan, but I'll never forgive myself."

NINE

"She's too big, Mom," Maddie says, shuddering in her night-gown. "Look at her teeth."

Bernice strains against her red collar, which still says A. GRE-GORIAN; her wagging tail swats my thigh with each beat.

"But I'm holding her, honey. She won't hurt you, she can't. Just come over and let her sniff you. She's all clean now." I bathed Bernice right after I bathed Maddie, using green flea shampoo they sold me at the dog pound, along with a leash, two steel bowls, and a thirty-dollar trowel for shoveling a megaton of dogshit.

"*Rrronononr*," Bernice grumbles, a guttural noise that makes Maddie's blue eyes widen in fear.

"What's that?"

"She's talking to you, honey. She wants you to love her."

"But I don't love her. I don't even like her." Maddie tugs anxiously at the end of a damp strand of hair; her hair looks brown when it's wet, more like my mother's original russet color than her own blazing red.

"Aw, can't you just give her a little pat on the head? Her hair's washed too." I scratch Bernice's newly coiffed crown and she looks back gratefully, her tongue lolling out. "See? Look how happy she is to be with us."

"But why did *we* have to take her?"

"Because nobody else would. They all have apartments that don't allow pets. We're the only ones with a house who could have a pet."

"They could move."

"No. Now come closer."

She doesn't budge. "Why couldn't you just leave her there? In the dog pound."

"You know what would happen to her. You saw *Lady and the Tramp*."

"They don't do that right away, Mom. They wait about six or five weeks."

"No, they don't wait that long."

"Somebody else could have adopted her."

"I don't think anybody would have. You should have seen her in the cage." I flash on the scene at the pound; Bernice penned by herself, barking frantically next to a streetwise pit bull. "Nobody would have taken her, Maddie. Most people like puppies, not dogs."

"I like puppies. Little puppies."

I sigh. I got my second wind when I washed Bernice, but the day's awful events and my own fatigue are catching up with me.

"It's not *my* fault, Mom." Maddie pouts. "She's scary."

"I know, you're being very brave. How about you go up to bed now? You look tired."

"I'm not tired. You always say I'm tired when I'm not."

"All right, you're not tired, but I am. Go up to bed, and I'll be right up."

She makes a wide arc around Bernice, then scurries upstairs, and I take the disappointed dog into the kitchen and put her behind an old plastic baby gate. She whimpers behind the fence, but I don't look back. I reach Maddie's room just as she turns off the light and hops into bed. "She's so big, Mom," she says, a small voice in the dark.

I sit down at the edge of the narrow bunk bed and let my weariness wash over me. I smooth Maddie's damp bangs back over the uneven part in her hair. It reminds me of Sally Gilpin, and I feel grateful to have my daughter with me, however terrified she is of big dogs. That much is right in the world. "I understand, baby."

"Where will she sleep?" Maddie says, digging in her mouth with a finger, worrying a loose tooth from its moorings.

A good question, only one of the hundred I haven't answered. "I have it all figured out."

"Mom, look," she says with difficulty, owing to the fist in her mouth. Her eyes glitter in the dim light from the hallway. Huge round eyes, like Sam's; my color but his shape. Across the bridge of her nose is a constellation of tiny freckles too faint to see in the dark.

"Look at what?"

"Look." She moves her hand, pointing at one of her front teeth, which has been wrenched to the left.

"Gross, Maddie. It's not ready. Put it back the way it was, please."

"Everyone else has their teeth out. My whole class."

"But you're younger, remember? Because of when your birthday is."

"*Duh*, Mom."

"*Duh*, Mads."

She punches the tooth back into place with a red-polished fingernail. "It doesn't even hurt when I do that tooth thing. I like to stick my tongue up in the top." Which is exactly what she does next.

"Stop, Maddie."

"You know how there's like the top of your teeth? And you can stick your tongue in the top and wiggle it around?"

"Kind of."

"Well, I like to stick my tongue in there and make like buck teeth."

"Terrific. Just do it with your tongue, not your finger, okay? And don't show it to me or I'll barf."

"Why can't I use my finger? It works better."

"You'll give yourself an infection."

"No, I won't."

"Fine. Don't blame me when your mouth explodes."

She giggles.

"You think that's funny?"

She nods and giggles again, so I reach under the covers and tickle her under her nightgown. "No. No tickling!" she says.

"But you love to be tickled."

"No, I hate it. Madeline likes it. You can tickle her." She fishes under the thin blanket and locates her Madeline doll, which she shoves at my chest. "Tickle her."

I look down at the soft rag doll with its wide-brimmed yellow felt hat. Madeline has a face like a dinner plate, with wide-set black dots for eyes and a smile stitched in bumpy red thread. Her orange yarn hair is the same color as Maddie's, but we didn't name Maddie after the Ludwig Bemelmans books, we named her after Sam's grandmother. When I gave Maddie the doll at age three, they became inseparable. "You really do look like Madeline, you know?" I say. "Except for the hat."

"No, I don't. She looks like me. I look like myself."

I laugh. "You're right." I lean over and give her a quick kiss. Her breath smells of peanut butter. "Did you brush?" I ask, second-rate sleuth that I am.

"I don't have to brush if I don't want to."

"Oh, really? Who said?"

"Daddy. He told me it was *my decision*." Her tone elides into the adolescent sneer that comes prematurely to six-year-old girls.

"Don't be fresh."

"Don't be fresh. Don't be fresh. Daddy says you can break the rules sometimes."

"Oh, he does, does he?" Easy for Sam to say. After his highly suspect charitable deductions, fidelity was the second rule he broke. Sam is a high-powered lawyer who lost interest in me at about the same time I became a mother and quit being a high-powered lawyer myself; ironically, I thought that was just when I was getting interesting.

"Gretchen says that if your tooth comes out too soon, you have to wait a long time for a new tooth to grow." She twists a hank of Madeline's yarn hair around her finger.

"Is Gretchen a girl in your class?"

"Gretchen knows about bugs and gerbils. She knows about why it's a hamster and not a gerbil. She has three teeth out. Madeline likes her."

"Then she must be nice."

"She is. She has long hair, really long. Down to here." She makes a chop at her upper arm. "She wears a jumper."

Like Madeline. "Do you eat lunch with her?"

"Sometimes. Not usually. Usually I'm alone."

"Why?"

"I don't know that much people, so nobody ever sits next to me."

I try to remember what I read in that parenting book. Talk so your kid will listen, listen so your kid will talk; it's catchy, but it means nothing. "What can we do about that?"

"I don't know." She shrugs.

I forget what the book says to do when they shrug. "Would you like to have Gretchen over? Maybe one of the days I'm off from work?"

"She won't come."

"You don't know that unless you ask."

"But I don't know her exactly as a best friend, okay?"

"But, honey, that's how you get to know someone."

"Mom, I already told you!" She turns away.

I am at a loss. There is no chapter on your child having no friends. I even spied on her at recess last month after I went food shopping. The other first graders swung from monkey bars and chased each other; Maddie played by herself, digging with a stick in the hard dirt. Her Madeline doll was propped up against a nearby tree. I found myself thinking, If she's digging a grave for the doll, I'm phoning a shrink. Instead I telephoned her teacher that night.

"She'll be fine," she said. "Give her time."

"But it's March already. I'm doing everything I can. I help out in the classroom. I did the plant sale and the bake sale."

"Have you set up any play dates for her?"

"Every time I suggest that, she bursts into tears."

"Keep at it."

"But isn't there anything else I can do?"

"Let it run its course. She's on the young side."

"But she was fine last year, in kindergarten. She was even younger."

"Weren't you home then?"

Ouch. Then my alimony ran out and almost all my savings; with child support, I can swing part-time. "Yes, I only work three days a week, and she has her grandmother in the afternoon. It's not like she's with a stranger."

"She's just having some trouble with the adjustment."

Well, *duh*, I thought to myself.

But I didn't say it.

Bernice's ears prick up at the sound of a soft knock at the front door and she takes off, barking away, back paws skidding on the hardwood floor. In a minute, there's the chatter of a key in the lock; it has to be Ricki Steinmetz, my best friend. She's the only one with a key besides my mother.

"Rick, wait!" I shout, but it's too late.

The door swings open and Bernice bounds onto Ricki's shoulders. *"Aaaiieee!"* Ricki screams in surprise.

"Bernice, no!" I yank the dog from Ricki's beige linen suit, leaving distinct rake marks in the shoulder pads, and hustle Ricki and Bernice inside before my neighbors call the landlord.

"Is that a *dog?*" Ricki says, backing up.

I hold a finger to my lips and listen upstairs to hear if Bernice's barking woke Maddie. Ricki understands and shuts up, her mouth setting into a disapproving dash of burgundy lipstick. There's no sound from Maddie's room. Bernice chuffs loudly on Ricki's cordovan mules.

Ricki gasps. "Did you see that? She threw up on my shoes!"

"She just sneezed."

"These are Joan and David!"

"Come in the kitchen, would you?" I take Bernice by the collar and walk her like Quasimodo into the kitchen. "What are you doing here? It's almost nine o'clock."

Ricki snatches a paper napkin from the holder on the dining room table and follows me into the kitchen. "Didn't your mother tell you I called? I wanted to come over and see how you were, after what happened," she says, wiping her shoe. Ricki is a family therapist who takes clothing as seriously as codependency. She still looks put together even after a day of seeing clients; her white silk T-shirt remains unwrinkled, her lips lined. In fact, she'd look perfect if she didn't have those rake marks on her shoulders and that goober on her shoes.

"It'll dry."

"Disgusting." She slips on the shoe. "It's the judge's dog, isn't it?"

"Yep."

"Tell me you're taking it to the pound."

"Nope. I own it. Her."

She stands stock-still. "You're kidding me."

"Don't start with the dog. I heard it from my mother, I heard it from my daughter. You came over to be supportive, so start being supportive." I sit down on one of the pine stools at the counter in my makeshift eat-in kitchen, and Bernice stands beside me, tail wagging. I scratch her head.

"Sorry. You want some coffee, on you?"

"I'll make it." I start to get up, but Ricki presses me onto the stool with a firm hand.

"Sit!" she says.

Instantly, Bernice plops her curly-coated rump onto the floor.

"Wow," I say, astonished. "I never saw her do that."

Bernice pants happily, her long tongue unrolling like a rug.

"Cute," Ricki says.

"And pedigreed, too. When can I drop her off?"

"No way." She opens the freezer.

"But you have more room than I do. You need a Swiss dog. Think of the boys, if they get lost in the mall."

"I'm ignoring you." She rummages through the boxes of frozen vegetables. "Where's the coffee?"

"On the door." I give up and watch my new dog lie down at the foot of my stool, shifting once, then again, to get comfortable on the tile floor. She needs a dog bed, but I'll be damned if I'll buy that, too.

"What happened to that cappuccino decaf I gave you?" Ricki shouts from inside the freezer. Icy clouds billow around her chic wedge of thick brown hair.

"It's gone. Use the Chock full o' Nuts."

"You don't have flavored?"

"I have coffee-flavored. Now close the door."

She grabs a can and shuts the door. "I'm going to understand your crummy mood because you're entitled to it. You have a good reason to feel crummy."

"Is this the supportive part?"

"Yes. I'm validating you."

"Like parking, you stamp my ticket?"

"Just like that." She pries the plastic lid off the can and spoons the coffee into the basket, then pours the water into the coffeemaker. I watch her as if I've never seen this done, my brain stuck in a sort of stasis. The red light on the Krups blinks on: a machine, highly reliable and predictable. People are not machines, and so they do unpredictable things. Things that strike like a bolt from the heavens, stunning you where you stand.

"You okay?" Ricki asks.

I watch the coffee dribble into the glass pot. "I still can't believe it."

"I know." Ricki puts her arm around me, but I don't feel her touch, not really. A spring storm howls outside, rattling the loose storm windows. These things seem like they're happening around me, and not really to me. "It's a shock," she says.

I think of Armen. His hand in my hair. How easily he lifted me to the couch. The weight of his body, the strength of it. He was lovely. "It's just not possible."

"I know," she says, stroking my hair.

He was happy. I know he was. "He didn't even own a gun."

"I read it was registered to his wife."

Susan. She's the one who found him. He was going to tell her about us. "She put Bernice in a *dog pound*, Rick. What kind of a woman does that to her husband's pet?"

Ricki glances at Bernice, comatose on the floor. "I can see it."

"They had a terrible marriage, no matter what she says. They were going to divorce."

"How do you know all this?"

"He told me."

"He told you about his marriage? Since when?"

"And Sarah, one of the law clerks, worked on Susan's campaign. I think she came by chambers late at night. She got nervous when I told her about the tapes."

"Tapes?"

"It was a bluff, but it worked." I hear myself sounding slightly hyper. "Then there's Galanter."

"Galawho?" Ricki steps away from me, concerned.

"Judge Galanter, who becomes chief now, for the next seven years. He'd never have gotten to be chief if Armen hadn't died. He would have been too old to be eligible, past sixty-five. I wonder if he drinks."

"A judge, drinking? A federal appellate judge?"

"What, it's confined to the trades?" I experience it again, as a flash of insight: the fighting, a woman's fists pounding futilely against a man's bulky shoulders. My mother and my father. I can't remember any more than that. I was six when he left.

"Grace, you're losing it." She looks at me like I'm crazy, and maybe I am. I feel it welling up inside of me.

"Is it possible that he didn't commit suicide? Is it possible that he was murdered?"

"What?" she says.

I tell her the whole story, about Armen and me. She looks drained when I'm done, but still caring, and I imagine that's what she looks like after a session with one of her flakier clients. She sets down her empty coffee mug with finality. "I'm worried about you, Grace. You've lost a man you cared for, and not for the first time. There was Sam."

"What's Sam have to do with it?"

"It's a loss."

"No, it isn't. It's not a loss when you lose someone who doesn't want you. Happily ever after, just not together."

Ricki crosses her arms. "You don't mean that."

"I sure do. You may not think my life turned out so great, but I do. I'm okay. At least I was until this happened."

"Maybe Armen's death is kicking up a lot of stuff for you."

"What stuff?"

"Abandonment. Loss. Think of your father."

"My father?" I almost laugh. I hate it when she turns into a shrink. "How do you guys make these connections? My father was a drunk. Armen was wonderful."

"But they both left you. It makes sense that you're having trouble accepting it."

He left you. It hurts to hear her say it; that much is true. "I don't think that's it. I can accept that he's gone, Ricki. What I can't accept right now is that he committed suicide. At least I can't accept it without question, like the rest of the world. I don't understand it, okay? Not yet, anyway."

She holds up two neatly manicured hands. "Okay. Okay. I'll shut up. After all, you're the cop here."

"What'd you say?"

"You heard me."

But she's right. I did, and it gives me an idea.

TEN

EXECUTIVE PARKING LOT, says the sign on the steel racks of Samsonite briefcases. It's the only spark of humor in the grim police station, from the aging alcoholic asleep in the lobby to the battleship-gray paint peeling off the cinder-block walls. Detective Ruscinjki blends in here, with his gray hair and gray eyes. He folds his furry arms behind an ancient typewriter in the bustling Central Detectives' office and looks up at me. "You sure you're not with the media?" he asks.

"No."

A black detective in shirtsleeves and shoulder holster walks by, ignoring us.

He looks unconvinced. "We got lots of calls from the media on this case. Print media. Electronic media. They'd say anything to get past the desk, anything to get the gory details."

"I'm not a reporter. I told you, I worked for Judge Gregorian. I have court ID if you want."

He leans back in his chair at a long table in the common room. "All right, Miss Rossi, so you're not with the media. You're not his lawyer, either, or a member of the family. That means I tell you what I tell the reporters. The case is closed. We have no reason to believe that the judge's death was anything other than a suicide." A lineup of battered file cabinets sits behind him, solid as the stone wall he's putting up for my benefit. Or detriment.

"I was just wondering how you can be so sure. Is there some physical evidence you found?"

"Not that I intend to discuss with you. Trust me, it was a suicide. I saw it."

I feel my mouth open. "What? You *saw* Armen?"

He frowns, confused for a moment. "The judge? I was on the squad Monday night, I got the call. That's why you asked the desk man for me, isn't it?"

"I didn't ask anybody for you. I just said I needed to talk to one of the detectives about Judge Gregorian."

He takes one look at me and seems to sense there was something between Armen and me; he's not a detective for nothing. "I'm sorry," he says, softening. "Sit down."

So I do, in a stiff-backed metal chair catty-corner to him.

"Listen to me," he says, leaning on the typewriter. "I've been a detective for nine years now, spent twelve years on the force before that. I don't rule it a suicide unless I'm one hundred percent. On this one, I was one hundred percent. So was the ME."

"ME?"

"Medical examiner. He was there himself, since the judge was so prominent, husband of the senator and all. They'll have the toxicology reports in a month, and the autopsy results. But I tell you, we agreed on the scene, him and me."

A medical examiner; an autopsy. I can't even think about it, not now anyway. "What was the evidence?"

He shakes his head. "I couldn't tell you that even if I wanted to."

"I read a lot about it in the newspapers. They seemed to have plenty of information."

"An important man, a case like this, the papers will know a lot. We may have a leak or two, there's nothin' I can do about that. But none of it comes from me."

"I read in the paper that the gunshot wound was to the right temple. Armen—the judge—was right-handed. Is that the type of evidence you look for?"

"One of the things."

"The papers said the gun was his wife's."

"She kept it in the desk. Felt very bad he used it that way. Cried a river."

"The paper also said the doors and windows were locked. So that's something you look for too, right? In a suicide."

"Yes. Generally."

"In the *Daily News* they said it was a contact wound. What does that mean? Like you said, 'generally'?"

"Miss Rossi, I'm not going to tell you about this case. I can't."

"Just generally, not in this case. Does it mean a wound where the gun makes contact?"

Ruscinjki purses his lips; they're as flat as the rest of his features, and his receding hairline is a gentle gray roll, like a wave.

"How can you tell that it made contact?"

"I can't say—"

"I'm just asking a question. Not in this case or anything. Hypothetically."

"Hypothetically?" A faint smile appears.

"Yes. If I were to say to you, How can you tell if something is a contact wound, what would you say?"

"How we know it's a contact wound is the gunpowder residue. If it's a contact shot it sprays out like a little star. A shot from a coupla inches away, the gunpowder sprays all over."

I try not to think about the gunpowder star. "Okay. What else do you see with a typical suicide? Educate me." I imagine I'm taking a deposition of a reluctant witness, and I'm not far wrong.

"Gunpowder residue on the hand, and blowback."

"Blowback?"

"Blood on the hand that held the gun. Blood on the gun, too."

I try not to wince. "Okay. Anything else?"

"Cadaverous spasm."

"And that is?"

"The body's reaction to the pain of the blast, the shock of it."

"How does the body react? Generally?"

"The hand grips around the gun and stays that way. After death."

"Is there anything else?"

"No. That's mostly all of it."

"I see. Now. If you don't have this type of evidence, the three things you mentioned, the case is not one hundred percent. Is that right?"

"Right. In a case where there's no note."

I almost forgot. "Is it odd there was no note? I mean, in the typical case do you see a note?"

"Most times there is a note. Most suicides lately are your AIDS people, people who know they're going to die. They leave a note. They prepare."

"So if there's not a note, does that tell you it's not a suicide?"

"Not at all. It doesn't tell me anything, one way or the other. Lots of suicides leave their notes way in advance—depression, preoccupation, withdrawal." His tone grows thoughtful, more relaxed; he'd rather talk psychology than pathology. So would I.

"But Judge Gregorian wasn't depressed."

"According to the secretary, he did become depressed about this time of year. Something about Armenians." He brushes dust off the typewriter keys. "The press was all over him because of that death penalty appeal. Not that I'm talking about the actual case." The sly smile reappears, then fades.

"But he seemed to handle that fine."

"The senator said his mother committed suicide. It runs in families, you know."

"But it's not inherited."

"They get the idea. All of a sudden it becomes a possibility. It's like kids in high school, they come in clusters." He looks sad for a moment. "People kill themselves all the time, for lots of reasons we can't understand. Who can understand something like that, anyway?"

I consider this and say nothing, sickened by the image of Armen slumped over, his lifeblood seeping out. A lethal black star on his temple. His own blood spattered on his hand.

"The judge had a watchdog, too. A good watchdog."

Bernice. "What about his dog? Did you see her that night?"

He laughs. "I would say so, it tried to take my arm off. We had to lock it in the bathroom, wouldn't let us near him. I read the wife donated it to the Boys Club."

So much for his detective work; Bernice is in my wagon out front, she fussed so much I decided to take her with me to work. "So you figure that in, right? The dog would have attacked a stranger."

"Yeah. Sure."

"But not someone she knew."

He shrugs. "So?"

"So if he was killed, the killer was someone he knew."

"He wasn't killed. All the evidence is consistent with him killing himself."

"It's only consistent with him putting a gun to his right temple. What if someone made him do it?"

He shakes his head. "There would be signs of a struggle, or a forced entry, and there aren't any."

"But it's possible."

"I doubt it."

"But is it possible? Hypothetically?"

He gets up with an audible sigh, pushing down on his thighs like a much older man. "You know, there are support groups."

Support groups. Therapy. He sounds like Ricki.

"Listen, Miss Rossi. You may never understand it. Doesn't mean it didn't happen."

I meet his cool eye. He's a detective, an experienced one. Maybe he is right about Armen. Still, maybe he's not.

I leave the police station and walk to my wagon, parked at a meter across the street. Bernice has escaped from the cargo area and is nestled officially in the driver's seat, but she doesn't notice me coming toward her. She's watching a thick-set man get into a black boxy car a couple down the line.

Odd, he looks like someone I saw yesterday in my neighborhood.

I watch the car pull out quickly. A new car, American-made. The license plate is from Virginia.

Strange.

"*Roarf!*" Bernice says, startling me.

"Get back, beast," I say to her through the car window.

You're no fun, say her eyes.

Christ. I fish in my blazer pocket for my car keys, but they come out with a folded strip of legal paper. I figure it's an old shopping list until I open it up:

> Grace—
> *This is only the beginning for us. I love you.*
> Armen
> P.S. *I hope you find this before your dry cleaner.*

I look at the note in disbelief. I read it again. Armen.

I love you. My God. I feel a wrenching inside my chest.

It's his handwriting; it always looked like he was writing in Armenian, even when he wasn't. How did this get here? When did he write it?

Of course.

The last time I wore this jacket was Monday, the night we were together. It was slung over the back of my chair.

I check the other pockets, but they're empty. When did Armen leave this note? Then I remember. I used his bathroom before we left. My jacket was at the conference table.

This is only the beginning for us.

I shake my head. Not the sentiment of a man intending to kill himself. Not at all.

"*Roarf!*" Bernice barks again, trying to stand in the seat. Her slobber has smeared up the window.

I look back at the police station and consider running back inside. No. I'd have to tell the detective everything, and he'd find a way to dismiss it anyway. He's one hundred percent, he said.

I look down at the note in my hand, feeling a surge of pain inside, and with it, a certainty. Armen didn't commit suicide. He was murdered. I know it now. I'm holding proof positive. Exhibit A.

Unaccountably, I think of the black car. I look down the street, but it's long gone.

Someone's life is at stake, Armen had said. *Get involved.*

I put the note back in my pocket and slip my car key in the door. There's going to be an investigation, but it'll have to be my own. Because I'm involved, starting now.

As soon as I can get into the driver's seat.

The intercom buzzes on my telephone as soon as I get to my desk in the vacant clerks' office of the judge who lives in North Jersey. It's lined with case reports and lawbooks, and furnished in a cheap utilitarian way, with a wooden desk, side table, and chair. "Yes?"

"Grace? I've been calling you at home, it's your day off, isn't it?" It's Sarah. My heart gives a little jump.

"Yes, but I'll be in every day for a while, and today I have to look at that marshals' tape."

"That's what I wanted to talk to you about. I'll be right over."

My heart pounds as we hang up. Jesus, is she going to confess to murder? What will I do? I open my desk drawer, and a gleaming pair of scissors glints from a logjam of yellow pencils.

I put the scissors near my right hand on the desktop, feeling idiotic for arming myself against a baby lawyer from Yale.

"Knock knock," Sarah says. She leans confidently against the doorjamb. A filmy skirt billows around her freckled ankles; a melon sweater complements her hair.

"That was fast."

"We need to talk, you and I."

I let my hand linger near the scissors. "I'm listening."

She slides into the hard leather chair across from my desk and crosses her long legs in the drapey skirt. "You might as well say it. You know I'm on the tape."

"I haven't seen it yet, so I don't know that. Why don't you tell me what I'm going to see?"

She tosses her hair back. "I have a better idea. Why don't you tell me what I saw that night in Armen's office? On the conference table and the couch, as I recall."

I feel myself stop breathing. *I love you.* "What you saw was none of your business. You were spying."

"You were fucking your boss."

I rise to my feet involuntarily behind the desk. "What were you doing there?"

She doesn't bat an eye. "What's the difference what *I* was doing there? You were *fucking* him, Grace."

The mouth on this child. "Stop saying that."

"You two were having an affair, I knew it all along. That's why he wanted you on *Hightower*. When he told you he wouldn't marry you, you threatened to blackmail him. Tell the papers, ruin his reputation. You and Ben put so much pressure on him that he killed himself the same night."

I look at her in astonishment. "That's ridiculous, all of it. Where did you get *that* from?"

"I figured it out."

Typical Yale grad; totally impractical—or smart enough to know that the best defense is a good offense. "It's crazy."

"You should be ashamed of yourself," she says. Her voice rises in anger, but I can't tell if it's an act or not.

"Wait a minute, Sarah, what were you doing in chambers in the middle of the night? You were supposed to be in bed with Artie."

"I knew Armen would be working late. I was bringing him a sandwich."

"You left Artie to bring another man something to eat?"

"Artie wouldn't mind. He loves Armen."

"So you told him?"

She looks uncertain. "Not exactly."

"Of course you didn't. You didn't care if Armen was hungry, Sarah, you knew I'd be working late with him, and you wanted to see if anything was happening that shouldn't be. If he was cheating on Susan, your friend."

"Are you kidding?" She laughs abruptly. "I knew their marriage was over."

Part of it is true, leaving me dumbfounded. "How do you know that?"

"I practically ran her campaign, remember? I'll be her chief aide after this job. She tells me everything."

"Then why were you so worried about the tapes?"

"Because I knew I was on them."

It doesn't square. "So why is that a problem, if you have nothing to hide? A tape of you with a sandwich, so what?"

Her blue eyes freeze like ice. "You don't know what you're talking about. What are you accusing me of?"

I don't even know, but she's getting angrier, so I spin a plausible argument out of the meager facts I've been dealt, making something out of nothing, like any good lawyer. "All right, how's this? You come to the office and see Armen and me on the couch. You're so enraged you can't sleep. You go to his house, and he lets you in. Even Bernice is happy to see you, so she doesn't make a fuss."

"Ridiculous."

My hand inches over to the scissors. "You scream at him, lose control, like you did the other morning with Ben. He tells you he loves me and you go even crazier."

"Why would I do all that?"

"Because you're in love with him."

Sarah's mouth drops open, and before I can stop her she's lunging right at me. I feel the sting of a hard slap across my cheek and stagger backward, the scissors slipping from my hand. She comes at me again, her face contorted with uncontrollable rage. I know that expression, have seen it before on someone else, and for the first time in my life I realize I've been slapped before, with that much force. I slide down against the bookshelf, then am caught by strong arms. My father's. Sarah's.

"Grace!" Sarah yells. "Oh, God, are you all right?"

Grace, are you all right? Are you all right?

The room is spinning, and fear runs cold in my stomach. "No, no," I hear myself saying.

"God, Grace, I'm so sorry! Here, wait," I hear Sarah saying, as if through a fog. The next thing I feel is a warm splash on my face. Wetness dribbles down my cheeks and onto my blouse. Sarah comes into hazy focus as a familiar odor brings me around. "Are you okay? Are you conscious?" she asks.

I wipe my face, then smell my wet hand. "Is this *coffee?*"

"Yes. Here, sit up." She helps me to a sitting position against the bookshelf and kneels on the rug opposite me.

"Why did you throw coffee at me?" Dazed, I watch as a full cup sets into a brown Rorschach blotch on my white blouse.

"I thought you were going to pass out. It was the only thing around. Not that you didn't deserve it," she adds, a trace of resentment wreathing her voice.

"I deserved it?"

"You shouldn't have said I loved him."

"You did, didn't you?" I wipe my cheeks on my sleeve; the blouse is a goner anyway.

"Don't say that, it would hurt Artie so much. And what you said, about me killing Armen, that was awful."

"I didn't say you killed him."

"You were about to." Her eyes well up as suddenly as Maddie's. In all her bravado, inside she is a child. A sheltered, spoiled child. "I would never kill Armen. I would never kill anyone. It's inconceivable."

I consider this. "I do think Armen was murdered," I say, hearing it out loud; it sounds right and horrible, at the same time.

"Do you really?" She blinks back her tears.

"You know Susan, right? If she came in from Washington and he told her about me, could she have killed him, in a jealous rage? A crime of passion?"

"Never. Never in a million years. She's not like that, emotional like that." She shakes her head.

"I want to talk to her."

"She's leaving for a fact-finding mission."

"Fact-finding? When?"

"Any day now, she's not sure."

"Where?"

"Eastern Europe, Bosnia. Investigating the genocide there."

A regular genocide hobbyist, that woman. "Don't you think it's odd for her to leave the country right now?"

"No. I think it's good for her. She needs to get away."

Suddenly I hear Bernice barking loudly, a fierce, threatening bark, one I haven't heard before. Someone shouts in the hallway; then a louder voice, Eletha's, screams, "No! No!"

"What's that?" Sarah says, alarmed.

"Trouble." I scramble to my feet. Sarah's right behind me as we tear toward chambers.

ELEVEN

"Bernice, no!" I shout, but she pays even less attention than usual. Driven by instinct, her brown eyes lock onto her quarry, whose pin-striped back is quite literally against the wall.

"Somebody get this animal!" Galanter bellows, jowls flapping, arms splayed out like the Antichrist. A half cigar smolders between his fingers.

"Bernice, no!" I shout again, but her glistening black lips retract to display a lethal set of canines, only three feet from Galanter's belt buckle. She growls, and I feel a bolt of fear inside. She has the power to tear him to pieces and, apparently, good cause.

"Rossi, control this animal! Now!" Galanter sputters, his face a hot red.

"Just relax, Judge," I say, approaching Bernice slowly from behind. I have no idea if she'll bite me if I try to stop her.

I call to her softly, but she growls again and drops her head to crotch height. Galanter's blue eyes flare open in fear, and Artie begins to laugh.

"Hold still, dude," he says. "You got nothing to lose. She won't even find it."

"You're out of a job, mister!" Galanter says.

"Tell me about it," Artie says. "Grace, be careful now."

"Bernice won't hurt me. Will you, Bernice? You wouldn't hurt your mommy." I reach her glossy hindquarters with my fingertips and stroke my way up her back to her collar.

She growls again, baring more of her canines.

"She's going to jump!" Galanter shouts.

"No, she won't." My hand inches up to Bernice's neck and I grab the red leather collar securely in my hand. "Don't move yet, Judge."

"Hold her!" Galanter screams, slipping away from in front of Bernice.

"No, wait!" I yell, as Bernice lurches after the fleeing judge. My arms almost tear loose from their sockets and my heels skid along the carpet. Sarah throws her arms around my waist as Bernice thrashes in my grip, torquing her enormous body left and right in desperation. Her frantic barking reverberates in the tight corridor. I bury my face in a mountain of fur and hold on for dear life.

"SuperJew to the rescue!" Artie shouts. He tackles Bernice in midair, and she yelps in pain and frustration.

Galanter scrambles down the hall, pant legs flapping. He reaches his chambers and slams the door.

I release my grip on the dog, and so do Artie and Sarah. Bernice explodes out of the pileup and races to Galanter's chambers. She leaps onto the closed door and barks wildly.

"Jesus." I collapse next to Sarah and Artie, both flat on their backs on the carpet. I can't catch my breath; the coffee stain heaves up and down. Bernice has never acted that way before, and you don't have to be Oliver Wendell Holmes to figure out why.

"Can you believe that?" Eletha says.

"It's his aftershave," Artie says. "Or his personality."

Sarah rolls over and looks at me grimly. "What do you think, Grace?"

What do I think? I think I may not be able to complete my

fact-finding mission on Susan, but I know where to find Galanter. I think the new chief judge will be needing an assistant. With experience.

"How do you know all this?" I ask Ben at the end of the day, in Armen's darkening office.

"That's what I've been wonderin' too," Eletha says, without looking up from the folders she's been filing. On the cardboard box it says DEAD FILES. "Why does Mr. Safer here know every damn thing before I do?"

"One of Judge Galanter's clerks told me, the only one who's still speaking to us after what Bernice did." Ben casts a cold eye at the dog, sleeping soundly where Armen's area rug used to be.

"But how can they hold phone argument in *Hightower*?" I ask. "You use the phone for status conferences, little things like that. Not for argument on a death case."

"Why not?" He crosses his arms, his oxford shirt a crisp white.

"Death is different, that's why not."

He looks up at the ceiling, searching the recessed lights like other people gaze at the stars. "Where have I heard that before?"

"Anthony Amsterdam, when he argued before the Supreme Court in *Gregg v. Georgia,*" Eletha says. " 'Death is final. Death is irremediable. Death is unknowable; it goes beyond this world.' "

"How did you know that, Eletha?" Ben says with obvious surprise.

"Oh, I been workin' in de big house for a while now, Mr. Ben." She laughs naughtily. "It was in one of Armen's articles. I typed it and I never forgot it." Her smile fades and she returns to the box. "Hand those folders to me, Grace, the ones in front of you."

I slide the case files and appendices along the smooth table-top. "Ben, when are they going to hold this phone argument?"

"Tonight at seven." He checks his watch. "An hour and a half."

"After the close of business?" Curiouser and curiouser.

"They have to do it tonight, to leave time for the Supreme Court to decide the appeal. It's Hightower's fault. He caused it by waiting until the last minute."

Now I understand. "It doesn't have anything to do with the timing or the Supreme Court. Galanter doesn't want argument during regular business hours because that would be public."

"Not necessarily."

"No? You think the newspapers would let the panel hold a closed argument in this case? The first death case here in *decades?* They'd be upstairs with motion papers before you could say First Amendment."

"As is their wont, but—"

"Galanter won't have that, so he calls a phone conference when the evening news is over. When the newspapers are sold out. Everybody will be watching *Home Improvement.*"

"You've become quite the cynic, Grace." Ben unrolls a shirt-sleeve and twists the cuff button closed expertly. "In fact, I heard the most outlandish thing about you today."

"What?"

"It's so absurd I can barely bring myself to repeat it." He sets to work on the other shirtsleeve, unfolding one three-inch panel after the next. "I heard you think the chief was murdered."

Eletha looks over at me in surprise.

"I do. Call me crazy."

"You're crazy," Eletha says. She lets the file slip into the box, where it lands with a *tick.*

"I thought you had more sense than that." Ben fastens the button at the cuff, then holds both arms out and inspects them. "Well, I have to go. I'll leave you to your conspiracy theories."

"I didn't say it was a conspiracy."

Ben gasps in a theatrical way. "Maybe it is. Maybe the entire federal judiciary is in on it. Maybe they all conspired to kill him because he was—tall!" He turns on his heels, laughing, and walks out of the room. I watch him head into the clerks' office where he turns off his computer, then the lights. I listen for the sound of the door closing as he leaves. I know Eletha well enough to know she's waiting too.

"What the fuck you doin'?" she says, as soon as the chambers door clicks shut.

"Don't be shy, Eletha."

"Are you serious about this?"

"Yes."

"Is that what was goin' on with those marshal tapes yesterday?"

"Yep."

"They don't tape, do they?"

"Nope."

She shakes her head. "So what are you up to?"

"It doesn't make sense that he would kill himself."

"What are you sayin'?"

So I tell her, leaving out the most important part, the part about Armen and me. When I'm finished, she leans on the file box and looks directly at me. "Look, Grace, I knew he was in love with you. I knew about it before you did. He told me."

I feel my face redden. "You did? He did?"

"Mm-hm." She nods. "I have to admit, I told him not to get involved because you two work together. You know what he said? He told me he didn't give a good goddamn."

I smile. It warms me inside.

"So I know why you're thinkin' what you're thinkin'."

"Then why'd you tell me I was crazy?"

"Because Ben was here."

"What a good liar you are. Jeez, Eletha."

"Thank you, thank you." She curtsies prettily, then straightens up, rubbing her lower back. "Ow. Damn, I'm gettin' old."

"So what do you think? You knew him longer than any of us. Would he commit suicide?"

She sighs. "I worked for Armen for thirteen years, but I can't figure it out. It's hard to believe I wouldn't have seen something like that comin'. Like a sign."

"But the police say you said—"

"How do you know what the police say?"

"I went there this morning. They're sure it's a suicide. The detective was quoting you, things you said."

An angry frown contorts her features. "They didn't listen to me. That white cop askin' me those questions? He knew what he thought and he didn't want to hear anything different."

"I wanted to ask them about Susan. It was her gun."

"I can't get over what she did to Bernice. Dang, that woman's cold!"

"Do you think she would've—"

"Possible. It's possible. I wouldn't put it past her." She nods. "And today with Galanter, that was wild."

"You mean Bernice? She shoulda bit it off. I'd put it down the garbage disposal myself."

I smile. "Has Bernice ever done that before?"

"Are you kidding? That dog is a doll baby." She shakes her head. "So you workin' with the police or something? They gonna reopen the case?"

"No. I'm on my own. Single Moms, Inc."

"You're talkin' about murder? Accusing a senator? Galanter? Shit, Grace."

"Not accusing, just asking questions. Developing theories. Being a lawyer."

She sighs and stretches backward with a tiny grunt. "Oh, my back."

"You all right?"

"It hurts. The lifting doesn't help."

I feel a pang of guilt. She's been packing by herself since Armen died; the office is littered with boxes, some taped closed, some still open. A lifetime of paper stored away; his whole career. It makes me sad, and it has to be hard on her, too. "I should have helped you. I'm sorry."

"Nah, s'all right. It's a lot of stuff, though. He saved everything, I swear." She points to the back of the office, to the long mahogany credenza behind Armen's desk. "We got all the personal stuff back there, the articles and stuff. Then we got the academic stuff and old case files against the side wall."

"Why don't you go home? I'll finish the box."

"Why you pushin' me out, girlfriend? You wanna look around?"

"I wasn't thinking of that, but it's a good idea."

She picks her sweater off the back of the chair. "All right, don't stay too late. Tomorrow, baby." She knocks hard on the wood, and Bernice wakes up with a startled bark. We both laugh.

"Dog almost ate a judge," I say.

"Smartest thing she ever did."

"Second smartest."

She pauses at the doorway and smiles softly. She knows the first: loving Armen. I suppress a stab of pain as I listen to her lock up her desk and gather her handbag and newspaper.

"By the way, El, have I got a man for you," I call out to her.

"You know I'm seein' Leon."

"Time for a change," I say, but she's out the door. It closes harshly, accentuating the stillness of the suddenly empty office.

I look around at the boxes and files filling the room. The brocade throws are folded into neat squares and stacked on a chair for packing. I never asked Armen where he got them or even what they were. Most of the other Armenian artifacts have been wrapped in bubble paper. I step between the boxes to his desk and find myself running my finger along its surface, leaving a wake in the dust like a light snow. I laugh to myself. A wonderful man, but not a neat man.

I look at Armen's chair and try to imagine him sitting in it again. It's so hard to believe he's gone. Murdered. It tears at me inside. Maybe there are clues here. Something. Anything.

I look over from the chair to the credenza beyond. None of its doors are open; Eletha hasn't started on it yet. What had she said was in there? The personal stuff. I walk around the desk and kneel on the carpet in front of the cabinet.

You were raised better, says my mother's voice, stopping my hand on the gold-toned knob.

"No, I wasn't," I say. I slide open the thin door and take the first paper off the top of the stack. Its typeface is faded and old-fashioned, from the days of Smith-Coronas.

TOWARD AN ARMENIAN IDENTITY
by Armen Gregorian

I brush the dust away. He wasn't a judge yet; it doesn't say if it was published. I sit down and skim the short article. Well-written, heartfelt. I reach for the next paper in the cabinet, but as I slide it out, a pack of old check registers falls to the carpet, bound by a dirty rubber band. I slip one out, skimming the entries: Food Fare $33.00, Harvard Coop $11.27, Haig $6.00 (for Chinese food). Judging from the sums, it was a long time ago, though Armen didn't bother to date the entries or keep a running tab of the balance.

Typical. It would have driven me crazy over time, but time is something we didn't have. Time was taken from us. From him.

I feel a lump in my throat and slip the register hastily back under the rubber band. I shove it next to another checkbook. It looks newer than the other papers in the cabinet, so I pull that one out.

It's a maroon plastic checkbook, fake alligator on the front and back. At the lower right corner it says PHILADELPHIA CASH RESERVE in gilt-stamped script. The checkbook looks brand-new. I snap it open, anxious without knowing why.

The balance is staggering: $650,000. I had no idea. I look at the name and address and hear myself gasp.

Greg Armen. The address is an apartment in West Philadelphia.

What apartment is this? Armen lived in Society Hill, in a townhouse he owned with Susan. I look again at the name on the checks. Greg Armen. Obviously an alias. But why?

I hear my mother's voice inside my head: Come on, kid. A judge with a secret bank account? A false address? An alias? *A bribe.*

Impossible. I push the voice away and flip through the checkbook. There are no entries since the initial one, which is undated.

Was Armen involved in something? Does it have anything to do with his death?

I swallow hard and think twice before committing theft. Well, once maybe. Then I take the checkbook and close the cabinet.

TWELVE

Only an hour later I have crossed the threshold into another world. A scented, serene world, where the colors are chalky washes of pastels and the air carries the scent of primrose. Is it heaven? In a way. It's the Laura Ashley shop at the King of Prussia mall. I called Ricki to discuss the checkbook and she agreed to meet me here. I trail in reluctantly behind her, holding her bags like a pack animal. "So what do you think?"

"I told you what I think. I think you should go straight to the police. Show them the note from Armen and the checkbook." She plucks a frilly blouse off the rack and holds it against her chest. "You like?"

"For you or for me?"

"I don't need blouses, you do. That coffee stain is so attractive."

I tug my blazer over the brown blotch. "I have enough blouses."

"No you don't. You have the yellow one you wear over and and over, and the blue." She slips the blouse back onto the rack. "But it is a lot of money."

"The blouse or the bank account?"

"The blouse."

"So's the account."

"I wonder if he declared it, the crook."

"Don't say that." I look around the small store, but it's empty. Nobody can afford this stuff, not even in King of Prussia. "He's not a crook."

"You sound like Richard Nixon."

I set the bags down beside the rack. "I bet it has something to do with his murder."

"Murder? You're losing it, Grace. I told you. The checkbook doesn't mean he was murdered. Maybe he committed suicide in regret over taking a bribe." She snatches a blouse from the rack and her hazel eyes come alive; it's off-white, with billowy sleeves and a Peter Pan collar. She hoists it proudly into the air. "This is perfect."

"For what? Punting on the Thames?"

Ricki puts the blouse back onto the rack. "You have a bad attitude, you know that?"

"But we don't know it's a bribe, Rick. All we know is that it's a checking account of some kind."

"A boatload of money under an alias? Come on." Her concentration refocuses, laserlike, on the next ruffled blouse on the rack. She picks it up and appraises it. "This is nice."

"What about the note?"

"What about the blouse?"

"Where am I going to wear it, Rick? Tara?"

She slaps it back onto the rack. "Maybe we'll have better luck with the dresses." She turns smartly away and heads over to a lineup of dresses whose skirts are so voluminous they puff out like parachutes. Ricki extracts one with an expertise born of practice and waves it at me from across the store. "Very appropriate, don't you think?" she says.

I pick up the bags and follow her. "No feathers? I want feathers. And a headpiece."

A young saleswoman, more like a saleschild, perks up from

behind a counter littered with fragrant notecards and sta-
tionery. She looks like Alice in Wonderland in a black velvet
headband and a white pinafore. "That's one of our most popular styles," she says.

"I hate it," I whisper.

Ricki looks daggers at me. "Give it a chance, Sherlock."

"No."

The saleschild's face falls.

Ricki slaps the dress back in place. "You are so stubborn. So
stubborn."

"Rick, listen."

"You said you wanted me to help you."

"This isn't what I meant."

"Why do I bother? You call me up and I come. My one
night without clients and here I am. I should have gone food
shopping. There's no milk in the house." She puts her hands on
her hips and glares at me.

There's no milk in the house. The all-time low watermark of
motherhood.

I put my hands on my hips and we face off at opposite ends
of the dress rack, the High Noon of Mothers. No milk in the
house, and Ricki is the most organized of women; it must
gnaw at her conscience like an overdue library book. I feel the
first pang of guilt, which means she's quicker on the draw.
"Give me the goddamn dress," I say.

"Good." She plucks it from the rack and pushes it at me.

"I'm not promising anything."

"Fine."

The saleschild comes over. "Can I help you?" she says
brightly. Too brightly for minimum wage.

"Yes," Ricki says. "My friend needs dresses. With her eyes,
I think a royal blue would be nice."

"Rick, I'm standing here. I can speak."

The saleschild looks from Ricki to me.

"I don't want anything fancy," I say.

"Not fancy?" The saleschild looks puzzled; fancy is all they sell. They have a monopoly on fancy.

"She doesn't mean fancy," Ricki says, "she means fussy."

"No, I mean fancy. Empire waistline, hem to the floor. I'm too old for puffed sleeves."

"Fussy," Ricki says again.

The saleschild looks at Ricki, then at me. The poor girl's getting dizzy. I hand her the dress for balance.

"Where are the business-y dresses?" Ricki asks.

"I'm out of a job, Rick."

"Then you need interview clothes."

"Follow me," says the saleschild. She pads in ballet slippers to a rack of dresses and takes three from the rack. Any one of them would work at my coronation, but Ricki badgers me to try one on. We squeeze together into the flowered dressing room. Ricki always comes into dressing rooms with me; she doesn't realize this was okay when we were in high school but now that we're almost forty, it's a bit odd.

"Are we having fun yet?" I mutter, stepping into the billowing dress.

"Let me zip it up for you," Ricki says.

"It's the least you can do."

She zips the dress more roughly than necessary and I regard myself in the mirror. The style makes me look tall and thin, which must be some sort of optical illusion. Still, all I can see is that my eyes look too small and my nose looks too big; my father's Sicilian blood, acid-etched into my features. I look terrible.

"You look stunning!" Ricki says from behind me.

"Uncanny. That's just what I was thinking."

"The neckline is so pretty."

I look down at my chest and catch sight of the scalloped bra, barely covered by the dress. It reminds me of Armen, of that night. *This is the beginning for us. I love you.* "What about the note he wrote me, Rick?"

But she's busy picking up a flowered scarf and tossing it around my neck. She's caught brain fever from the shopping, like early man, blood-lusting after the kill. She found the right dress, now the whole village can eat. "Here, if you're not in love with the neckline."

"Rick, what do you think about the note?"

"What note?" She drapes the scarf to the left, then squinches up her nose.

"The one I found in my pocket."

She rearranges the scarf over my shoulder. "Are we talking about that again?"

"Yes."

"I'm trying to take your mind off your official police duties, but you're not letting me."

"Just tell me where the note fits in, huh? Is that the act of a man who would kill himself a few hours later? You're a shrink, you tell me. You must have handled suicide in your practice."

"Only one, thank God." She crosses herself quickly even though she's Jewish.

"But depressed people, right? You must see tons of depressed people."

"Oh, they ship 'em in."

"Rick, will you help me? You may actually know something here."

"Why, thank you."

"You know what I mean."

She ties the scarf around my neck. "Okay, so you're asking me? Professionally?"

"Yes."

She pats the knot and steps back, squinting at my costume like a movie director. "I think your friend the judge was a very interesting personality, and I think his behavior was totally consistent with suicide. Even the note."

"But how?"

"Let me ask you this. How well did you know this man?"

"Armen? I knew him well."

"You worked for him for three months. Part-time."

"We worked closely together. I knew him well."

"Think about it," she says. "You didn't know he loved you. You didn't know he was sitting on a pile of money. You didn't know he had an apartment."

"But I knew what mattered, what kind of man he was. Everybody knew that. And what's this have to do with psychology anyway?"

"Everything. He was a very important judge, a powerful judge, and the husband of a United States senator. On top of that, he's a *macher* in the Armenian community. A hero, right?"

"Yes." I feel vaguely like I'm being led where I don't want to go.

"So people like that, they're managing constantly under the pressure to live up to very high standards. The standards of others, of the community. It's tough to keep that veneer perfect, to keep up appearances. They begin to keep secrets, like he did, and pretty soon what they know about themselves grows further and further away from what the world thinks of them. In the right circumstances, a person like that falls apart. The veneer cracks, and so do they."

"But it wasn't a veneer. He really was—"

"Perfect?"

I feel it inside. "Yes. In a way. He believed in things. He cared, really cared, and he fought hard."

"Don't you think you're idealizing him, Grace?"

"No, I'm not idealizing him." My throat tightens, but it could be the scarf. "Take this frigging thing off. I feel like a Boy Scout in drag."

She avoids my eye and unties the scarf. "You worked for him for a short time. You had a business relationship with him until one night. Now you're charging around, going to the police, ransacking his office for clues."

"I wasn't ransacking."

"You're acting like it was a fifteen-year relationship, like he was your husband. But he wasn't. In fact, he was somebody else's."

Ouch. "That's beside the point. The man was murdered, Ricki."

"You don't know that. It's not your job to investigate it, even if it *is* true. If you were my client, I'd ask you why you're doing all this. What would happen if you didn't?"

"His killer would go free."

"And what's the matter with that?"

I look wildly around the frilly dressing room. "What's the matter with murder? It's very bad manners, for starters."

"Don't be snide, I mean it."

"But what kind of question is that, What's the matter with murder?" I hear my voice growing louder.

"No, the question is, Why does it matter if his killer goes free?"

I hold back my snidehood. "It's terrible. It's *unfair*."

"Then it's the unfairness that strikes you."

"Yes, of course."

She purses her lips. "You're a person who's been treated unfairly. By your father, then by Sam. You had a baby, he wanted out. He broke the contract."

I feel a churning inside. "Yeah, so?"

"So maybe it's not *this* unfairness you're fighting about, maybe it's unfairnesses in your past. Ones you can't do anything about."

"Oh please, Ricki."

"Think about it. Keep an open mind."

"The man is dead, Rick. Am I just supposed to ignore that?"

She folds her arms calmly, like she always does when I get upset. Therapists never have emotions; that's why they want to hear ours. "How long have we known each other?" she asks.

I boil over. "Too damn long."

"Well, that's a very nice thing to say."

"If you wouldn't analyze me at every turn—"

"You asked me to."

"I asked you to analyze *him*, not me."

"Why do you need me to analyze him if you know him so goddamn well? Hmm?"

I have no immediate answer. The word *uncle* comes immediately to mind, but I push it away.

"Well?" A triumphant smile steals across her face. "I should've been a lawyer, right?"

Right. Or a personal shopper.

The red-lighted numbers on the clock radio say 4:13 A.M.; they're oddly disjointed, constructed like toothpicks laid end to end. It flips to 4:14.

The house sleeps silently. The dishwasher stopped cranking at 1:10, leaving only the clothes dryer in the basement. A wet bathroom rug thudded against the sides of the drum, keeping me awake until 2:23. Since then I have no excuse except for my own feelings, tumbling as crazily as the rug in the dryer. The fury, grief, and confusion cycle: it comes right after spin-dry.

Maddie's in the next room, her door closed against Bernice, who sleeps in my bed like a mountain range bordering my right side and curling under my feet. This must be why they call them mountain dogs. I shove her over, but she doesn't budge. My thoughts circle back to Armen.

He said he loved me, but there's obviously much he didn't say. A secret bank account. An alias. I sit up and shake two powdery generic aspirins from the bottle, then swallow them with some flat seltzer from a bottle on my night table. I flop back in bed and stare up at the white ceiling with its cracked paint, trying to put away my emotions.

But I'm having less success than usual. Anxiety makes my chest feel tight. I wonder vaguely if they have a drug for that, and then I remember that they do.

Alcohol.

The thought warms me like brandy. I throw off the covers, slip on a terry bathrobe, and tiptoe down the creaky stair. Bernice looks up but doesn't follow; she won't go in the kitchen now unless she's dragged into it.

I flick on the kitchen light and dim it down, then open up the tall kitchen cabinet that was built into the wall sixty years ago. My landlord let me strip the old paint away, and underneath was a fine bare pine, which I scrubbed and pickled white. I love this cabinet, a true old-fashioned larder, which finds room for every grocery I buy on its five shelves. The liquor is at the top, like a penthouse above the stories of oversized cereal boxes, cans of soup, and baked beans.

I grab a stool, climb up on it, and pull down a thick shot glass, one of the multitude my mother gave me a long time ago. Half I threw out and half I stowed in the basement until Maddie found them. I eventually had to sneak them away from her, finding something unseemly about a child's tea party with shot glasses and a steel jigger. I hid them up here, where they line up like pawns guarding the liquor bottles.

I peer at the dusty bottles and try to make a decision. What shall I treat myself to? It's all left over from my wedding, the last time I had more than two drinks. Alcohol goes right to my head, but that's suddenly what I want.

A bottle of Crown Royal stands like a king behind the pawns. The lattice blown into its glass catches even the dim light. I pick the bottle up by its gold plastic crown and climb down from the shelf.

I am going to get drunk. This strikes me as a daring and powerful act, something a man would do. I am going to have myself a drink, yessir, I am going to tie one on. I put the bottle on the counter and crack open the cap, which sticks slightly. The bottle's almost full. I take a whiff.

Fragrant. Sweet. Tangy. Strong.

I remember this smell, and it brings a memory down on my

head. My parents fighting again, shouting. My father, lurching out the door. My mother, crying alone. A bottle of Crown Royal sitting in the center of a kitchen table, eye level with me: It's so majestic, glinting like gold. A regal beacon in a world where Daddy is gone and the future is a mystery.

I pour myself a shot.

THIRTEEN

My head buzzes with liquor from the night before; my stomach gurgles like a polluted stream. Getting drunk isn't as manly as I thought it would be. At least not the next morning.

You don't have to be hung over to be seeing double. Even triple. There are judges everywhere in the grand ceremonial courtroom: circuit judges, district judges, bankruptcy judges, magistrate judges. They gather like ravens in ebony robes on either side of the dais and in the reserved section in front of it. Twenty representative judges from the circuit and district courts fill the dais in two tiers. Crows on the power lines.

The audience, relegated to the back rows, is standing room only. Lawyers, academics, and reporters clog the courtroom. Standing in the back are older men in shabby overcoats, the courtroom junkies dressed up. Shake and Bake isn't here, but one of them, in a dark overcoat, looks familiar. Thick and bulky, like a thug. I try to think where I've seen him before.

Outside the police station? Maybe the man in the black car with Virginia plates.

I crane my neck to see him better, but he disappears behind a group of Armen's closest friends, the Armenian men in his dinner club; they cleave together, olive-skinned and outnumbered. Susan has been doing what she can to cut them and everybody else out, flying Armen's body to Washington for a funeral tomorrow. Meanwhile she sits dry-eyed in the front row, sucking up all the attention by saying nothing, like a vacuum.

Does she know about Greg Armen?

It makes me sick to my stomach. Everything does.

Ben has joined Galanter's clerks, up front. Artie sits with Eletha, comforting her before the service begins, but he looks like he needs comforting himself. He's more unkempt than usual, his hair uncombed and his rep tie wrinkled. Sarah is next to me in the row behind them; she and Artie don't exchange a word during the ceremony. Is there trouble in Paradise? I haven't been paying attention.

Chief Judge Galanter begins the memorial service from the coveted center seat. His statement is ruthlessly generic, and over as soon as it starts. A few of the other judges make short speeches, their words shaky, their sentences halting. They mourn, but it's a peculiar sort of mourning, characterized by bewilderment. One of their own, a suicide. Only Judge Robbins says the word, his eyes red-rimmed behind rimless spectacles. I close my mind until the service is over, hoping my head will stop thundering.

When it's over the judges adjourn to the robing room, and some of Armen's Armenian friends linger near the dais, waiting for a chance to talk to Susan. At the periphery of the crowd are reporters, interested in the same thing. Susan doesn't seem to mind talking to anyone and doesn't shed a tear. Her own husband's memorial service. What had the detective said? *Cried a river?*

A wild-haired reporter with a day's stubble gets close to her and says, "Senator, just clear up one thing for me. Senator, over here."

She looks up, but her smile vanishes when she seems to recognize him. "One question, Sandy. That's it."

"Is it true that you and the judge were having marital problems?"

Shocked, the well-wishers turn and look at him.

Susan's mouth sets into a thin line. "I'm fine. Thanks for asking." Instantly, a tall, preppy aide in expensive eyeglasses takes her elbow and hustles her through the crowd to the robing room door.

"Have some decency!" an older lawyer says to the reporter, who takes off through the crowd after Susan. Two marshals, Mutt and Jeff, head after him; the big one, McLean, takes the lead.

"What an asshole," Sarah says, but I watch the reporter until I lose him in the crowd. "Let's go."

Sarah and I bobble together in the mass of people leaving the ceremony. I whisper to her, "How do you think he knew?"

"Lucky guess. He's been hustling since the campaign, trying to get a real job."

I consider this, but it hurts my head to think. I keep seeing the checkbook, hidden now in my underwear drawer.

We pour out of the courtroom doors into the marble walkway that connects the north half of the federal building to the courthouse. I let the crowd carry me past the plant-filled atrium on the right, which the court employees use to smoke in. A hunchbacked man sweeps up the discarded cigarette butts with a broom.

"You'd think we could find him something better to do," says a man's voice beside Sarah. The wild-haired reporter. Up close, he looks sweaty and his curls are permed. "Remember me, Miss Whittemore?"

"What happened to the marshals?" Sarah says, and picks up the pace next to me.

"I'm Sandy Faber. I write for a lot of newspapers in the city."

"Where do you get off asking a question like that?" Sarah says, barreling ahead.

The reporter falls into her brisk stride. "Did I upset your client, Miss Whittemore?"

"I don't have any clients, and you don't fool me for one minute. You're the one who wrote that victim's rights story. You called Armen a killer."

"I didn't call him a killer, I merely quoted—"

"I don't want to hear it."

The reporter scrambles over to me and grabs my arm. "Ms. Rossi, it'll just take a minute. I know you cared about the judge."

"We all did," I say, wresting my arm back.

"Somebody didn't. The person who killed him."

It stuns me in my tracks, but Sarah reacts instantly. "How dare you!" she says. "You want me to call the marshals?"

"Take a look at your co-counsel here, Miss Whittemore. She's not so sure it's a suicide either."

I feel my gorge rising, only partly from the alcohol. I look past the crowd for the ladies' room and spot it at the end of the gleaming hall. "I have to go."

"Grace, are you all right?" Sarah asks.

I wave her off. "See you upstairs."

"Ms. Rossi?" calls the reporter, who takes off after me, opening his skinny steno pad as we walk. "You were close to Judge Gregorian, weren't you?"

Does he suspect anything about me and Armen? I hurry past the crowd. The rapid motion makes me seasick. I'll never drink again; I don't know how my father stood it.

"Did you know that the judge and his wife were having marital problems?"

I try to ignore him and make my way through the crowd to the ladies' room. I zigzag left and right, like a sunfish trying to tack in a hurricane.

"Can you shed some light on that, Ms. Rossi? Ms. Rossi?"

I reach the door and pull its stainless steel handle with all my might, but the reporter stops it with his hand. He's breathing heavily; he smells like cigarettes.

"Grace, are you gonna let somebody get away with murder?"

I look into his face with its sheen of sweat. I feel a stab of confusion and nausea. I yank on the door. "I have to go."

"Is that the way it's gonna be? Is it?" he calls after me, as the heavy door closes between us.

I lurch into an empty stall, lock it, and drop on to the seat until the wave of nausea passes. I hang my head, examining the speckles in the floor tile; gray, black, and white fragments tumble together like a kaleidoscope. Between each tile is a steel line where the grout would be, but it wiggles from time to time. I right myself and wrestle with the oversized dispenser for a square of toilet paper.

Are you gonna let somebody get away with murder?

I wipe my face with the thin square and decide to stay there until the earthquake stops. I listen to other women flush the toilets, wash their hands, and leave. I wait until all the hands are washed and all the women have gone. In time, the voices outside the bathroom diminish, then disappear altogether.

I think of the checkbook. I think of Armen. I'm not sure if I can't move or won't. I stay a long, long time at the bottom of the tall, glistening courthouse, sitting on the john in silence, thinking about my murdered lover. The judge with the alias.

What does that reporter know?

I hear the bathroom door open.

Shit. Who's coming into my bathroom? I feel intruded upon. I hate to share a public bathroom with the public, especially when my stomach is barely parallel to the floor.

Whoever it is walks farther into the bathroom. There's no sound of pumps on the floor; she must be wearing flats. I lean over and squint through the slit where the door meets the jamb, but I can't see anybody.

I know someone is there, but she's not going into a stall. She doesn't turn on the water, either, or strike a match for an illicit smoke. Maybe she came in to fix her makeup or brush her hair. I listen for the sounds, but nobody's fumbling in a handbag.

Still, someone is there. I heard the door. I feel a presence. I squint through the slits but see nothing.

Then I hear the faintest sound, of human breathing.

Someone is standing right in front of my door.

Panic floods my throat. I rise involuntarily.

There's a shuffling outside the stall as the presence moves closer in response. I lean next to the door, every nerve taut, straining to listen.

I hear the breathing, louder now.

I look underneath the door to my stall.

Planted there is a pair of large black shoes.

A man's.

FOURTEEN

"Who's there?" I shout, terrified.

"Are you all right?" says the man. Concerned, professional. "You've been in there awhile."

"Is that you, Faber?"

"No, I'm a special agent with the FBI."

"In a ladies' room?" My voice clatters off the tile walls. "Go away or I'll scream, I mean it! Right now!"

"Wait, relax. I swear to you, I *am* an FBI agent. Our office is here in the building. Seventh floor."

"Anybody would know that. It's on the directory."

"I'm with the agency for ten years now. I trained at Quantico. Eighteen months, not counting in-service training."

"Quantico, Virginia?" I think of the man at the memorial service, the car with the Virginia plates.

"Yes. Listen, I don't have much time. Here's my ID." A hand materializes above the shoes, carrying a card-size plastic wallet.

I start to reach for it, then draw back. What if he grabs my wrist? "Drop it. Near the toilet. Now." I sound ridiculous, even to myself.

"All right, all right." He tosses the wallet into the stall like a Frisbee; it banks against the toilet and settles at my feet. I'm not close enough to the door for his hand to reach under, so I pick it up. My hands have stopped trembling. So has my stomach. I open the billfold like a tiny book. On one leaf is a photo of Tom Cruise and on the other is a Pennsylvania driver's license.

"What is this, a joke? Where's your FBI badge?"

"I can't carry my creds, I'm undercover."

"Sure you are. You a friend of Tom's, too?"

"It goes with my cover. Look at the license, at least you'll see who I am."

I look at the driver's license. His features are nondescript in the state-sponsored mug shot, and it says that he's six feet one, 185 pounds. His hair is dark brown, eyes blue. It could be the man with the Virginia plates, but I had only a glimpse of him. "What's your name?" I ask.

"It's right on the license."

"Maybe you stole the license. What's your name?"

"Oh, a test. I get it. Abe Lincoln."

"You think this is funny? You scared the shit out of me. If this is standard FBI procedure—"

"It isn't, believe me. They'd have my ass. I wouldn't do it unless I were absolutely desperate."

That rings true. "So what's your name, desperate?"

"Thaddeus Colwin."

I strain to read the name on the driver's license. Thaddeus Colwin III. "Thaddeus?"

"It's Quaker."

"A Quaker cop?"

"A good cop, a bad Quaker. Call me Winn anyway. Thaddeus is my father."

"Wait a minute, if you're undercover, why are you carrying around your real license?"

"I knew I'd be contacting you after the service, and I knew you'd bust my chops."

"How'd you know that?"

"You're a lawyer. Duh."

Hmmm. "Do you have kids?"

"No, and my favorite color is yellow. This is getting kind of personal, isn't it? We just met."

A comedian. "What's your address?"

He sighs. "Twenty-one thirty-three Adams Street, Phila-del-phia. Pennsylvania."

"Social security number?"

"What?"

"Tell me your social security number or I scream."

"What is it with you?" he says, amused no longer.

"I'm somebody's mother, that's what it is with me. If you kill me, my daughter's stuck with a dog. For a father."

"166-28-2810."

It matches the driver's license. Maybe he *is* for real. "What do you want anyway?"

"Can you come out? I need to talk to you. I don't have much time. Somebody could've seen me come in here."

"Why do I have to come out? Why can't we talk like this?"

A huge sigh. "Artie told me you were like this."

"Artie? Artie who?"

"Weiss. The law clerk."

"You know Artie? How?"

"We play ball."

"Where?"

"At the Y. Now I have three minutes left. Will you please open the goddamn door?"

"Where did Artie go to school, if you know him so well?"

"That's a no-brainer, it's the first thing he tells any-body. Now open the door, I'm backing up against the wall. See?"

I look through the slit but see only the dark edge of a coat. "Go over to the sink and turn the water on. Keep pressing on the faucet top, so I know you're at the other end of the room, away from the door."

"Very clever. You go to Harvard too?" I hear the sound of footsteps, then the water being turned on.

"Are you pushing the top?"

"What?" he shouts. "You know I can't hear you when the water's running."

I'm beginning to hate this guy. I open the thumbscrew and peek out of the door. I freeze on the spot. I can't believe my eyes.

It's Shake and Bake. He's standing at the faucet in the ladies' room, complete with beard, cellophane rain bonnet, and black raincoat.

My God. A paranoid schizophrenic. I slam the door closed and bolt it. He must have stolen the driver's license. "Get out! You're not supposed to be in the courthouse! I'm going to scream!"

"Fuck!" I hear him shout. I look through the crack and watch him release the faucet in disgust, then slap it. "Fucking fuck!"

"You're not allowed in here!"

He turns toward the closed door. "It *is* me, I'm with the FBI," he says, in a voice as cultivated as someone named Thaddeus Colwin III would have. "Look, I ran the water, didn't I? Would a crazed killer do that? Open the door. Please."

"You? Shake and Bake? A federal agent?" I watch him through the crack.

"Open the door," he says. He slips the rain bonnet off the back of his head like a major leaguer after a strikeout. "Please."

"If you're an FBI agent, why did you make that scene at the oral argument, with the bomb?"

"It was part of my ingenious master plan."

I can't tell if he's kidding. "What plan?"

"Trust me, I'm smarter than I look."

"Smart? It got you banished from the courthouse."

"But it got me in good with the reporters, and that's very useful to me right now. Please come out. We don't have much time."

"We?"

"*Please.*"

I open the door a bit. "So you're a federal agent or a schizophrenic impersonating a Quaker."

His expression settles into businesslike lines behind the grimy beard. "You were close to Armen, right?"

I can't get over the incongruity of such an educated voice coming out of a bag man. "A reporter just asked me that."

"Were you close to him?"

"Wait a minute. Does Artie know about you?"

"No. No one does, except you."

"Why me?"

"Because I need you."

"What for?"

His eyes look slightly bloodshot in the harsh overhead lights. "This is confidential. All of it."

"Fine. What?"

"Are you going to work for Judge Galanter?"

"Possibly. How did you know that?"

"You told Sarah, Sarah told Artie, Artie told me."

"They teach you that at Quantico? Whisper down the lane?"

"Hey, whatever works. It's the only rule in this game." He breaks into a crooked grin, but I don't like his insouciance. Or his scummy teeth.

"You know, Artie really likes you. He worried about you when you were in jail."

"I know."

"He risked his career pretending to be your lawyer."

He purses his authentically parched lips. "Don't worry about me and Artie, okay? I have a job to do, he'll understand."

"Oh, I see. Manly men, ye be. So what's the story?"

"I'm undercover in an investigation supervised by the Justice Department. I can't tell you the details, I shouldn't even be meeting with you myself. All I can tell you is that it concerns charges of official corruption."

I feel my nausea resurge. "Corruption?"

"In the judiciary."

I think of the checkbook nestled in my Carter's at home. Armen's checkbook. "What kind of corruption?"

"Bribery, obstruction of justice."

Oh, God. "A federal appellate judge? Those are impeachable offenses."

"They're also crimes, so I couldn't care less if he loses his job. I need you to help me look for certain evidence."

"What's the matter with a search warrant?"

"I don't have enough for probable cause, not yet." His face grows tense. "What time is it anyway? I can't wear a watch on this job."

I glance at my wrist. "Noon."

"Shit. I have to be at the shelter, otherwise they run out of sandwiches. If you'd come out of the goddamn stall earlier—"

"What kind of evidence are you talking about?" I say, but he's busy yanking out the bottom of a ratty T-shirt so that it shows under his faded WHITE WATER KINGDOM SWEATSHIRT.

"Do I look pathetic enough? I only made seven bucks yesterday. All this bullshit about not encouraging us."

"Tell me more about the investigation. Is Galanter the only suspect?"

"No, and that's all you need to know. Don't tell anybody we talked. Give me back Tom Cruise." He slips on his rain bonnet and ties it under his chin like a babushka. "After all, I'm the Rain Man."

"I get it." I hand him the wallet, which he slips into a pocket sewn into the folds of his trousers. "What if I want to call you?"

"You can't. I'm homeless, remember?" He pushes his pants down around his hips and starts to leave the bathroom. "I have to go. I'll explain it all later."

"Do you think Armen was murdered?"

His face falls suddenly behind its hobo's mask. "Why do you ask?"

"Why don't you answer?"

"Maybe."

I feel my heart pounding. "Do you think it has to do with your investigation?"

"Maybe."

I think of Armen, lying face forward on his desk. Did he really take money for a case? There are so many questions, and only one thing is clear. It hurts inside.

"I miss him too," the agent says. Then he opens the ladies' room door and slouches out.

FIFTEEN

Maddie's gone outside to play, and my mother hands me her dinner dish for rinsing. The child left more peas than I thought. Puckered now, they careen randomly on the surface of the dish. "Let's talk about Dad," I say, taking the plate.

"Let's not," my mother says. She walks back into the dining room without meeting my eye. I watch her receding form, soft and shapeless in a pink acrylic sweatsuit. The back says NUMBER-ONE GRANDMA. She bought it for herself.

"Why not?" I call after her.

"It's not that time of year yet."

At least she's in a good mood. "What do you mean?" I maneuver Maddie's plate into the wire dishwasher rack. Bernice, standing at her now-customary place at the dishwasher door, sniffs the plate, disappointed to find it clean already.

"You're early," my mother says, returning with my messy plate of waxy mashed potatoes. "You usually don't start with those questions till Christmas." Her mouth is a tight smile; wrinkles radiate like tiny scars from the edges of her lips.

"I could be late, did you ever think of it that way? I mean, is the glass half empty or half full?" I take the plate and she turns silently on her heel. "Depends on your perspective, Ma, right?" I watch the water splash harmlessly off an insoluble potato mound, then stow the dish in the rack to let Bernice finish the job.

My mother comes back as Bernice is in mid-meal. "Don't let the dog do that, Grace! It's unsanitary. We eat off those dishes. Shoo, shoo!" She bangs a glass down on the counter and takes a swipe at Bernice, who backs up, confused.

"It's all right, Ma. It's going into the dishwasher."

"They're not even cheap dishes, they're expensive dishes. It's unhealthy. The germs."

"The hot water kills the germs."

Her frown deepens as she eyes Bernice, who's licking her chops sheepishly. "When I sit at your table, I don't like to think I'm eating off a dog dish."

"It's not like I feed her from the dish."

"It's the same thing. You're lucky my mother can't see this. You know what she would do? She would set your place at the table with the dog's dish."

She never talks about her childhood. "Your mother would do that?"

"She sure would. My mother was spiteful. She'd explain it to you this way. If your dish is good enough to feed the animal, then you don't mind eating out of the dog's dish. Believe me, Grace, she would." She shakes her head and walks into the dining room. "It's so common."

I would remind her that we're common, that she manicured nails to support us, but this is family history long since revised; she tells people she was in the beauty industry, whatever that is. "Is the table clear, Ma?" Bernice trots back to the dishwasher, but I wave her off.

"One left." She comes back in and hands me her own plate. It doesn't need rinsing; you would never know anybody ate off it.

"Tell me about my father."

Her frown is replaced by a cynical smile. "What do you

have to know? He had dark hair, he wore it slicked back. He was Sicilian, he might as well have been black. He was younger than me, so I should have known. End of story."

"Do you miss him ever?"

Her smile, weak to start out with, now fades completely. "No."

"Were you ever happy?"

"No."

"Not even before he started drinking?"

"He always drank. He drank from the beginning."

"So tell me—"

"There's nothing to tell."

"Tell me about his drinking, then. It's hard to remember."

"Good. It's better you don't." She does an about-face and heads out of the room. I brace myself as she returns with another glass.

"I remember that he drank Crown Royal."

Her face reddens but her expression remains rigid. She sets the glass down. "He drank everything. Beer. Wine. Whiskey. Cough syrup." She pushes back a steel-colored curl. "You know all this. Why do we have to go over and over it?"

"I remembered something about Crown Royal. It used to come in a purple sack with gold letters."

Her eyelids flutter. "It still does. You know that from now, not before."

"He gave me the sacks for purses," I say, the sentence popping out of my mouth of its own force, a memory I didn't know I had until this very moment. "For dress-up." I scan her face for verification, but it's a perfect blank. "Remember?"

"No."

"The purses? The gold braid on the side?"

"No."

"There was a drawstring."

She turns to go, but I grab her arm. My grasp is rougher than I intended, and in the half second she looks back I catch a fleeting expression on her face. This one I can read: fear. She's afraid I'm going to hit her. Suddenly I understand.

"Did he hit you, Mom?" I ask, horrified. Outraged.

"Why are you doing this?" Her forehead creases with anxiety. She tries to wrench her arm free but I hold her tighter, almost involuntarily.

"I have to know. Did he hit you?"

"It's *my business*." She yanks her arm from my grasp and backs unsteadily away from me toward the refrigerator door. Behind her is a jumble of crayon rainbows and happy-face suns. Maddie's drawings. "*My* business."

"It's my business, too!"

"No, it isn't."

"Mom, there's no shame in it. It's not your fault."

"None of this is your concern."

"I knew he left us, I never knew why. Is that why? Did you throw him out because he beat you? I'm not blaming you, I just want to know."

"Stop! Stop it right now!" She holds up a veined hand, her finger pads curled over like the tines on a hand rake. Years of nicotine, the doctor told her.

"Ma—"

"You let me be!" She hurries out of the room but I follow her, almost panicky. To make it better, to make it worse, I don't even know.

"Ma, it's just that I've been wondering—"

She whirls around and silences me with a crooked index finger. Her face, for the first time in my memory, is full of pain, and she fights for control. "Let it drop. What's done is done. Going over it doesn't do me any good, doesn't do anybody any good."

"Did he hit *me* too, Ma?"

"What are you talking about?"

"Something happened the other day at the office, and I remembered."

Her chest heaves like a boxer's under the silly sweatshirt. "Grace Deasey—"

"Grace Deasey *Rossi*, Mom. I had a father, and I would like to know what he did to me. That *is* my business."

She snatches her purse from a chair and almost runs to the front door. "You're out of your mind. You'll drive me out of mine if I let you. But I won't let you."

"Ma—"

"No," she says simply, and walks out.

NUMBER-ONE GRANDMA winks at me as the door slams closed behind her.

SIXTEEN

"Let's do it," Eletha says grimly as we encounter the first wave of reporters along the wall of the outer lobby to the courthouse.

"Grace! Grace Rossi!" one of them shouts.

Shocked, I turn toward the voice. It's the reporter from the day before, Sandy Faber. He's wearing the same sport jacket and more stubble. "Remember what I said, Ms. Rossi?"

"Which judge does she work for?" one of the women reporters asks. He ignores her, so she shouts at me. "Who do you work for, Ms. Rossi? Do you have any comment on *Hightower*? Why did it take so long to get the transcripts of the oral argument?"

"Holy shit," I hear Eletha mutter beside me.

I push forward away from the reporters, but the lunchtime crowd is barely trickling out the narrow courthouse doors.

"Come on, Ms. Rossi!" Faber shouts. "You gonna talk to me? Come on. Gimme a break here."

The heads of three other reporters snap in my direction. I feel Eletha's hand on my forearm.

"Who do you work for? Judge Meyerson? Judge Redd?" the woman shouts at me. "I can find out, you know."

"No comment," I say.

"Aw," the woman says, "just tell me who you work for. It's Simmons, right? That's who? Simmons?"

I feel Eletha's talons dig into my arm; she seems shaken. I press ahead, pushing in line for the first time in my life as a good girl. It works. The crowd surges forward, and Eletha and I squeeze out the door and into the crowd outside the courthouse.

"You all right?" I say to Eletha, but she can't hear me over the Hightower supporters to our left. *"No justice, no peace!"* they chant. Their signs read: DEATH PENALTY = GENOCIDE OF AFRICAN AMERICANS! ABOLISH THE DEATH PENALTY! SUPREME COURT ADMITS "DISCREPANCY CORRELATES WITH RACE!"

"Let's just get out of here," Eletha says.

"I'm trying, El." One of the signs is a picture of a young black teenager with smooth clear skin and a shy smile. He wears a red varsity football jacket. Hightower. The sound of the chanting resounds in my head.

At the front line of the swelling Hightower contingent is a prominent black city councilman and members of the black clergy. An older black woman standing next to one of the clergymen catches my eye; she's heavyset but dignified in an old-fashioned cotton dress, a calm eye at the center of a media hurricane. I recognize her from TV: Hightower's mother, Mrs. Stevens.

"Are you surprised by the amount of support that's being shown for your son?" a TV reporter says to her, thrusting a bubble-headed microphone in front of her face.

Mrs. Stevens looks startled, then the black councilman steps closer to the microphone, obstructing her from view. "We are going to hold a round-the-clock vigil to protest the death penalty, to show that it has always been racist in this country," the councilman says. "The Baldus study shows that African

Americans are more likely to receive the death penalty than whites."

"Push, Grace," Eletha says.

"Okay, okay," I say. I force my way past the man in front of me, but find myself face-to-face with Mr. Gilpin, who's standing in my path. Even in the midst of the hubbub, his face relaxes into a smile.

"Hello there, my friend," he says, loud enough to be heard over the din. "Is this pretty lady a friend of yours?"

A tall black man in an X baseball cap chants over his shoulder, and behind him is the TV reporter and the black councilman. Gilpin acts like none of this is happening, as if it's a squabble over a suburban fence, not an incipient race war.

"Mr. Gilpin, this is Eletha Staples," I say.

Eletha extends a hand reluctantly. "Hello, Mr. Gilpin."

"Call me Bill, Eletha. You girls goin' out to lunch?"

"No justice, no peace!" booms a clear voice behind him, and the crowd begins to shove me aside.

"We'd better go, we're blocking the way," I say. I edge forward, but Eletha gets jammed between one of the Hightower supporters and a TV technician.

Gilpin grabs her arm and pulls her lightly to her feet. "Are you all right?" he says.

"Get me out of here, please. I hate crowds." She places a hand to her chest and starts breathing in and out. I'm worried she's going to hyperventilate and Gilpin must see it too, because in one swift movement he scoops us up by the elbows and drives through the mob. He deposits us at the curb and brushes back a pomaded hank of hair. "I played football in high school," he says.

Eletha tugs a handkerchief from the sleeve of her sweater and dabs at her forehead. "Thanks a lot."

Gilpin's eyes skim the crowd unhappily. "We started this, I know. But it'll be over soon."

Which is when it occurs to me. The politics of the new *Hightower* panel is all over the newspapers; Galanter and Foudy aren't closet conservatives. Gilpin must realize that Hightower's going to lose, and he's about to see his daughters' murder avenged. I wonder if Gilpin is happy that Armen was killed. Suddenly I like him less. "We'd better be going," I say.

He nods. "Sure enough."

"Thanks again," Eletha says, recovering.

We cross Market Street and the chanting trails off into the noontime traffic, making me suddenly aware of Eletha's stone silence. She chugs along the sidewalk like a locomotive and I tense up, feeling like a curtain has fallen between us: white on one side, black on the other. We come to the corner of Sixth and Chestnut and she squints up at the light. An executive takes a second look at her, then stares right at my breasts. My tension, pent up, bubbles over. "They're a B-cup, okay?" I spit at him. "Any other questions?"

The man hurries past us, and Eletha bursts into startled laughter. "I can't believe you said that!" she says.

"Neither can I. It felt great. Absolutely great." I laugh, suddenly lighthearted. "I've been wanting to do that all my life."

"So have I."

I meet her eye. "Are you mad at me, girlfriend?"

She shakes her head, still smiling. "I'm getting over it." The traffic light turns green and we cross Chestnut.

"It's not my fault I'm white."

She laughs again. "It's not that. It's that I can't believe you're messin' with Gilpin. You know better than that."

"I'm not messin' with him. He talked to me the first day."

"You shoulda walked away."

"I couldn't walk away, he's a person."

She holds up a hand. "I don't want to know he's a person, and I don't want to know Hightower's a person. These are names on a caption, not people. If you start thinkin' they're people, you won't be able to do your job. Look what happened to Armen."

"What?" We stop in front of Meyer's Deli, the only place she'll eat; Eletha's not Jewish, but she practically keeps kosher. "What do you mean by that, about Armen?"

She looks warily at the lunchtime crowd. "Let's talk inside, okay?"

We head into the noisy deli, with its old-time octagonal tile floor and embossed tin roof. Meyer's is always mobbed, but the line moves quickly because everybody inhales their food; the clientele consists almost exclusively of hyperactive trial lawyers. The hostess accosts us at the door and hustles us to an orange plastic booth against the wall. Our waitress, Marlene, appears at our table from nowhere. "You havin' the tuna fish?" she says to me, already writing down #12 on her pad.

"Only if you call me 'honey,' " I tell her. "I want someone to call me 'honey,' and not just for my body."

Eletha smiles. "Do what she says, Mar. She just attacked a man on the street."

"Okay, honey," Marlene says mirthlessly. She tears off the check and puts it face down, like we're at the Ritz-Carlton. "You havin' the whitefish on bagel, Eletha?" she says, scribbling on the order pad.

"Yes," Eletha says.

"What's goin' on at the courthouse, girls?" Marlene says. She rips Eletha's check off the pad and slaps it face down on the table. "They gonna kill that kid?"

Jesus. "We have no comment," I say.

Marlene scowls as she slips the ballpoint into her apron pocket. "I'm sick of the whole thing anyway," she says, and vanishes.

Eletha leans forward. "So. I've been thinkin' about what you said, about Armen. About him being murdered."

"What?"

"Just accept that he's gone, Grace. That's hard enough. Anything else is a waste of time."

"I don't understand. You don't think he was murdered?"

"I'm not so sure."

Now I really don't understand. "Since when? That's not what you said yesterday."

"I know what I said. But last night I tried to quit school, and they told me Armen paid already, in advance."

"What are you talking about? You go to school?"

"Night school, at the community college. I got two more years left, and I've had it up to here." She draws a line across her throat.

Marlene materializes with our food. "Enjoy," she barks, and takes off again.

"Eletha, I didn't know you went to school."

"I thought Armen might've told you." She picks up a bagel half and spackles it with whitefish salad.

"He didn't, but why didn't you?"

"It's a secret." She bites into her sandwich, but I'm still too surprised to start mine. "In case I flunk out."

"You won't flunk out."

"You never know. The whole damn thing was Armen's idea. Now he's gone."

"But I think it's wonderful, Eletha."

"You don't have to do it, girl. Three nights a week I get home at eleven o'clock. I gotta take two buses, then transfer to the subway. Malcolm's in bed, I don't even get to see him. If I'm lucky, I got an hour left to fight with Leon. I figured if I got an associate's degree, maybe I could transfer the credits and go on to college, then who knows."

"Maybe to law school?"

She smiles. "Maybe."

"That sounds great. I think it's great."

She puts down her sandwich. "Nah, it was a pipe dream.

The only reason I didn't quit was Armen. He'd have been on my case forever, like he was till I quit smoking. That man was too much. He paid my tuition for me, clear through to graduation."

"But why does he pay it at all, if I can ask?"

"I couldn't afford to, so we had an agreement. He lent me the money and I paid him back in installments. When they told me it was all paid off, I started thinkin'. Maybe it *was* a suicide. Maybe he was fixing it so I couldn't quit after he was gone."

It can't be. "Maybe he just wanted you not to worry about it."

She shakes her head. "I feel like quitting anyway."

"Don't. He wouldn't want you to."

"I know that." She bites into her sandwich.

"El, can I ask you a question?"

She nods, her mouth full.

"How much money are we talking about for your tuition?"

"Couple thousand a semester."

"Where would Armen get that kind of money?"

"He makes a fine livin', hundred thirty thousand a year, and he saved like a fiend. He never spent a dime, that man."

It doesn't make sense. Why would Armen save if he had over half a million dollars? "He was a saver?"

"Always. But he was cheap, they all are."

"Who's they? Judges?"

"Armenians. You should see, when they'd have a dinner, I'd be countin' dimes on my desk. Who had the iced tea, who had the wine. I'm serious."

"That's racist, El."

"I know. But it's true." She laughs.

"Did his family have money?"

"No. Susan's did, but he didn't."

"So how much did he have saved, do you think?"

"Maybe fifty-sixty thousand. He told me not to worry about

it, he'd take care of Malcolm's college. I worried plenty, but I don't make enough to save shit. Why?"

I look down at a half-eaten pickle. "Just curious."

We split up after lunch because Eletha has to run an errand; she promises me she'll take the back entrance into the building, because there's no demonstration there. As I reach the courthouse, I consider doing the same myself. The mob has grown. People spill out past the curb and into the street, filling the gaps between the TV vans and squad cars. The police ring the crowd, trying vainly to keep it out of Market Street.

I cross against the traffic light, which turns out to be advisory anyway. A gaper block stalls traffic up and down the street. As I get closer to the courthouse, I see that something seems to be happening. The chanting stops suddenly; the crowd noise surges. Reporters and TV cameras rush to the door. I pick up my pace. It looks like breaking news, maybe the panel decision. My pulse quickens as I reach the edge of the crowd. I look for the hot orange cones that mark the walkway into the courthouse, but they've been scattered.

"What's going on?" I say, but am shoved into a woman in front of me. I turn around to see who's pushing. A cameraman stands there, and a lawyer with a trial bag.

"Sorry," says the lawyer, sweating profusely behind horn-rimmed glasses. "It's this person behind me."

"No!" someone screams at the head of the crowd, and then there's more shouting and pushing. The mob's moving out of control. I feel a sharp elbow in my back. It knocks me off balance.

"There's a decision!" someone shouts up front; then there's more yelling, even screaming. I feel panic rising in my throat as the crowd swells toward the door, carrying me with it, almost off my feet.

Suddenly there's a painful whack at the back of my head. I feel faint, dizzy. Everything gets fuzzy. My arms flutter, groping for anything to stay upright.

Gunshots ring out like distant firecrackers, and there's screaming and shouting, also far away. Strong hands catch me from behind. Someone says in my ear, "This is a warning. Let the judge rest in peace."

The words and the pain melt together.

And then slip beyond me.

SEVENTEEN

I wake up on a green plastic couch in a room I've never seen before. My head hurts, but I can see everyone clearly. Standing over me are Eletha and the law clerks. Behind them are a few marshals I don't know, and the big mustachioed one, Al McLean, who was on duty the night Armen was killed. I'd been meaning to talk to him. His shrimpy sidekick, Jeff, sits silently in a chair nearby.

"Auntie Em, Auntie Em," Artie says, but nobody laughs.

"Hey, baby," Eletha says soothingly. She sits on the couch beside me.

"What happened?"

"You got caught in a riot, child. I shoulda walked back with you."

"Fifteen people were wounded," says Ben, from over Eletha's shoulder. "They ran out of ambulances, that's why you're here."

"Where?"

"Our lounge," McLean says, which explains the odor of stale cigarettes.

"I still say she should go to a hospital," Eletha says loudly, in McLean's direction. It takes me only a second to picture the fuss she must have made before I woke up.

"Somebody had a gun," Sarah says. "Two people were shot. Demonstrators."

The gunshots I heard. "Are they okay? Are they dead?"

"I don't know. Nobody knows."

Then I think of the warning just before I blacked out; it sends a chill through me. Was the person who warned me also the shooter? "Did they catch who did it?"

"No. No suspects, either. They don't know if it was a demonstrator or just some nut."

"And *Hightower,* the panel affirmed?"

"Names on a caption, Grace," Eletha says.

My head begins to pound dully. "Which means Hightower dies."

"Not so fast," Sarah says. "Robbins dissented. It'll be appealed to the Supremes."

"*Finis est,*" Ben says with satisfaction. "All they have to do is find a vein."

"Ben, stop it," Sarah snaps.

Eletha helps me to a sitting position. "You need to see a doctor, honey."

Behind her, Sarah says to Ben, "Don't be so fucking cocky. I didn't think it was such a good opinion. Galanter blew the ineffectiveness issue. Nothing Hightower's lawyer said to that jury could have made up for the failure—"

"Please, you two!" Eletha says, half turning toward them both. "This not the time or the place. Grace is hurt, and all you can do is argue!"

I squeeze her arm to calm her. "I'm fine, El. I just got a bump, that's all." My fingertips root through my hair to find the Easter egg on the right side. *Let the judge rest in peace.* I must be on the right track because somebody's worried about it. But who? I didn't recognize the voice. It sounded like a man, but it could just as easily have been a woman speaking low.

"You might have a concussion," Eletha says.

"I feel fine." I struggle to sit up.

"I told you she don't need no hospital," McLean says. Jeff watches from the chair.

"You shouldn't be sitting up," Eletha says.

"Fine. I'll stand." And I do, to stop her from worrying. The room spins a minute, and Artie steadies me with a strong arm.

"Grace!" Eletha shouts.

"Eletha, please. You're giving me a headache." I cover my ears and Artie laughs.

"She's okay, El," he says. "I got her."

"Somebody warned me out there," I say, slightly woozy.

"What do you mean?" Artie says.

I stop myself; I shouldn't say anything, not yet. "I thought I heard somebody warn me to be careful. I guess about the crowd."

"Did you see him?"

"No." I shake my head, and the fuzziness isn't hard to fake. "I guess it was nothing."

Eletha reaches out for my other arm. "You should go to the hospital. You look white."

"I am white."

"Excellent!" Artie says, laughing, and I convince Eletha that I'll survive if she lets me leave the marshals' lounge. I don't feel especially comfortable around McLean or Jeff anyway.

The courthouse lobby is almost vacant, like it was before the *Hightower* case started. No reporters or gawkers are in sight, just a handful of lawyers and witnesses, watched over by a platoon of marshals. "Where are all the reporters?" I ask, as we walk through the lobby.

"They cleared the building," Ben says.

"She picked up on that, dude," Artie says. "The mayor filed for a restraining order to block the press from in front of the courthouse. The DOJ applied for one inside."

"They won't get it," Sarah says.

"Yes, they will," Ben says. "It's within the police power. They'll get it because of the shootings."

We reach the elevators and the marshals make us walk through the metal detectors, even though Eletha threatens their life. Or maybe because she threatens their life. "You okay?" asks Ray, when I emerge on the other side.

"Sure. Thanks."

"Good." He looks relieved. Relieved enough to wave to Eletha.

We ride up in the elevator in silence. The law clerks seem uneasy, and I feel stone scared. People have been shot; it may or may not have to do with the warning. But the warning was real; it came from a killer, maybe Armen's killer.

"You'd better go home, if you're not going to a hospital," Eletha says as we step off the elevator.

"Maybe I will," I say. Ben is the first to find his keys, and he unlocks the exterior door.

Eletha pulls me by the arm, and we troop down the hall together. "First we'll get some ice on that bump, like the nurse said," she says. We push open the door to chambers, and standing in the middle of the room is Senator Susan Waterman.

I blink my eyes once, then again. She's still there.

Bernice, the dog who's been driving my station wagon, stands disloyally at her side.

"What are you doing here?" Sarah shouts, letting out a squeal of delight that reverberates in my brain. She rushes over to Susan and gives her a warm hug. "I thought you were in Bosnia!"

"I delayed the trip. We leave tonight."

Ben tightens his tie. "Senator Waterman," he says, extending a stiff hand, "please accept my condolences."

Susan breaks her clinch with Sarah. "Thank you, and I'm pleased to finally meet you," she says to Ben, pumping his hand so vigorously that her silver bangles jingle. Ben seems to forget that he's a Republican for a minute as he takes in the aura of power that envelops the woman. It's undeniable, despite the offhand way she wields it. "My husband told me so much about you, Jim."

Ben withdraws his hand. "I'm Ben. Ben Safer, Senator."

Her clear blue eyes focus on Artie. Tiny parentheses at the corners of her lips deepen into a smile. "Then *you* must be Jim," she says, vaguely off balance.

"Artie Weiss, Senator. I'm sorry about Armen." He can barely say it; he must still be hurting.

"Good God, I'm zero for two," she says with a light laugh. "Wait, I know. You're the basketball player."

"Right. I think Jim was one of last year's clerks," Artie says uncomfortably.

"Of course." She shakes his hand and then looks at Eletha. "You look wonderful, Eletha. How are you?" She extends a hand.

Eletha shakes it, obviously underwhelmed. She complained all morning about the funeral arrangements, or lack therof.

"Fine," she says. "How was the funeral?"

A flicker of pain crosses Susan's face; the first sign of grief I've seen. "Beautiful. I'm sorry you couldn't be there, El," she says, then her gaze focuses on me, direct and strong. "You must be Grace. My husband spoke about you all the time."

I bet he did. Did you kill him for it? "I'm sorry—"

"Thank you." She extends a hand and squeezes mine hard; I squeeze back just as hard. We have both proved our manhood. "And thank you for adopting Bernice. I was so surprised to see her here, I called the refuge and they told me. I couldn't possibly keep her, with my schedule."

I'm sure. "She's fine with me."

"Grace got caught in that mess down there," Eletha says. "Hit on the head. I keep telling her she should go home."

"By all means you should. I'll lend you Michael, he'll put you in a cab." She gestures to the tall aide with the expensive glasses, standing by Eletha's desk. I remember him from the memorial service.

"I feel fine, I really do."

"Nonsense." She marches me over to Eletha's chair and plops me down in front of the monitor. "El, would you get us some ice for this bump?"

"I was about to."

Bernice trots over to me and burrows under my hand, trying to make up for her inconstancy. Her brown eyes roll up at me like marbles. "Good dog," I say, softening, and pat her head.

Eletha returns with some ice wrapped in a paper towel and hands it to Susan, who brandishes it like Nurse Ratched. "Where's the bump?" Susan says.

"In the back."

"Remember when Malcolm fell off his bike, Eletha?" Susan asks. She probes my head with a large hand and presses the ice into my noggin—not exactly a mother's touch. "He needed stitches, didn't he?"

"Twelve of 'em."

"Twelve stitches, can you imagine? Poor kid. He was four, right?"

"Five," Eletha says.

"I think that's enough ice," I say.

"Be still," she says. I want to hit her.

"Did you hear what happened out front?" Sarah asks. "Two shootings? You weren't down there, were you?"

"Of course not," Susan says, over my head. "I was up here, waiting for you."

"I didn't know you were coming in."

"I should have called, but I was en route and the shuttle was a mess. I came to pick up a few boxes. Are those all the boxes, Eletha, in the office?"

"For the most part. I still haven't packed all the case files yet."

"I was looking for some of the older things, his personal things, but I couldn't find them."

"What things?" Eletha asks. "The personal stuff is still in the credenza."

I think of the checkbook; I found it in the credenza. Is that what Susan is looking for?

"I looked, but all I found were school papers," Susan says.

"I think I'm done with the ice, Susan." I take her hand and move it away. "What are you looking for exactly? Maybe I saw it." I watch her face.

She looks down, mildly surprised. "Oh, maybe you have. Memorabilia, mostly. Pictures from our honeymoon, things like that. Special, personal things. I guess you haven't seen anything like that."

Is this a code? "No, I haven't seen anything special. Or personal."

She leans over me with the wrapped cube. "More ice?" We have ways of making you talk.

"No, thanks." I take the ice and toss it into the wastecan, then rise unsteadily, feeling her aide hovering at my shoulder. Is he the one who hit me? I wonder what his voice sounds like.

"Are you sure you're well enough to stand, Grace?" she asks.

Boy, she's good. I can't tell if what's beneath her smooth exterior is evil or just a smooth interior. "Sure. Thanks."

"Well, I'd better get ready. I'm holding a press conference before we go."

"Press conference?" Sarah says.

"Since I'm in town, considering what happened. Then we go. In two hours, isn't that right, Michael?"

The aide checks his Rolex and nods, apparently mute, at least in my presence. I need to hear his voice. I say, "You look so familar, Michael. Did you go to Penn?"

He shakes his head but doesn't say a thing. A man of few words.

"Where did you go to college?"

"Brown," he says quickly. Too quickly for me to hear his voice.

"Where are you from? Maybe that's where I know you."

"Maine."

"Oh? Where in Maine? My ex used to like Blue Hill in the summers."

"Bath."

It's still not enough. "Oh. Well, what's your last name? You look so much like someone—"

"Robb."

Eletha shoots me a quizzical look and I give up; I'm out of questions and Michael's out of syllables. "I guess it was somebody else."

"Guess so," Susan says, with a faint smile.

EIGHTEEN

Bernice rests her chin on the top of the plastic gate like Kilroy over the fence. My mother shifts the ice pack on my head. "How's that?" she says.

"Ma, will you stop? I'm fine."

"You're not fine," she says, practically hissing. Her breath is a mixture of denture cream and stale cigarettes. She hasn't mentioned our skirmish last night; we're both pretending it didn't happen. "You shouldn't have been there."

"I had to eat, Ma. If I didn't eat you'd be yelling, 'Why didn't you eat?'" Of course, I didn't tell her about the warning. It's been worrying me since it happened, but I still can't remember any more than I already have. From the local news, it looked like the shooting had to do with *Hightower,* so the person who warned me wasn't the shooter. I hope.

"Here's the lady," Maddie says. Her eyes are fixed on the portable TV on the pine hutch. The national news comes on, and the first story begins with a miniature head shot of Susan, floating to the right of a graying Tom Brokaw. "She looks like she's in the movies, Mom. She's pretty."

"I heard she's ugly in person," my mother says.

"She's not." Especially for a killer. But by now she's in the air, heading out of my jurisdiction with monosyllabic Michael.

"Look, Mom," Maddie says. "She's gonna talk again." She points to the television, and I focus on the screen as the news runs part of Susan's speech.

"What happened in Philadelphia today, only a block from Independence Hall, makes a mockery of the Constitution. The framers envisioned that the First Amendment would create open, free, and robust debate. They did not anticipate that words would be replaced by gunfire and thoughts drowned in human blood."

"I don't like that part," Maddie says solemnly.

"Me neither," I say, absorbed by Susan's tiny image. Her star is on the rise, her career jump-started by her husband's death. The papers keep talking about her strength under fire; presidential timber, says the *New York Times*.

"I am happy to announce that the condition of the two shooting victims is now stable. However, we should use this near-tragedy to consider how we, as citizens of a free and democratic country, can exchange ideas through peaceful means, without resort to violence."

"What's she saying, Mom?"

"Nothing."

My mother laughs. "So what else is new? She's a politician."

The ice pack shifts on my head, and I seize the moment to grab it away. "I'm fine now, thanks. Please go sit down."

"I'm trying to help you."

"I know. I said thank you." I drop the melting ice pack next to the spaghetti bowl.

"Shhh!" Maddie says, staring at Susan.

"Was that a Chanel suit she had on?" my mother says, as she takes her place at the dinner table.

The broadcast cuts to scenes outside the courthouse: film of Mrs. Gilpin crying in the arms of a friend and her husband looking on with relief and happiness. He says to a woman reporter, "Now we can see justice done. Now we can close the book."

In the background is Mrs. Stevens, but Gilpin doesn't seem to make the connection that she's about to endure the same pain he had. The camera cuts to her, standing next to the black councilman. "How do you feel, Mrs. Stevens?" comes a shotgunned question, a reporter's drive-by.

"How do you think she feels, you jerk?" I say to the TV.

"I don't understand, Mom," Maddie says, but I hold up a finger.

On the TV, Mrs. Stevens swallows visibly. "I think my boy done wrong, but I don't think he deserves to die. He's still young, and the young—"

"Justice was not done here!" the councilman interrupts. "Thomas did not have a fair trial! We will appeal to the Supreme Court without delay, because time is running out. Meanwhile, two African Americans were shot here today, showing support for their young brother. . . ."

The camera focuses on Mrs. Stevens's numb expression, then a commercial for Rice-A-Roni comes on.

"So Senator Waterman makes the national news," my mother says, arching an eyebrow plucked into a gray pencil line.

"She calls these things press conferences, but she never takes any questions." I get up stiffly and turn off the TV.

"Aw, can we leave it on?" Maddie asks.

"No, honey, not during dinner."

"But we just watched during dinner."

"That was special." I sit down.

"I don't see what the big deal is," my mother says, half to herself.

Of course she doesn't. When I was a kid, we ate dinner on spindly trays in front of a console television. At least Walter Cronkite didn't hit us. "We've already discussed this, Mom."

Maddie resettles sullenly on top of the Donnelley Directory. "Grandma lets me watch TV during snack."

"I think it was a Chanel suit," my mother says quickly, chopping her spaghetti into bite-size pieces. She refuses to twirl it: too Italian. "Did you see?"

"See what?"

"The buttons. That's how you know it's Chanel."

"I didn't see."

"How's your head?"

"Full of important thoughts."

She frowns. "I still say you should report what happened. You were attacked."

"It's not worth it."

Maddie shifts on the phone book. "Are they gonna catch the guy that did it, Mom?"

"I don't think so, babe."

"Why not?"

"They don't know who did it."

"Serves them right." My mother snorts. "They're the ones with all the guns—"

"Wait a minute. That's enough," I say, and she quiets; we have a specific understanding. I wouldn't let her baby-sit for Maddie unless she agreed to suspend her two favorite activities: racism and smoking.

"What, Mom?" Maddie asks, confused. "What happened to the guy?"

"They think he ran away, honey."

"Where did he run to?"

"Somewhere in the city. Not near here."

Maddie nods knowingly and digs into her salad. "It's dangerous out there."

"What?" I laugh. "Where did you get that?"

"Don't you know?" she says, with a mouthful of iceberg lettuce.

"Finish chewing and then talk, okay?"

She chews the lettuce like a little hamster.

"Don't let her do that," my mother says, but I wave her off.

"How's that tooth, monster girl? Ready for the Tooth Fairy?"

Maddie swallows her food. "Almost ready. There's only one of those thread things. Wanna see?"

"No. Please."

Her face grows serious. "There are bad people, Mom, didn't you know that?"

"Really?"

"Uh-huh."

"What are you watching in the afternoons, *Dragnet* reruns?"

"*Care Bears!*" Maddie says, and grins at my mother. My mother winks back, and I decide to let them have their secrets.

"All right, so tell me how school was."

"Okay." She shrugs, shoulders knobby as bedposts in her white blouse.

"Did you have art?"

"Yeah."

"Yes. Did you make anything?"

"Yes."

"What did you make?"

"A picture."

"What is this, a deposition? What was it a picture of?"

She perks up slightly. "Trees. You stick little sponges in the paint and then on the paper. It makes fake leaves for the trees. It's scenery. It's for our play."

"You're going to be in a play?"

Maddie nods and sips her milk, leaving a tomato-sauce stain on the rim of the glass and a milk mustache on her upper lip. Then she grabs her napkin in a professional way and wipes her mouth.

"What's the play about?"

"Spring."

"That sounds nice. Is it a musical?"

She rolls her eyes. "No, Mom. That's in the olden days. We don't do anything as dumb as that."

"What a relief. Jeez."

Maddie squints at me to see if I'm kidding. I squint back, and we squint at each other like moles for a minute.

"Maddie told me some good news today, Grace," my mother says. She turns to Maddie. "Tell your mother how you made a new friend."

"You made a friend?" It's too much to hope for.

Maddie beams. "At recess."

"Terrific!" I feel my heart leap up. "I propose a toast. To Maddie and her new friend." I hoist my glass in the air, and so does my mother. The heavy tumblers clink loudly.

"She won't tell me any more about it," my mother says. "She says she's only allowed to tell you."

"Oh, a secret! So you played with this friend at recess? What did you play?"

"Digging."

"Like with Madeline?" I think of the day I watched her near the edge of the playground.

"Yep. He likes Madeline."

"Oh, he's a boy, huh? Is he cute?"

She wrinkles her nose. "Kind of. He's big."

"How big? Like a second grader?"

"No, bigger than that. Almost as big as Daddy."

My mother laughs. "That means fifth grade."

"What's his name?"

"It's a secret. He's my secret friend."

I wonder if he's imaginary. "But he's real, right? Not like Madeline. A real boy."

She looks confused. "He's a man, Mommy, not a boy. He helped me and Madeline dig a hole. He's strong."

"What? A man?"

My mother puts down her fork in surprise. "Not a stranger!"

"Maddie knows not to talk to strangers." I turn to Maddie. "Right, honey? He's not a stranger, is he?"

Her face flushes red. "He *knows* you and that's not a stranger."

"Who is he?"

"He said it's a secret. I told you. He knows you and your work. He knows your judge and the lady on the TV. That's not a *stranger*."

"What did he look like, Maddie?" my mother says, her voice thin with anxiety. "Tell Grandma."

Maddie looks from my mother to me, becoming uncertain. "I didn't do anything bad, Mom. He said he was my friend, and you said make a friend."

"Of course you didn't do anything bad," I say as calmly as I can. "Which recess did he play with you, Mads? Recess in the morning or recess after lunch?"

"He knows things. He said it's good to be careful, like you say. He said, Tell Mommy too."

I feel my gut tense up. "Tell me to be careful?"

"Maddie, what are you talking about?" my mother says. "How could you—"

"Ma!" I snap at her. "Let me talk to her."

My sudden anger makes Maddie's lower lip buckle. "Mom, I didn't do anything wrong." Her eyes well up with tears.

"It's all right, baby," I say. I scoop her out of her seat and she burrows into my neck. I think of the man and my skin crawls. Is this for real, and does it have anything to do with this afternoon? "Can you remember what he looks like, Maddie?"

"No," she sobs.

"That's okay. It's all right, now." I hug Maddie close and catch sight of my mother over the top of my daughter's tousled red head. Her face has gone gray and drawn with fear; her gnarled fingers shake as she reaches for her water glass. "You okay, Ma?" I ask her.

She looks up, startled. "Fine," she says.

Later, after we've cleaned up and Maddie's safely in bed, my mother makes coffee in silence while I call the principal at Maddie's school and tell him what happened during a recess that's allegedly supervised. He reminds me that the back field is huge, that there are only two playground aides for 350 children, and that Maddie was playing at the far end. I suggest politely that he hire more aides, then show my fine upbringing by not threatening grievous bodily harm, although I let him know a lawsuit is always an interesting alternative. Then I call Maddie's teacher, who mentions that Maddie has a vivid imagination. Not that vivid, I say to her, before I hang up.

I call the police in my tiny borough to report the incident; they seem happy to leave their game of checkers to come over and do real police work, like on TV. One even has braces on his teeth. My mother lubricates them with hot coffee and I give them free legal advice, so they promise to cruise around the house tonight and the playground tomorrow and the next day. I decide not to tell them about Armen's murder or what happened to me at the courthouse; it's out of their distinctly suburban league.

But I'm getting the message the killer is sending, loud and clear. Someone is using everything they can—including my six-year-old—to warn me off, but it won't work. It only makes me want to fight back harder. Where do they get off threatening my child? They haven't met up with the fury of a single mother. Especially one who's run out of alimony.

NINETEEN

The phone rings after the police leave. "Grace." It's a man's voice, almost in a whisper. "It's Winn."

"Who?"

"Winn. Shake and Bake. Get down here fast."

"What? It's eleven o'clock at night."

"Please. I can't talk long."

"Listen, you, somebody tried to grab my daughter today. And somebody hit me from behind."

"Are you all right?" He sounds stricken, but not as stricken as I am and only half as stricken as my mother.

"She's fine, we both are."

"Was she hurt?"

"No, but only because she was at school. I can't have this, Winn."

"I'll protect her. I'll get somebody on her."

"Who, kindergarten cop?"

"I'll make him a teacher. A janitor."

"That's not the point."

"I can't talk now, just come down here. It's Artie. He needs help."

"Artie? Where?"

"Northern Liberties."

Not one of Philadelphia's showcase neighborhoods. "What are you doing there?"

"We're at Keeton's. On the corner, at Third. There's a sign."

"Is Artie okay? In danger?"

"Nothing like that, but come now." He hangs up.

I hang up slowly, looking at the phone. I hate to leave Maddie tonight, after what happened to her, nor am I excited about driving around, after what happened to me. On the other hand, it might help to talk to Winn, and Artie's in trouble. There's a caffeinated couple of cops driving circles around my house and a bulldog of a grandmother seething in the living room; my daughter has never been safer. I decide to go, mumbling an excuse to my mother, like in high school.

I drive into town with an eye on the rearview mirror, and no one appears to be following me. I reach the warehouse district in a half hour. The streets are wider here than they are in the rest of Philly and almost deserted. Trash mars the sidewalk, and the homeless beg from the traffic on the expressway ramp. One man, apparently crazy, is draped in a blanket despite the warm, breezy night. I look away until I remember that it's an apparently crazy man I'm looking for. I look back, but it's not Winn.

I drive around the block, past a graffiti mural on an electrical wholesale store, until I find a ratty tavern. An old-time window of thick glass block is stuck into a dingy brick facade. Over the black-painted door a pink neon sign glows KE TON'S. Artie is lying in front, passed out under a dim streetlight. Winn is propped up against the lamppost, fuzzy-faced and dressed in a raincoat, looking oddly like a degenerate Paddington Bear. I pull up to the curb and get out of the wagon.

Winn smiles vacantly when he spots me. "Harvard's sick, Miss Rossi."

I kneel over Artie. There's stubble on his formerly handsome face, and his clothes are a mess. But then they always are. "Artie? You okay?"

Artie opens one eye, then covers his startled face with his hands. "It's alive! Make it go away, Grace. It's heinous!"

Winn smiles. "Harvard drank too much."

"I figured."

"I figured you figured." Winn claps his hands. "I figured you figured I figured you figured."

"He's crazy as a fuckin' loon, Grace," Artie says, his eyes still closed. "Sarah was right."

"Bye-bye, Sarah," Winn says.

Artie looks up at me, his mouth curving down in Pagliacci's exaggerated frown. "Sarah went bye-bye, Grace."

"I'm sorry, Artie."

"She was in love with Armen, she admitted it." His eyes fill up with drunken tears. "She never loved me."

Poor kid. "I'm sorry."

"I knew it all along, Grace. She thinks I'm stupid, but I'm not." He licks his dry lips. "I knew from the way she looked at him."

I grab the folds of Artie's denim jacket; it occurs to me that I have picked up a drunk before. This drunk budges only an inch.

"Armen was my friend, Grace. He was my friend."

"I know, Artie."

"I was right! I am a genius! I made law review!" he rails into the night, then his head lolls to one side. A piece of wax paper rolls over him like urban tumbleweed.

I struggle to move him but can't. "Would you help me, Shake and Bake?"

"No." Winn wags his head back and forth, ersatz autistic before my eyes. "I'm busy."

"That's funny, Shakie." My lower back begins to ache; I'm too old for this and in no mood. I straighten up and glare at Winn. "Now get up and help Mommy."

Artie's eyes fly open suddenly, like a corpse reanimated. "Look, Grace! Look what I got!" He starts to unbutton his fly.

Oh, Christ. "I know what you got, Artie. Keep it in your pants."

"No, no, Gracie! Something totally awesome! Look!"

I look down. Artie's work shirt is yanked up to his neck. Directly north of his stomach, between two rather erect nipples, sits a basketball, regulation size. Its surface is brown and pebbled, and in the center, in familiar script, it says *Wilson.* "What is that?" I say, aghast.

"I got a tat! Isn't it so *excellent?*"

"A tat?"

"Artie has a tat-toooo," Winn says, singsong.

"No pain, no gain," Artie mumbles. "Today I am a man."

"I got one, too," Winn says, getting up. He brushes off his soiled pants, which does nothing to improve them. "Two tats. One for Harvard, one for me."

"Terrific."

"*Barukh attah Adonai,*" Artie says, "*Eloheinu meleckh haolam.* Let's light the candles!" He waves his hand in the air, then it flops back against the cracked sidewalk.

"Want to see my tattoo?" Winn asks, standing a little too close for comfort. He smells like cheap beer and body odor.

"Keep your shirt on, Shakie," I say.

"Grace's being mean to me, Artie," Winn says, pouting.

"Don't be mean to him," Artie says, eyes closed, from the pavement.

I look at Winn, unamused.

"Two points," says Winn. "For me."

Artie caterwauls in the shower while Winn sits forward on the beat-up couch in Artie's apartment, quizzing me about what happened to Maddie and me. He looks uneasy when I finish the story and takes off his rain bonnet to run his fingers through his greasy hair. "This is too dangerous for you, for your daughter. I never should have gotten you involved in it."

"So why did you?" I sit back on a folding chair in front of a secondhand coffee table.

"I had no choice. I had nothing on the leads I was running and I know something's there."

"What do you think's going on? You said Galanter's not the only judge involved." I sip a Coke to hide my anxiety.

"Everybody dance now!" Artie sings in the shower, to C + C Music Factory.

Winn glances at the bathroom door, then leans close enough to give me another whiff of his rich stench. "Allegedly involved. I'm not sure yet, but I think Galanter's in on it and maybe Townsend."

I feel stunned. And no Armen. "A conspiracy?"

"It happened before, in this circuit, in the nineteen forties. Judges Buffington and Davis, together they sold a group of cases. One of 'em was working with a Second Circuit judge, too, who took half a mil. You could buy a lot of justice for that much money back then."

I think of the $650,000. "But that was then."

"Last year, Judge Aguilar in California told a Teamster who was embezzling union funds about one of our wiretaps on him. And Judge Collins, my personal favorite, took a hundred thou to give a drug dealer a lesser sentence. Both federal judges. Collins even collected his salary during the six years he spent in jail."

"This a hobby of yours, judicial misconduct?"

"It's what I do. All I do, in fact."

"Like a specialty?"

He nods. "It's fun, it's brainwork, and it's mostly bloodless."

"The Quaker part."

"In a way. I like taking these guys down. They've had every advantage, every privilege, and still they go bad. They're hypocrites. They've got no excuse except greed."

It doesn't sound like Armen.

"Now it's Galanter's turn. It's a scandal, Grace. It'll blow the courthouse wide open."

My heart sinks. For the court and for Armen, when they find out about the bank account.

"You still upset about today? You look kind of sick."

I chug some Coke. "Just the gal for undercover work."

"You're not working undercover anymore. I want you out of it. Clear."

"Why?"

"You need to ask, after today?"

"You're assuming I want to get out. Tell me what you think is going on."

"You remember the case that was argued Monday, the one I blew up? *Canavan?*"

"The racketeering case, with the florists."

"Yes. The Mob *was* behind it. The lawyer just couldn't figure out how."

I force out the words. "The Mob?"

"I believe they got to the judges and paid somebody off to make it come out their way, either Galanter or Townsend or both. Artie told me the judges vote right after the cases are argued, and I needed more time to gather evidence. So I had to make sure the argument didn't happen. *Ticktickticktick.*"

I put down my Coke and look at him with wonder. "They did postpone that argument."

"Of course they did, and I got more time to watch everybody play the game. I told you I'm smarter than I look."

I feel my pulse quicken. If Winn is right, the $650,000 couldn't have been a bribe for *Canavan*. Armen would have voted to reverse, sending the defendants to jail: clearly not the desired outcome from the Mob's point of view. "I don't understand something. Does this have anything to do with Armen's death?"

"I think so. He may have been killed to prevent him from voting in *Canavan*."

"My God. Who killed him?"

"Somebody they paid to do it. Some scumbag."

"Or Galanter."

"What?" He rears back slightly. "That's not how these cases work."

"Maybe this one did. There was no break-in, and Bernice wouldn't have let just anybody in." I tell him how Bernice attacked Galanter, getting excited as I speak; it renews my determination to work for him.

"Where's the *Canavan* case now?" We both hear Artie turn off the water in the shower; Winn looks worriedly at the bathroom door. "Has it been scheduled for argument again?"

"I don't know, it was Sarah's case. It'll probably be listed with the next sitting, a month from now. What is it you want me to do, when I work for Galanter?"

"Do you have the job already?"

"No, but I'll get it."

"Don't. I told you, I want you out."

"I'm going ahead, so you might as well tell me what I'm looking for. I want to find out if Galanter killed Armen."

He rubs his gritty forehead. "I knew this was going to happen. I must've been crazy to—"

"All I need is for you to protect Maddie at school. I'll be with her the whole weekend. Plus I have the local police."

"You what?"

"I want you to park a car right across from the school field. Here's her picture." I fish one out of my wallet and hand it to him. "It's not a new one, she's actually cuter than that."

"Freckles. I like freckles." He smiles at the picture and slips it into his pocket. "I'll have her watched, but I still want you to bow out. Quit now, I'll handle Galanter. You're too exposed. I don't like it, Grace."

"Tell me what I'm looking for. Where do I start, the *Canavan* record?"

He looks directly at me. "Are you really going to do this?"

I think of Armen. He loved me; he was murdered. And he didn't take any goddamn bribe. "Yep."

"Christ." He rubs his beard. "All right. If you insist on this, then all you should do is keep your eyes and ears open around his office. Try to answer the phones. That's it."

"Why? What am I looking for?"

The toilet flushes in the bathroom and Winn snatches a *Times* crossword puzzle from the debris on the coffee table and scribbles in the blank squares. "Call me if Galanter gets phone calls from any of these characters. Or if he has lunch with them, meets with them at all. That's all I want you to do, got it? I'll take it from there." He tears out the puzzle and hands it to me. "I also wrote down the number of the pay phone at the shelter. I'm there most of the time now. If you call, say you're my cousin. Ask for Rain Man."

I look at the crossword puzzle. After a phone number, reading down is THESAURUS, and reading across is SPOOL. Underneath that is a list of names, all as Italian as mine. I feel a twinge of shame, then fear. A mobster, that close to my child?

The bathroom door opens and Artie steps out wearing a red Budweiser bath towel around his waist. "Everybody dance now!" he sings, and thrusts his pelvis expertly at us.

"Artie!" Winn shouts idiotically, lapsing instantly into character. "You're all better!"

"I *am* better!" Artie strikes a muscleman pose, his wet biceps glistening with leftover water. In the middle of his chest is a slick basketball.

"You look good!" Winn says, applauding. He leaps to his feet with joy and bunny-hops over to Artie. "Everybody, everybody, everybody dance!" They form a conga line and dance around me on the sofa.

I sit back and laugh, marveling at how deceptive appearances can be. The man playing the fool is really a shrewd federal agent; the Ivy Leaguer is dumb enough to engrave a basketball onto his chest. And what about me? I'm somewhere in the middle, definitely involved. It's a surprise when I realize why.

I want justice.

Everybody dance now.

TWENTY

Needlepoint is usually surefire therapy. I take refuge in it at the most stressful times and have come through a divorce and even Maddie's hernia operation with a few very nice pillows. I'm hoping needlepoint will get me through high crimes and misdeameanors, but this may be too much to ask of a hobby.

I tug a pristine silver needle through a tiny white square. The yarn comes through with ease, filling in an infinitesimal block of emerald green in a rolling English landscape. I favor the smaller scrims; they demand more concentration. I stitch another itsy-bitsy square and look behind me for the local squad car, parked across the street. The skinny cop in braces sits in the front seat, engrossed in the newspaper; he looks even younger than last night, if such a thing is possible.

I check on Maddie. She swings on a swing, pumping her legs back and forth. I can see her smile broaden with pride as the swing goes higher. She's still learning to coordinate the pumping action; it's not as easy as it looks. I wave to her, but she doesn't see.

I return to England after a careful glance around the neighborhood playground. No felons anywhere, just a few children playing in the sandbox and a mother here and there. It's not busy today; it's Saturday and everybody's out running errands, which is what I would be doing if I weren't somewhere in Northamptonshire.

I look up at Maddie, still on the swings on the far side of the fenced kiddie area of the playground. She was deliriously happy the day she hit six and graduated to the big kids area, but I don't like it much. The swings are too damn high for my comfort level, and my park bench is too far away. If you think I was protective before, you should see me now.

"You're dead!" screams a little boy, and I jump. The child runs by, chasing another boy with a toy Uzi. "You have to lay down, I killed you!"

This is why I'm glad I don't have boys.

England waits while my blood pressure returns to normal. I watch the boys chase each other in the dappled sunshine around a white hobbyhorse on a steel coil, then double back around the sandbox and out toward the swings. Of course they run right in front of the swings, directly in harm's way. Don't these monsters have mothers? They survive the gauntlet of swings and run past the bench out by the tennis courts. A man in a black sweater sits on the bench; his head barely follows the boys as they run by him.

Odd.

I didn't see him when we came. There's a newspaper on his lap, but he's not reading it. I take another stitch and yank the yarn through quickly. I look up at the man on the opposite bench.

He's still there, but too far away for me to make out his features. His hair is dark, and he seems broad-shouldered underneath the bulky V-neck sweater. Something about him looks familiar. Then I remember. He looks a lot like the man I saw at the police station and the memorial service, but I can't be positive.

Still.

I turn around to the police car. It's there, but it's empty. No adolescent cop, no newspaper. I swallow hard. The cop was here a minute ago. I look down the street. He's standing in front of the borough library, talking to an old woman carrying a stack of books. He's too far away to see or hear me.

Jesus. Stay calm.

I look back at the man on the bench, watching him as he scans the playground, apparently harmlessly. His sweater is much too heavy for such a balmy day, and it's bulgy enough to accommodate a gun in a shoulder holster. He could be with the Mob; he looks the part. Is he the same man as at the police station?

That man had a black car with Virginia plates.

I take a quick stitch and casually look over the cars along the street. There's my wagon, then another wagon and a minivan. His car isn't there; so far, so good. I glance at the library lot next to the playground. The chrome grill of a dark car peeks at me from around the library, glinting in the sunlight. I bite my lip. It looks like the black car, but it also looks like a zillion other American cars. It's parked with the front end facing me, and there are no license plates in the front. Maybe it's from Virginia, maybe not.

I can't stand this. I feel more nervous by the second.

I take another stitch and peek over at the cop. He's nodding as the old woman unloads her pile of plastic-covered books into his arms. Terrific. My yarn snags; a notch of kelly green explodes through a yellow thatched roof. I hate needlepoint.

I stare at the man. He's still sitting there, but now he's checking out the swings. Maddie's not the only child on them, but he appears to be watching her. I look back at him, then at her. She's between us, but he's closer to her than I am.

Relax, I tell myself. You handled back labor, you can handle this. I weave the needle into the scrim border for safekeeping.

Maddie sails back and forth, her cotton skirt billowing each time she swings forward. The man in the sweater watches her, unsmiling.

What the hell? Is he the man from the school playground? Is he the man from the police station? Why is he watching my daughter?

Suddenly, the man takes the newspaper off his lap and stands up.

I set my needlepoint aside and stand up.

He looks up at the swings and so do I. With a start, I see that Maddie's swing isn't going nearly as high as it was; she's beginning to slow down. She slows to a low arc, dragging an untied Keds on the ground, kicking up loose, dry dirt. She's getting ready to jump off.

My heart starts to pound.

The man takes a step toward the swings.

The cop rearranges the books. The old woman takes his arm.

I feel breathless. I open my mouth to scream but nothing comes out.

The man walks right toward Maddie. Unmistakably.

My scream breaks free. "Maddie! Maddie!" I shout. I'm off in a second, running toward the swings. "Help, police!"

Maddie looks confused, then terrified. The man glances back at me, then sprints in the opposite direction.

I pick up my pace, running as hard as I can. "Help! Police!" I scream, full bore.

My panic sets off the other mothers. One of them gathers her children together, hugging them to her legs. The other, a young mother, takes off like a shot after the stranger, who's fleeing across the grassy common. She's a short-haired woman in bicycle pants, and she passes me in no time. "I got that bastard," she says, hardly puffing as she whizzes by, cowlick flying.

I keep running until I get to Maddie, who's frozen with fear in front of the swings. I scoop her up and hug her tight. Over her shoulder I watch the young mother almost on the heels of the man. I pray to God he doesn't have a gun as she grabs him by the sweater and they both fall hard to the ground.

The cop comes running from the entrance to the playground, but the young woman doesn't need his help. She clambers onto the man's back and wrenches his arm behind him. A group of teenagers playing basketball at the far side of the playground stop their game and come running over. It's a done deal by the time the cop and the teenagers reach the middle of the huge field, which is when I guess the young woman must be an undercover cop, sent by Winn just in case.

"What's happening, Mommy?" Maddie says in a small voice. "What's going on?" She wraps her arms tighter around my neck.

"That man who was running, was he the one you saw on the playground at school?"

"Yes."

I watch as the basketball players ring the prone man. "It's okay now, baby. It's all over."

"What are they gonna do?"

"They're gonna put him in jail."

"Why?"

Because he's a killer, I think to myself, and hug her even closer. I pick her up and walk over to the crowd around the man. The cop has handcuffed him and flipped him over on his back. The woman has her running shoe at his Adam's apple. She gives me a brusque wave as I approach.

"We got him," the cop says.

Please. "You had an assist, I think, from the FBI."

The cop and the woman exchange looks over the unconscious man. "Are you with the feds?" the cop says.

"Me? Are you kidding?" The young woman laughs. "I'm a librarian."

"What?" I say. "But the way you tackled—"

"*Arrgh,*" the man moans, regaining consciousness. He's older up close but still a scumbag, like Winn said.

"He's wakin' up!" one of the ballplayers says.

The librarian presses her ribbed toe into the man's throat. "Stay right there, asshole."

"Grace?" the man says, disoriented, looking up from the grass.

"How do you know my name?"

"I gave it to you, for chrissake."

"What?"

He spits grass out of his mouth. "I'm your fuckin' father."

Bernice glares through the gate of her Fisher-Price prison, eyeing with canine distrust the stranger who is my father.

"Lucky for me that dog wasn't with you today," he says. Underneath his sweater is a ropy gold chain; no shoulder holster, as far as I can tell. "That's a big mother dog."

"Watch your language."

"Sorry."

"You want coffee or not?"

"Yeah." He holds up his mug.

"How do you take it?" I pause over him with the pot of coffee. Maybe he needs a hot shower.

"Black is fine." He looks up at me with blue eyes that eerily mirror my own, which stops me short. I can see the years on him; the deep crow's feet at the corners of his eyes and a softening around the jowls. He must be over sixty, but he looks fifty. His hair is jet black, like Robert Goulet's; I wonder if he dyes it. I pour him some coffee, then myself, avoiding his eyes.

"You're mad, aren't ya?" he says.

"You know me so well, Dad."

He winces when he sips his coffee. "Christ, this is hot!"

I stop short of saying, Good, you burn yourself? "So what are you doing here? In the neighborhood, thought you'd drop by?"

He frowns at my sarcasm but evidently decides not to send me to my room. "Look, I wanted to see my granddaughter."

"Why?"

"I just wanted to see her, okay?"

"Why now? She's been around for six years. It's not like she's been booked up."

"I just retired." He clears his throat, but his voice still sounds like gravel. "I moved back to Philly."

"So you *were* in the neighborhood."

"I figured it was time to settle up, you know?"

"No, I don't."

"When you're my age, you'll know." He slurps his coffee, wincing again.

"We have a telephone. You could have called."

"I know, I looked you up in the phone book. That's how I knew where she went to school." He glances into the living room, where Maddie's teaching herself to make a cat's cradle with a pink string he brought her. "She's a little lady. Just like you were," he says wistfully, but I have no patience for his wistfulness.

"You scared her, you know. And me."

"I'm sorry."

I pull out a chair at the side of the table, two seats away from where he sits. Even from here I can smell his aftershave, something drugstore like Aqua Velva. He doesn't say anything for a minute, staring down into his mug. I'll be damned if I'll fill this silence. I sip my coffee.

"Okay, so it wasn't the best way to go about it," he says finally.

"On the contrary. It was the worst possible way to go about it."

"Now I got your Irish up." He laughs softly, but I'm not laughing.

"You want a drink? Little sweetener for that coffee?"

He looks at me, stung. "I haven't had a drink in a long, long time."

"Right."

"It's the truth."

"Good for you. Where do you live?"

"Philly, now. South Philly."

The Italian neighborhood. "What do you do?"

"I used to teach."

"You were a *teacher*?" I can't hide my surprise. I would have figured him for a bartender, maybe a trucker. But a teacher? "What did you teach?"

"English."

"*What?*" He can barely speak it. I almost spit out my coffee.

"You're surprised at your old man, eh?"

"Please. Let's not leap ahead with the 'old man' stuff. Where did you teach?"

"In high school. In Virginia."

It was his car, the black one. It's parked out in front of my house like an official Mafia squad car. "Have you been following me?"

He shifts heavily in his seat. "Not exactly. Just watching, a little."

"Why?"

"Tryin' to decide, you know. When to make my move. In the beginning, I just wanted to see what you looked like." He appraises me for a minute. "You grew up nice, pretty. Very pretty."

Let's change the subject. "So they let Italians in Virginia. You like it there?"

"No. No *calamar'*, no nothin'. I had nothin' keepin' me there, so I came back. That's my life story."

"Never remarried?"

"No."

"No other kids?"

"Not that I know of." He laughs, then spots my glare. "No."

I shake my head, and another silence falls between us. We have nothing to say to each other, we have everything to say to each other.

"You're a lawyer?" he says.

"Yes."

"Here's a good one. You're in a room with Adolf Hitler, Genghis Khan, a lawyer, and a revolver loaded with two bullets. What do you do?"

"What are you talking about?"

He waves his hand. "It's a joke."

"Okay, what?"

"Shoot the lawyer twice." He laughs, but I don't. "Okay, strike one. Here's another. What's black and brown and looks good on a lawyer?"

"Listen—"

"A Doberman." He laughs again, his eyes crinkling at the corners. An attractive man for his age, with a kind face. Except that he's a wife beater. Did I mention that appearances are deceiving?

"You beat my mother, didn't you?"

"Did she tell you that?"

"In a way."

He exhales heavily. *"Madonn'."*

"Well?"

"I never laid a hand on your mother. Never." He points a thick index finger at me.

"Bullshit. I remember."

"You remember wrong, lawyer."

"The hell I do. Don't you dare come here and tell me what I remember," I say, my voice rising. "I know what I remember."

"Mom?" Maddie calls uncertainly from the living room. The child has been traumatized enough; now her mother is going off the deep end.

"You want to go play outside, honey?"

"No."

"You want to watch a tape?"

"Even though I watched cartoons this morning?"

"Yes."

"Yeah!" She leaps off the couch.

"You know how to put it in?"

"I do it all the time, Mom. Jeez." She rummages under the TV for her tapes.

My father watches Maddie slip a tape in the VCR. "Smart little girl."

I feel a knot in my chest. "She sure is. So was I."

He pushes his mug away and folds his hands. "You want to know why I left?"

"For starters."

He looks down at his wrinkled hands, the only giveaway as to his age. "I met your mother at the Nixon, at Fifty-second and Market."

"We're beginning at the beginning, I see."

He gives me a dirty look. "As I was saying before I was so rudely interrupted, the Nixon was one of the biggest ballrooms around. Cost a couple bucks to get in. Had a mirror ball, spotlights, ten-piece band. Soup to nuts. You had to wear a tie and jacket."

"Very classy."

He nods, missing the irony. "*Very* classy. Why your mother was there that night, I still don't know. She was from Saint Tommy More. She was a great dancer, the best."

"My mother, dancing?" I blurt out. It's inconceivable, she barely smiles.

"God, yeh." He nods. "I was there with the goombahs, the boys from the corner. Louie, Popeye, Cooch. She was there with the Irish girls. They were all in a corner, talkin' to each other. The Italians never asked the Irish to dance, the Irish never asked the Italians to dance. They weren't from the neighborhood. Lady of Angels." He smiles, lost there for a minute. "I remember her eyes, she had gorgeous eyes. Bedroom eyes."

"So?"

"So I asked her to dance, but she wouldn't dance with me. I

kept after her for the slow dance. Finally she did. I remember the floor was slippery from the powder."

"Powder?"

"Yeh. Talcum powder, on the floor. Made it even more slippery, for slide dancing. Slow dancing, you know. Big band. Ah, your mother was good. So was I. You had to be good; otherwise you'd slip on your goddamn ass." He laughs thickly. "They had a contest, too, for the best jitterbug. We won some money, coupla bucks, I forget how much."

I hear the first strains of *Cinderella* coming from the living room and Maddie jumps back up on the couch, already lost in the fantasy world of Disney. Someday my prince will come. I should burn those tapes.

"Then we went outside for a drink. You couldn't drink at these things, but we found a way to drink. We always found a way to drink. Then we got married and you came along." His smile fades. "I decided to stop then, went to AA, the whole bit. But she didn't."

I don't understand. "You mean *Mom* drank?"

"I tried to get her to stop, but she couldn't." He leans back heavily in his chair.

"But Mom doesn't drink. Not even beer."

"Maybe not now, but then she did. I tried everything. Hiding the bottles, throwing them away, pouring that shit down the toilet. I dumped her whiskey and she came at me—"

"Came at you?"

He reddens slightly. "That was the last straw. I couldn't take it anymore. I knew if I stayed, I'd go down with her. So I left. Took off. The only thing I did wrong, the thing I regret, is I left you."

My chest grows tight. I can't say anything.

"I can't even tell you I tried to get custody, because I didn't. They wouldn't have given it to me, not in those days, but that's no excuse. I heard she stopped drinkin' after I left, but I still didn't go back. We were bad for each other, we would've gone down together. And you too."

I swallow hard, disoriented. This isn't my family history. My history is altogether different: a father who drank, a no-good, and a mother who suffered. A victim, a saint. I don't know whether to believe him. I can't look at him. "You should go," I say.

"I'm not so dumb that I expected everything to be all right with us. I came because I wanted to make it up to you. I have a little money. Maybe I can help out."

"You can't. You should go."

"Maybe you need to think about it. I know I sprung this on you. You can call me any time." He puts a card down on the table. EMEDIO "MIMMY" ROSSI, CERTIFIED ESL INSTRUCTOR. "I'm startin' a little business. I teach English as a second language. To Koreans, Vietnamese, like that."

"Am I supposed to clap?"

"You're tough, you know that?" He gets up to go, but I still can't look at him. I have a thousand questions for him, but only one keeps burning in my head.

"Did you hit me?" I ask, when he's past me.

"What do you mean, hit you?"

"When you drank, did you hit me?"

"No. Never." His voice sounds louder; he must have turned around to face me. "Why?"

"I'm remembering things."

He's silent for a moment. "You'll have to ask your mother about that," he says. I hear him call good-bye to Maddie and leave by the screen door.

It closes with a sharp bang.

"*Roarf!*" Bernice says.

TWENTY-ONE

I spend a long time at the dining room table, feeling awful as Maddie sits enchanted by her tape. What is he saying? That my mother drank too? That *she* was the one who hit me?

It never even occurred to me.

I'm not sure what to do; I can't process it all fast enough. I can't even deal with the fact that I have a father now. What does a grown woman want with a father? And is there room for a mother, especially one who would wallop a child? Then a more urgent concern pops into my head.

Maddie. Has my mother beaten her, ever? My God. I close my eyes. From time to time Maddie gets bruises, but she told me they were from falls. And first grade has been so difficult for her; her first year in my mother's care. It all fits, and it sickens me. Would my mother really hit Maddie? It would be beyond belief, except that she apparently hit me, too.

When I was Maddie's age.

What's been going on in my own house? Maddie knows, but I have to pick the right time to ask her. It preoccupies me as I cook and serve dinner. Afterward, I clean up the dishes and let Bernice slobber over every plate, a silent payback.

Later, at bathtime, Maddie relaxes in a full tub of Mr.

Bubble. She makes a blue rubber shark swim among plastic goldfish, hidden beneath the sudsy meringue. I sit down on the lid of the toilet, watching her. Now might be the right time.

"How's that water, button?" I say.

"Want to see a tornado?"

"A tornado? Sure."

She grabs her nose and turns over once in the tub. The water swirls around her and she comes up smiling, wet hair stuck in tendrils to her cheeks and chin. "Did you see?"

"Amazing."

She looks askance. "You weren't watching."

"I *was* watching, it was cool. Like a whirlpool, right?"

She sinks into the bubbles up to her chin.

"So Mads," I begin, as casually as possible, "what do you and Grandma do in the afternoons?" The shark plunges into a swell and Maddie doesn't answer. Maybe she's avoiding it; maybe it's a child's typical inattentiveness to adults. Or hers to me. "Mads?"

"What?"

"Do you have fun with Grandma while I'm at work?" Dumb. A leading question.

She nods and the shark leaps across her tummy.

"What do you guys do?"

"Watch TV."

I'm relieved at this answer for the first time ever. "Cartoons?"

She nods at the shark, who nods back at her.

"Tapes, too?"

"Yeah. *Yes.*"

"Don't you ever just play?"

She nods again. The shark nods, too.

"What do you play?"

"Can I have Madeline in the tub?"

"Of course not, she'll get wet," I say reflexively, then think again. Maybe Maddie can say something through Madeline that she can't say to me directly. "I'll let you this time, but not in the water, okay?"

"Yeah!" The shark dances for joy as I fetch the doll from Maddie's room and bring it back. I sit cross-legged on the rag rug beside the tub.

"Hey, Maddie," I make the doll say.

"Hey, Madeline," Maddie says cheerily. She abandons the rubber shark.

"What games do you play with your grandma?" the doll says. "Gimme the dirt."

Maddie giggles. "What's 'the dirt' mean?"

"The gossip. The news. The real truth. I want to know everything." The doll's yellow felt hat bobs up and down.

Maddie sits up in the bathtub, focusing on the doll as if she were real. "We play lid," she says.

"What's lid?"

"It's a game, with a ball and a lid."

"That sounds boring."

Two slick knees pop through the bubbles; she wraps her arms around them. "She chases me around when she loses."

"My grandma does that, too. She's a bad sport. I hate her."

"Does she pinch you? My grandma pinches me."

I feel my heart skip a beat. "Pinches you?"

She nods. "She chases me around and pinches my butt."

"Hard?"

She shakes her head. "Just for fun. When she loses. Anyway, she doesn't catch me ever because I'm too fast. I'm faster than the boys. Do you like boys?"

"No, I hate them more than grandmas. Does your grandma ever get mad at you and yell?"

She looks blank.

"Tell me!" the doll screeches. "Tell me, you little brat! Tell me everything!"

She giggles and unsticks a wet strand of hair from her cheek. "It's a secret," she whispers, growing serious.

LISA SCOTTOLINE: THE FIRST TWO NOVELS

"A secret?"

"A *real* secret. Something Mommy doesn't even know." Her blue eyes glitter.

"A secret from Mommy?"

"Grandma said she would never find out."

I feel sick inside. "I know. Mommy's so stupid. Tell me."

"I can't. Grandma said Mommy would be mad if she found out and yell at me."

"I bet she wouldn't." The doll flops up and down in frustration, cloth mitts falling at her side.

"Uh-huh," she says emphatically. "My mom yells a lot. She says it's because she has to do everything and I don't help."

Guilt washes over me like a tsunami. "My mom yells all the time, too. She's a jerk. A big, fat, stupid jerk."

Maddie covers her face, laughing. "My mom yells *all* the time. She yells when I don't put my clothes in the hamper and she has to pick them up. She bends over twenty times a day. If she had a nickel for every time she bends over she'd be rich."

"She sounds like a big fat jerk, too."

"But know what I do?"

"What?"

"I go in the closet and take off my clothes."

"What? Why do you do that?"

"That's where the hamper basket is. I stand in the basket and my clothes fall right in." She smiles and so do I; I picture her standing in the closet in a Rubbermaid bin.

"You're pretty smart, you know that?"

"I am. Really." She rubs her nose with the palm of her hand.

"Do you love me?" the doll asks.

Maddie reaches over and arranges a strand of the doll's too-red yarn hair. "Yeah."

"Then tell me your secret!" the doll explodes, jumping around frantically. "RIGHT NOW!"

"All right, all right! Calm down!" she says, a tenuous cross between laughter and true concern. "The secret is that Grandma smokes."

"What?"

"On the porch. During *Tom and Jerry.* My mom thinks she doesn't smoke when she baby-sits me but she really does."

"That's the secret?" I try not to sound disappointed, although I didn't know my mother did this. She'd told me, with an absolute straight face, that she holds off for three hours. A good liar, from years of practice.

"Isn't it a good secret?"

"Yep. You got any other secrets for me?"

Maddie looks up, thinking. "Nope."

"I'll tell you one."

"Okay." She straightens out her knees in the tub.

"My mom gets so mad sometimes that she hits me. Like this." I squeeze the doll and bounce her head off the ledge of the tub. "Like this and this. Owww!"

"Really?" Maddie's eyes grow wide and she looks at the doll for confirmation. I make the doll nod.

"Really. It hurts."

"That's mean."

"I know. She does it when she's mad or when she drinks."

"Drinks?"

"Like a beer. Like wine or whiskey. Does your mommy do that?"

"No." Maddie shakes her head, mystified. "She just yells."

"Does your grandma?"

"No."

"Never?"

"No."

"Do you ever see her drink anything?"

"Water."

"No whiskey? It's yellow."

"No. She just smokes. It comes out her nose like a dragon."

"Yuck."

She nods gravely. "Yuck."

I feel my pulse return to normal. So the unimaginable didn't happen, and my daughter is safe in her grandmother's care. It's just the past I have to deal with. My past.

I'll get to it right after I'm finished with the present.

TWENTY-TWO

It's Sunday, and Bernice, Ricki, and I sit on the bottom row of the hard steel bleachers, watching Ricki's favorite son play soccer. Ricki's eyes remain glued to Jared while I tell her how Shake and Bake turned out to be Winn and about my father. She looks at me only when I tell her about the hit on the head in front of the courthouse, but I think that was because Jared took a water break.

"Way to go, Jared!" she shouts, cupping her hands to her mouth. "Did you see that? He almost scored!"

"He's the messiah. I'm convinced."

"Hey, watch it."

I look around the lush suburban field almost reflexively; my paranoia hasn't diminished, even though the Italian stalking my daughter turned out to be her grandfather. Apparently, there's nothing to be worried about here. Bryn Mawr, where Ricki lives, is one of the wealthiest communities on the Main Line. No killers here, only color-coordinated parents watching their kids kick the shit out of each other. I'm safe as long as I stay off the field.

"Are you gonna see your father again?" Ricki asks.

"Not if I can help it."

"You should, you know. I think it's very healthy."

"Give me a break, Rick. It's a horror show."

The wind blows a strand of hair into her lipstick and she picks it out. "I like that he came forward and found you. He's dealing with it, or trying to. Credit where credit is due."

"Please. The guy looks like Elvis. On the stamp they didn't pick."

"You should talk to your mother about what happened when you were little."

"Another winner. Masquerading as Rose Kennedy. What a joke."

She watches Jared kick the ball to his teammate. "Nice pass, honey!" She covers her mouth. "Damn. He told me not to say that anymore. Anyway, talk to her."

"I have bigger problems." I think of Armen. His killer is still out there, and this is my only Sunday without Maddie, who's at Sam's.

"You mean the judge?"

"I told you it wasn't suicide, Rick. Even the FBI thinks so."

"Don't be unbearable, please."

"You mean because I was right and you were wrong?"

"Yes, already."

"Do you say *uncle?*"

She claps loudly. "Way to go, Jared! Way to go!"

"Sometimes a train really is a train, Ricki. Trains and bagels, bagels and trains."

"Go, Jared, you can do it!" She claps. "All that matters is you getting out of that mess. You're right to let the FBI take over, it's their job. You should never have been involved in the first place."

So I lied. It was a white lie, a little white lie. Why worry her?

"I don't know what made you think you could investigate a murder all by yourself. With the Mafia yet."

Silly me. "Uncle," I say.

"Maybe I'm finally getting through to you. All that free therapy, paying off." She smiles at me, then gets distracted by the action on the soccer field. "Hey, ref, what about it? Wake up, you jerk!" The woman next to her glances over. "I heard on the radio about that death penalty case."

"Yeah, the Supremes still have it. They haven't decided yet."

"Go, Jared, charge him!"

I think of Hightower, sitting alone. I read they moved him from death row to a special cell near the death chamber. The death warrant runs out tomorrow morning at 9:03. I wonder what Mrs. Stevens is doing today. How many mothers know the exact time and place of their child's death? Besides the Gilpins?

"The radio said they were locking down the prison tonight," Ricki says. "What's that mean?"

"It means all the prisoners have to stay in their cells."

"Isn't that what prison is?"

"They do it before executions, so the population doesn't riot."

Ricki leaps to her feet. "He scored! Way to go, honey! Way to go!" Applauding wildly, she looks down at me. "Clap, you! He scored!"

So I clap for Jared, who truly is a fine young man, all wiry legs in his baggy soccer trunks. He throws his arms into the air and beams at his mother and me, his mouth a tangle of expensive orthodonture. But somehow when I look at his face, flushed with adrenaline and promise, I think about Hightower, who had no suburban soccer field, no fancy jersey or hundred-dollar cleats. One will go to Harvard; the other will be put to death.

No justice, no peace.

Empty rhetoric, until I think of Armen and his killer.

That very night I'm on the warpath, rattling toward West Philadelphia in the dark. I'm heading for Armen's secret apartment. Someone killed him; maybe the answer is there. And I'm the only one who knows about it, so it's relatively safe. I decide to go, especially since Maddie is with Sam. I make the most of baby-sitter time; if you have children, you'll understand. I've known couples to drive around the block just to enjoy that last fifteen minutes.

I've disguised myself as the high-priced lawyer I used to be, just in case anybody's watching me: a monogrammed brief-case, overpriced raincoat, and pretentious felt hat. I check out the rearview mirror on the way to West Philly, but everything looks clear.

I open the car window into the cool night air. It still smells like hoagies at the corner of 40th and Spruce, like it did twenty years ago. I swing the car into a space and step out into a curb-ful of trash. Some things never change.

I lock the car and walk down Pine Street, which used to be lined with Victorian houses full of expensive apartments with hardwood floors and high ceilings. The richer students lived here when I was in school; it looks like they still do, judging from the cars parked along the street, bumper to exported bumper.

I reach the address on the checkbook and stand outside the brownstone in the dark. It's a three-story Victorian, with high arched windows and a mansard roof. A light is on on the bottom floor, showing through closed shutters in what would be the living room. I straighten my hat, climb the porch steps, and ring the bell to the front door.

A porch light comes on. An older woman appears at the window, behind bars. Her gray hair is plaited into a long braid and she wears thick aviator glasses. "What is it?" she shouts at me, through the bars.

"I'm a lawyer," I say, brandishing my briefcase.

She does an about-face. The light goes off.

Good move. I take another tack. "Please, I'm a friend of Greg Armen's."

The light goes on again and she reappears, friendlier in a colorful Guatemalan shirt. "What do you want?"

"I need to come in. I'm meeting him here. My name is Grace Rossi."

She squints and I smile in a toothy way. She unlocks the several locks on the door and opens it, welcoming me into the foul odor of Indian curry. "Smells good," I say.

"Do you work with Greg?"

"Yes. I was supposed to meet him, but he's late. Do you know a way I could get into his apartment? To wait for him?"

I hear a cat meow from inside her apartment. "He didn't come today. He always comes on Sundays."

"I know, he got tied up. He asked me to stop by tonight. We just started seeing each other."

"You want to surprise him?"

"Right."

"Interesting. Hold on," she says, winking at me in a stagey way. "He gave me a key in case he forgets it." She scuffs into her apartment in Birkenstocks and returns with a key on a ring. "He does forget it sometimes. He's kind of strange, in that cap and sunglasses all the time. I like her, though."

"Her?"

"Whoops! You didn't hear it from me! Give him hell!" she says, slapping the key in my palm; then she turns on her heel and scuffs inside. I hear the cat meow again as she closes the door.

I trudge up the stairs with a sense of dread. *I like her, though.* Who is she? The shabby carpeted stair winds around to the left, and at the top are two doors, 2A and 2B. The checkbook said 2B, so I slip the key into its lock. It opens easily, eager to reveal its secret, even if I'm not so eager to know it.

The room is dark, except for a streetlight streaming through the bay windows at the other end of the room. It looks like an efficiency, with a single bed against the wall. A chain hangs down from an overhead light, and I yank it on.

What I see shocks me.

All over the apartment, everywhere I look, are toys. Against the wall are white IKEA shelves full of stuffed animals. A plush tiger. Pinocchio. A Steiff lion. Mickey Mouse. They're crammed onto the shelves in all directions, sticking out by their cartoon feet and white-gloved hands. The lower shelves are stacked with an array of games. Candyland. Don't Break the Ice. Clue. Monopoly.

Stunned, I close the door behind me.

A child's room. Does Armen have a child? The woman downstairs said he comes on Sundays, like lots of divorced fathers. Like Sam. Is Armen divorced? Was he married before?

What is this all about?

I walk stiffly to the middle of the room and pick up a stuffed Dalmatian puppy from the couch. It looks back at me, round-eyed, blank.

Who is this child? Who is this woman?

I rummage through the stuffed animals on the shelves, then the games. Toy cats and teddy bears fly off the shelves in my wake. I feel myself getting angry, losing control. Who is this woman? Who is this child?

I tear the plastic lid off a white toy box full of blocks and root to the bottom. Nothing, except for plastic beads and a pirate's scabbard.

I move to a bookshelf next to the toy box, also white. It's full of children's books, more than most libraries, and many in hardback. I snatch them out, one by one, enraged. Why didn't he tell me, that night on the couch? I hear the sound of my own panting and watch with satisfaction as *Goodnight Moon* and *Where the Wild Things Are* fall to the soft carpet, littering it.

I take the next book from the shelf. *Eloise.* There's a pang deep within my chest; I know this book, but I have yet to buy it for Maddie.

How do I know *Eloise*?

I open it, going through it page by oversized page, trying to remember. I come to a page that at first looks ripped but unfolds at the top. I trace the trail of Eloise from a distant memory, my nail running along the dotted red line that goes up and down on the elevator. I remember a thick fingernail tracing these same travels. *See, here she goes.* The finger is yellow-stained at the edge with nicotine, and the hand is warm as my own hand rides around on top of his. My father's hand. *See, Princess?*

And then he left.

I love you.

Liars, liars all. I let the book fall to the floor.

Suddenly, I hear a noise at the windows behind me. I turn around, but nothing's there. I hear the noise again, like a rustling outside. I reach overhead and turn off the light. The room goes black just as a figure climbs onto the porch roof outside the bay window.

I back up against the wall.

The figure creeps toward the window, silhouetted in the streetlight. I feel my hackles rise. Someone is about to break in. Who knows about this apartment? Armen's killer?

The figure removes the portable screen from the window and places it on the roof without a sound. A professional. The streetlight glistens on his black leather jacket, stretched tight over a powerful back. I watch, dry-mouthed, as he jiggles the center window and it comes open in his hands.

I reach for the apartment key in my raincoat pocket, ready to drive it into his eyes. I feel the scream rising in my throat but suppress it.

The figure opens the window halfway and climbs into the room, landing silently at the foot of the single bed.

I back toward the apartment door in the dark, every nerve strained with tension. I can't see who the intruder is and I don't care. I must have been out of my mind to come here. I take a step back. Suddenly, I slip on a book and let out an involuntary yelp.

In a split second, the dark figure is barreling across the room toward me. He slams into my chest with the impact of a freight train, knocking the wind out of me. I cry out in pain and fall back on the hardwood floor. My head cracks hard where it was bumped before.

I try to scream but a hand clamps down across my mouth so cruelly it bring tears to my eyes. The hand forces my head back down against the floor. His body climbs up on mine, pinning me to the floor. I try frantically to knee him but he's too strong. A flashlight blazes into my eyes, blinding me.

"Grace!" says the voice behind the light. "What the fuck?" The hand releases my mouth.

"Who?"

"It's me. Winn." He shines the flashlight on his bearded face. "What are you doing here?"

My head begins to ache. "Why did you attack me?" I ask him, wincing. "You hurt my head."

"What did you break in for?" He backs off of me.

"What did *you* break in for?" I pull my tweed skirt down, trying to recover my dignity. "Jesus H. Christ, I've never been so banged up in all my life. Ever since I met you."

He stands up and helps me to my feet. "Why didn't you say who you were?"

"I didn't know it was you. Why didn't you say who *you* were?"

"I didn't know it was *you.*"

"Where's your raincoat?"

He looks down at the leather coat. "Underneath." He pulls out an edge to show me, but it's too dark to see. "I found this in a Dumpster a block down, can you believe it? It must've cost a couple hundred dollars."

"You've been undercover too long. Where's your rain hat?"

"I don't wear it on B and E's. You should sit down. Come

on." He eases me onto the couch and tilts my head back on a crinkly bandanna he pulls from his pocket. "Rest a minute. I'll find some ice."

I grab his lapel before he gets up. "No. No ice. I hate ice."

"You need ice."

"No. What I need is to yell at you, then I need to sue you. Then I need to yell at you and sue you again."

He laughs and sits heavily on the couch next to me. The streetlight illuminates the oil slick coating his nose; I could never go undercover, my pores couldn't take it. "I'm sorry I jumped you like that," he says, "but you surprised me."

"I surprised you? I'm lawfully on the premises."

"How was I supposed to know that? I've been watching this place for over a month. The light is never on at night. I came in to catch a killer."

"Didn't you see me go to the door?"

"I didn't recognize you. You don't wear hats, and I never saw you with a briefcase. I thought you were here to see the old woman downstairs. You're off the reservation, Grace. Way off. Who's staying with your daughter?"

"She's at her father's. Sunday is father's day, apparently."

He reaches around the back of my neck. "Lift up. I want to fix this thing." I oblige and he folds the bandanna in two.

"I hate men."

"I know, we're bums. Look at me."

"Exactly."

He laughs. "Which do you hate more, men or ice?"

I feel myself smile, the adrenaline ebbing away. "Men. Armen in particular. So he was a father? Who's the mother?"

"Don't you know?"

"Of course not."

"Then how do you know about the apartment? I thought he told you."

Hurt and humiliated, the combination platter. "So whose child is it? Tell me."

He pauses. "Were you in love with him?"

I'm glad he can't see my face. "No. I was in lust with him. I didn't know him at all, obviously. If my daughter ever does what I did, I'll kill her."

"You were lonely."

"How do you know?"

"Artie told me."

I wince. "Terrific. On to more important topics. Is it his child?"

"Yes."

"And the mother?"

"You want to know? Straight up?" I feel his eyes on me.

"I can take it, doc."

"The mother is Eletha."

I gasp as if the wind were knocked out of me again. I can't say anything for a minute.

"Grace?" He touches my arm, but I move it away.

"The mother is *Eletha?* The child—"

"Is Malcolm."

Oh, God. "How do you know that?"

"She dropped him off here."

My mind reels. I think of Malcolm's picture on Eletha's desk. His lightish skin. Why didn't I think of it? Armen paid for her tuition, even. "They were married?"

"No. I checked. Never married."

Malcolm, born out of wedlock? "Does Susan know?"

"I don't know, I've never seen her here. Armen met Malcolm every Sunday."

"Since when?"

"I don't know that either. They played inside, sometimes he took him to Clark Park. Places he wouldn't be recognized. He was a good father."

My stomach turns over. "Oh, please. He was a liar."

"That's unfair."

"How do you know? What was he, Clarence Thomas? God, was I blind."

"Don't judge him until you have all the facts. I knew Armen, too. He was a good man. He went out of his way for me. He got them to let me into the Y, even got me a locker. He didn't care that I was homeless."

"You're not. And he was a piece of shit."

"You don't believe that or you wouldn't have protected him."

"I protected him? How?"

"You didn't tell me about the money. The $650,000. That's how you knew about the apartment, isn't it?"

I sink back into the couch. My head hurts even more. "How do *you* know about the money?"

"The IRS found out about the account. It was a fraction of that last year, when he declared it. Gained a lot of weight in twelve months."

"It couldn't be a bribe for *Canavan,* you know. Armen wanted the case to come out the other way."

"I know that and you know that, but the money convinced my boss it was Armen who took the bribe. They figure it's the reason he killed himself, he couldn't live with it. He killed himself in April—tax time, they figure. They're gonna pull the plug on this investigation any day now. The bad guy is already dead."

"But you saw Armen at the argument. It was him against Galanter."

"They think that was just for show. He hadn't voted yet, he was killed before he could. If I don't turn up something very soon, the investigation is over. Armen's gonna be smeared in every newspaper in the country."

"But his killer would go free."

"I know, and the world will think Armen was dirty. Including his son."

I feel stunned. It was awful before, and now it's worse. Now it's Armen and Eletha, my lover and my friend. Were they still seeing each other, sleeping together? What did she mean to him? What did *I* mean to him? "I don't know if I'm still in."

"I want you out, I told you. You're in danger."

"It's not that." I tell him about what happened with Maddie, even about my father. He's a good listener and stays quiet for a minute after I finish; the last man who listened to me that intently was Armen.

"So you're hurt," he says.

True. "I always thought he was so honest, so honorable. But here, this place. A child, Malcolm."

"He would've told you sooner or later."

"I don't know."

"Let me take it from here, you're in way too deep. All I wanted you to do was answer Galanter's phone. Now you're breaking into apartments."

"I didn't break in, I talked my way in."

He smiles. "You lied your way in. Not illegal, just immoral."

It reminds me of Armen, and our talk that night, over *Hightower*. Law and morality. *You can't separate them, why would you want to?* Then I think of his broad back slumped over his desk. Armen was murdered, and murder is wrong. Illegal and immoral. Nothing I've learned tonight changes that, and I'm still the only one who has a chance of getting to Galanter. I rise, unsteadily. "Maybe I'm not out, Rain Man."

Winn takes my elbow. "Aw, come on, Grace. I worry about you."

"Good. Somebody should."

"I mean it."

His voice has a softness I'd rather ignore, at least for the time being. "You want to walk me out or you gonna play Batman again?"

I get no answer, not that I expected one. We end up leaving by the conventional method. He waits for me on the sidewalk while I stop downstairs to return the key. The old woman opens the door carrying the cat, a chubby orange tabby. "I heard you moving the furniture!" she says slyly.

"Moving the furniture?"

She plucks the key from my hand. "You're a nineties woman, I'll tell you that!" The woman shuts the door, and the cat meows in belated agreement.

TWENTY-THREE

Monday morning I push open the glass door into the court-house lobby. It's mercifully clear of reporters and crowds, but it looks like martial law has been declared. There are double the number of marshals, and even the lawyers and court employees have to go through the detectors. I join one of the lines, predictably the slowest moving.

"What gives?" I say to a skinny marshal, when I reach the middle of the line. Jeff stands at his side.

"New rules, on account of that circus last week."

"A little late, isn't it?"

"Tell the AO that."

In front of me in line is an older woman, thin and tall, with marvelously erect posture. Her gray hair is swept into an elegant French twist and the air around her smells like lilac bushes in June.

"Line up, now!" roars McLean, at the head of the line. His booming voice sets the woman in front of me trembling. "All bags on the conveyor belt! All bags on the belt! Sir, *sir!*" he shouts at a heavyset man in a red Phillies windbreaker.

"Shit," the man says. He surrenders the wrinkled paper bag to the conveyor belt of the X-ray machine.

"Say what, sir?"

Ray looks over from behind the machine. "Don't be roughin' up the Phils fans, McLean. We need 'em all, after last season."

The marshals laugh, including the fan. But not McLean. "I'm not roughin' nobody up. I'm doin' my job." The fan lumbers through the metal detector, and McLean motions distractedly to the woman in front of me. "You don't know who's carryin' a piece," he says. "You can't tell by lookin'."

The older woman quivers like Katharine Hepburn.

"They still haven't caught the guy who did those shootings," McLean continues, watching her place a wristwatch with a black cord band into the bin. "You can pack anywhere, even your boot." He shouts over her head to the marshal at the monitor, "Billy, you remember that joker, the one with the boot?"

Billy peers over the top of the monitor. "The cowboy."

"Yeah. Some cowboy," McLean says. "Put your purse on the belt, ma'am."

The woman watches with apprehension as her purse disappears into the maw of the machine. As the light turns green, McLean propels her through the metal detector and looks at me. "How's your head, Ms. Rossi?"

"Fine, thanks," I say warily.

"Put your purse on the belt. Go when the light turns green."

"You be nice to her, McLean," Ray says. "She's my girl. Grace, you takin' care of that matter we discussed?"

Damn. I forgot to talk to Eletha about him. How can I broach it now, when I can barely look her in the eye? "I'm workin' on it, Ray." I walk through the metal detector, but it explodes in a ringing alarm.

"Come back on through," McLean says. I walk back through the metal detector and the clamor subsides.

"What's the deal?"

"Turned up the sensitivity. Have to do our jobs right." He winks, but it's not friendly. "Take off your watch and try it again."

I snap off my Seiko, and it clatters into the bin on the counter. I start through the metal detector, but no sooner do I hit the black rubber carpet than the detector erupts in another cacophonous warning. The people in line break ranks to see what's going on.

"I think she's okay," Ray says, "even if she *is* a lawyer." The other marshals laugh.

"No, can't take any chances. Ms. Rossi's been a busy lady, checkin' up, makin' sure we're doin' our jobs."

I glance at Ray, but he looks as surprised as I do. "I was checking security."

"I know what you were doing. You wanted to know who was on duty the night Judge Gregorian bought it. Well, you're lookin' at him, and I didn't see nothin' unusual. Earrings in the box."

I drop my hoops into the bin. "Do you check the hallways?"

"Sure, I patrol."

"Did you check our hallway, on eighteen?"

"Sure did. Nothin' there."

"At what time?"

"About eleven o'clock, then again around four or so."

My mouth goes dry. By four o'clock Armen and I were on the couch. "Did you come into chambers either time?"

A smile plays around his lips. "Don't remember."

"You don't remember?"

"Is there an echo in here?"

I grit my teeth. I've deposed bigger bastards than this. "Do you usually go into chambers?"

"I check the doorknobs. If the door's unlocked, I go in. I forget if that one was open that night. Now you better get through the detector. We got a line here."

I walk through the detector, trying to remember if the door was unlocked that night. I have no idea. The alarm sounds again.

"Come on back, Ms. Rossi."

I walk back through and the noise stops. My handbag sails past me in the opposite direction. McLean looks over his shoulder at Jeff. I can't see his face but I can see Jeff's, and he's smiling.

"Now your belt, please, Ms. Rossi."

"Cut her a break, man," Ray says.

"You ain't my boss and I ain't your man," McLean snaps, then looks at me. "Only one thing left. Stand up and put your hands out straight from your sides."

"Get real. You know I'm not a security risk."

"You want to get to work today?" he says. From behind the counter he produces a hand-held metal detector, which looks like a cartoon magnifying glass. He switches it on in front of my chest.

Biiinng! It screams to life, even louder than the other metal detector. All eyes are on me, or more accurately, on my breasts. Shame and fury restrict my breathing.

Biiinnng! Biiinnng!

McLean holds the magnifying glass in front of my left breast, then moves it slowly in front of my right. It's all I can do not to hit him.

Biiinnng! Biinng!

"I thought so," he shouts, and turns off the noisy alarm. "Underwire bra." One of the marshals laughs out loud, then quiets.

I look McLean in the eye. "If this is some kind of game, pal, you won't win."

"I don't know what you're talking about," he says, unfazed.

I grab my earrings and bag and stalk ahead to the elevator, where the older woman is holding the door for me. "Here, dear," she says, in a comforting way.

I slip inside and punch the button for eighteen. "Thank you."

"What an unhappy man," she says, looking up at the lighted numbers. The elevator doors open on the second floor and she extends a bony hand. "It was very nice meeting you. My name's Miss Pershing, by the way. Amanda Pershing."

"Grace Rossi."

Her hooded eyes light up. "Are you Italian?"

I think of my father. "No."

She looks disappointed as the elevator doors close behind her. Her perfume lingers, and I travel heavenward in an elevator filled with lavender and rage. Did McLean see Armen and me together? Where was he when I was hit on the head?

I head for chambers but hear noise down the hall, coming from Galanter's chambers; it sounds like a party.

I pass the judges' elevator and linger for a moment in the hall. The sound is coming from the office of Galanter's law clerks. Maybe they're celebrating Galanter's ascension; maybe I can learn something about *Canavan*. I walk down the hall and stand in the open doorway.

There are no judges, but the clerks' office is packed with twenty-five-year-olds, crowding among the federal case reporters, laughing and talking. One of Galanter's clerks has two party hats crossed on his head in a coarse caricature of a woman's breasts.

"It's time!" somebody shouts, and then everybody starts blowing horns and noisemakers, like New Year's Eve.

"Ready for the countdown?" shouts a pretty blonde in a dark suit. She checks her watch, as do several of the others.

"Ten! Nine! Eight! Seven!"

The kids all shout, growing giddier with each second. I have no idea what is going on.

"Come on in, the water's fine!" says one of the partyers, who's older than the others. He takes me by the hand and pulls me inside. "Count with us!"

"What for?" I yell, over the din.

"Six! Five!" shouts the crowd in unison. "Four! Three! Two!"

"What are we celebrating?"

"Justice!" He raises a plastic glass. "The Court denied the stay in *Hightower*. This is the big day! 9:03!"

"One! *Zero!*"

"Good-bye, Tommy!" shouts the blonde, next to a familiar head of wiry hair.

Ben. He sees me in the doorway, and his shocked expression freezes for a moment. Then he turns his back on me.

TWENTY-FOUR

"You had a phone call, Grace," Eletha calls out from Armen's office, as soon as I get into chambers. "From that reporter."

"Reporter?" I pause in the doorway to Armen's office, taken aback by the sight. Everything has been packed up. There's not a trace of Armen still visible; none of the books he loved or the objects he collected. Even the cudgel he kept on the wall has been wrapped. I feel a sharp twinge inside.

"That stringer, the one who was givin' Susan such a hard time after the memorial service." She pushes a stiff strand of hair out of her eyes, looking beautiful without even trying. No wonder Armen loved her. "The curly guy, who needed the shave. Faber."

Are you gonna let somebody get away with murder? "I know the one. Did he leave his number?"

"You're not gonna call him back, are you?"

"Why not?"

"He's an ass. He called here, buggin' Ben, even Sarah. Artie hung up on him." She strips some wide packing tape from a roll and presses it onto a box. "I can't be bothered. I got another asshole to deal with. Did you see?" She steps aside, presenting the chair behind her like Vanna White. A long Indian headdress is draped over the chair. Its feathers are a brilliant cardinal red, with orange in the center, and the pointy tips of each plume are black. It's easily eight feet long and makes a gaudy caterpillar onto the carpet.

"What's that doing here?"

"It's Galanter's, he's the chief now, get it? Think he'll wear it behind the goddamn desk?" She shakes her head. "Meanwhile, check out what's going on down the hall. You won't believe that either."

"I saw."

"They should be ashamed of themselves. I called the clerks' office upstairs. They'll stop 'em."

"Was Galanter in?"

"He's been gone all morning."

"Where?"

"Damned if I know. He left some typing for me, like I'm his goddamn secretary."

I turn to go. "I gotta check the mail."

"How was your weekend?" she calls after me.

I think of my newfound father, then the secret apartment full of toys. "Same old, same old."

"You're talkative this morning." She's puzzled by my coldness, and I decide to level with her in a way she didn't with me. Or maybe I want to pick a fight.

"Actually, I had an interesting weekend, El. Went up to West Philly."

"You? In my neighborhood? What's up there?"

"Armen's apartment."

Her mouth forms a glossy chestnut-stained O. "Say what?"

I close the door behind me. "I thought I knew you, El, but it turns out I don't."

She eases down onto one of the boxes. "Now don't say that."

"What am I supposed to say?"

"How'd you find out about the apartment?"

I hadn't thought about that. "I came across some papers in here the other night. A lease."

"I thought I packed all that stuff."

"You didn't tell me about Malcolm."

"You expected me to?"

"Of course, we're friends. I thought he was yours and your ex's."

She points an electric nail at me. "I never told you that. You assumed it."

"You *let* me assume it."

"You'd've blamed me."

"Blamed you? It's him I blame."

She frowns. "Armen? Why?"

"Hitting on women who work for him. First you, then me."

"Armen wasn't like that."

I look away at the bookshelves, empty and hollow. "Come on, El. I wasn't born yesterday and neither were you. It's the same old shit, just in a black robe."

"It wasn't like that."

"Wasn't or isn't?"

"Wasn't," she says firmly. "It's ancient history."

"Good. So he wasn't cheating on me, just his wife."

"We ended before he met Susan, Grace."

It sets my teeth on edge. "Then why didn't he marry you?"

"Because I said no."

"What?" It's a surprise.

"The bottom line is"—she pauses, then laughs and throws up her hands—"we fell in love, then we got pregnant. He wanted to make it legal, but I couldn't see marryin' him, takin' him away from everybody he loved. His mother. His community."

"What community?"

"The Armenians. The dinners, the church, the whole thing. It was the center of his life." She looks down. "You think his mama liked it when she met me, my belly big as a watermelon? I'm half the reason she killed herself."

"Is that true?"

"I don't know. Armen always blamed himself. So when he asked, I said no." She sighs. "Don't think I haven't regretted it, plenty of times. I even felt a little jealous of you."

"Me?"

She waves it away. "Water under the bridge. It was the right thing. I didn't fit in his life."

"Did Susan?"

She wrinkles her stubby nose. "Not really, but he fit into hers. Now *you* were different, you woulda been the one. You fit into his life and he fit into yours."

I feel a lump in my throat. I know that, inside.

"With him and me, we were betwixt and between, both of us. My family wasn't in love with the situation either. It never would've worked."

"So you took Malcolm yourself and raised him?"

"Not on my own. Armen was in on every decision, we talked about Mal all the time. He was a great father, Grace. The best."

"How'd you swing it financially?"

"Armen paid Malcolm's expenses. Now I don't know what'll happen." She flicks some imaginary dirt out from under a nail. "It's part of the reason I'm thinking about quitting school. To get another job at night."

I think of the checkbook. "Did Armen leave a will or anything?"

She laughs. "For what? He had no extra money, it went to us. You saw the apartment, he bought that boy everything. I told you he saved. Well, it was Malcolm he was saving for, for his college."

"How much had he saved?"

"About fifty-sixty grand, like I told you. Not bad, huh?" She smiles proudly, and the irony hits me full force. I can't shake the image of the $650,000, socked away in a money fund. Did Armen hold out on her and Malcolm?

"Let's say he did have money, Eletha. Do you think he had a will? Did Susan say anything?"

"Not that I heard."

"Does she know about you and him?"

Eletha's eyes widen comically. "You crazy, girl?"

I smile, feeling my hostility subsiding. Maybe I wouldn't have told me either. "Why not?"

"Uh-uh." She shakes her head. "I didn't want to tell her, and he promised me he wouldn't. She has no idea."

"But how did he get away every Sunday?"

"How do most men get away? Work. Clubs. It became his Sunday off. We were careful during the campaign, laid low, and she found plenty to do, believe me. She was into him early on, but when she caught Potomac fever she left him behind."

"Is that when he asked for a divorce?"

She looks at me like I'm crazy again. "Armen? Never. He loved her in his bones. She's the one who called it quits."

I don't understand. "*Susan* was the one who ended the marriage, not Armen? But he told me she'd asked him to stay with her."

"Through the campaign, because she needed a hubby to smile pretty for the pictures. Otherwise, that woman didn't need him at all."

I sit down in one of the chairs at the conference table. "I don't know what to think, El. I don't understand Armen. I don't understand anything."

"You're takin' this bad, girlfriend," Eletha says. "What don't you understand, baby? Mommy make it better."

"I don't know if Armen was a bad guy or a good guy."

"A good guy. Next question."

"I don't know who killed him."

"He killed himself. Next."

I look at her in bewilderment. "How can you say that? You had a son with him."

"That's right."

"You said he was a good father."

"He was. The best."

"How could he be? What kind of father leaves his own child?" I think of my own father, though I hadn't started out thinking about him. Suddenly I need to know the answer to the question, burning like hot lead at the core of my chest. "Tell me that, Eletha. How can a father turn his back on his own flesh and blood?"

"Because he has no choice. Maybe the pain is too great to stay." She shakes her head. "Look, you left your husband, didn't you? Why?"

"He cheated on me," I say, the words dry as dust in my mouth. "It's not the same."

"Yes, it is. You loved him, didn't you? But you left."

"I had to."

"Right. You had no choice. Just because you left doesn't mean you didn't love."

I feel a catch in my throat. I can't say anything. I think of Sam, Armen, then my father. I need Ricki, fast.

Eletha folds her arms. "And I always thought you were so smart. Fancy degrees and all."

"You just assumed wrong," I say to her, and she laughs.

The marshals' smelly gym is empty; it's midafternoon. Against the wall is a huge mirror and racks of chrome free weights. A treadmill stands at the end behind some steppers. On the far wall hangs a poster of Christie Brinkley and beside it one of the electric chair. At the bottom it says: JUSTICE— FRIED OR EXTRA CRISPY? I kid you not.

"How can they have that there?" I ask Artie, who's flat on

his back, pumping a barbell up and down over his chest.

"Have what?"

"That poster." I point, and his eyes follow my finger.

"Christie? She's a babe. An old babe, like you."

"The other one, whiz."

He hoists the barbell up and down, exhaling like a whale through a blowhole. "I never noticed it. They let me work out here, Grace, I don't give a shit about the artwork. Which rep am I on?"

"I don't know."

"You're a lousy spotter." He presses the barbell into the air.

I can't take my eyes from the poster. The newspaper said that Hightower's last meal was steak and an ice cream sundae. He ate the dessert first. After dinner he played Battleship with his guard, and the guard won. "Artie, if you were playing Battleship with a man who was condemned to death, wouldn't you let him win?"

"What?" The barbell rises and falls.

"Wouldn't you let him win? I mean, the man's going to die."

"I don't know, would you?" He grunts with effort, his bangs damp from sweat.

"Of course. I let Maddie win all the time. What's the difference? It's a game."

"Games matter, Grace."

"Excuse me, I forgot who I was talking to." I look back at the poster. The witnesses at Hightower's execution said he shook his head back and forth as the lethal chemicals flowed into his veins. His feet trembled and his fingers twitched for about three minutes, and then it was over. Final, unknowable, and beyond this world. "Artie, what do you think about the death penalty?"

"What is this, menopause? Hot flashes and questions?"

"Come on. Tell me what you think."

"I don't think about the death penalty."

"But if you had to say, how do you come out?"

He presses the barbell all the way up to a hook on a rack behind him, where it falls with a resounding *clang*. "It's no biggie." His arms flop over the sides of the bench.

"I thought you were against it."

"That was when I was fucking Sarah. Now that she's fucked me, it's just fine."

"You don't mean that."

He pushes his wet hair away from his forehead. "Yes, I do."

"But think about the act. The actual act of killing someone."

"I could do it, if he deserved it."

"My, we're in a macho mood."

"You started it. This isn't why I asked you to meet me in my branch office."

I laugh. He has been spending a lot of time here, I gather because he's out of work and avoiding Sarah. "All right. What did you want to talk about?"

"I wanted to tell you I was sorry about the other night. I drank too much. I wasn't making any sense."

"It's okay. I understand why it happened." Drowning your sorrows. I've done it exactly once.

"Thanks, Mom." He rubs his chest, and sweat soaks through his thin T-shirt. I remember the basketball underneath.

"You still got that tattoo?"

"Until I find a blowtorch." He sits up, straddling the bench, then sighs heavily. "Lifting sucks. I miss hoops."

"You're not playing anymore?"

"Nah. The team broke up." He wipes his forehead with the edge of his T-shirt. "You know, before Sarah dumped me she told me something. She said you thought Armen was murdered."

"I do."

"Really?"

"Really. Why, what do you think? You gonna laugh at me?"

"No. I even thought of it myself, for a minute. After the way Galanter's been acting."

It surprises me. "You suspect Galanter?"

"I didn't know about suspecting him, but if anybody did it, he did."

"Why?"

"Besides the fact that he's a dick?"

"Yes."

"Because he wanted to be chief judge. He would never have been chief if Armen hadn't died." Artie straightens up, rallying. "And remember how Bernice went after him?"

"Do you think becoming chief judge is enough of a motive?"

He snorts. "What are you, funny? It's the same as Battleship. It's *winning*."

"People don't kill to win."

"Sure they do. Plenty of people—mostly men, I admit—would kill to win. It's ambition. Raw, naked, blind, cold. Ambition."

I think of Galanter taking a bribe in *Canavan* and killing Armen to guarantee the result. That makes sense to me, in a perverse way. "I don't agree. I think people kill for money—or love."

"Love? Not Galanter, what does he know from love? He's not even married, he lives for the frigging job. He has an Indian headdress, Grace. The man is not fucking kidding."

"True."

"As chief judge, he'll get on all the Judicial Conference committees. Get to go to D.C., hobnob with the Supremes. It even positions him for the next appointment to the Court. Look at Breyer, he was chief."

The Supreme Court. I hadn't thought of that.

Combined with *Canavan*, that's one hell of a motive.

"It's a place in history, Grace."

I remember that Galanter has a collection of first editions in his office. "He would love that."

"He sure would. It's the top of the profession. They ain't final because they're right, they're right because they're final."

"But Galanter's a Republican appointee."

"The Dems won't be in forever, babe." He looks down, then shakes his head. "Justice Galanter. That's so beat. Can't you just hurl?"

I consider this, and he's right. I could just hurl.

TWENTY-FIVE

I slip my master key into the doorknob. It turns with a satisfying *click*, admitting me to the darkened chambers. No one's there, as I expected; it's too late even for geeks. I told my mother I had to work late, killing two birds with one stone: avoiding her and poking around. I enter the reception area and close the door quietly behind me.

The computer monitors are on, standing out like vivid squares of hot color in the dark, wasteful but helpful. ORDER IN THE COURT! WELCOME TO THE THIRD CIRCUIT COURT WORD PROCESSING SYSTEM! guides me through the reception area, where the blinds are down.

The chambers are laid out like ours, with the judge's office to the left. I walk into Galanter's office; even at the threshold it stinks of cigar smoke. The far wall is entirely of glass, like Armen's, overlooking the Delaware. The lights from the Camden side make bright wiggly lines on the black water.

In the light from the wall of windows I can make out Galanter's glistening desk, also of glass. I walk to it with more nervousness than I want to acknowledge and whip out the flashlight I keep in the car; it says WALT DISNEY WORLD. Official burglary tool, patent pending.

I flick on the flashlight with an amateurish thrill and flash it around the room. Next to Galanter's desk are the same shelves we have, where Armen used to keep the current cases. Galanter does it the same way. I look over the shelves. The circle of light falls on each stack of red, blue, and gray briefs, the colors regulated by the Third Circuit's local rules. Attached to the briefs with a rubber band is the appendix in each case and the record. That's what I'm looking for.

I sort through a bunch of criminal cases, all sentencing appeals, and a commercial contract case; the Uniform Commercial Code seems less interesting to me than it used to. Underneath the stack, at the very bottom, is *Canavan* and its record. I tug the *Canavan* papers off the shelf and settle down on the floor.

I pull off the briefs and appendix to get to the record. I expect to find a stack of blue-backed pleadings bound at the top, but the papers are stuffed in a yellow envelope. SEALED COURT DOCUMENTS, says a forbidding red stamp on the envelope. A court order is taped underneath.

Why would a district court seal this record? In any event, it doesn't apply to me, at least not tonight.

I plunge into the envelope, pulling out the first part of the record. On top is the complaint, which alleges that Canavan Flowers was driven out of business by a group of local flower retailers. The defendants listed Bob Canavan on their FTD-like telephone network but never sent him any orders to fill. The complaint is a poorly drafted litany of the ways Canavan was starved out, but never explains why. The young lawyer couldn't flesh out the Mob connection. Neither can I.

A ring of florists? Galanter laughed.

I flip past the complaint and skim the appendix until I come to the names of the wholesalers. I take the crumpled crossword puzzle Winn gave me from my pocket and compare it with the papers, sticking the flashlight in my armpit. None of the names are the same. The list of wholesalers' names reads like white bread, the list of mobsters' names like Amoroso's hoagie rolls. I put the pleadings aside in favor of the depositions. If there's gold to be found, it'll be here. Something that isn't what it seems.

I read the first deposition, then the second and the third, fighting off a sinking feeling. None of the names are the ones on the crossword; none of the allegations amount to anything other than common law fraud by a bunch of rather hard-assed florists. Isn't that what Townsend said? *How is it different from a case of garden-variety fraud?* Was he speaking from the casebook or the checkbook?

I start the next deposition, given by one of the vendors. An inadvertent reference to a deliveryman sounds familiar. Jim Cavallaro. I look down at the short list on the crossword puzzle:

James Cavallaro.

It must be the same man. I think a minute.

Of course.

The Mob couldn't care less about the carnations; it's in the delivery. In the trucks and the truck drivers. In an operation that runs by phone orders, the delivery is where the money is to be made. It doesn't matter what's being delivered, even something that smells like roses.

I leaf back to the other depositions, looking for references to the truckers. I scribble down the names, but there's only a few. My next step is to check Galanter's phone log to see if any of them made calls to chambers, or if there's any other connection to Galanter.

Suddenly I hear the jiggling of the doorknob in the reception area to Galanter's office. I freeze, listening for another sound, but by then it's almost too late.

The door opens, casting a wedge of light into the reception area. I flick off the flashlight and shove the record back onto the shelf. If this is Winn, I'll bludgeon him with my Pluto flashlight.

Where can I hide? I look around the room.

Galanter's private bathroom. Right where Armen's was, off a tiny hall leading from the office. I scoot into the bathroom and slip behind the door, willing myself into stillness.

Whoever's coming in has a flashlight of his own.

He strides into Galanter's office as if he doesn't have any time to lose. He casts the flashlight this way and that, throwing a jittery spotlight at the bookshelves, then at the couch and back again. All I can see of him is that he's big-shouldered, an ominous outline above the blaze of the flashlight. Too heavyset to be Winn. I withdraw behind the bathroom door, afraid.

The figure strides to Galanter's desk. His back is to me as he aims the flashlight on the papers piled neatly on the glass surface. He touches each pile; his hand is hammy as it falls within the flashlight's beam. He seems to be looking for something, rapidly but with confidence. He's been in this office before, it seems. He had a key, unless he picked the lock.

His hand moves over the desk like a blind man reading Braille. He finds something and picks it up. I squint in the darkness. He holds a wrinkled piece of yellow paper in the beam of the flashlight. It must be a phone message; we use the same ones. They're printed on thin paper so they'll make a carbon copy. They tear constantly.

"Fuckin' A," the man says, in a voice I almost recognize. He takes the paper and slips it into a pocket.

Who is this man?

I get my answer when he turns around. In one terrifying instant he passes in front of the bathroom on the way out. I don't see his face clearly, but the mustache is a giveaway, as is the glint of an official marshal badge.

Al McLean.

My mouth goes dry. I hold my breath as I hear the outer door to chambers open, then close behind him. He jiggles the doorknob to make sure it's locked.

McLean. Christ. And he was the one on duty the night Armen was killed. I wait in the bathroom a minute, not surprised to be perspiring. I wipe my forehead and tiptoe into the office. I want to know what McLean was looking at, and what he took.

I walk over to the polished desk, stand in the same position he did, and flick on the flashlight. Everything is upside down, all the papers and correspondence that tie a circuit judge to the outside world. In a stack on the middle pile is a group of yellow message slips, written in the careful script of Galanter's secretary, Miss Waxman. The first two messages are from Judge Foudy and Judge Townsend. PLEASE CALL BACK, the secretary has checked. But the three messages after those are from Sandy Faber.

The reporter. The same one who's been phoning me and everyone in our chambers. The latest message, recorded at 4:58, says IMPORTANT! in letters so perfect they could be printed.

What did Faber find out? And whose message did McLean take?

It could be Faber's, since the three preceding it were from him. But it ain't necessarily so; the odds are worse than a flip of the coin. I decide to check the phone log tomorrow; it will have copies of each message. It's too risky to stay tonight.

I set the messages down the way I found them. Underneath is a small squarish envelope, its address the tiny Gothic typescript characteristic of only one institution: the Supreme Court of the United States. *Hobnob with the Supreme Court*, Artie said. *Position himself for the next appointment.* I open the stiff envelope.

What's inside is a surprise.

A note from Associate Justice Antonin Scalia, thanking Galanter for his recommendation letter on behalf of Ben Safer. Incredible. Ben doesn't even clerk for Galanter. I read it again, then slip it back in the envelope. I stack everything up the way it was, three-inch messages on top, small cards under that, letters next, then briefs. Strict size order, calibrated to telegraph CONTROL.

Boy, am I going to hate working for Big Chief Galanter.

TWENTY-SIX

Galanter's office gleams in the morning light, all sparkling surfaces with sharp edges. Glass glistens in front of the many photos of him with other judges; his collection of rare books rots behind locked glass doors. Even the furniture is shiny, covered with a polished cotton in navy stripes. It's more the domain of a corporate CEO than a judge with a public-record income of $130,000. I always thought Galanter had family money; I never knew it was money from the Family.

The problem is, he isn't hiring.

"I have my own clerks," he says, looking down at me from behind his desk chair. His cigar sits in a Waterford ashtray on the desk. "They're all full-time."

"But you get a part-time assistant as chief judge. It's in the budget already, for the administrative work."

"My law clerks can handle it until I hire one. Judge Gregorian waited several months to hire you, as I recall."

"The Judicial Conference meets soon. You'll need to be briefed."

"I can read." He thrusts my memo at me, a heavy hint to scram. I rise from the stiff-backed chair.

"I'd recommend that they get to the misconduct complaints first, then. There are eight backed up, and Washington likes us to stay on top of them."

"Washington?"

"They monitor the complaints, even keep a report on their disposition by all the chief judges. You don't want to make that list, it's a black mark. In Washington." I turn to go, hoping he'll call me back. I get as far as the door, ten feet farther than I predicted.

"You say there are eight, eh?"

"Last time I looked. We set them aside to do *Hightower*, and they just kept on coming."

"How long do they take?"

"The research, a while. Then we get the record and review it. That takes time too. At least a week per complaint."

He puts his hands in his pockets, rocking slightly on his heels. "I don't have the space for you. I'm gutting your office when I move. It needs redoing."

Fuck you very much. "I can work in your law clerks' office."

"No."

Good thing I have a strong ego. "I can work in the library on the first floor."

He examines his nails. "Of course, I would hire my own assistant eventually."

"I want to get back to practice anyway."

"I'd have no time to supervise you."

"I don't need supervision, just a paycheck." A sympathetic note, to make him feel like the regent he thinks he is.

"Miss Waxman?" he calls out the door. His oppressed secretary materializes at the other entrance to his office; she's probably been hovering there, waiting for him to bark. A civil service retirement is the only reason this sweet-faced soul would stay with such a tyrant. "You two have met, haven't you?" Galanter says.

"Sure. Hello, Miss Waxman."

Built like a medium swirl of soft ice cream, she nods at me but says nothing.

"Give her the drafts as you finish them, then I'll take it from there. If I need you, I'll call."

"Fine." I start to go, then do Peter Falk as Columbo. "Where should I put the drafts so I don't have to bother you? I used to put them in a box on our secretary's desk."

He looks at Miss Waxman. "Miss Waxman, make a place on your desk for a bin."

She nods.

"I could show you what I mean, Miss Waxman," I say to her.

She glances at Galanter for permission, and he dismisses us with a wave that says: Women, so concerned with the details! Then he picks up the phone. "Close the door," he says.

I close the heavy door and meet Miss Waxman at her desk in front of the door to the law clerks' office. Next to her computer keyboard is the phone log I need to see, with the standard four message slips to a page. Galanter couldn't have gotten too many calls this morning, so the copy of the message McLean took should be on the top page.

"I thought it would help if I knew where to put the papers," I say, moving closer to the open log book. "I don't know how you do things here."

She nods slightly. Her bangs are arranged in tiny spit curls around her face; an aging Betty Boop, down to the spidery eyelashes. "We do them the way the judge wants them," she says in a soft voice.

I look at the log. The top four messages are: Judge Richter at 9:00, Judge Townsend at 9:15, Chief Judge Wasserman of the Second Circuit at 9:16, and one at 9:20 from Carter at the Union League. Damn; a busy morning. It's not on the top page; it must be on the page underneath. I touch the spot next to the log. "Do you think it should go here? It just might fit."

"If you think that's okay, Miss Rossi."

"Please, call me Grace."

"I wouldn't feel comfortable."

"Please. We'll be working together."

She nods deferentially; the master-slave relationship, she understands it perfectly. This I can't abide. "Where would *you* like to put the box, Miss Waxman? It's your desk, after all."

"I don't know." Her brow knits with worry, cracking her pancake makeup into tectonic plates. Sometimes free will is not freeing. "I just don't know. Whatever you think, Miss Rossi. Grace."

I pat the surface near the log again and spot a photograph of a wicker basket full of silver toy poodle puppies, with frizzy gray pompadours. "Maybe here?"

"No!" she blurts out. "But, I mean, if you want to."

"No, that's all right. Whatever you want."

She touches her cheek. "It's just that . . . my dogs are there. Their picture. I like to see them when I work."

"I'm sorry. I don't want to hide the picture."

"But still, if you—"

"Please, I understand. I have a dog too." And now I have an idea. A wonderful, nasty, awful idea. I feel like the Grinch. "It's a big dog, though."

"I like big dogs too," she says. Interest flickers in her pale gray eyes.

"Actually, I adopted Judge Gregorian's dog, Bernice."

"You did? I heard she was given to the Girl Scouts."

"No. She was at the Morris Animal Refuge."

A horrified gasp escapes her lips. "Why, that's a *dog pound*."

"I know."

She gazes at me with an awe better directed at Madame Curie. "Well, aren't you kind!"

I look away guiltily and pick up the dog picture. Its frame is flimsy, from a card shop. The puppies look at me with abject trust, like their mistress. "They're so cute, Miss Waxman."

She beams with a mother's pride. "They do all sorts of tricks. I taught them. They're smart as whips."

"They look it." Coal-black eyes, little button noses.

"This one grew up to be a champion." She points at the one in the center, but how she can tell them apart I'll never know; each one looks as yappy as the next. "That's Rosie, my baby. My champion."

"A champ? Really?" I take an invisible deep breath and let the picture slip from my fingers. It hits the carpet and the frame self-destructs on impact. I feel like shit on toast, but it had to be done.

"Oh! Oh!" Miss Waxman exclaims, hands fluttering to her rouged cheeks. She bends over instantly to rescue the picture, and I flip the top page of the phone log over.

"I'm so sorry," I say, reading the four preceding telephone messages, recorded in carbon copies. All four are from Sandy Faber. I counted only three messages from Faber on Galanter's desk, so that means the one McLean took was from Faber too. "I hope it's not broken."

"It came apart," she wails.

"I feel terrible." I flip a page back, then another. A bunch of judges. Cavallaro and the other Mob names would be farther back, presumably before the *Canavan* argument, but I don't have time to look now. I turn back to the top page. "Here, Let me help."

"That's all right, I have it." Waxman finishes gathering up the frame, and when she straightens up, her eyes are glistening with tears.

I feel awful. "Let me fix it, Miss Waxman. If I can't, I'll replace it. I'll buy you fifty, I swear." I take the assembly from her with a gentle tug.

"It doesn't matter. I can get another," she says, ashamed of her reaction.

"Let me try." I replace the piece of plastic in the square well, then put the photo over it and close the back. One of the brass clips has gotten bent, so I bend it back with a thumb. I breathe a sigh of relief for my immortal soul. "There you go. I really am sorry."

She turns it over in her hands. "Why, it's good as new!"

"It wasn't hard."

"I could never have done that."

"Of course you could have, Miss Waxman." I touch her shoulder, soft in a nubby chenille sweater. "Maybe we can have lunch sometime."

A look of horror skitters across her face. "Oh, no, I eat at my desk."

"Every day?"

"Yes."

"Why?"

"The phones. I have to get the phones." She nods.

"Can't the law clerks get the phones? We take turns in our chambers, so everyone can have lunch."

"Judge Galanter doesn't think law clerks should answer the telephone."

"Why?"

She looks blank. Ours is not to question why.

He wants to keep the calls confidential, I bet. "I guess he has his reasons."

She purses her lips, inexpertly lined with red pencil. "He says you don't need a legal education to answer a telephone."

I wince at the insult to her, but her expression remains the same. "We'll see about that, Miss Waxman."

She smiles uneasily.

I spot Artie making copies at the Xerox machine on my way back to chambers. "Just the hunk I want to see."

"The Artman. Making copies. Copy-rama," he says, lapsing into an old routine from *Saturday Night Live*. "At the Xerox."

"How are you doing, handsome?"

"Gracie Rossi. Single mother. Former lawyer. Very horny." He grins and makes another copy.

"I get it. Now cut it out."

"You're no fun," he says in his own voice. He flips a long page over and hits the button. "What are you doin' in the enemy camp?" He leans over confidentially. "Find any evidence?"

"Not yet. Listen, you busy tonight?"

"Me? It's atrophied, babe. It's fallen off. It's lying in the parking lot across the street. You know that speed bump? That's it." He laughs.

"Artie, you'll be okay. You'll fall in love again."

"I'm not talkin' about love, Grace. I'm over love. I'm talking about jungle fuckin'."

I pretend not to be shocked, it dates me. Besides, I have something to accomplish. I need to talk to Winn, face-to-grimy-face. "Listen, since you're free, how about you come to my house for dinner tonight? You can even bring your sidekick."

"She broke up with me. Had a crush on my friend, what can I say? I had her body, not her heart." He shakes his head. "Can you believe I loved her for her *mind? Me?* It's gorky."

"You're growing up. Anyway, I meant Shake and Bake."

"The Shakester. The Shakemeister. Shake-o-rama," he says, singsong again. "Real smelly. Schizophrenic."

"Wash him up first, okay? So he doesn't terrify Maddie. Or Bernice."

"The Madster. Little cutie. In the first grade."

"Artie, stop."

He comes back to reality and hits the button. "You really want me to bring Shake and Bake?"

"I thought it would be nice. Do my part, sort of." White lie number 7364.

"Is your kid ready to meet the oogie-boogie man?"

"I married the oogie-boogie man, pal."

He smiles. "What are you makin' for dinner?"

"What do you care? I can beat Frosted Flakes."

"Hey, last night I had Cocoa Krispies, from the Variety Pak. You know those little boxes?"

"Maddie likes those, too. So come to dinner. You can have Lucky Charms for dessert."

"You want to make me a good-bye dinner?"

"Good-bye? I didn't say that." I feel a pang: too many good-byes lately.

"Yes, ma'am. I'm outta here. Headin' for the junk blondes in NYC. I picked out a crib this weekend." He doesn't look so happy about it. "This is the lease."

"So when do you go?"

"Next week. Cravath's taking me early."

"You're in the army now."

"Tell me about it." He looks at his lease with contempt. "You have to be a lawyer to understand this friggin' thing."

"You *are* a lawyer, Artie. Starting next week, people will pay a hundred and fifty bucks an hour for your time." I think of the basketball on his chest.

"Suckers." He laughs. "So will you look this over for me?" He holds up the lease, a standard form.

"The landlord always wins. That's all you have to know."

"That's just what Safer said." He shakes his head. "What a dick. He's in there, sittin' by the phone."

"Why?"

"Waiting for that call from Scalia."

"They call?"

"Except for Rehnquist. He got turned down once, so he makes his secretary call."

I think of the letter I saw on Galanter's desk. "Think he'll get it?"

"The 8 Ball says yes. Isn't that so lame?"

"It's a toy, Artie, remember?"

He looks at me, dead serious all of a sudden. "It's always right, Grace."

I almost laugh: $150 an hour. Don't say I didn't warn you.

Later, after work, we drive to my house together. Artie sits in the front seat and Winn sulks in the back, in an apparent psychotic funk because Artie made him take off his rain bonnet. When we reach the expressway, Artie turns to the news station for the basketball scores, but Winn wants the Greaseman, another misogynist with a microphone. He reaches between the seats and presses the black button for the Greaseman's station.

"On!" he says. "We want the Greaseman."

Artie punches the KYW button. "No Greaseman. Greaseman sucks."

"Greaseman. Greaseman!"

"Be good, Shakie," Artie says.

The news comes on as we sit stalled in the bottleneck going west. The expressway narrows to a single lane at the Art Museum, even though it's easily the most heavily traveled route west out of Philly. A row of red taillights stretches out in front of me all the way to Harrisburg. "Why would they design a road like this? It makes no sense."

Artie looks out over the Schuylkill, the wide river that runs alongside the expressway. Its east bank is home to a lineup of freshly painted boathouses; the white lights trimming them glow faintly. Single rowers scull down the river and disappear into the sun, now fading into a dull bronze. Here and there an eight picks up the pace, with a skiff running alongside it and a coach shouting through an old-fashioned tin megaphone. "I'll miss this shitburg," Artie says.

"It's not a shitburg."

"How do you know? You never lived anywhere else."

"Why would I want to?"

"KYW . . . news radio . . . ten sixty," Winn sings, in unison with the radio jingle. "All news all the time. All news all the time."

Artie turns up the volume. "Go Knicks."

"Go Sixers," I say, and catch Winn sticking his tongue out at me in the rearview mirror. His face changes as soon as we hear the first news story.

"A Caucasian male," the announcer says, "found murdered in the early morning hours, has been identified as Sandy Faber, a reporter who worked for several Delaware Valley newspapers. The Mount Laurel, New Jersey, man was beaten to death after he used an automated teller machine in Society Hill. Police have no suspects, though they believe robbery was the motive."

My God. I find myself gripping the steering wheel to keep my wits. Faber, killed. And McLean in Galanter's office last night, taking his phone message. I look at Winn in the rearview mirror, but he's still in character.

"Bye-bye Greaseman," he says sadly. "All gone."

TWENTY-SEVEN

I tell Winn the story while I pop chicken with rosemary into the oven and check on Maddie, who's in the backyard shooting hoops with Artie. Artie's hogging the ball again, so I knock on the window. He coughs it up with reluctance while I start to scrub some new potatoes, then drop them into hot water and finish the story.

"Back up a minute, Grace. What were you doing in Galanter's office?" Winn says, pacing in front of the counter. His ratty clothes are clean so he looks merely poverty-stricken, more like a grad student. "It could've been you that was murdered last night, not Faber."

"He was after Faber, not me. He knew just what he was looking for. I bet Faber was getting closer to Armen's killer. I wonder if McLean was working with Galanter somehow."

"You shouldn't have been there."

"Do you think he was working with Galanter or not?"

"You're not a professional. You have no training." He paces back and forth in the cramped kitchen; Bernice watches him, swinging her massive head left, then right.

"But if McLean were working with Galanter, why would he

have to steal the phone message? Galanter would just give it to him, wouldn't he? Unless they thought of it later, after hours."

"Grace—"

"But Galanter could've called Faber at the paper, using a general number." I look out the window, thinking. Maddie is shooting foul shots, none of which reach halfway to the basket; Artie, retrieving the balls, is learning to take turns. "No. Faber wasn't a staffer. He was a stringer, he works on his own. So he couldn't be reached at the paper. But why didn't they call him at home, look him up in the phone book?"

"Grace, you're not listening." Winn stops pacing and folds his arms. Bernice rests her head on her front paws.

"Neither are you."

"Yes, I am. Faber wouldn't be in the Philly phone book because he lived in Jersey. They said it on the radio."

"There you go! So maybe Galanter did have something to do with Armen's death, he wanted to be chief judge so bad. Or maybe McLean was working alone."

"Grace, you have to slow down." He rakes a hand through his hair; it looks a lighter brown now that it's been washed. "I told you not to go prowling around at night. First Armen's apartment, now Galanter's office."

"I work there now. It's my office, too."

"No, it isn't."

I open the oven door and check on the chicken. Bernice sniffs the air with interest. "I thought I did pretty good. I even figured out the Mob connection."

"That was my end of the deal, not yours. You could have called me. I would have explained it to you."

"I couldn't have read the *Canavan* record in the daytime. What did you expect me to do?"

"I told you to keep your eyes and ears open at work. That's all I wanted. I didn't think you were going to turn into Wyatt Earp."

"Nancy Drew. My role model, not yours."

He frowns deeply. "Look, the phone log was okay, the breaking and entering was not. Got it?"

"What are we fighting about? We just caught the bad guy. Let's call the police."

He throws his hands up in the air. "Grace, I don't want you in any deeper. How you gonna explain what you were doing in Galanter's office? I don't want you identified."

"All right, then you report it. Call your boss."

"My boss, why? We think McLean may have murdered a reporter at a money machine. It doesn't have anything to do with the DOJ investigation. Murder's not even a federal crime."

I sit down on the stool next to Bernice, curled up in her new sixty-dollar dog bed. The aroma of rosemary chicken fills the room, but it doesn't suffuse me with the homey feeling it usually does. "I have an idea. How about you report it to the Philadelphia police and I'll be your confidential informant? I tell you what I know, you get an arrest warrant for McLean. Just keep me confidential."

"You, an informant?"

"Why not?"

"Confidential informants are slime."

"You don't know what I'm capable of. I knocked over a picture of poodles today—on purpose."

He smiles. "Life on the edge."

"It'll be enough for probable cause for Faber's death. It's a start."

He rubs his beard thoughtfully. "We could take it a step at a time. *I* could take it a step at a time."

"Do we have enough for a wiretap? It's the same standard, isn't it?"

"Down, girl. Wiretap of who? McLean, maybe, but not Galanter. All we have on him is a marshal going into his office, which is what he's supposed to do."

"But he took a message."

"That doesn't prove anything about Galanter, even assuming McLean fesses up. Trap-and-trace procedures are strict, Grace, you know that. It's not like on TV, with phone taps installed as soon as you suspect somebody. Remember the Fourth Amendment?"

I pull a pad out of the junk drawer. On the top it says DENNIS KULL—YOUR REALTOR IN MONTGOMERY COUNTY. "Let's start already. Take a letter, Maria."

"What?"

"Take a statement from me, okay? Let's get to work before the kids come back in."

He takes the pad grudgingly and begins to write.

"Wait, I didn't dictate yet."

"Oh, you didn't, huh? Well I'm dictating, not you. Sign this." He tears off a piece of paper and slides it along the counter to me. At the top it says CONTRACT. Underneath that it says, I PROMISE NOT TO GO ON ANY MORE SECRET MISSIONS OR WINN CAN TAKE ME TO THE PARTY OF THE FIRST PART.

I smile.

"Sign," he says, handing me the pencil. "I'm not interested in losing my most confidential informant."

"It's not a valid contract. There's no consideration."

"Ha! You'd take money from a homeless man?"

"It doesn't have to be money, it could be anything of value. Not that you have anything of value either."

He reaches into his pocket and offers me his battered photo of Tom Cruise. "My most prized possession. Now sign."

"You're kidding."

"Nope."

"If I sign your statement, will you sign mine?"

"Yes."

So I sign. It's not enforceable anyway.

The kitchen fills up with the homey smell of fresh-baked rosemary chicken.

*   *   *

Winn's phone call comes at the worst time, when I'm rushing like a madwoman to get Maddie to school. I leave her at the front door holding her Catwoman lunch box, run back to the kitchen, and struggle over the gate penning Bernice in the kitchen.

"They arrested McLean this morning," he says.

I feel a thrill of excitement. "They got the bad guy! All right!" Even Bernice wags her tail.

"Your identity remains a secret. Even from my boss, the president."

I'm juiced up, like I just won a jury trial. "So tell me what happened."

"Mom, we have to go," Maddie calls from the door. I've been pushing her all morning, and now she's going to push back.

"Tell me fast," I say to Winn.

"They picked him up at home, no muss, no fuss. He denies taking the message. He's mad as hell."

"You saw him?"

"Through the two-way mirror. The man has a temper and a history of some pretty rough street fights."

"I'm not surprised. He doesn't deny being in the office, does he?"

"Mom," Maddie says, coming into the dining room, far enough from Bernice to feel safe. "We have to go."

I hold up my index finger, the universal sign for please-let-Mommy-talk-on-the-phone. Bernice sticks her head over the gate, begging for Maddie's attention.

"He admits to being in Galanter's office," Winn says, "but he claims he was just checking. He was on duty that night. Said he heard a noise."

"I take offense. I didn't make any noise."

"I know, master burglar. He has no good alibi for the time Faber was killed. Says he was off by himself, fishing."

"In Philadelphia?"

"On the Schuylkill."

I laugh. "Real believable."

"Right. The boats fuckin' dissolve, the fish don't stand a chance."

Maddie says, "Mom, I'll be late. I don't have a note."

I check my watch. She's right. "Wait a minute, Winn. When does he say he was fishing?"

"At dawn, the same time Faber was killed."

"Also the same time Armen was killed."

"That doesn't mean anything."

"What's the connection to Armen? Did they find out anything?"

"No."

My heart sinks. "But then why would McLean kill Faber? I thought it was because he was investigating Armen's death. Getting closer."

"Wrong motive, and I'm not sure Galanter had anything to do with it either. We may be back at square one."

"What?" It comes out like a moan.

"McLean had it in for Faber. Turns out they had a couple of run-ins last week, with all the press coverage of *Hightower*. Faber stepped over the line trying to get a story and it pissed McLean off. He's an ex-cop, you know. They all are."

I remember McLean taking off after Faber at the memorial service.

"Last month, McLean caught Faber bothering the U.S. Attorney and roughed him up. Faber reported him for it and they were considering discipline. McLean was about to lose his job."

"Jesus." I think of the reporter, beaten to death, and reality sinks in. Catching McLean doesn't bring Faber back or erase the violent way he died. And Armen is still a question mark.

"Mom, she's staring," Maddie says, watching Bernice anxiously. "Is she gonna bite me?"

I scratch Bernice's head. "No, honey, she loves you."

"You love me?" Winn says. "I knew it. Tell me what it was that turned you on. Was it my body odor? The tartar on my gums? My tattoo?"

I laugh. "Basketball tattoos don't do it for me, pal."

"It's not a basketball. You don't know what it is."

Maddie narrows her eyes. "Is that your boyfriend, Mom?"

I silence her with a glare. "I gotta go, Winn. I have to take Maddie to school."

"But we love each other!"

Maddie dances around, singing, "Mommy has a boyfriend, Mommy has a boyfriend." Bernice watches her, wagging her tail harder.

"Is that Maddie?" Winn asks. "What'd she say?"

"Nothing."

"She likes me, you know. She told me after dinner."

I hold the phone close to my chin and wave to Maddie to stop, but she doesn't. Who raised this child? "I have to go, Winn. We're late."

"All right, but stay out of trouble. Call if you have to, cuz."

"Fine."

"No more funny stuff, remember our contract. Things are heating up. Anything can happen. If McLean didn't kill Armen, whoever did is still out there."

Maddie skips around the dining room table. "Mommy has a boyfriend, Mommy has a boyfriend." As soon as I hang up, the child says, giggling, "I'm telling Daddy."

"The hell you are," I say, and chase her around the table.

TWENTY-EIGHT

Wednesday is my alleged day off, but I decide to go in until Maddie gets out of school. I drop her off, still the only mother who walks her child all the way into line, and drive into town.

I rack my brain about McLean and Armen the whole way in; somehow the two must be connected. Al McLean was a cop, Winn said. Where do a cop and a judge meet up?

In court.

Cops are in court all the time as witnesses. Maybe Armen let a defendant go free on appeal, somebody that McLean had testified against in the trial court. It's just a hunch, but it's not a bad one. I hit the courthouse with my brain churning.

The marshals look grim at their stations behind the security desk and at the X-ray machine. They have to know about McLean's arrest. Ray is nowhere in sight, only Jeff. He barely nods as I walk through the detector. I head upstairs alone and unlock the door to my office. I want to do some research on Lexis before going into chambers.

The joke is on me.

I open the door to my office and it isn't there anymore.

The bookshelves, previously full of duplicate case reports and green pebbled volumes of Pennsylvania statutes, are empty. Dismantled overnight. The rug has been torn up, exposing a cement floor covered with yellowed streaks of sticky gum. All the furniture is gone; only my desk and computer remain, not counting the view.

I'm gutting your office, Galanter said. He even paid overtime. He must really like me.

I step through the tacky goop, my pumps sticking at the soles, until I reach my desk. I sit with my feet stuck straight out until I find a legal pad to rest them on. At least my papers and computer are still there. I log on to Lexis and the modem sings to me. A glittering double helix comes on, the logo of the legal research company. Don't ask me why.

WELCOME TO LEXIS! says the screen. Machines greet us everywhere in the modern workplace; it's the people we can't find. PLEASE TYPE IN YOUR SEVEN-DIGIT IDENTIFICATION NUMBER.

I watch the polite sentence disappear. Ben, computer maven, has rigged it so we don't have to log on each time. The only downside is you have to erase the last user's research.

YOUR LAST SEARCH REQUEST WAS FREE SPEECH AND ARTNETT. DO YOU WANT TO CONTINUE WORKING ON IT? Y OR N?

Probably Sarah's. I press N, then punch in GENFED, then 3CIR, to retrieve only cases in the Third Circuit.

The screen says, READY FOR YOUR SEARCH REQUEST.

"Give me a minute, whiz," I tell it. I'm not as speedy on this program as I should be; Lexis was born about the same time Maddie was, and my refresher training's no match for a 486 chip. I squeeze my eyes shut and think. Assume Armen decided a case when McLean was a cop, and McLean was a witness of some kind. That means I need cases that will contain both names. I open my eyes and type in AL MCLEAN AND WRITTENBY (GREGORIAN).

In a nanosecond the screen says, YOUR REQUEST HAS FOUND NO CASES.

Shit. So there's two possibilities: a dry hole or a lousy drill. Guess which is likelier. I double-check the search request. Wrong. Al's name is probably Albert, or Alan. If he testified in court he would use the more formal name. I type in AL! MCLEAN AND WRITTENBY (GREGORIAN). It should retrieve all incarnations of Al imaginable. I sit back, proud of myself.

Not for long. YOUR REQUEST HAS FOUND NO CASES.

Damn it! I sigh at the computer. It's in there somewhere, I feel it. Every judge has enemies; they make at least one with each case. In desperation, I type in MCLEAN AND WRITTENBY (GREGORIAN).

The computer says, YOUR REQUEST HAS FOUND ONE CASE.

"Yes!" One case is all I need. Excited, I squint at the template above the keys and hit .fd, which is computer for gimme gimme gimme!

Clermont v. Brewster comes up. An old case, 1983. Armen was on the panel and wrote the opinion. But it's not a criminal matter. I don't understand.

I type in .fu, which stands for full case and not what it usually stands for.

The case comes up in full. I type .np to get to the next page, then the next, deflating slightly with each new screen of white-on-blue text. There's no police testimony in it at all; it's a medical malpractice case. A woman, Elaine Brewster, sued a doctor for not diagnosing her skin cancer early enough to save her life. A jury awarded her a whopping $15 million. On appeal, the Third Circuit reversed. Armen, writing for the panel, found the evidence of the doctor's negligence was insufficient to go to a jury, a sympathy vote but legally indefensible.

I hit .np and the next page pops onto the screen.

Then I see it. Highlighted in bright yellow by the computer. Mr. McLean.

A man who testified in the trial court about the plaintiff's pain and suffering, but not in his capacity as a cop. He testified that the plaintiff had been a beautiful woman, spunky enough to keep her own name after marriage. Elaine Clermont. The disease reduced her to an invalid, her skin blackened and eaten away.

The woman was his wife.

McLean lost his wife to cancer and he lost $15 million to Armen. That's it.

I ease back into my chair, staring at the screen. I should be happy, but I'm not. Too much pain, too much death. I imagine McLean going to Armen's to kill him. Bernice would have known McLean from the courthouse. So would Armen; he would have let him in without question. But Armen wouldn't have remembered McLean from a ten-year-old case. He never saw McLean testify in the first place; the appellate court bases its decisions on a record. Armen would have assumed McLean was his protector. He would have assumed wrong.

But why would McLean wait ten years to get Armen? I don't know the answer, but I intend to find out.

My hand is shaking as I pick up the phone to call Winn. It's not hard to convince the young girl who answers the phone that I'm Winn's cousin, I sound pretty depressed. I tell Winn the story and after he gets over the initial surprise, his tone turns cautious. "How do we know it's the same McLean?" he says.

"What do you mean?"

"You said the computer searches the name exactly, right?"

"Right."

"So how do we know it's the same man?"

"How many Mr. McLeans can there be who had a case before Armen?"

"Maybe one, but that's not the point. The question is, can we charge this McLean just because a guy with the same name had a motive to kill Armen?"

"But it's *him*."

"McLean is a common name."

"Not really." It sounds feeble, even to me. I went to high school with one.

"Does it at least say he was a cop?"

I scroll through the case. "No. It identifies him as the husband, that's all. He's only mentioned in the opinion for a paragraph."

"Does it say his age?"

"No. But the wife was thirty at the time. That would be about right."

"Only if you assume she married a man about her age, but an assumption's not enough to charge a man with murder. The whole thing could be a coincidence. After all, why would McLean wait ten years to kill him? Can't we verify it somehow, get the actual record instead of just the opinion?"

Of course. I should have thought of that. "The record will have the trial transcripts, all his testimony. Address, work history, the whole thing."

"Where's the record now?"

"The case was from the Eastern District of Pennsylvania, so the record would be downstairs in the district court file room. It's in this building, unless it's archived."

"Can you get it? I mean without your standard B and E."

I smile. "We order district court records all the time. We call on the phone, they deliver them to chambers."

"When will you have it?"

"In four hours."

"Four *hours?* I thought you said the file room was downstairs."

"This is the federal government. They have to fill out forms and type up receipts. If I went downstairs and got it myself, I'd have the answer in fifteen minutes."

"Do it the normal way. I want everything by the book."

"It's not a Miranda warning, Winn."

"McLean's already in custody, what's the difference? It's more important that it be done right."

"I'd do it right. It's perfectly safe. Let me get the file."

"Grace," he says, "I want no suggestion that you tampered with the records. I want the chain of custody to be clear. Order the record, please. Keep the reason to yourself. Don't go running in and telling everybody you caught Armen's killer."

"Come on."

"You come on. Now order the record and call me when it comes in."

"Mighty pushy for a Quaker."

"You love me anyway."

"Bullshit."

"And one other thing. There's a loose end."

"What?"

"It doesn't explain Armen's bank account. Or *Canavan*."

"Do I have to do everything for you?" I say to him before I hang up.

Then I look at the phone, thinking. He's right. It doesn't explain the money, but that was *his* investigation. My investigation is just about over.

We celebrate Ben's big news at a picnic lunch on the grassy mall between the Liberty Bell and Independence Hall, just catty-corner to the courthouse. Ben got the call from Justice Scalia this morning and was so delirious he even became likeable, helping all of us box the last of the case files. For a time it was like when Armen was alive and we all worked together, despite the clerks' bickering. My spirits were high, fueled by my certainty that the record would prove me right about McLean. I felt so good I sprung for hoagies all around.

"They call this a sub in New York," Artie says, inspecting his sandwich with a frown.

"What do they know? We invented it," I say, wiggling my toes in the grass. Behind my digits is Independence Hall, the most beautiful building in the world, in its own subtle way. Its muted red bricks have a patina that only two hundred years can bring, and its mullioned panes of glass are bumpy; perfectly imperfect even from here. A long line of schoolchildren piles two by two out of Congress Hall, the right wing of the building, where Congress used to meet.

"Look around you, Artie. This is a real city, a city where people can live. It's beautiful, and there's history everywhere."

"Except for that," Sarah says flatly, her long granny skirt spread out on the grass. She points over Ben's shoulder at the new housing for the Liberty Bell, a structure of sleek concrete with corners that stab out onto the cloudless sky. "I hate that building. They call it a pavilion, but it looks like a Stealth bomber."

"Something the matter with Stealth bombers?" Ben says, smiling.

Eletha picks a paper-thin onion out of her hoagie, her nails working like pincers. "It's not that bad, Sarah. It's just new." She drops the onion onto a pile of its brethren.

"That's the problem." Sarah raises her voice to be heard over the tourist buses gunning their engines next to the pavilion. "It should be compatible with the surrounding architecture and it's not."

"I agree, they should've left the bell where it was. It belongs in Independence Hall." I remember how angry I was when they moved the Liberty Bell from Independence Hall. Now Independence Hall has to face its bell's new home; it's like sitting across the table from your ex's trophy wife. For eternity.

"You mean they didn't consult you?" Artie says. "You, Miss Philadelphia?"

"Isn't it terrible? I don't know why they think they can run this city on their own." I tear into my cheese hoagie.

"So Ben," Eletha says, "the clerkship begins in September?"

He nods and sips his coffee.

"What'll you do till then?"

"I'm working on an article."

"What about?" she asks, fishing out another onion.

"The European Convention on Human Rights."

"Human rights? You?" Sarah says, bursting into tactless laughter.

Ben smiles easily; not even Sarah can bother him today. "I've been doing some thinking on the subject."

"*You?*" she says, still laughing.

"Real nice, Sar," I say. "What are *you* going to do next? And you better say join the Peace Corps."

"How about joining Susan's staff? Is that good enough?"

"Not since she got my name wrong," Ben says, and Eletha laughs.

"Is she still in Bosnia, finding facts?" I ask.

Sarah nods, and I hope she forgets that I accused the woman of murder. Nancy Drew, my ass. She had a roadster, not a station wagon.

"So Artie," Eletha says, "are you all ready for Wall Street? You pack your toys?"

Artie looks down at his hoagie. He seems out of sorts today, quiet. "Guess so. Off to peddle my soul."

"For how much?" Eletha asks.

"You don't want to know, girlfriend."

"Yes I do. Hit me with it."

"Just shy of one hundred large."

Eletha almost gags. "You're kiddin' me!"

"Not including the endorsements. Justice. Just do it."

"Justice?" I say. "On Wall Street?"

"*Isjdjr! Keidnbu!*" shouts a young man with flyaway blond hair, who troops with a park ranger onto the lawn behind Ben. Suddenly, a group of tourists is thronging around the man and the ranger, a bobbing mass of blond heads. "*Keird ishdsn!*"

"What the fuck is this?" Artie says. "Our neighbors to the north?"

"I would like to propose a toast," I say, ignoring the interruption. I hoist my Diet Coke in the air. "To all of us, even Ben. And to justice." I'm thinking of McLean, behind bars.

"Perfect!" Sarah says. "To all of us, even Ben. And to justice!" She hoists her Evian bottle to Eletha's paper cup.

"To all of us, even Ben," Eletha says. "And to justice, and happiness."

Artie raises his bottle of Yoo-Hoo. "There is no justice or happiness. To all of us, even Ben, and to Patrick Ewing."

"*Kirs eushjk!*" shouts the young man. He points to the Liberty Bell, visible through the pavilion's glass wall. Crudely embossed letters at its top say ALL THE LAND AND UNTO ALL THE until the sentence disappears around the cast-iron curve. Tourists encircle the bell, but a park ranger will prevent them from touching the rough-hewn letters. I touched the letters once, when the ranger wasn't looking; they felt cool and ragged.

"Thank you, all of you," Ben says. "It's very nice. You're all very . . . kind."

Artie bursts into laughter. "Don't choke up or nothin', dude. It's not like we meant it."

"Artie, be nice," I say. "Good things happened today for a change." I think of my successful Lexis search. Wait until they find out Armen was murdered. Will it make it worse or better? Which way does it make me feel?

"God knows, we needed it," Eletha says, taking a slug of her iced tea.

"Welcome to Philadelphia, ladies and gentlemen," the park ranger booms, then launches into his spiel with official enthusiasm. The tourists frown up at him almost instantly. Either the sun is bright or they don't understand English with a Philadelphia accent. My guess is they've seen the sun before.

"I have some good news of my own," Eletha continues, shouting to be heard. She sets down her cup in the grass and inhales deeply. "I'm a free woman, as of today. I broke up with Leon."

"Really?" I say. I was wondering what she meant about happiness.

"I told him this morning, no more shit. Life is too short to take shit from any man."

"Good for you!" Sarah says, drawing a sharp look from Artie. There's an awkward silence, and I think of my promise to Ray.

"Don't hang it up too fast, Eletha," I say. "Have I got a man for you."

"So have I," Ben says, leaning over. "Chief Judge Galanter is single."

Eletha laughs. "That'll be the day! Shoot me before I get to that point. Shoot me, child!"

I think of Armen and stop laughing slowly. The others don't seem to notice.

Sarah says, "No, Eletha, you got it backwards. Shoot *him*."

They all roar with laughter, even Ben. I force a smile. What does it feel like to be shot? What is the last thing Armen felt? Did McLean hold the gun to Armen's temple? Force him into the chair? I look away to where the park ranger is addressing the tourists and tune him in.

"There were no bell foundries in the colonies at that time period," the ranger says, "so rather than send it back, these resourceful colonists, who had previously made only pots, pans, and candlestick holders—"

"Grace?" Artie says. "You with us?"

I push it out of my mind. We got him now. That's justice, even if it doesn't bring Armen back. "Sure."

"Who's bachelor number one?" Eletha asks.

"What?"

"Who did you want to fix me up with?"

"Oh. One of the marshals."

Eletha shudders. "One of the marshals? Forget it!"

"Back in the saddle, Miss Thing," Artie says. "I love a man in uniform."

"What's the matter with a marshal?" Sarah says.

Eletha leans forward. "You know what I heard? One of the marshals was arrested this morning. For the murder of that reporter."

Sarah pales. "You mean the stringer? The one who was calling us?"

"What?" Ben says, setting his hoagie down in its shell of waxy paper. I concentrate on the grease spots soaking the paper from the inside and try to look as shocked as he does.

"That's unbelievable," Artie says, between mouthfuls of corned beef. "Which marshal?"

"Al McLean, the big one."

"How did you hear this?" I ask her.

"Millie, from the clerk's office. So no marshals, honey. Not for me. No way."

"But it's Ray Arrington. He's a teddy bear."

"Ray? A *what*?" Artie says, chomping away. "Gimme a break! You ever see him on a basketball court? The man is a maniac. He almost knocked Shake and Bake out."

"Ray?"

"The Shakester had a bruise all down his side."

"Poor schizophrenic," Ben says. He stows his empty coffee cup in his hoagie wrapper and rolls them up together. "We should get back to the office. It's been over an hour."

Eletha and Sarah look at each other and laugh. "What are they gonna do, fire us?" Eletha says.

"I want to work on my article."

But Sarah doesn't hear him. "We're free. We have no work, no job, no office." Her face falls suddenly. And no boss, is the thing we're all thinking, but nobody says it. Artie wraps up the remains of his lunch in silence and Eletha watches him, her eyes unfocused. I feel a lump in my throat and raise my can in a silent toast.

"I agree," Sarah says softly, and touches her drink to mine.

Eletha raises hers, too. Only Artie doesn't say anything. I can't catch his eye.

Ben clears his throat. "We'd better go back. Grace still has a job, you know."

"Don't remind me." I've indentured myself for nothing, unless I want to help Winn's bribery investigation. "Anyway, today I'm off duty."

"So why'd you come in?" Sarah asks. She gets up, then helps me up.

"I don't know. We don't have much more time together. I thought I'd say good-bye." It comes out of its own force; and even though it's not the reason I came in, I realize how true it is. The lump comes back.

"Awww," Sarah says, and to my surprise gives me a warm hug, which Eletha joins.

"Group hug!" Artie says, rallying. He wraps his long arms around Eletha and presses us all together. I'm somewhere in the middle, trying to swallow the damn lump.

"Come on in, Mr. Human Rights," Sarah calls out.

"I'll pass," Ben says, but I hear the smile in his voice.

"*Isjdhyk mejsgr!*" shouts the young man. "*Kkkrk!*"

TWENTY-NINE

I sit at my desk with the form letter in my hand, reading it to Winn:

> *We have been unable to locate the record in this matter in our archives or file room. This is not out of the ordinary with older case files and we will continue our efforts to locate it. We regret any inconvenience this may have caused you.*

"You know McLean took it, don't you?" I say.

"Possibly."

"Possibly?"

"The government never loses anything?"

"A court record? Not often."

"Ever?"

"Not often."

Winn is silent.

"Charge him anyway, Winn. The lawsuit existed. His wife existed. He can't hide the facts, even if he can steal the record."

"Fuck. This slows us up."

"How? Ask him about it. Say to him, Did your wife die of skin cancer? Did she sue the doctor? Was the fifteen-million-dollar award taken away by Judge Gregorian?"

"He's not answering questions, Grace. He's got a lawyer already."

Shit. Of course. Shoot the lawyer twice. It stumps me for a minute.

"You say we don't need the record, but if the record doesn't matter, why would McLean steal it?"

"Because he's stupid. Because he didn't count on anybody doing legal research on him."

"How would he steal it? Would he be able to?"

"Sure. The marshals have master keys, that's how he got in Galanter's office. The files are kept in number order by year. Even an idiot can find a record."

"Fuck!"

"Let me be the confidential informant again. I'll make another statement. Describe everything that happened in Armen's office, the way McLean acted to me at the metal detector, even my research and the clerk's letter. It's enough to charge him, isn't it?"

"It's a close question."

"Winn, he killed Armen because of the court case, then he killed Faber because he was close to finding out. A verdict that big would make the papers. Faber probably did his homework and found out about the wife's case. Hell, he could find it easily on Nexis. I could do it myself, right now. Faber was calling our chambers all day."

"Relax, Grace."

"Charge him. It's enough. I'm a lawyer, I know. Are you gonna let him get away with murder?"

"It's close. I don't want to go in half cocked."

Man talk. "You got another idea?"

"Yes. Is there any other place records would be?"

The thought strikes like a thunderbolt. "The appendix! The

appendix is a duplicate of the record. For a trial with that much money at stake, I bet it's complete."

"Where would the appendix be?"

"Every judge on the panel would have gotten one, including Armen. It's an old case but Eletha would know if we have it." My brain clicks ahead. I didn't see the older cases in the boxes we packed this morning, but Eletha could have packed them earlier. "She said Armen saved everything. We just finished packing this morning."

"Go get 'em, tiger."

"It's about a million boxes."

"Dig we must."

Easy for him to say. He doesn't have to deal with Eletha's reaction when I tell her what I'm going to do.

"You want to do what?" Eletha shrieks at me, astounded. She stands protectively in front of the boxes that stack almost to the ceiling in Armen's office.

"Shhh!" I look toward the clerks' office, even though the door is closed. "You can go home. I'll do it. I already called my mother to pick up Maddie at school."

"Are you out of your goddamn mind?" Long fingers clasp at her chest and she breathes deeply, in and out.

"Eletha, don't do the Lamaze thing, not for me. You can go."

"You want to rip open all my boxes? We just finished!"

"I'll put everything back."

She shakes her head. "No. I won't let you do it. No way. No file is important enough to ruin all that work."

I wish I could tell her why, but Winn made me swear. "I'll redo it."

"Galanter wants this stuff out of here! I told him we'd be done tomorrow, you know that. That's why I worked my ass off all morning! All *week!*"

"I know, but I need it."

"What for?"

"A misconduct case."

"What misconduct case is ten years old? Don't bullshit me, Grace. We're friends."

I take her by the shoulders. "Listen, trust me. I can't tell you anything more."

"Why not?"

"Eletha, it's the most important file in the world."

"No file—"

"This one is."

"Are you outta your mind?" Her dark eyes watch me with hope.

"No."

"But I got class tonight, and Leon sure ain't gonna sit anymore."

"That's all right. I have to do it myself."

"Galanter wants in—tomorrow. It'll take you all *night*."

I remember the last time I was here in this office until dawn. "That's okay."

I look around at the boxes and so does she. It's daunting, like moving an entire house in only one night. Twice. I wonder if I'll be able to get it done in time. If I can't, screw Galanter. He may not be a killer, but he's still a jerk.

"I know what you're thinkin'," Eletha says to me, wagging a finger. "It's gotta be done by morning. GSA is comin' in to take up the rug."

"All right, all right."

"You want me to come back after class? It's over at ten."

"Nope. You got Malcolm."

"I'll bring him. He can sleep on the couch."

"No, thanks."

"Suit yourself." She shakes her head, mystified. "Start with those boxes against the wall." She gestures to about forty-five boxes, taped closed and stacked up like children's blocks. "Those are the case files. Everything over there"—she points against the back wall behind Armen's desk—"is old stuff, papers, and some older files. There could be some older case files in there, too."

"Okay." I eyeball the boxes in the back. Thirty, easy. Christ. I remember when I left Sam: all my stuff and Maddie's in a storage bin, and it still wasn't that high. "No problem."

She points at the conference table and the chair against the window, both of which are heaped with brown paper packages. "That's all the Armenian stuff. I put bubble paper underneath that brown paper, you know. You won't be needin' any of it, so don't unwrap it."

"I won't." Each package is labeled in black Magic Marker, some cryptically. STATUE. ANOTHER STATUE. PRAYER RUG. FRAMED THING. BIG THING. I laugh at BIG THING, lying horizontally across the chair near the window. "What's that one?"

She wrinkles her nose. "You know, that big thing?"

"No, I don't, El. I have no idea."

"You do too. That wood thingie he had hangin' up, like a baseball bat."

Now I remember. The cudgel. "Oh, yeah. That big thing."

"Right. It weighs a ton. Leave it alone, all of it."

"I will. I promise. Hey, where's the Indian headdress?"

"Oh, that?" She grins. "I lost it."

"You what?"

"I can't remember where I put it, for the life of me. I guess it just got lost in the shuffle." She scratches her sleek head, then bursts into laughter.

"Eletha, what did you do?"

"It serves his ass right, doesn't it?"

I have to agree.

"Okay. I gotta go, but I'm gonna do one thing for you. Make you a pot of coffee."

"Deal," I say, and get to work.

I open box after box, digging into each with cheap government scissors. I go through the case files; each is a manila folder containing Armen's notes, a set of briefs, and an appendix. Unfortunately, they don't seem to be in chronological order, or in any order at all; I don't stop to read Armen's notes, even those not written in Armenian. I can't afford the time; I'm trying to nail his killer.

The afternoon wears into the evening and I go through cup after cup of coffee and box after box of files. Eletha pops her head in to say good-bye when she goes; then Artie, Sarah, and Ben, who's still carrying a briefcase. I tell them I lost some papers, and they all offer to help, even Ben.

I check my watch. Maddie's bedtime. I decide to call home, then Winn after that. I punch in the numbers to my house.

Maddie answers the phone, then proceeds to work me over. "But *why* do you have to stay, Mom?" she asks, her thin voice rising on the other end of the line.

"I told you, honey. Because it's an important case. I have to work on it."

"Why can't somebody else work on it? Why does it have to be *you*?"

"Because I'm the only one who can."

"Are you with your boyfriend?"

I laugh. "Of course not. I don't have a boyfriend, I'm working. Now tell me what you're gonna read with Grandma before you go to bed."

"I'm too sick to go to school tomorrow, Mom. Madeline feels sick too, her forehead's hot. She's *burning*."

I ease into the chair next to the conference table. "You'll be fine in the morning. You just need to sleep."

"But my head hurts. My neck is swollen."

"Honey, listen. We'll see in the morning, okay?" I tug a box over to the chair and cross my legs on top of it. "I'll check if you have a fever."

"You have to use the thing. The glass thing. Grandma says you can't tell with your hand, not really."

Thanks, Mom. "Maddie, I've never used a thermometer

with you and I've never been wrong. I can tell with my hand."

"No, you can't. It's not science."

I look out the window into the night. The orange lights are twinkling again, running in thin strips to the river, the way they were that night. I was sitting right here, but tonight is different from before. It's raining hard, a spring downpour, and Armen is gone. The streets below glisten darkly.

"Mom?"

"Tell you what. Remember last week, how you wanted to wear your party dress to school and I said no?"

"The purple one?"

"Yes. Well, I'll let you wear it tomorrow, just this one time, since it's a special occasion."

"What special occasion?"

I think of the case file; it's in here somewhere. "We'll make one up. Happy Thursday."

"You're silly."

"I am. I get it from you."

She giggles. "Mom, I have to go now. The commercial's over."

"What, are you watching TV? It's after nine o'clock!"

"It's Disney."

"Disney is still TV. What happened to reading?"

"Just Donald Duck, then we have to turn it off."

"All right, but after that it goes off. Now go get ready, you don't want to be too late to bed."

"Yes, I do," she says, hanging up.

I press down the hook and am about to try Winn when I see a dark form reflected in the window. Someone must be in the doorway behind me. I hang up and twist around in my seat.

The gun is the first thing I see.

I scramble to pick up the phone.

THIRTY

"Hang up, Grace," Ben says. He closes the door behind him and locks it from the inside. "Hang *up*."

The phone clatters uselessly onto the hook. "Ben?"

"Surprise! Did you find the file yet?"

"What? How—"

"Lexis. The computer saves the last search request, remember? I saw it after lunch when I logged back on. Nice search request, by the way. You're improving." He moves to the head of the conference table and points the gun at me.

I'm terrified. My mouth turns to cotton. No one is around. Eletha is at class. God knows where Winn is, or security. "How did you get that gun past the metal detector?"

"I took the judges' elevator." He smiles down at the gun, handling its heft with satisfaction. He looks strange, unhinged. "I bought this the other day. Isn't it nice?"

"What are you doing, Ben?"

"It's not what I'm doing. It's what you're doing." He slips a finger inside his jacket, pulls out a small piece of white paper, and holds it up. "Your suicide note. Sign it." He places the paper in front of a brown package that reads PHOTO OF A

MOUNTAIN. "Oops, I almost forgot." He puts a rollerball pen on top of the paper.

I don't touch the letter or the pen. I can't believe this is happening.

"Please sign, Grace. Make it easy on yourself."

My own suicide note. A fake suicide. Oh, no. "Did you kill Armen, Ben?"

"Yes."

I can barely catch my breath. I assumed wrong.

"I didn't plan to, if that's any consolation."

"But why?" It comes out like a whisper.

"Why did I kill him? What's the difference?"

"I want to know, to understand."

"I wanted that clerkship."

I stare at the paper. It's almost inconceivable. "You wanted a clerkship that bad? A *job*?"

"It's the Supreme Court of the United States, Grace. I've been preparing for it my entire adult life. I'll teach after that, then on to the appeals court. I intend to end up on the high court myself. I wasn't about to let *Hightower* stand in my way."

"It was Armen who stood in the way."

He flinches slightly. "Sacrifices had to be made."

Armen: a sacrifice for a young lawyer's ambition. "But you could've gotten the clerkship anyway."

"Why take a chance?"

I don't understand. I feel sick with fear and dread. "You got the clerkship, so why this? Why me?"

"It's your own fault. You were the one digging around. You dug up McLean, now there's a glitch. It's only a matter of time before he points the finger at me."

"Did McLean kill Faber?"

"The reporter? Yes, at my suggestion. Faber was too close to finding out."

Two men dead. I feel stunned. "Was McLean the one who hit me on the head?"

"No, that was me. Now open the letter and sign it. I want no question later that you wrote it."

I feel myself break out into a sweat. The lethal black eye of the gun barrel is almost at my head; I think of the gunpowder star the detective found on Armen. "What does it say?"

"That you hired McLean to kill the reporter. You see, Faber had found out that you had killed the chief."

I look up at him behind the large gun barrel. "Why would *I* kill Armen?"

"Sexual harassment is a terrible thing. He raped you that night in the office."

"He did no such thing!"

A smug smile inches across his lips. "I heard. You were very willing, McLean said."

"You—"

"Of course, McLean was all too happy to help you cover up the murder. He's been nursing his hate for a decade. He thinks the chief ruined his life, so it didn't take much convincing to get him on board. I bought him a few drinks and pointed him in the right direction." He levels the gun at me. "Sign, please."

I pick up the paper and unfold it. It's neatly typed, and the last line makes me sick inside:

I love my daughter very much.

I stare at the paper. *I love my daughter very much*. Maddie. She'll think I abandoned her. I know how that feels. I fight back the tears; I'd beg if it would do any good. "She needs me, Ben," I said hoarsely.

"You were the one who wouldn't let it lie."

I look at the note. The typed letters seem to swim before my eyes against a vast backdrop of brown packages. PRAYER RUG. STATUE. ANOTHER STATUE. Then I remember the label on one of the other packages. BIG THING.

The cudgel. It's on the chair by the window. Eletha called it a baseball bat. How will I reach it? I need time to think. Stall him.

"You have a problem, Ben. I don't have a gun like Armen did."

He laughs abruptly. "He wasn't very good with it, Grace. I had the letter opener, but he couldn't bring himself to shoot me. I grabbed his hand and pointed it at his own head. It was over in a minute."

Poor Armen. I imagine the scene with horror. I can't speak.

"Don't think too badly of me. I did give him a last chance to come out the right way in *Hightower*, even brought him a draft opinion. We discussed the case law for some time, even the policy issues. It was sort of a final appeal. For him, and for me."

He makes me sick, outraged. "How are you going to pull this off, Ben? You going to make me shoot myself, too? Your fingerprints are all over your gun."

"Oh, you won't use my new toy, Grace. You'll jump."

I feel my mouth fall open. My mind reels. "From where?"

"The window." He gestures with the gun barrel.

I wheel around toward the window, petrified at the thought. Then I glimpse the cudgel right near the window, on the chair. Armen said it was used to kill. Can I kill? "Ben, you don't mean this."

"Yes, I do."

My blood runs cold. "But the windows."

"I'll break them. They're just a single layer of glass, not even Thermopane. This building was built in the sixties."

"But the marshals will hear it."

"Not from inside. We're eighteen floors up. Even if someone sees it, they'll think it's the wind from the storm and phone GSA. They should be here by tomorrow morning." He cocks the trigger on the gun and it clicks smoothly into operation. "Sign the paper. Now."

He's thought of everything. I feel a stab of stone cold fear, then will myself to stay calm. Remember Maddie. Use the cudgel. It destroyed families, now it will protect one. "I'll sign it," I tell him, "but ease off the trigger. You want them to find me shot?"

"Now you're thinking." He relaxes on the trigger and I pick up the pen. My hand is trembling as I read the letter one last time. What if I can't get to the cudgel. What if I blow it? "Hurry, Grace."

I scribble my name, then lift the pen from the paper. Just in case, underneath I write, *I love you, Mads. You are the best.* I blink back the tears that seem to come.

"Get up," Ben says. "Stand near the window."

Good, you bastard. That's just where I want to be. My whole body shivers. Get a grip. I'm not within arm's length from the cudgel, not yet. It's too close to the window.

Still aiming the gun at me, Ben crosses the room. He picks up a chair and swings it into the wall of windows. The huge panel shatters instantly into brittle shards; cracks race all over the pane like nerve endings, electrified. Breathing like a madman, Ben hurls the chair into the cracked window again, at full speed. It bounces off with a crashing sound. The glass explodes into a million pieces. Slivers fly in all directions. The window collapses and falls away, hurtling down the side of the courthouse, leaving a jagged opening like the mouth of a dark cave.

Wind and cold rain blast into the office, gusting hard off the Delaware. Glass particles and loose papers flutter wildly around the room in crazy currents. My hair whips around. The rain soaks my face and clothes. Glass stings my cheek, my forehead. The room seems to hang in the middle of the thunderstorm. Wind buffets my ears.

"Walk to the window!" Ben shouts against the wind.

I brace myself and step closer to the cudgel near the window. The wind howls. The rain drenches me.

"Now, Grace! Jump or I push you out! Your choice!"

I take another step to the window. The city glitters at my feet. The cudgel is at my right, and behind it is Independence

Hall, lit up at night. I face the wind and take one deep breath, then another. One, two . . . three!

I grab the wrapped cudgel by its end and whip it full force into Ben's face. It makes contact with a dense, awful thud. I drop the weapon, horrified.

Ben staggers backward, shrieking in pain and shock, blood pouring from his mouth and teeth. His jaw hangs grotesquely and his hands rush to it. His gun slips onto a pile of broken glass. I dive for it a second before Ben does and scramble to my feet, my own hands cut and slippery with blood.

I point the gun at him as he lies on the floor, in the whirling holocaust of splintered glass and paper. "Stay down!"

But he won't. He staggers to his feet, moaning in agony. It's a wild animal sound, as loud as the wind. Blood runs in rivulets between his fingers.

"Stay back! Stay away!" I can barely look, but he keeps coming toward me, backing me up against the conference table. I hold the gun up. I don't want to shoot him, please don't make me. "Ben, stop!"

Suddenly, he stops and shakes his head, still cupping his chin. His suit is heavy with rain and blood. His dark eyes brim with tears as they meet mine, and for an instant he looks like the Ben Safer I remember.

"Ben, I'm so sorry." I start to sob. "You'll go to a hospital, they'll fix it."

He shakes his head again, then turns toward the window. I feel a cold chill as soon as I understand what he's going to do.

"*Ben! No! Don't!*" I scream into the rain, but he won't hear me.

He runs headlong toward the darkness, and when he reaches the edge of the carpet, he leaps mightily into nothingness and the thunderstorm.

The next sound I hear is a heartless clap of thunder, then the shrillness of Ben's scream.

And my own.

THIRTY-ONE

I wake up in silence and semidarkness. There's a bed table at my side and a boxy TV floating in the corner. Moonlight streams through the knit curtains, casting a slotted pattern on a narrow single bed. A hospital room. I lie there a minute, flat on my back, taking inventory.

I am alive. I am safe. I wiggle everything, and everything works.

I hold up my hands in the dark. There are bandages on some of my fingers. My face aches, the skin pinching like it doesn't quite fit. I can only imagine what I look like. My fingers go instinctively to my cheeks. The surface is rough underneath, cottony. More bandages.

I hear myself moan, remembering slowly how I got to be here.

It comes back to me like a gruesome slide show, with hot white light blinding me between each freeze frame. Ben, entering with the gun. *Click.* The suicide note. *Click.* The cudgel at the window. *Click.* Independence Hall at my feet.

Oh, God.

Poor Ben. I hurt him, and he died a horrific, painful death.

And Armen, dead too. Even Faber, beaten to death. It's too awful to dwell on. I feel wretched and totally, miserably alone, until I turn over. There, asleep in a shadowy corner near the door, her silvery head dropped onto a heavy chest, is my mother.

Who else. She has been here for God knows how long. She probably arranged for Maddie to go to Sam's.

I lie still and look at her sleeping in a hard plastic chair. Even in the dim light I can see she's fully dressed. A matching sweater and slack set, cheap leather slip-ons, and stocking knee-highs, which she buys in gift packs. Her chest goes up and down; her shoulders rise and fall. In her hand is a paper cup, sitting upright on her knee, even though she's sound asleep. On the cup I can make out a large blue circle.

I know that circle. Pennsylvania Hospital, at Eighth and Spruce.

My mother was born in this hospital in 1925, and it was here that she gave birth to me, and I, in turn, to Maddie. One after another, each picking up the thread and advancing it, like an unbroken line of stitching in a fabric's seam. Three generations of us, each making her own way. Raising her daughter in her own way, without men. A tribe of three women only.

How curious.

Our blood, our very cells, must be constitutionally different from other families. Families of four, for example. Or families that go on camping vacations in minivans and watch their kids play Little League. Families that leave the city they were born in, to divide and scatter.

Normal American families.

We're not like them, like on TV, with a mom and a dad. Nor are we ethnic Americans: happy-go-lucky Italians or the truly Irish, raucous on St. Patty's Day. We are not of those tribes, of those races. We are something else entirely. We are our own invention. We are what we do.

And what we do, what one of us in particular is doing, is sleeping. In an inhospitable chair, clutching a full cup of water. The full cup of water is significant, an act unto itself, and my heart tells me who the water is for.

For me, when I wake up.

It will be the first thing she offers, because she cannot say *I love you* as easily as she can hold out something to drink. Because she cannot say *I worry*, she issues orders and commands. And when she felt pain and loss, she could not say that either, so she drank whiskey. And lashed out in rage.

I understand that now, watching her sleep in the chair. I understand, too, how blessed I am to have her wait while I sleep, with a cup of water on her knee. I don't feel a need to confront her any longer. There's no reason to shake my fist in her face, to call her to account. That much is past, not present.

That much is over.

Let it go.

The door opens and a nurse comes in, luminous in a white uniform that seems to catch and hold the moonlight. She walks directly over to the bed and looks at me with concern. She bends over and whispers, "Are you in pain?"

I am not in pain. I was in pain when my face looked fine. I shake my head.

"Are you hungry?" A single lustrous pearl dots each earlobe in the darkness. She smells like Dove soap and White Linen.

I shake my head, no.

"Do you need anything?" Her teeth are white and even. Her breath is fresh, like peppermint Life Savers.

"No. Thanks."

She pats my shoulder and leaves.

I feel myself smile at her receding silhouette. This is her job and she does it well, but her shift will end soon. My real nurse, the one snoozing at the switch, stinks of cigarettes, but ten to one she's been sitting there for a long, long time. Her shift never ends, as mine will not.

I should let her sleep, but I owe her a rather large apology.

"Ma," I say, and she stirs.

"Honey?" she says hoarsely.

Her eyes aren't even open before she offers me a cup of water.

THIRTY-TWO

"Will you look at that!" Artie says in amazement at the kitchen window. We all gather around and look out at my backyard. I'm so happy my face hurts.

"I can't believe it," Sarah says. "She never did that before, even for Armen."

"She's gonna do it again," Eletha says, casual today in a sweater and jeans.

We all watch as Bernice rolls over like a champ and comes up smiling. Miss Waxman stands over the dog like the Ubersecretary and gives Bernice a treat, delivered professionally to the mouth. Bernice snarfs it up and sniffs the grass for leftovers.

I open the window and yell through the screen, "Way to go, Miss Waxman!" It stings my cheeks, but the woman is working miracles out there. "Isn't she great, Maddie?"

Maddie rolls her eyes. *Duh*, Mom.

"Wish I had a dog like that!" Eletha says. "Boy are you lucky, Maddie!"

"*Roarf!*" Bernice sits and barks at Miss Waxman, who frowns at her charge.

"No!" Miss Waxman says, her voice resonant with authority. Her transformation is as radical as Bernice's, and probably as ephemeral. "No talkie!"

Artie shakes his head. "Did she really say that?"

I elbow him in the basketball. "Give her a break, it's working. What have you done for me lately?"

"I brought you a get-well present."

"You did? Where?"

"It's in the living room. Wait." He runs heavily out of the kitchen and Sarah laughs.

"Wait'll you see this."

"What is it?"

"You'll see." She smiles as Artie lumbers in with a package wrapped in Reynolds Wrap.

"Nice paper, Weiss," Eletha says.

Artie thrusts the present at me. "It was either this or the Hanukkah paper."

"Thanks, Artie," I say, peeling back the foil like a microwave dinner. Underneath is a shiny black plastic I've seen before. "A Magic 8 Ball all my own!" I'm actually touched, which shows how soft I'm getting in my dotage. I give him a hug.

"It's mine, you know," he says, smiling.

"Really? Yours?"

"Putting away childish things, Artie?" Sarah asks.

"You know me better than that, Sar. I got Etch A Sketch now."

Sarah laughs, and so do I.

"What? It's more fun than Legos, and it doesn't hurt when you step on it."

Sarah and I exchange looks. Her expression is unreadable as usual, but mine is full of deep and powerful significance. My eyes telegraph: You are crazy to let this wonderful man leave your life, because there are not that many wonderful men around. I'll tell her later if she doesn't read eyes.

"Of course, the Etch A Sketch is okay," Artie says, "but it's still not my favorite toy." He grins at Eletha. "Doctor, lawyer, Indian chief."

"Don't you tell on me now," she says, laughing evilly.

Sarah looks from one to the other. "What are you two talking about?"

It takes me a full minute to figure it out, but that's because I'm such a stinky detective.

"Look, Grace!" Miss Waxman calls from the backyard.

We all look out the window. Bernice is heeling perfectly as Miss Waxman walks her back and forth. This is not what it looks like when Bernice walks me.

I wave to Miss Waxman. "Unbelievable. The dog is Rin Tin Tin."

"Who's that?" Sarah says.

"Forget it."

"Tell her about the Edsel, Grace," Eletha says.

"One more wisecrack and the dog is yours, El. And I know what you did," I say, pointing my newly bejeweled fingernail at her. Eletha painted my nails while I was in the hospital, and each one is a masterpiece of turquoise polish with a sapphire in the center.

"Hey, girl, you owe me, from that fix-up with Ray."

"You went out with him?"

"Lunch. Then he pounced." She shudders.

"Oh, no."

"Told you," Artie says. "Man's an animal."

"I'm sorry, El. I thought he was nice."

"He slobbered worse than Bernice." She snaps her fingers. "Wait a minute. I just got an idea."

"What?"

"Maddie hates Bernice?"

"Right."

"Ask Miss Waxman to take her."

I look at Eletha, astounded.

The perfect solution.

* * *

Tears pour from her eyes. Her face is flushed. She hiccups uncontrollably. I'm afraid she's going to lose dessert, right there at the dining room table.

"Mads, I don't understand. You hate Bernice."

"I don't hate Bernice!"

The dog looks over the plastic fence, forlorn as a child in a custody fight.

Miss Waxman, shaken, sets down her teacup. "I'd give her a good home, dear. She could play with my poodles."

"She'd be happier, Mads," I say. "She wouldn't be so lonely during the day." And I wouldn't have to hurdle a fence every time the phone rings, or share my bed with the Alps.

"She'd have friends, Maddie," Artie says.

"She doesn't need friends!" Maddie cries.

"Everybody needs friends," Sarah says.

Maddie only cries harder. They have no way of knowing it, but we're not talking about the dog anymore. I hug Maddie close.

"Maybe we should keep Bernice," I say.

Miss Waxman nods. "Of course, whatever you want. She's a very fine animal."

"A *fine* animal," Eletha says. "If Bernice were my dog, I'd never give her up."

Maddie's sobbing slows down and she buries a tear-stained face in my neck. "I can be her friend," she says.

"Now there's an idea. You sure can."

"Can I go upstairs now?" she whispers.

"Sure." I pat her on the bottom and she runs out of the room. I plop into my chair and take a slug of frigid coffee.

Artie snorts. "Way to go, girls. Called that one right."

"Sorry, Grace," Eletha says sheepishly.

"It's not your fault," I say. "I should have known."

"I'm so sorry," Miss Waxman says. "It's all my fault. It's my inexperience with children."

"No, it's my fault." I touch her hand. "My child, my fault."

"Only women have conversations like this," Artie says. He digs into the apple pie Eletha brought.

"Well, it's all right now," I say. I push my hair back and drink the icy coffee. "We have the dog. Someday she'll get out of the kitchen." I look over at Bernice, and her tongue rolls out. "Maybe."

Miss Waxman looks at Bernice indulgently. "Maybe if you take it a step at a time."

"How?"

"Move the animal into the dining room, let the child play near her when she's in the living room so they get used to being around each other."

I think of what Maddie said. *Maybe I could be her friend.* "Then what?"

"You might want to buy her some toys."

"She has plenty of toys."

"I think she means the dog," Sarah says, smiling faintly. "Don't you, Miss Waxman?"

Miss Waxman nods and sips her tea with delicacy.

Oh. I knew that. Add it to the bill.

"Of course," Miss Waxman continues, "not everyone takes to animals, but it seems like Maddie will."

"I'm sure," I say. Just not in my lifetime.

"Like Judge Galanter," Artie says ruefully. "Bernice almost ate him, did you know that, Miss Waxman?"

Miss Waxman shudders. "Judge Galanter was *quite* unhappy about that."

"I bet he was. He almost lost his nuts."

Miss Waxman clears her throat, and a frown crosses Sarah's face. "Why was she after him, I wonder. Remember that, Grace?"

"Yeah. Odd."

"Dogs don't like Judge Galanter," Miss Waxman says.

"Neither do people," Artie says. "Does he have any friends, Miss Waxman?"

"Artie," Sarah says, "don't put Miss Waxman on the spot."

"She can tell me to pound sand if she wants to." He turns to Miss Waxman. "You can tell me to pound sand if you want to."

"Tell him to pound sand," Eletha says.

Miss Waxman's mascara'd eyelashes flutter briefly. Ten to one, she's never heard the term.

"Does he have a friend in the world?" Artie asks.

"Well, he doesn't have . . . many friends."

"I heard he eats alone. He doesn't even meet anybody for lunch."

"Like Ben," Sarah says. Eletha winces and so do I, at the fresh memory of that horrible night. Artie blunders on, retriever puppy that he is.

"Name one for me, Miss Waxman. One friend."

She thinks a minute. "He has an older brother, a banker."

"Beep!" Artie says, like the buzzer in *Jeopardy*. "Doesn't count, that's family. Anyone else?"

She pauses. "There's a Mr. Cavallaro. He met him for lunch, once or twice."

I look up. I am hearing things. "What did you say, Miss Waxman?"

"A Mr. Cavallaro? Mr. James Cavallaro?"

But I'm already running for the kitchen drawer, where I keep the crossword puzzle.

I have a feeling it's on its way to being solved.

THIRTY-THREE

I sit in the darkened back row of the courtroom, where Winn sat that first day. Susan will be speaking here in not too long, at yet another press conference, this one about the bribery scandal. Galanter has been indicted and will be impeached if he doesn't resign. The entire Third Circuit feels the sting of disgrace collectively. Even the court crier is somber as he stands aside, watching TV technicians adjust the lights that will illuminate the dais; interlopers, spotlighting our shame.

Senator Susan Waterman leans on the back of the pew in front of me. She looks sophisticated in a checked Chanel suit, with her hair smoothed back into a classy French twist. Power hair. "How do you know about the money?" she asks.

"I found the checkbook. How do *you* know about the money?"

"You're wondering where he got it." She doesn't answer my question, but I'm not the one in control of this meeting even though I asked for it.

"Yes, I'm wondering where he got it."

"He got it from me."

"Why?"

"For the child." She glances at her preppy aide, the laconic

Michael Robb of Bath, Maine, who's discreetly guarding the courtroom door. "His child with Eletha. Did you know he fathered a child?"

"You know about Malcolm?"

"Of course."

"Eletha thinks you don't know."

"I know that. Armen agreed not to tell me, and he never did. My campaign manager found out before I ran for office, during my vetting. He's the one who told me. I kept it from Eletha—even from Sarah."

"But not Armen."

"Of course not."

"Were you hurt?" She seems so cool, I can't help but ask.

"No. It was before we met, how could I be? He always wanted children and I didn't, so I couldn't begrudge him."

Eminently reasonable. "Why did you give him the money?"

"For the child's education."

"How much did you give him?"

She checks her new Rolex. "Six hundred thousand. The rest he saved."

"Six hundred thousand dollars? That much?"

"He needed it for the child. I'll make sure Malcolm gets it when the estate is settled." She claps her hands together to end the meeting; I notice that her funky silver bangles have been replaced by a thick gold bracelet. Power jewelry.

"You gave him six hundred thousand dollars for the education of a child he had with another woman?"

"Yes."

"I find that hard to believe."

"That's your problem."

"Come on, Susan, let's talk. It's just us girls. What did Armen have that you wanted, that you paid him for?"

She checks her watch again. "I don't have time for this."

Which is when I finally figure it out. Remind me not to quit my day job. "That's it, isn't it? Time."

"What?"

"Armen gave you a year. You wanted him to stay with you through the campaign, and you knew he needed money for Malcolm. So you paid him. You bought him for a year."

"I needed him," she says, and I see a glimmer of the lethal ambition that drove Ben.

It scares me. I say exactly what I'm thinking, unfiltered. "What did Armen see in you?"

"I'm an idealist and so was he."

"An idealist? What are your ideals?"

"I am a liberal, freely admitted. I'm working for child care—"

She doesn't want children.

"For the poor—"

That jacket is double my rent.

"I'm working for the American family."

"You can't *buy* a family."

The courtroom door opens and the preppy aide lets Sarah slip through, but Susan doesn't seem to notice. "You resent me," Susan says.

I get up to go. "No. Mostly, I don't understand you."

"Do you know how important it is for women to get into government? Do you realize the effect we have, the role models we provide?"

"I think I do."

Sarah comes over, looking vaguely senatorial herself. "Grace, how are you?"

I give her a warm hug. "Get out while you still can, Sar."

She looks at me, puzzled, as I head for the swinging doors.

"Good-bye, Michael," I say brightly, on the way out.

"Good-bye, Grace," he says. "And have a nice day."

I do a double-take.

His gaze is direct; eyes clear and intelligent, with a hint of crow's feet at each corner. His mouth, now that I can see it without the underbrush, looks full, even sweet. His brown hair is trimmed, with longish sideburns. He's not hard to look at as he sits at the conference table, next to the FBI bureau chief, the U.S. Attorney, Senator Susan Waterman, my favorite mayor, and the acting chief judge of the Third Circuit, Judge Morris Townsend, awake for the occasion.

"*That's* Shake and Bake?" Sarah says, crossing her legs.

"Isn't he awesome?" Artie says, with an admiring grin. "You oughta see him play. As fine as Earl the Pearl."

"He does look . . . different," Miss Waxman says.

Eletha cracks up. "Real different."

Susan gets up and makes a speech, blah blah blah; the U.S. Attorney and the others all make speeches, blah blah blah. God knows what they say, and who cares. It all sounds the same, each one taking full credit for an investigation in which I heard it was Winn who ended up strapped to a body mike, pretending to be Nick the Fish. On a tip by a secretary who trains toy poodles.

Please.

The FBI bureau chief takes the podium again and a thousand flash units go off, motor drives whining like locusts. He sips his water and says, "I would like to introduce Special Agent Thaddeus Colwin, who has been investigating this matter in an undercover capacity. You'll understand that we can't give you the details, because every secret we divulge is one less weapon in our arsenal against crime. Suffice it to say that we are extremely pleased with the results of the investigation. Special Agent Colwin?"

Winn gets up, and the courtroom bursts into applause. He smooths down a pair of wool pants uncomfortably, and by the time he reaches the podium he's blushing. "There's something I have to say before you start shootin'."

The crowd laughs.

Sarah recrosses her legs.

"I'm happy that this investigation turned out so well, but I can't take the credit for it. The real credit should go to two other people."

I feel nervous; they promised to keep me out of it. The FBI chief looks as worried as I am; Winn is supposed to hand the credit up, not down.

"One of these persons chooses to remain anonymous, and I keep promises to my confidential sources. However, I have made no such agreement with the other person, and she is one of the kindest and bravest ladies I ever met. She testified yesterday at the government's probable cause hearing, so now her identity can be divulged. Her name, friends, is Miss Gilda Waxman."

I look over at Miss Waxman. Her hands fly to her cheeks; her eyes brim with astonished tears.

"Please stand up, Miss Waxman," Winn says. He claps for her, and so does everybody else.

"Oh, my. Oh. Oh," she says, from her seat. The woman has never had a moment in the spotlight in her entire life. She looks as if she's about to have a heart attack.

"Stand up, Miss Waxman!" I say, half rising to grab her soft arm and pull her to her feet.

"No, I couldn't. Really." She tries to sit back down, but Artie covers the seat cushion with his large hand, palm up.

"Come on, good-lookin', sit down," he says, wiggling his fingers. "I dare you."

She swallows hard, then faces the courtroom and her fans. She looks uncertain for a minute, then breaks into a shy smile.

THIRTY-FOUR

I turn the Magic 8 Ball over in my hands and read the bottom.

Yes, definitely, it says. Its white letters float eerily to the black surface. I'll try again. There are only twenty possible answers; it shouldn't take that long to get the answer I want, and I am a patient woman. I shake the ball and look at the bottom.

It is certain.

Where are all the negative answers? Must be defective. I listen to the stone silence coming from Maddie's room. She's boycotting me because I won't let her invite her grandfather to her class play. Should I invite him? I shake the ball and turn it over.

Most likely.

Hmmm. I'll rephrase the question; I didn't go to law school for nothing. Should we never see Maddie's grandfather again? I shake the ball harder, then rotate it.

My reply is no.

"Damn!" I say aloud, and Bernice raises her head. "Why don't we take him, Bernice? He and Grandma could duke it out in the auditorium. You bring the camcorder. We'll be on *Funniest Home Videos*."

I set down the 8 Ball next to the card my father sent Maddie today, which started this whole thing. A short hello, then a list of Italian words, with their meaning. Girl: *ragazza*. Dog: *cane*. Cat: *gatto*. Seems that Emedio "Mimmy" Rossi and his grandaughter got to talking about languages at recess that day. Now Maddie is convinced she wants to learn Italian.

Love: *amore.* I have to admit, it's a pretty language.

"Mom?" Maddie calls faintly from upstairs. Bernice looks toward the stairway at the sound.

"What?"

"Can you come up?"

"Sure." I put down the card, and since Bernice is still *cane non grata* outside the kitchen, I climb over the gate. It catches me neatly in the crotch. Either Bernice goes free or I get taller.

I head up the stairs to Maddie's door, which is plastered with stickers of butterflies, frogs, porcupines, and metallic spiders. Here and there is a much-valued "oily," the goopy stickers that are all the rage with the younger set. Me, I had crayons, eight in all. "Did you want me, Mads?"

"You can come in," she says grudgingly.

"Good." I turn the knob, but the door doesn't move much. "Maddie, is something blocking the door?"

"Wait a minute." I hear her dragging things around inside. She must have barricaded the door again with her Little Tikes chairs; they never show that particular use in the catalog. "Okay," she says. "You can come in now."

I open the door and it shoves aside the clutter behind it, including a chair, a white stuffed gorilla, and about three hundred multicolored wooden blocks. "So, how are we doing up here?"

She holds out her palm. "Look."

In the center of her hand is an ivory nugget. I pick it up in wonder. The front edge is the bevel I recognize and the other end is a fragile circle tinged with blood. "Wow! Your first tooth, Maddie."

"It didn't even hurt."

"How'd it come out?"

"I pulled it out."

I recoil. "Really?"

She nods.

"Let me see your mouth. Smile."

She snarls in compliance, and sure enough, there's an arched window where her front tooth used to be. Then she snaps her mouth shut like a baby alligator. "I'm still mad, you know. This isn't a make-up."

"I understand. Let's get the tooth ready for the Tooth Fairy."

"I'll take care of it. It's mine. Give it back." She holds out her hand.

"Don't be fresh." I put the tooth in her palm.

"Thank you," she says, and walks over to her play table. It's covered with play lipsticks, plastic jewelry, art supplies, and old scarves I've given her for dress-up. She plucks a blue paisley scarf from the pile and wraps the tooth up in it. Then she writes with a crayon on a scrap of pink construction paper.

"What are you doing, honey?"

"I have to write a note."

"No, you don't. You put the tooth under your pillow, and the Tooth Fairy leaves you some money."

"I wasn't talking to you."

So cute. My daughter's first tooth and we're not on speaking terms. "That's quite enough, miss. Would you like a time-out?"

"Well, I *wasn't* talking to you. I was talking to myself."

"Fine, but you may not be rude."

She turns around in her bare feet and thrusts the paper at me. It says, in wobbly red letters: I DON WAN $. T R T G RD. THAN YU. "I don't do lower case."

"It's very nice. What's this part say?"

"It says, I don't want money." She points to the end. "Thank you."

"Why don't you want money?"

"I want her to bring my grandfather to the play."

I sigh in the martyred way my mother taught me. "Why, Maddie? Why does it matter so much?"

"Because everybody else will have a daddy there and I won't. Everybody else will have a grandpop there and I won't. Everybody else has sisters and brothers and I don't." Her lower lip trembles. "All I have is stupid old red hair and freckles that everybody makes fun of."

I look down at her blue eyes, on the verge of welling up. There's nothing in the book about this.

Suddenly, I hear a rustling down in the kitchen, then the *click-clack* of nails on the stairs. I turn around just in time to catch Bernice before she plows into Maddie. She must have jumped the gate.

"She's out!" Maddie screams, backing up against her play table.

"I got her. So you busted out, huh, Bernice?"

"Put her back in the kitchen!"

I hold Bernice by her new ten-dollar collar with its gold electroplate heart: G. ROSSI, it says. The dog wriggles with joy at her liberation from the kitchen. Her tail wags so hard that her hindquarters go with it, a living example of the tail wagging the dog.

"Aw, Maddie, let's leave her out a little. She's sick of the kitchen. She wants to be with us."

The dog swings her head from me to Maddie. It may be my imagination, but Bernice's expression is as close to hopeful as a draft horse can get.

"She's staring at me again," Maddie says. "Why does she have to stare?"

"She wants you to be her friend."

"I can see her teeth."

"So she has teeth, Maddie. You have teeth, she has teeth. Dogs lose baby teeth too. Did you know that? Just like you."

"So what?"

A tough nut. "Why don't you ask her to sit, like Miss Waxman taught her?"

"She won't do it for me."

"How do you know? You never tried. Give her a chance."

Maddie looks at me, then at Bernice. "Now you *sit!*" she shouts.

Miraculously, Bernice sits. Right on the spot. Her tail goes *thump thump thump* on the hardwood floor.

"She did it!" Maddie says.

"She's a good girl. Ask her to do something else. What else did Miss Waxman teach her, do you remember?"

Maddie locks eyes with an excited Bernice. *"Roll over!"*

Bernice drops heavily to the floor and rolls over an array of wooden blocks; she finishes lying flat on her belly and begging for more.

"Look at that!" I say. "Now tell her she's good."

"Good dog!" Maddie says sternly.

"Now see if she'll give you her paw."

"What do I say?"

"Say, 'Give me your paw, Bernice.'"

"What a stupid name," she says, but even her pseudo-cool can't hide her excitement at Bernice's response. *"Bernice, give me your paw."*

Bernice looks blank but scrambles to a sitting position, panting. Her eyes remain on Maddie, rapt.

I rack my brain. What did Miss Waxman say? "Try 'Shake.'"

Maddie straightens up like a toy soldier. *"Shake! Now!"*

I begin to wonder about the dark side of my little angel, but Bernice doesn't seem to mind. On cue, the dog lifts a furry foreleg and paws at the air between her and Maddie.

Maddie's eyes grow panicky. "What's she doing?"

"She wants you to take her paw."

Bernice puts down her paw, then raises it again.

Maddie looks at me, then back at Bernice. "Will she bite me?"

"Of course not. Come on, Maddie, just touch it. She won't bite you. I promise."

Bernice puts down her paw and raises it again in the air.

Maddie reaches out tentatively with her fingers, her child's hand just inches from Bernice's soft white paw. I flash on Michelangelo's depiction of God creating Adam, which doesn't seem half as significant for western civilization.

"Just touch her, Maddie. She wants to be your friend."

Maddie bites her lip and reaches closer to Bernice's paw.

Bernice whimpers and rakes at the air.

"Go ahead. *Touch* her, Maddie."

"Can I?" she says worriedly.

"Yes, go ahead."

And finally, she does.

THIRTY-FIVE

We sit uncomfortably in the darkness, on the carpeted steps that serve as seats in the elementary school auditorium. To the left is my mother, her face carved from a solid stratum of granite, like the dead presidents hewn into Mount Rushmore. Her hair has been sculpted into curls and is as rigid as her gaze, which does not waver from the stage, much less look at me. I figure that we will speak again in the year 3000 or when she quits smoking, whichever comes first.

Making a cameo appearance to her left is Tyrannosaurus Ex, Sam, in a Burberry suit with a stiff white collar. I told him I would picket his law firm if he didn't come today. He gives me a billable smile when I look over.

Next to him is Ricki, looking entirely entertained, and not only by the class play. She has brought along her three sons so the requisite brothers will be present, and has even offered me half price on the therapy I will need to recover from today. That's what friends are for, she said with a smile. And she forgives me for lying to her, and even for returning the blue Laura Ashley dress.

To my right, of course, is a man who looks like Robert Goulet and smells like the perfume counter at Thrift Drug: my father. He's the only one having fun at this thing. He guffaws at all the punch lines and claps heartily after all the songs. He nudges me in the ribs four times, whenever Maddie enters in her costume, knocking the camcorder into the back of the man in front of me. When I finally ask him to stop, he says out loud: "Wadja say, doll?"

So I don't ask again. I put the rubber rectangle of the camcorder to my eye and watch my daughter take center stage. Dressed as a carrot, naturally, she joins hands with her new friend, Gretchen the tomato, and they take the hands of a bunch of broccoli and several tulips to sing about the things that sprout up in the spring, tall and proud in the warm sun.

Like children.

In no time at all I'm in tears, looking through the rubber eye of the camcorder, hating that it will record my sniffles with Japanese high fidelity. In the background will be a group of first graders warbling faintly about springtime.

I find myself thinking of Armen, then Sam and my father. And how sometimes it doesn't turn out like it's supposed to.

Love dies, people die. Mothers and fathers break apart, the ties that bind unraveling as freely as a ball of yarn, with one tie remaining: the microscopic skein of DNA that resurfaces in our children, in permutations never imagined. Maddie's the only tie between Sam and me; I'm the only tie between my parents. We all relate to our children, but none of us to each other.

The tears wet the eyepiece of the costly camcorder, and I have to set it down in my lap. My father puts his aromatic arm around me, and then my mother does the same, which only makes me cry harder.

For all we lost.

For all we never had.

Sam passes me a monogrammed handkerchief and I try to recover, grateful for the darkness. Meanwhile Ricki looks like she wants me on Prozac, and the carrot is hugging the tomato. The house lights come up, threatening to expose my hysteria, but in the light I can see that everyone else is crying too. I'm just another hysterical mother in an audience of hysterical mothers applauding their baby vegetables.

Maddie finds me in the crowd and grins, gap-toothed.

I clap loudly for her, hands over my head. I look over and my father is doing the same thing. Scary.

My mother puts a note on my lap. On the front it says GRACE ROSSI. "What's this?" I ask her.

"Sam passed it down to you."

"Sam?" I look over at Sam, but he's whistling for Maddie, doing his best impression of a real father. I pick up the note and something falls into my lap.

It's a new photo of Tom Cruise. The note says:

> *Roses are red,*
> *Violets are blue,*
> *Maddie's adorable,*
> *Wanna see my tattoo?*

I look past Sam and over the parents, teachers, and kids. Underneath the EXIT sign, in the back row of the auditorium, is a handsome man in a black raincoat.

And no rain bonnet at all.

ACKNOWLEDGMENTS

Kay Thompson's wonderful character Eloise likes to make things up. So do I, which is important to keep in mind as you read this book. Even though I have worked for the Third Circuit Court of Appeals, doing the very same job as my character Grace Rossi—indeed, in the very same courthouse—*Final Appeal* is fiction. None of the characters are real, although they are realistic, and the plot, though plausible, is entirely imagined.

The first thanks go, as always, to my agent, Linda Hayes, and to my editor extraordinaire at HarperPaperbacks, Carolyn Marino. I am blessed in knowing these terrific women and in becoming their friend, even if I never write another book. But since I intend to write other books, I'll be the grateful recipient of their judgment in knowing what makes a book work, their insight into how to improve a manuscript, and their commitment to me and my writing. Not to mention their sensitivity to my care and feeding. The Old Testament would call what they have loving-kindness, which is proof that there is still some writing that cannot be improved upon.

Heartfelt thanks also go to my boss, Chief Judge Dolores K. Sloviter, who is the absolute best the federal judiciary has to offer. Her dedication to public service is an example for me every day, and we are all lucky to have her. I mention her here especially because she has been more supportive of my part-time writing and full-time mothering than I could ever have hoped.

Thanks, too, for their support, to Martha Verna, Anne Szymkowski, Mary Lou Kanz, and the law clerks, Seth, Theresa, and the strikingly handsome Jim (and before them Alison, Larry, and Jessica). I am grateful as well to the other employees of Third Circuit—Bill Bradley being the ringleader of a conspiracy that includes Marisa Walsh and the staff attorneys; Toby Slawsky, Lynne Kosobucki, Pat Moore, and the Circuit Executive's Office; Doug Sisk, Brad Baldus, and the clerk's office; and the librarians, who have been so supportive.

Thank you very much to Alison Brown at HarperPaper-backs, a whiz of an editorial assistant who made some dead-on suggestions about an early draft, and who has helped in many other ways. Many thanks to Laura Baker at HarperPaperbacks and my local publicist, Laura Henrich, who are both wonderful. Janet Baker, my copy editor on all two occasions, is awesome; even from afar, she never forgets Philadelphia. A quick story: in *Everywhere That Mary Went*, Janet corrected me on exactly where along Route One you begin to smell the cow manure. This is a copy editor you can only dream about, and she is mine.

When Grace Rossi wandered out of my range of expertise, I sought help from United States Attorneys Joan Markman and Amy Kurland (who was kind enough to let me collar her on Fifth Street), Special Agent Linda Vizi of the FBI, Detective McGlinchey and others of the Philadelphia police, the federal marshals and court security officers (Messrs. King and Devlin, as well as Tony "Hole-in-One" Fortunato and his cohorts), and the staff at the medical examiners office of Philadelphia. Not to mention Brian J. Buckelew, man of many talents, and my friend David Grunfeld. All errors and omissions, of course, are mine. By the way, needlepoint really does relieve stress, and you're guaranteed one pillow for every life crisis. Ask Barbara Russell of Barbara Russell Designs in Chestnut Hill.

Special thanks, too, to Reverend Paree Metjian and his family, who taught me about Armenian pride and culture. I feel honored to have been even a fictional member of that community.

Finally, I am indebted to my friends, especially Rachel Kull and Franca Palumbo, who found the time to read an early draft of this book and to offer suggestions and encouragement. I owe them both a tankerful of milk, and much more.

As for my family, they are where it all started and where it all ends.

ABOUT THE AUTHOR

LISA SCOTTOLINE is a *New York Times* bestselling author of eleven novels and a former trial lawyer. She has won the highest prize in crime fiction, the Edgar Award, and has lectured at law schools and bar associations on issues of legal ethics. She is an honors graduate of the University of Pennsylvania and its law school, where she was an editor of the *Law Review* and won the Loughlin Prize for legal ethics. Her books are published in more than twenty languages, and she remains a life-long resident of the Philadelphia area. Visit her at www.lisascottoline.com.